PRAISE FOR TOM LOWE
AND *SPIN*

"Jim Asher is a postmodern Great Gatsby, naive at heart, wending his way toward political status in California politics. And the book asks a serious question: Can one play the political game and remain honest?"
—*Chicago Tribune*

"*SPIN*'s Jim Asher is Jerry Maguire meets Dirk Diggler of *Boogie Nights,* and from the first page, he won't loosen his frantic grip on you."
—*Los Angeles Daily News*

"Tom Lowe is preparing himself for instant celebrity status. . . . *SPIN* is certain to amaze."
—*The London Times*

"[A] political potboiler."
—*Denver Post*

"Sex! Money! Republicans! It's all here."
—*San Jose Mercury News*

"A racy and fast-paced debut novel. . . . Lowe writes a fast if somewhat foul-mouthed prose and has a quick if somewhat prurient imagination."
—*The Weekly Standard*

"This first novel jangles with edgy realism. . . . The story crackles with lusty energy and shimmers with steamy emotions."
—*Library Journal*

"*SPIN* is a fast-paced, exciting read."
—*Sacramento News & Review*

SPIN

A NOVEL BY

tom lowe

POCKET BOOKS
New York   London   Toronto   Sydney   Tokyo   Singapore

POCKET BOOKS, a division of Simon & Schuster Inc.
1230 Avenue of the Americas, New York, NY 10020

Copyright © 1998 by Tom Lowe

Originally published in hardcover in 1998 by Pocket Books

ISBN: 0-671-01924-4

First Pocket Books trade paperback printing July 1999

10 9 8 7 6 5 4 3 2 1

POCKET and colophon are registered trademarks of
Simon & Schuster Inc.

Cover design by Jeanne M. Lee

Printed in the U.S.A.

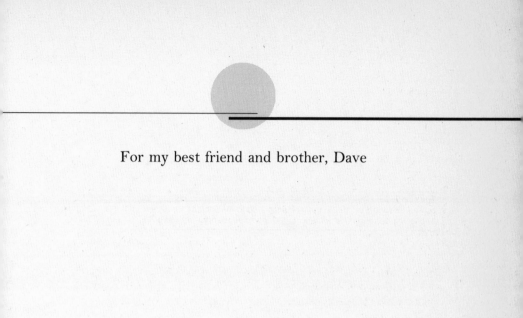

For my best friend and brother, Dave

AUTHOR'S NOTE

Thankfully, *Spin* is a total and complete work of fiction. Although I borrowed backdrops from recent California political history, none of the characters in this novel or their actions are real—period.

The human brain is an imperfect instrument built up through long geological periods. Some of its levels of operation are more primitive and archaic than others. Our heads, modern man has learned, may contain weird and irrational shadows out of the subhuman past— shadows that under stress can sometimes elongate and fall darkly across the threshold of our rational lives. Man has lost the faith of the eighteenth century in the enlightening power of pure reason, for he has come to know that he is not a consistently reasoning animal. We have frightened ourselves with our own black nature and instead of thinking, "We are men now, not beasts, and must live like men," we have eyed each other with wary suspicion and whispered in our hearts, "We will trust no one. Man is evil. Man is an animal. He has come from the dark wood and the caves."

—Loren Eiseley, *Darwin's Century*

If you know what life is worth, you will look for yours on earth.

—Bob Marley

SPIN

PROLOGUE

Something was tugging on my shirt. I rolled over and opened my eyes, but all I could see was a smudge of light. I pressed hard on my eye sockets. The glittery stars soon gave way to the face of a Highway Patrol officer looking down at me. He had a neat mustache and smelled of strong aftershave. I tried to sit up, but I couldn't move my right arm—I must have slept on top of it. I pinched it hard, but it had lost all feeling.

"Are you okay?" the officer asked.

"Where am I?"

"The capitol building. You're in the speaker's office. This place is a disaster."

I looked around. Brett's fine, antique mahogany desk was completely trashed. The Captain Morgan bottle from the night before lay shattered against the wall, leaving a puddle stain on the Oriental rug, right near the pulverized picture frame of Brett's son. A cigarette butt with a very long ash had burned into the polished wood floor beside me. The office's tall rectangular windows overlooking the capitol lawn were already glowing with early blue light.

"My arm, officer, it won't move."

The officer touched it. "Wow . . . it's really cold." He moved the arm around to get some circulation going. When he let go, it flopped limply.

"Oh fuck. I think it's dead," I said. I pounded it on the hard wood, but it felt like a corpse's limb.

"What the hell happened in here?" he asked.

"I don't know."

The officer was young, and aside from his military-cropped hair, he seemed friendly enough. "You better get that arm looked at, buddy."

I was scared, remembering stories of drunks losing limbs after accidentally sleeping on them. I saw it happening to me. Just then I felt the first painful tingle in my fingers. I tried to curl my thumb, and my muscles finally responded. My luck had come through again—the angel was still on my shoulder.

"You better clean this place up," the officer said. "It's almost seven o'clock." He lifted me to my feet, but I couldn't stand without holding on to his shoulder.

"Why don't you lie down on the couch," he said. "Looks like you guys threw one hell of a party in here last night. I saw Speaker Alexander leaving at about two in the morning."

Great. He thought Brett was involved in this mess. I laid back on the couch and played along. "Yeah. I guess we all got a little out of hand."

"You all right now?" he asked.

"I'll be fine, thanks."

He walked out. I knew he wouldn't record this incident in his security log; most of the CHP officers in the capitol were good Republicans, so they always covered for me. My boss, Assembly Speaker Brett Alexander, was the most popular Republican in the state. Basically, it allowed me to do what I pleased—a life without consequences.

I searched under tables and in corners for Natalie, but she was gone. I didn't remember her leaving; I was terrified of what might have happened. But right now it was the least of my problems. When I reached down to pick up the shards of broken rum bottle, blood rushed to my head and I collapsed to my knees. I wanted to die. I stumbled into Brett's private bathroom; the vile state of my body seemed sickeningly worse surrounded by the pristine white marble floor and shiny brass fixtures. When I looked in the mirror, I panicked. One eye was ringed black, its corner bloodshot solid red from a burst vessel, and a dark crusted cut lined my brow. My shirt was ripped and stained blue. My breathing was hard and labored, like a man dying. My mouth was an ashtray. When I turned my head, I noticed my hair was spiked up the side in a glob of dried vomit. I hadn't noticed vomit on the floor, but now I could taste the stale acid coating my tongue.

Just then, Brett walked into the bathroom. He stopped in the doorway behind me, holding the shattered picture frame of his son. A piece of its glass hit the floor. I looked up at him in the mirror. Brett's face slowly turned from confusion to outrage.

"What the hell is going on here?" he asked.

I closed my eyes. "I don't know."

"What the hell happened to my office, Jim?"

I didn't want to open my eyes.

"Jesus Christ. You've got to get out of here," Brett said. "We have the budget meeting in five minutes. The fucking governor is right outside the door here, Jim. Jesus H. Christ!" He walked back into his office mumbling swear words.

I needed to get out of there fast. I splashed water on my face and walked back into the office. Brett was staring at his desk in disbelief, one hand clutching his hair.

"Brett, I'm sorry."

"Just go, Jim."

I stood there, trying to think of something to say. "I'm really sorry. This will never happen—"

He pointed at the door, shaking his head, looking away from me.

I walked out through the conference room's back door right into a crowd of lobbyists and state legislators gathered in the hallway. Everyone was waiting for the big annual budget meeting, which I was also supposed to attend. In neatly pressed suits, their bodies were full of early morning energy. I tried to keep my head down as I passed through the herd, but I was noticed by a high-ranking assemblyman I knew and a reporter from the *Los Angeles Times*. It was deeply humiliating.

Downstairs in the basement parking lot of the capitol, I sat in my car for a long time, not wanting to move. I couldn't drive. I closed my eyes, but I knew I couldn't sleep. I was wide awake, hungover with poison coursing through my body. My stomach churned, then my mouth grew watery. I opened the car door and retched all over the concrete, vomit spraying out through my nose, making it sting. I closed off one nostril and blew chunks of pasty food out my nose. It made me throw up again. Somehow at that very moment I stepped outside my body, hovering just above the Lincoln. I had a clear view of myself hanging out the car door—like watching myself through a security camera. There I was, dressed in a tattered $1,800 Armani suit, one hand posted on the concrete holding me up, the other hand fighting to keep my tie from dropping into the puddle of yellow bile.

What had my life turned into? On the surface, only a few hours before, I had been exactly where I should have wanted to be. I was the youngest, hottest political consultant in the state. I had already changed the face of California politics. I was making so much money I wasn't even cashing my state paychecks anymore; I was spinning billion-dollar deals, annihilating opponents, both Democratic and Republican, sleeping with any woman I wanted. I was at the top of the political game yet nearing the bottom of my existence. I was a hypocrite, a liar, a goddamn fucking disgrace. I had completely humiliated myself in front of Brett. And right when we were preparing for the culmination of our dreams—the White House. Considering everything that had taken place in the last twelve hours—the dirty money, the sex, the dishonor—I felt like I couldn't go back to that life now. I was disgusted with what I had become. I thought of killing myself. It would be easy, and everything would go away. But then there would be nothing. And nothing was bad and you couldn't take it back.

I opened my glove box, digging around for what I needed. I pushed aside my Glock and grabbed a pint bottle of Jack Daniel's. As I pulled it out, something dropped onto the passenger's seat beside me. I picked it up: it was my business card from Edward Winston's US Senate race two years before, my first campaign. The card triggered a flood of memories—images of a time when politics was fresh to me, wide open, and exhilarating. It seemed like ten years ago, so far removed and distant from where I was now. With a trembling hand I twisted the cap off the whiskey and guzzled half the bottle. I looked back at the pistol through watery eyes. I threw back some more booze, my throat burning, and I lit a smoke. I held the cigarette lighter under the business card, letting the flames burn down until they singed my fingers.

PART 1

two years before . . .

ONE

I had just returned from a summer in Europe and had no idea what the hell I was going to do with my life. After four years on my own, with little to show for it, I was back living with my parents. But with Disneyland ten minutes away, Hollywood just up the 405, and the waves pounding the shore right off our porch, Newport Beach was my kind of town—larger than life, self-mythologizing.

I came in from the beach one weekday afternoon and hosed off my surfboard. My mom was reading on our back porch.

"How's the water, sweetheart?" she asked.

"A little chilly," I said. "Nothing like the Mediterranean in June." I draped a towel over my shoulders, sat down at the patio table, and poured myself an iced tea. "Why are you home from work so early, Mom?"

"I had a parent conference this afternoon. One of my kids is having some emotional problems; he's been kicking other students."

"Fun."

My mom was a counsellor for severely handicapped kids at the local high school. I had worked as an aide in her classroom when I went there. Of course, she always gave me great recommendations. I loved my mom more than anyone; she seemed perfect in all respects.

"Have you given any more thought to what we were talking about?" she asked.

"Yeah, I guess. I mean, I like kids, and being a teacher sounds pretty good, but there's no money in it."

"Well, that's true. But, Jim, you wouldn't have to do it forever. I could help you get your credentials in about two months, and then you could just teach until you decide what you really want to do. You'd have your summers off."

"I guess. I'm still thinking about it. But I don't wanna live at home forever. I need to make some real money, so I can get out on my own."

"You know you're welcome here as long as you need a place, sweetheart. Another thing is, a lot of politicians get their start by teaching, if you're still thinking about that for a career. Mayor Preston was a teacher for ten years before he ran for the city council. I'll bet the mayor would even let you volunteer in his office during your summer breaks. That could be your foot in the door."

"I'll think about it. Thanks, Mom."

I walked inside and sat down to watch TV with my brother, Jake.

"So, what's up for this weekend, bro?" he asked.

"There's a big party Friday, down on Forty-second. I heard they're getting two kegs. I don't know what's up Saturday. I'm getting kinda sick of the same old parties, though—same chicks, same brawls, same stupid conversations."

Jake nodded. He was a sophomore in college, so he was still in full party mode—every Friday and Saturday night, every weekend, guaranteed. But to me the weekends had all been blurring together lately. Sometimes it felt like I was just going through the motions, acting out the role expected of me, waiting for something real to happen in my life.

"Hey, wanna go backpacking next weekend?" Jake asked. "Hit the Sierras?"

"Maybe. Let me see what's going on with all these job applications. I'm pretty much broke. My ATM is more like a slot machine these days. I put my card in and I have absolutely no idea what's gonna come out. I'm always like, 'Come on, baby, twenty for daddy!'"

Jake smiled. "That's why we should go now, before you get stuck working."

"True. A few days trekking through Yosemite does sound pretty good."

I kicked my feet up on the coffee table, dusting its top with sand from the beach. I leaned back and relinquished my brain to the television, ready to burn away a few hours. Just then, a clever political ad came on for Edward Winston, labeling his opponent, California Senator Dana Steadfield, as "the liberal Democrat who loves to spend your money."

I was a political junkie, so I always kept up with everything in politics, but my time in Europe had put me slightly out of the loop. "Who is this Edward Winston guy?" I asked Jake.

"He's some rich guy running for the Senate. He has like four hundred million dollars. He's been destroying Senator Steadfield with these attack ads all summer. I think she's starting to slip in the polls."

"Good. It's about time someone stepped up to the plate. Steadfield is such a big liberal bitch. I'd love to see her get booted out of Washington."

"Dude, you'd be amazed at all the ads Winston is running. You can't even turn on the TV without seeing one. I heard he's gonna spend whatever it takes to win."

Now that would be a cool place to work. I walked into my bedroom and dialed information.

"Hello, what city, please?" the operator asked.

"Uh . . . I don't know," I said.

"What listing, please?"

"Winston Senate campaign."

"Hold, please . . ." A few seconds passed. "I don't have anything for that."

"Okay, give me the Republican Party's phone number in Orange County."

"Hold, please . . ."

I called the GOP headquarters and got the address for the Winston campaign office in Santa Ana, only ten minutes away. I threw on some cheap slacks with suspenders and a tie—I wanted to look like Michael Douglas in *Wall Street*—and drove to Santa Ana. I was feeling spontaneous. What did I have to lose?

Once I found the correct address, I parked my Ford Probe and strolled up to the three-story building, which looked like any other mirrored office complex. I went through the lobby and up to the third floor. My heart was pumping. An engraved gold plaque on the door read: EDWARD WINSTON, US SENATE. When I walked through the door, I saw all kinds of commotion—everyone was running around talking to at least two or three people at the same time; dozens of fax machines were whizzing and screaming; a camera crew from Channel 4 was setting up to interview someone; and the beautiful young receptionist was staring at me, as if to say, *Do you have any idea what you're getting into?*

After sitting around for an hour, I was shuffled into the volunteer coordinator's office. He was a short guy named Ted. Pictures of Ronald Reagan wallpapered his office. I was very nervous as I sat down.

"So," he said, "the receptionist tells me you want to volunteer, huh?"

"Well, actually, I'm looking for a job."

"We don't hire people off the streets. Um, that's not to say you're a street person . . . uh . . . how did you hear about the campaign?"

"I saw one of those ads you're running on TV."

He grinned. "Pretty awesome, aren't they. Did you see the illegal alien one?"

"No. I saw the 'Democrat who loves to spend your money' one."

He laughed out loud. "That one's great! God, do I love that one!"

He had me smiling. This Ted guy, sitting there in his Ralph Lauren shirt, flanked by images of Reagan, was the real deal: a big-shot political player. But at the same time, I was keenly aware that I could do his job better than him. Not to brag, because there are extreme downsides to being a highly intelligent and lucid thinker—Dostoyevsky called it a curse—but since my earliest memories, I had always been aware of my abilities, and I always believed that if I was given a fair chance, in any situation, I could excel past everyone.

"Well," Ted said, glancing down at my résumé, "Jim . . . Well, Jim, it says here you were in the army."

"Four years."

"You're a Persian Gulf veteran, eh?"

"Yep."

"Well, you guys did a great job over there, I gotta tell you. I used to stay up all night watching CNN. Amazing. So, anyway, what other campaigns have you worked, Jim?"

"Actually, this will be my first. But I've been into politics ever since I can remember. In fact, when I was a kid, I would always skip *Voltron* or *Tom & Jerry* to catch *Brinkley* or *Face the Nation*. My neighborhood buddies thought it was a little strange."

"I know what you're saying. Great. And I see you have an English degree. Where do you picture yourself ten years from now, Jim?"

"Probably in the White House."

"What, as president?"

"No, no. I'm not exactly sure; maybe a spokesman. I've just always wanted to work in politics, especially at the White House."

"We have several people on this campaign who've worked at the White House."

"Really?"

"Really. So, Jim, why are you a Republican?"

"Well, my parents are Republicans. I've always been a Republican. I grew up here in Orange County. I hate high taxes, gun control, illegal immigration, welfare . . ." Not very eloquent so far.

"What do your parents do?"

"My pop works for UPS and my mom's a schoolteacher."

"That's respectable. Well, you seem bright. I think our issues director, John Griggs, could use some help. Are you interested in that?"

"Sure," I said, not really knowing what an issues director was.

Ted led me through the bustling hallways like a safari guide. The campaign took up the entire third floor. "That's Jeff," he said, pointing to a short, nerdy guy. "He does Edward's and Mariella's scheduling."

"Who is Mariella?" I asked.

"You don't know Mariella?"

"No."

"You will," he grinned. "She's the candidate's wife."

"Oh."

Ted pointed out everyone along the way. There were advance people, media people, field people, mail people, advertising people. Everyone looked at me when I walked by. Not friendly, not mean. Yet not too busy to stare.

"Where is the main campaign headquarters?" I asked.

"This is it, buddy. You're in the eye of the storm here."

Wow, I thought. This was exactly the opportunity I had been waiting for.

We found our way to the issues office. The place was a wreck, with newspapers, coffee cups, three-ring binders—there was shit everywhere. Sitting behind the desk was a man in his late twenties, moderately good-looking, about six three, built like a football player a few years after playing football, with messy hair and a friendly smile.

"John Griggs," Ted said to him. "This is Jim Asher. He wants to volunteer."

I trampled across the cluttered floor and shook John's hand. He had a pen behind each ear, hundreds of highlighted books and magazine articles scattered on his desk, and a purple juice stain on his shirt.

"Nice to meet you," I said nervously.

"Hey," he said. "How's it going."

Ted seemed eager to get back to his work. "You guys hang out and get to know each other. John here does all the issues and some of the speech writing for Mr. Winston. Come see me before you leave, okay, Jim?" Then Ted was gone.

"So," John said. "You want to do issues?"

"Sure."

"Good. I can really use the help. This campaign is kind of crazy. The candidate is spending millions of dollars, but you'll notice that things are a bit disorganized. Sometimes the elbow isn't talking to the hand, if you know what I mean."

I nodded. I didn't know if now was the time to ask, but I did anyway. "Is this a paying job?"

"Um, I don't think so." He paused. "But let me give you some advice. A smart guy once told me this, and one year later I was working at the White House—"

"You worked at the White House?"

"Three years, for Bush."

"What did you do?"

"I was in the White House communications office. I wrote the president's news summary every morning."

"So you must have worked under Marlin Fitzwater, then?"

"That's right," John said. He looked pleasantly surprised that I should know such a thing. "So, anyway, here's the advice: make yourself useful and you'll make yourself indispensable."

"Who told you that?"

"Bill Bennett."

"Impressive. So, when do I start?"

"Six o'clock tomorrow morning," he said. "I'll start you out going through newspapers, searching for clips. You'll cut out and photocopy any article about this campaign, or any issues that might be relevant—crime, welfare, illegal immigration, whatever. It's not that difficult, just time-consuming. And who knows, if you work hard and show up on time every day, they might even hire you to do the clips full-time."

"That'd be great. Thanks a lot, Mr. Griggs. I'll be here at six."

"Just call me John."

I drove home singing. I felt high and full of energy. It wasn't a paying job, but it was a foot in the door, and I knew that was all I needed. The 55 freeway was bumper to bumper with traffic. Some asshole in a Lexus cut into my lane, but I didn't even flip him off. Normally, when someone snaked me on the freeway, I would dream of hanging out through my sunroof with a rocket launcher. I would push the trigger, and the rocket would streak through the air and slam into their trunk, tearing through the sheet metal, then ripping through the backseat before the secondary charge exploded and turned the entire luxury car into a two-ton fragmentation grenade, blasting the discourteous driver into hundreds of flying scraps . . . but not today. No. Instead, I smiled and turned up the radio. I had something new and exciting in my life.

When I got home I told my mom about the campaign and everything I'd seen.

"That's great, Jim. How much does it pay?" she asked.

"Nothing at first. It's kind of a volunteer thing for now. But if I work hard, my new boss, this guy named John Griggs, who worked at the White House, said they might hire me full-time. And then, who knows . . ."

"That's terrific, sweetheart. Your father and I figured you'd probably find your way into politics sooner or later. Why don't you call him at work and tell him the good news."

"It's not that big a deal, Mom. I'll just wait till he gets home."

"Well, *I'm* proud of you."

"Thanks. I think I'm gonna hit the mall and start reading some newspapers and magazines. I need to get up to speed on politics if I'm gonna be a big wheeler-dealer."

My mom smiled.

"By the way, could you spot me a twenty until I can pay you back? My car's out of gas."

"Sure." She got her purse and gave me the money. "Just add it to the tab. You can pay me back when you're rich and famous."

"Thanks, Mom." I hated asking, but I was flat broke.

Fast-forward a month to a Thursday night in Hollywood. I was now working full-time for the Winston campaign. The candidate's lovely and ambitious wife, Mariella, had moved me from the issues office to the press office. She seemed to like me. Even the campaign manager, Chuck, had to be informed of my new position. Things happened much faster than I had expected. All I had to do was pledge my loyalty as a conservative through informal conversations around the office, demonstrate that I was one of them, work very long hours, be smart and useful to as many people as possible, and I was absorbed into the campaign. Just like that. For all they knew, I could have been a Democrat spy. There was no official screening process that I saw.

On this particular night, the campaign had rented out the Billboard Live nightclub for a campaign event called "Winston Rocks LA." A pretty lame attempt at courting so-called Gen-X voters, but at least I was out of the office for a few hours. I had spent the whole day pitching reporters on the telephone: "Hello, this is Jim Asher from the Winston campaign, and I just wanted to let you know that Edward Winston is holding an important event tonight at Billboard Live . . . blah, blah, blah." Unfortunately, most of my pitch calls were cut off by a quick slam of the reporter's phone, making me feel like a slimy cold-calling stockbroker. I was terrified that no one would show up. But luckily, every station in town sent a camera crew, and most sent reporters as well. My job was to kiss the reporters' asses and say nice things about Edward Winston. Easy enough.

I had a folding table outside, where another press assistant named Michelle and I issued passes to the media. Limousines were lined up in a stalled parade near the entrance. A jet black Humvee pulled into the VIP space, and out stepped an actor in his early twenties. I had watched this guy grow up on *The Wonder Years.* Three gorgeous party girls climbed out behind him. I thought to myself: one of these days, Jim, one of these lost and lonely days, that will be you, pal.

A female reporter walked up to our table. Her cameraman stood near the curb.

"Is Jim Asher here?" she asked.

I was surprised. "I'm Jim Asher."

She smiled wistfully, batting her eyelashes. "Well, I told you I'd show up. I'm Samantha Gellhorne from Channel Seven."

"Great." I remembered her. She was the only reporter who had taken a minute to talk with me earlier on the phone—a random, blistering conversation about Kerouac's *On the Road*. Samantha was in her midthirties and quite attractive, with long cinnamon brown hair and green eyes. I could tell from her loose mannerisms and sultry voice that she'd been around the partying side of town. A lot.

"If I remember right, Jim, you owe me a drink," she said.

Michelle shot me a concerned glance.

"Oh, that's right," I said. "I'll see you inside. Thanks for coming, Samantha."

She took her press pass and disappeared into the bar with her cameraman.

Michelle turned to me. "You promised her a drink if she would come?"

"I was afraid nobody would show up."

Michelle was clearly perturbed. She was a strict conservative, raised in a Mormon family and married to a Republican lawyer in DC. She thought reporters were scum and only tolerated them to the extent necessary.

"Well, I guess it worked," she said. "But you better be careful, Jim. Samantha Gellhorne covers our Senate campaign, and she was obviously flirting."

"I'll be careful."

Michelle and I moved inside when the event began. It was my first sip of after-hours politics—my first taste of how things *really* work. We sat down at a small table.

"Do you want a drink?" I asked Michelle.

"I don't really drink. My husband doesn't like me to."

"Just one. Most of our work's done. We just have to keep an eye on the reporters now."

"Okay," she said. "Just one."

I brought back four rum and Cokes. Michelle was pretty. She was only twenty-one, and she had already worked as a copywriter for CNN. She didn't seem to like or trust people much—at least not in the normal superficial way—but she seemed willing to give me a chance.

"Jim, I understand you graduated from high school early," Michelle asked.

"Who told you that?"

"Ted and John. The office isn't that big, you know. Word gets around fast. Everyone's always scoping out the new person, trying to size them up. I'm just glad it's you now, instead of me. I've been the new person for the last two months."

"Happy to ease your burden," I said. "Yeah, I did graduate early. And I've heard the same about you."

"GATE program," she said. "I graduated when I was fifteen."

"I was sixteen. I'll never forget my first day of college. Everyone seemed so old; they had beards, and families, and houses. I barely had my driver's license. I felt so out of place."

Michelle nodded.

At this point, I had not even met our candidate, Edward Winston. The campaign had hundreds of employees scattered around the state, and Winston had been on the trail for weeks. I really wanted to make a good impression whenever I finally met him. Just having a conversation with a multimillionaire Senate candidate would be a cool experience. When Winston finally came onstage for a short speech, I couldn't even hear him over the rowdy bar crowd. Then he was whisked away to catch a flight for New York. Michelle and I, being the only press staffers at the event, decided to try our hands at "spinning" the reporters. We strolled down to the press stage, where all the cameras were set up.

Michelle asked me if I had ever spun reporters before.

"Not really," I admitted.

"It's easy," she said. "Just make small talk. Then slip in a few nice words about Winston."

"Okay. I'm a pretty smooth talker."

The reporters were busy gossiping among themselves and drinking beer. Now I knew why so many had shown up: all they had to do was file a quick fluff piece, beam it back to their stations, and they were free to party the night away. I gathered my confidence and walked up to a bearded reporter, interrupting his conversation with a cameraman.

"Hi, I'm Jim Asher from the Winston campaign. How did you like the speech?"

He looked me over with a condescending grin. "Whatever, kid."

I nodded, said, "Nice to meet you," then slithered away. I felt like a fool. Who was I kidding? These reporters didn't fuck around. I wandered around the press area, afraid to approach anyone. Meanwhile, Michelle was chatting up some cameraman. I knew I was out of my league—a punk kid in a $189 Men's Wearhouse suit trying to play grown-up.

Then Samantha grabbed my arm.

"What about that drink, Jim?"

Her lovely smile vaporized the humiliation. "Sure."

She tucked her arm through mine, and we walked to the bar—I strutted. Samantha seemed to know everyone as we passed through the buzzing suits and cocktail dresses. She stopped behind a balding man who was the centerpiece of his circle. She reached down and pinched his ass; his head spun sharply, but when he saw it was Samantha, he smiled.

"Hello, Dick," she said, kissing his cheek.

He squeezed her waist. "Hi, honey."

She turned and introduced me, but I already recognized him.

"Jim Asher," Samantha said, "this is Los Angeles Mayor Richard Tarken."

My hand shot out. "Very nice to meet you, sir."

He barely glanced at me before turning back to Samantha. "Another boy toy, Samantha?"

She rubbed my arm. "He works for Winston."

The mayor grinned at me. I got the picture.

Samantha and I finally made it to the bar. The crowd was swarming three deep for drinks.

"What'll it be?" I asked.

Samantha stood up on a bar stool and waved to the busy bartender. He dropped what he was doing and rushed over.

"Hey, Samantha." He leaned all the way over the bar and kissed her cheek. "How's my favorite party girl–reporter?"

"Good, Freddy," she winked. "We'll have six tequila shots and two Pacificos with lime."

I don't know if my chin actually hit the bar. "You don't mess around, huh?"

"Not at my age, babe. I live like I want to. If you wanna do well in this game, you'll do the same. Take it from Samantha. Don't try to spin these reporters with a bunch of shit. They'll chew your cute little ass off. You haven't been around yet."

I nodded. I was being schooled on exactly what schools don't teach.

"Here's to Jim Asher," she said. "You're gonna go far, babe. I've got a sense about these things."

I had watched this woman on TV since I was in junior high. She was one of the top reporters in the LA market. But somehow, from the start, it felt like Samantha and I were friends who'd simply been waiting to meet. We clanked glasses and slammed the shots. The tequila was smooth, almost pleasing. I reached for my Pacifico, but Samantha caught my hand gently.

"Not yet, Jimmy. Two more shots to get warm."

I knew I was in for it. "I've gotta be at work by five o'clock tomorrow morning, Samantha."

"Don't worry, I'll make sure you get there. Just tell 'em you were with me."
Like that would help.

We downed more liquor. Soon enough, she was hanging all over me, and I was hanging all over her. We were both smoking Marlboro red dogs, and the bar scene was blurring into a glittery surreal backdrop of melodic conversation. But people were beginning to notice, including some of Edward's campaign staff. I was making a spectacle of myself.

"Do you wanna get out of here?" she suddenly asked.

"Yeah. Hold on a sec. I have to check on something."

I searched the bar until I found Michelle, sitting by herself. "I'm taking off."

"Where?" Michelle asked.

"For a little drive." I tossed her my car keys; she had driven with me. "Just park it at the campaign. I'll catch a lift home."

She tilted her head and narrowed her eyes. "You're not going home with that . . . that *reporter*, are you, Jim?"

"Of course not." I kissed Michelle on the forehead and hustled back to Samantha, half expecting her to be gone. But she was still at the bar, now surrounded by a pack of middle-aged, chain-smoking male print reporters.

I approached the group hesitantly.

"Hey, there he is!" Samantha sang out to me. "My little Republican man." She stretched out her arms. "Come here, Jimmy."

The reporters eyed me suspiciously.

I had to act fast.

"How 'bout a round of beers," I offered. "Compliments of the Winston campaign."

Frowns and folded arms suddenly turned into smiles and slaps on the back. The reporters welcomed me into their distinctive circle. I took out the campaign's gold credit card, which I was authorized to use for "schmoozing."

A reporter named Paul Duran from the *Daily News* shook my hand. He was short and sloppy. This guy was a vintage old-school reporter—loose tie, rolled sleeves, cigar in his pocket, an alcoholic's nose.

"What do you do for Winston?" he asked.

"Press," I said.

"How long you been with him?"

"Not too long."

Paul pulled me aside. Samantha was busy talking to some reporter. "So, really, what's the guy like?" Paul asked.

"He's a great guy," I said. Of course, I hadn't met my own candidate, but I had to say something.

Paul glanced around, as if one of his reporter buddies might be eavesdropping. "Is Winston weird?"

"Weird?"

"You know." He held his hand out with a limp wrist. *"Weird."*

"Oh . . . Oh, no. I don't think so."

Paul's interest seemed to wane slightly. "It's just that we're hearing rumors."

"Oh."

Paul slipped me his card. "Thanks for the drink, Jim. Look, I don't have anyone inside your campaign yet. So gimme a call early next week."

Before I put the card in my pocket, I flipped it over. His home and cellular numbers were scribbled on the back in red ink.

An hour later, Samantha and I were flying a hundred miles an hour up Pacific Coast Highway, passing each other a hollowed-out pineapple full of tasty rum and juice—a parting gift from Freddy the bartender. The top was off her black Lamborghini Diablo VT, and the warm summer night's air was salty and alive as it rushed around me. Samantha drove the car recklessly, steering into sharp corners like we were in a slot car.

"Slow down!" I shouted over the engine.

She mashed down on the gas, pasting my head against the leather seat. We hit the next sweeping corner at eighty-five. I closed my eyes and clutched the handgrip, sure this would be my last breath.

"If we're gonna die," she shouted, "might as well be fast and drunk!" She actually accelerated into the turn, wheels screeching, flinging me against the door. The next thing I knew we were on a long straightaway. I let my breath out. Samantha cranked up Creedence Clearwater Revival's "Proud Mary" on the CD player and danced in her seat. I had never been in a Lamborghini before. And for some reason I wasn't worried about the police pulling Samantha over. I felt like we were above that, somewhere in that realm of celebrity where things are different than they are for those of us who drive Fords and eat drive-thru tacos.

"Isn't this fun, Jimmy?" she giggled.

I lit a smoke and laughed up into the bended dome of blurry stars. The whole night seemed wondrously out of my control. Samantha hung a sharp right off PCH and headed up into the hills overlooking the ocean. The Diablo's tires seemed to be coated with rubber cement as we raced up the narrow winding road, no guardrails. As we tore through the rich hills of Pacific Palisades, Samantha pointed out all the celebrity homes. She pulled into a long driveway. The house at the end was enormous. Its exterior was entirely stained wood, with large fern-draped balconies and a sprawling lawn that dropped into bleached white sea cliffs. Samantha parked behind a black BMW, flipped off her high heels, and raced up to the house.

"Come on, Jimmy. Come on!"

I raised the vertical door and climbed out of the low-sitting sports car. The house seemed too big for Samantha's television reporter salary. Then I saw a sparkling blue Lotus parked in front of the BMW in the open garage.

"Do you live alone?" I asked.

She smiled. "Come inside."

I took a deep breath and followed her up the brick path to the front door. When I stepped inside, I saw a huge bar in the middle of the living room. It was about thirty feet long, similar to the main bar at Billboard Live.

"Nice," I said sarcastically. "A bar in your living room?"

She grabbed my hand and dragged me over to a bar stool. "This is a very famous bar," she said. "Do you know that Jerry Woods used to be my bartender at parties, even when he was still governor."

"Wow."

She pointed to a picture on the wall. A nearby neon Budweiser sign lit up the frame—and sure enough, there was ex-California governor Jerry Woods mixing up daiquiris with Samantha kissing his cheek.

Samantha sighed. "The eighties were so much fun. Now everyone's too uptight." She pointed out the window. "See that Jacuzzi?" A redwood hot tub was perched on the cliff. "We used to throw wild coke parties out there, with all the governor's people, the mayor's people, movie stars, and a lot of your Republican friends."

At this point I wondered if Samantha knew how young I was. She was clearly drunk, but I could tell she had been there many times. In fact, she seemed to thrive there. Her clothes were attractive and her body was shapely. Chestnut freckles sprinkled her tan chest, but under her makeup, her pretty face was thinly lined from years of living this life I was seeing.

She walked behind the bar and flipped on the stereo. Led Zeppelin. She plugged in one of her five blenders. "How 'bout some margaritas?"

I glanced at my watch. "I've gotta be back in Orange County in four hours."

"That's why you need margaritas, babe. If you sleep now, you're fucked. Mornings are like corners, you've got to accelerate into them."

Seemed wise enough to me. "Mix 'em up," I said. I strolled around the downstairs with my hands in my pockets. The place was huge and well appointed—pool table, jukebox, big-screen TV. "So, this is your house?"

"Yeah. My father was a rich banker. When he died, he left everything to yours truly."

"So you've never been married?"

"Why would I?"

We finished off the pitcher. Then another. She sauntered over to my chair and sat on my lap, straddling me with her black skirt raised and crumpled around her hips.

"So what do you think?" she asked.

"About what?"

"About me." She kissed my neck.

"You're great," I said. "Fun . . . and pretty."

She kissed my cheek. "Let's go play in the hot tub."

Slowly, she pulled back and unbuttoned her silk blouse, letting it fall behind her. She leaned in, breathing seductively, and whispered, "Jimmy, can you make me moan tonight?"

I glanced over at the picture of the governor. He looked drunk now, and I pictured him passed out on Samantha's couch with some naked actress at his side. I thought about the others back at the campaign office. Did they know about this? Did they know about this side of politics—the fun side, the exciting side? If so, they had never mentioned it to me. I was operating on my own, making it up as I went. I could already see how politics was going to work. The power would come fast and loose if I could get in with the right people, like Samantha. Reporters and politicians needed one another. I pictured myself as the man in between. Why hadn't anyone else thought of it? Of course they had, but it's the kind of thing nobody talks about. It was at that moment, then, staring down at Samantha's naked white breasts, so far from where I was a month before, so close to my dreams I could literally touch them, that I saw my future—vividly.

I would streak to the top of the political arena with blistering speed, blowing a hole directly through the standard pay-your-dues career structure. I had no interest in paying any dues, wasting time. I wanted to be at the top—debating Democrats on talk shows, roaming the halls of Congress like I owned them, altering legislation with a single phone call, shooting the shit with senators, advising the president—and I wanted it now. I had a clear open road ahead of me. I knew I wasn't doing anything morally or ethically wrong; I was simply going at politics from a newer, faster angle.

I peeled off my clothes, slammed the icy froth at the bottom of the margarita pitcher, and followed Samantha outside. As I walked naked under the stars, the warm night air made me feel free. Samantha pushed the cover off the hot tub. Steam rose from the water as we plunged in. Within two seconds we were going at it, mouths locked together, hands racing over each other's bodies. Samantha panted in my ear and groped me. She reached up on the deck and grabbed the new full pitcher of margaritas. With one hand she pulled me up behind her. She bent over the edge of the tub slowly, seductively. Then she poured the thick drink over her shoulder, letting it run down her shapely back. She asked me to lick it off. Unbelievable.

TWO

Samantha pulled up to the Winston campaign office with a screech. 6:15 A.M. I was late.

"Thanks, Boo-Boo," she said. "You're a steam engine."

Now she was going to call me Boo-Boo. Who cared, I liked the steam engine part anyway. "It was fun," I said, squinting. To the southeast, the sun was washing orange over the Main Place Mall.

Samantha put on funky black sunglasses. "Call me at the station, Jimmy. My card's in your back pocket."

I reached down and felt its outline through my cheap slacks.

"I want an exclusive with Winston one of these days," she said. "Why don't you suggest it to him?"

"No problem," I said. Of course, I would have to meet him first.

Rubber squealed and the Lamborghini disappeared in a black blur around the corner. Samantha's custom license plate summarized her life: NO SLOW. I rushed inside. I had my own key because I was always the first one in the office. I dragged my shaky hand across the panel of switches, and the fluorescent lights hummed to life. The office always seemed weird when it was empty, like a high school classroom on the weekends.

My first stop every morning was the coffeemaker. I pulled out the plastic filter cup. It was full of coffee grounds from the night before. I poured a mountain of fresh grounds directly onto the soggy ones and filled the water container. I liked my morning coffee thick, like motor oil. I had work to do. I dragged a stack of newspapers from the front door to my small workspace and started tearing through them. My morning job was to clip newspaper articles—any stories mentioning our Senate race, either candidate, or campaign issues. I knew just where to look—page three, metro section, editorial page. Like everyone else in the world, I felt that my job was important; if I missed an article, the whole campaign missed it. I blazed through the *Los Angeles Times*, *Orange County Register*, LA *Daily News*, and the smaller local dailies. A private clipping service handled the other major markets, including San Francisco, San Diego, and DC. I had my own fax machine, which was already spitting out articles.

By 6:45 I had all the clips in one neat stack, leaving a scattered trail of mangled papers in my wake. This morning's bundle was thick. I had already learned that papers always dump positive political stories on Fridays. Sundays are also good, but you have to be careful; an unfriendly editor can fuck you by dropping your fluff piece on Saturday—the one day nobody gives a damn about politics.

I made ten copies of the clips and dropped them on the important desks throughout the office. Then I faxed copies to the high-powered consultants in DC and Sacramento. A Post-it note told me that Mariella was in Texas, so I faxed all thirty pages to her Marriott hotel, tying up their machine for twenty-five minutes. Mariella was fanatical about the clips. She always had to be on top of everything. The one time I had missed sending them, she went postal on me. I wouldn't make the same mistake twice. Mariella had given me every break and every key assignment at the campaign so far. She was a shrewd, enchanting, beautiful blond-haired whirlwind from Buenos Aires, comfortable throwing her imposing intellect around her husband's campaign. I was one of the only people in the office who truly liked her—or at least didn't rip on her behind her back.

By 7 A.M. the clips were done. People would start trailing into the office any minute. I staggered down the quiet hallway to the rest room. Each footstep on the marble floor felt like a cruel slap to my head. I walked into the rest room's foyer and nearly tripped over a big pile of clothes on the floor.

"Damn janitor!"

I went to kick the clothes aside but stopped myself. I looked down. Lying there on the floor, passed out like a recently destitute pauper, was John Griggs, the issues director. A stack of newspapers covered his head and upper body. His suit and tie were wrinkled, and his shoeless dress socks were shot with holes.

I reached down and pulled the papers off his face.

"John, are you okay?" I shook him, ready to check for a pulse. "John, wake up."

He grunted deeply and opened his eyes. He shook his head and rubbed his swollen eyes. "Where am I?"

"You're in the bathroom foyer," I said, laughing. "You okay?"

I helped him to his feet.

"Man, I don't remember falling asleep."

"What the hell were you doing?"

"I've been writing Edward's big immigration speech. Haven't slept in three days."

"Hey, I just made some ass-kickin' coffee in there, why don't you grab a cup, or the whole pot."

John checked his watch. "Shit, I've gotta finish the draft . . ." He dashed out the door and down the hallway.

I crammed the newspapers into the trash. This wasn't the first time I'd seen my new friend like this. Compared to John, the average fifty-hour workaholic was a slacker. The week before, I had discovered him snoozing under a folding table in the copier room at 5 A.M. I wondered if they had ever found him that way at the White House—passed out like a vagrant under Bush's desk in the Oval Office.

I went into the bathroom to check my look in the mirror. Just as I suspected: eyes bloodshot, suit filthy, hair going more directions than a compass in a room full of magnets. My clothes stank of cigarettes and tequila. My breath was unspeakable. I knew I was in for it when the campaign manager saw my sorry condition. I stripped to the waist and took a whore's bath in the sink. I didn't have a comb, so I used my fingers to tame my hair. When I got dressed, I looked in the mirror again. I still looked like shit. No amount of superficial sprucing could hide my disgraceful state. I was going to be in big trouble. I'd probably lose my job.

"Fuck it."

I walked out to my car, crammed seven sticks of Big Red in my mouth, and coated my suit with cheap-ass cologne from my glove box. I was ready for work.

I walked up to the conference room a few minutes late. The morning meeting had already begun. I peeked in through the crack in the door. Just my luck, all the big shot consultants were in the office this morning. I wanted to crawl under a vacant desk and hide out for a few hours. I really didn't want to get fired less than a month into my new profession. I would never be able to get another fresh start in politics. This was my one shot, and I knew I looked like a damn wreck. Just then, the receptionist walked by and gave me a strange look. Maybe I could run out the front door and call in sick? Then again, several people had seen me partying the night before.

I had to walk into the meeting. Only a coward would run out. I swallowed down my fear and opened the conference room door. I glanced around the polished mahogany table at some of the GOP's biggest players. Bud Raper, a man in his late fifties with a receding hairline, arched eyebrows, and a constant five o'clock shadow on his charismatic face, was the top political consultant in the world—Republican, Democrat, whatever. He had run dozens of campaigns, including Ronald Reagan's, and was a regular on CNN and the networks. Bud was royalty in the realm of spinmeisters. Next to him sat Sal Puchman, California's top GOP consultant, a behind-the-scenes wizard who had written many of Nixon's and Reagan's most memorable lines—including the eloquent

Challenger disaster speech. On the speakerphone were four of the highest-paid media and polling consultants in the business. In assembling his election team, Edward had spared no expense. This was indeed the Dream Team of GOP politics.

When I stepped into the room, everyone stopped talking and stared at me. I froze. Somehow even the speakerphone fell silent. Nazi death camp wardens looked friendly compared to these people. I knew I was in deep *shitzé*. My face flushed red, and I think I heard my gulp echo off the walls. I prepared to dive out the window. Suddenly Bud Raper sprang to his feet. "There he is!" he shouted, pointing at me. "The big press man!" He smiled proudly. "We heard about you and that reporter last night, buddy. Now that's what I call fuckin' media relations!"

He smiled and slapped me on the back, motioning to the empty seat beside him. "You're learning, kid," he said. "Sit down."

I couldn't believe it. Bud had barely ever spoken to me before. None of the big consultants had paid me much attention. But now they were all smiling and congratulating me. Astonished, but proud, I sat down next to Bud and the meeting went on.

My direct supervisor at the campaign was Winter Hallman, the communications director. Winter was a stunning twenty-seven-year-old former DKNY model. She was thin and strikingly beautiful, with long creamy legs, high cheekbones, a button nose, and flowing blond hair. Very pristine. She had graduated top of her class from Princeton, then worked as a speechwriter for President Bush when she was only twenty-three. Her claim to fame was writing the speech Bush had delivered in Japan just before he vomited on their prime minister and passed out like a wretched wino. Still, she had to be proud.

Winter had it all. Pleasing to the eye. Inspiring to the mind. She was one of those lucky few dealt a full hand at the genetics table. Mariella had booted the previous two communications directors and anointed Winter as the campaign's media princess. They were soul mates; they were both into meditation and spiritual mysticism of some sort. Once, late at night, I stumbled onto the two of them meditating in Mariella's office, surrounded by ghostly candles and hypnotic music. I didn't give it much thought. I figured that's what rich, brilliant people do.

After the morning meeting Winter gave me a few hours off.

"Get yourself together," she told me. Her voice was always calm and sweet when she talked to me; it could be piercing and shrill when she yelled at other staffers. "I need your help with a press release later, Jim. We've got this big immigration speech coming up tomorrow, and the media is clamoring to find out know where Edward stands on Prop. 187."

Proposition 187 was the hottest issue in California. Basically, if voters approved the measure in a statewide ballot, illegal immigrants would find themselves on the run in California. Proposition 187 would cut all government benefits to illegals, remove undocumented children from public schools, and require employers to report suspected illegals to the INS. Deportation would be made much easier. Liberals and Democrats opposed 187 as "cruel" and "mean-spirited." But most Californians, feeling violated and overrun by the estimated two million illegals in our state, favored 187. I favored it myself. For me, the key word was *illegal*. Every time I broke the law—speeding, parking illegally, or even taking a leak on a tree—I knew I was responsible for my actions, and the penalties. But illegal aliens were breaking the law every second of every day, by definition. If caught, I figured they should be deported. Certainly my tax money—my property—should not be used to educate their kids and pay for their medical bills. Not that I had anything against illegals as people. I sympathized with them. Hell, if I was a Mexican, I would have been jumping the fence and making a mad dash for San Diego myself. But the law was the law.

At his immigration speech the following day, Edward would announce his position on 187. There was plenty of speculation in the media; some thought he would court the Hispanic vote by opposing 187. But I had already known for two days that Edward would come out in favor of 187. Bud Raper was predicting a five-point jump in the polls, at least.

"I'll just take a quick shower and come back," I told Winter. "I don't want to leave you all by yourself."

"You might as well take a quick nap, Jim. We've got a long two days ahead of us." She patted my shoulder softly, holding on to my arm for just a second. "I need you to be one hundred percent."

"Thanks, Winter."

"Sure, sweetie."

I already had a schoolboy crush on her.

———————

When I got back to the campaign that afternoon the place was going mad. John Griggs rushed up to me.

"Did you hear the good news?" he asked.

"What good news?"

"A new poll just came out," he beamed. "Guess who's leading the California Senate race?"

I smiled. "Edward Winston?"

"You got it, playboy."

"That's fuckin' awesome," I said.

"Hey, by the way, Winter's looking for you. Everyone's in crash mode trying to get the good word out."

I found Winter in the office we shared. She had her headphones on, and her phone panel was lit up like a 911 switchboard. She pushed mute when she saw me.

"Jim, I'm glad to see you. Did you hear the fab news?"

"Yeah. Isn't it great that—"

"Listen, I'm juggling six reporters right now. Can you take a few press calls? John is pinned down with the immigration speech."

I had never taken a press call before. Besides Mariella, Winter was the only person authorized to speak on the record with reporters. Even Chuck, the campaign manager, could not be quoted. This was a huge break for me. But it also seemed like an affront to Chuck and some of the other senior staff. I was fully aware of all the politics *within* the office.

"Sure," I said. "I'll do my best."

She nodded, now a bit apprehensively. "Go get the spin from John Griggs," she said. Then she was back on the phone, in full spin mode herself.

I found John snacking on Dutch pastries in the kitchen. Mariella had the office on a fabulous European catering schedule. She had also hired a full-time masseuse on staff. The massage lady would wander around the office dishing out shoulder massages, and full body massages in one of the empty offices upon request. I thought it was a little weird, but who was I to refuse such lavish treatment.

"So what's our angle on this new poll?" I asked John.

"I talked to Raper ten minutes ago. He said we should really play it up. Make like Steadfield is on the ropes," he replied, with a mouth full of pastries.

"Okay. Thanks."

John crinkled his eyebrows. "Are you talking to the press, Jim?"

"Yeah—I guess."

"Wooow. Moving on up in the world."

"Yeah, right."

I walked up to the front desk and told the receptionist to direct calls from low-level reporters to the empty volunteer office. Thirty seconds later I had my first press call.

"Some reporter from the *Daily News*," the receptionist said.

"Put 'em through," I said. I tried to gulp down my anxiety, but when the phone beeped, my heart exploded. I was terrified I would say something stupid and everyone would read it in the clips the next morning. Reporters were still mysterious to me. My trembling hand reached for the receiver.

"This is Jim Asher."

"Jim Asher," the voice repeated slowly. "This is Paul Duran, *Daily News.* Didn't I meet you last night at Billboard Live?"

"Yeah," I said, "that's right." His familiar voice lifted a trillion tons off my shoulders. "Hi, Paul. Good to talk to you again."

"Great. Well, I'm calling about this new Field poll. Can you go on record?"

"Of course," I said.

"What do you guys make of it?"

"We're pleased."

Silence.

Did he want me to keep going?

"We're extremely excited," I continued. "We've known all along that our message of lower taxes, less welfare, and tougher law enforcement would appeal to the voters."

"Okay . . ." he said. I heard his fingers tapping a keyboard in the background. So far, so good.

"In the past, when Winston was trailing in the polls, your campaign discounted polls as 'unreliable.' Why are you suddenly embracing this poll?"

Shit. He had a good point. I didn't know the answer to that one. So I did what Bud and Winter had been teaching me: spin.

"Well, our internal polling here at the campaign has been showing us ahead for weeks. We've been tracking Steadfield's decline in the polls since July. Now the external polls are simply confirming what we've known all along: Californians are fed up with Dana Steadfield. They're fed up with her out-of-control spending habits, her weak stance on the death penalty, and her lack of concern for average hard-working folks."

"Perfect," Paul said. His keyboard was humming. "What's the feeling there at the campaign? What's Edward saying?"

As if I would know.

"We couldn't be more excited," I said. "There's a feeling of electricity here at the campaign. This is a big moment for Edward, and we're all tremendously proud of him."

"Thanks, that's all I need," Paul said. Then his tone changed. "Hey, by the way, did you bang Samantha last night?"

"Maybe," I said. "But that's off the record."

He laughed with a jolly smoker's hack. "Great. Let's go out for drinks one of these nights. I'll introduce you to some more reporters."

"Sounds good," I said. I was relieved. Everything I had said was simply regurgitated spin from the thousands of campaign stories I'd read doing the clips, or stuff I had picked up by listening to Winter on the phone. My eyes and ears were always wide open, and it paid off.

After three more calls from small-time local reporters, I went back to my desk in Winter's office.

"How'd it go?" she asked.

"Good. I don't think I messed up."

"I hope not," she said. "We'll find out tomorrow morning. The clips don't lie, sweetie."

Mariella Winston walked in, glowing. I hadn't seen her in weeks. She was tall and glamorous-looking, in a smart European way, and she always dressed magnificently. There was never a moment when Mariella didn't look completely prepared to step before a television camera; she even had a full-time hair and makeup lady who shadowed her everywhere she went.

"Did you hear the terrific news, Jimmy?" Mariella asked.

I smiled enthusiastically. "It's great news. I really think Edward's going to win."

Mariella walked over to my desk, practically floating, and kissed me tenderly on the cheek. "We don't 'think' he's going to win, sweetheart, we *know* he's going to win." Mariella still had a strong South American accent, but she also had an unbelievable command of English—much better than mine, and I'd been speaking it all my life. Mariella never paid attention to low-level staffers, except when they crossed her path. But she seemed to take an immediate liking to me. She was always telling me how handsome and smart I was. Whenever Mariella spoke to me, I felt a certain energy emanating from her—remarkably powerful, almost like gravity—and her piercing emerald eyes had a hypnotic effect on me. Although I never allowed myself to be completely sucked in, I felt compelled to do her bidding, and I always wanted to be a part of her world.

Winter pranced across the office and threw her arms around Mariella. "Isn't it wonderful."

Mariella kissed her warmly on the lips. "I know, honey. It's all happening like I told you."

Winter nodded. I noticed a watery glaze over her ice blue eyes.

"I have good news," Mariella said. "Let's get John, Renee, and the others together for a talk. We must build upon the positive energy we are all feeling now—we must harness it and channel it to transcend our current sphere of success. Edward is flying in from New York right now. We're going to dinner tonight—all the senior staff."

She turned to me.

"Jim, why don't you come along with us. You must meet Edward. I think you should develop a personal relationship with him."

"Thanks, Mariella."

"Sure, darling. By the way, why don't you call that reporter friend of yours, Samantha, and have her do a piece on this terrific new poll."

"No problem."

She kissed Winter again, then me. Mariella was affectionate in a graceful and flattering way that wasn't completely unsettling.

A minute later I was in the volunteer room—my secret cone-of-silence office. I dug Samantha's card from my pocket and immediately dialed her cellular phone.

She answered over a scratchy connection. "Gellhorne."

"Samantha, it's Jim, from last night—"

"Gotta go, babe."

The line went dead.

Shit. That was certainly the shortest friendship I'd ever made. I set the receiver back on the phone, feeling almost embarrassed. Damn—now Mariella was going to ask about the interview. She always followed up on everything. What would I say?

I moped down to the kitchen. John Griggs was snacking, this time on Chee-tos.

"How'd the press calls go, Jim?"

"Okay, I guess."

"Hey, did you hear? We're all going out to dinner with Edward tonight."

"Yeah. I really can't wait to meet this guy. It's kinda weird working for a total stranger."

"Politics is like that sometimes. I didn't meet Bush until I had been at the White House for five weeks. Everyone goes through it. Anyway, after dinner, we're all going to the Shark's Club for drinks. Wanna come?"

"Winston's going?" I asked.

"No. No way. He's not into that kind of stuff. But Chuck's going, and all the girls from the office too."

"Sounds dope."

Just then we heard angry shouts coming from behind Chuck's closed door.

"Hey, John, is there some kind of tension between Chuck and Winter? They don't seem to like each other."

"No comment, my friend. You'll have to make up your own mind on that. If you're smart, you'll stay out of office conflicts. That's what I do. Just do your work and keep to yourself."

"Yeah. You're probably right. No one ever messes with you."

"So, come on, what do you say about the Shark's Club?"

"Count me in, playboy."

The receptionist's voice came over the intercom. "Jim Asher, you have a call on line five: *Samantha Gellhorne!*" she giggled.

Everyone in the office grinned and chuckled at me. Apparently the joke had spread fast. With my face red, I dashed to the volunteer office.

"Hello."

"Sorry I had to hang up, Boo-Boo. I was sitting at a community meeting with the governor and the mayor. Your call brought the whole meeting to a screeching halt."

"Shit, I'm really sorry."

"Don't worry. So what's up?"

"Did you see the new Field poll?"

"I knew about it two days ago, Boo-Boo," she said. "Maybe next time I'll give you a heads-up, make you a hero at the campaign." Samantha seemed to drift easily between her role as a reporter and the woman who had licked cocktails off my stomach the night before.

"Can I get Winston?" she asked.

"Let me check . . . hold on."

I sprinted to Mariella's office. She was on the phone, but she held it aside.

"What is it, darling?"

"Mariella, can Edward do an exclusive with Channel Seven?"

"Is that your girlfriend's station?"

"Samantha."

"Emmm . . ." She paused. "His flight doesn't get in until five o'clock and then . . . oh, honey, why don't I just do it? Would that be okay with . . ."

"Samantha. I'm sure it would be."

I raced back to the phone.

"Samantha?"

"Babe."

"Edward's getting in late. How about Mariella, his wife? She's great on camera."

"Yeah, that's fine," Samantha said. "Actually from everything I've seen, she's an incredible woman. I caught her on the *Today* show last week. She was brilliant. I'd really love to meet her, but right now I can only send a camera for a canned statement."

"That's fine," I said.

"The crew will be there in an hour. Look, I've gotta run, Boo-Boo. Call me at the house tonight, okay?"

"Okay. Bye, Samantha."

Mariella always got tizzied over television interviews. Even though I told her it was only a canned soundbite, she immediately summoned the hairdresser and sent a female campaign aide to fetch a flashy scarf from Saks Fifth Avenue at the mall.

"Thanks for setting this up, sweetheart," she told me. Another kiss. "I think we need to make a new position for you, Jimmy. Maybe something like 'media relations' or 'media outreach specialist.'" She turned to Winter. "What do you think, Winter? Can we put Jim in charge of media outreach?"

Winter shrugged. "He seems to like it."

"Okay," Mariella said to me. "You will focus on relations with reporters, and booking Edward and me on television and radio interviews. Can you handle that?"

"Sure."

"Go tell Chuck about your new job," she said. "And how much are we paying you, sweetheart?"

"One thousand a month," I said, shamefully. I was the lowest-paid employee. Even the receptionist blushed when she saw my check.

"You'll have a lot more responsibility with your new job," Mariella said. "Go tell Chuck we are doubling your salary."

I nodded, speechless. Money was nothing to Mariella. The difference between one thousand dollars and ten thousand was like the difference between a penny and a dime to her. That's not to say she didn't understand its effect on people like me. She manipulated situations brilliantly, throwing me right in the middle of everything, to her own advantage. But I was game. I was watching my career take off before my eyes like a spectator at Cape Canaveral.

THREE

Chuck Hotchner, the campaign manager, was not pleased when I informed him of Mariella's unilateral appointment. He sat leaning half-cocked in his leather executive chair.

"Mariella told you *what?*" he fumed.

I explained the whole story—my new position and salary.

"I'm sorry, Chuck," I said. "I didn't ask her for it."

"I know," he waved me off. "This is personal, between Mariella and myself. It's just so fucking typical. I should never have let that woman walk into this office. She's like a rampant bacterial fungus disease. She just keeps eating away at your skin. I can't make one move without her approval now. I'm standing on stumps for legs. I can't run a fucking statewide campaign like this!"

He leaned all the way back in his chair, staring at the ceiling tiles with a faraway, dispirited look. Mariella had that effect on anyone who rubbed her backward. Chuck was in his late thirties, very handsome, with stylish clothes and hair. He was respected in the political world as a savvy, tough player. I also happened to know through the garrulous accounting girl that he was pulling down $35,000 a month running the campaign. I admired Chuck, and he had always been good to me from the first day. I hated to see him so dejected.

"Fucking bitch," he grumbled.

"Do you want me to leave, Chuck?"

He snapped to. "No. I've been meaning to talk to you, Jim. Look, about this reporter thing—Gellhorne. You've gotta be careful, buddy. I know it's fun and everything, but you could find yourself in a deep river of fast-moving shit real quick."

"I'll be careful."

"Don't tell it to me. Tell it to yourself." He leaned forward, resting his hands on the desk, fingers interlaced, his brown eyes solidly locked on mine. "I'm not preaching to you, Jim. Fuck, when I was your age, I would've told an old guy like me to go fuck a diseased goat. But that's the point. You remind me of myself ten years ago. In fact, when I was a hotshot young operative, I was pulling the same game you are, pal. And guess what? I was fucking the same reporter—Samantha Gellhorne. That's right. Only back then, her tits didn't sag. All I'm telling you is, there's no shortcut to the top."

I was paying attention, but not exactly listening. The part about Samantha hit home, and I could see where he was coming from. In fact, I could step outside myself and look at the scene from Chuck's perspective—talking to some young punk he knew was going to disregard his advice and live to regret it.

"That's all the preaching from Uncle Chuck today," he said. "Take from it what you will. Just go a little slower, Jim. Use your brain, and work your ass off. I see you coming in at five and leaving at midnight every day. That's good. You'll get there. You'll grow old and get rich like me. That's how it works. You establish yourself, earn a reputation, then these politicians will pay you anything you want. They'll think they can't win without you."

"I know."

"And by the way, watch your back with Mariella and Winter. Don't get tangled up with the wrong crowd, Jim. You've got friends on this side."

I nodded. "Thanks for the talk, Chuck."

I walked back to my desk, thinking the situation over. Winter had given me an identical talk about Chuck the day before, warning me not to "choose the wrong side." I was starting to understand. At some point, I would have to make a choice between Mariella's camp and Chuck's. In an office environment as dynamic as the Winston campaign, no one could sit on the fence and expect to find glory in the winner's circle. A fence sitter could survive, yes, but not thrive. And I *had* to thrive. But for the meantime, I would trim my sails to whatever winds blew through the office and keep my eyes focused on the prize—personal success.

That night we all met at the El Torito Grill in Costa Mesa. Edward was driving directly from the airport. Mariella, Winter, Chuck, John, and I waited for him outside. Also joining us was a press aide named Matt, and Renee Tumler, the fundraiser. Renee had been an Olympic two-hundred-meter swimmer at the '88 Seoul Games. She was pretty and whimsical—precocious—without a shred of the pretension one would expect from her ranks. I was meeting all kinds of interesting people in politics I would never have met otherwise.

Edward arrived a few minutes late in a black Lincoln Town Car. It was the first time I had seen him point blank. He was tall, with a distinguished and handsome face, and a marathon runner's lean frame. He wore sharply creased khakis and a yellow polo. His hair was neatly combed. As he walked up to the restaurant, followed by his personal assistant, his eyes were fixed dead on me.

"So, who is this?" he asked, holding out his hand.

I shook it vigorously. "I'm Jim Asher. Nice to meet you, sir."

"It's Edward." He smiled warmly, but his hand was cool and dry. "What do you do for me, Jim?" He turned to Mariella, as if to say, *Are you hiring more people?*

I was petrified. "Uh," I stammered, "I work in the press office and, um—"

Mariella swooped in and saved my pathetic ass. "He's doing media outreach, Edward," she said. "He's brilliant. It's so important that we make friendships with these reporters. Winter is too busy with the speeches to be proactive. Jimmy is wonderful with the media."

"Well," Edward said. "I've already spent ten million on this campaign so far. What's another ten." He threw his arm around me, probably sensing I was terrified. "Let's get something to eat," he said, rubbing his stomach. "I'm starving!"

I tried to sit as far from Edward as possible at the table, taking a seat in the corner next to John. Edward was unlike anyone I had ever met. Maybe it was the money. But I think there was something else about him, something very difficult to define. When you looked at his face it was objectively handsome, but under his skin I could always see his skeleton. As I watched him talking and joking awkwardly with his staff—people who barely knew him—I sensed that he was not enjoying the company; he was only putting up with it because he had to. All things considered, I couldn't blame him.

"Jim, come over here," Edward waved. "I'd like to talk with my newest employee."

Shit. Now I was going to get it—the hot seat. He would realize what a fraud I was. My masquerade in politics would be over. Edward kicked Matt out of the chair directly across from him and I sat down. To make the interrogation scene complete, an unshaded light dangled directly above my head.

"So, Jim, where did you go to school?" he asked.

All eyes were on me. I knew from reading articles that Edward had graduated from the prestigious Wharton School of Business.

"University of Colorado at Colorado Springs," I said.

"Mmmm . . ." He didn't seem impressed. "Why Colorado?"

"I was stationed at Fort Carson," I said. "I was in the military for four years."

"Oh," he said. "What branch?"

"The army. I was a reconnaissance scout. That's how I paid for college."

"That's terrific. You know, a lot of people think I grew up rich. I didn't. Our family didn't have much money until I was already at Wharton. In fact, I was one of the poorest kids in my freshman class, along with my first-year dorm mate, Donny Trump."

Everyone at the table smiled, obviously impressed.

"You see," Edward continued, "my dad's small electronics company in San Francisco didn't catch fire until my sophomore year; that's when he switched from making ten-dollar calculators to million-dollar mainframe computers."

"I didn't know that," I said.

"It's true. You need to learn these things about me, Jim. If you're going to be talking to the media, these are important things to get out."

Mariella chimed in. "Yes, I agree. Overcoming this image that Edward is some out-of-touch rich tycoon is going to be one of our biggest obstacles. Steadfield's campaign will try to label him as an empty suit who is trying to buy the election."

Everyone at the table nodded.

"I paid my own way through Wharton on track and field scholarships," Edward added. "But that's enough about me. So, Jim, what were you doing before you joined my campaign?"

Edward was asking me more questions than anyone else had bothered to ask in more than a month at the campaign. "Well, I was studying for the LSAT. I'm thinking of going to law school."

"You don't want to be a lawyer," he said. "I've got a dozen of them—they're all miserable. How have you been paying the bills?"

"I'm living at home, temporarily," I admitted. "And I've been modeling once in a while for spending money."

"Modeling, eh? Have you done anything I would have seen?"

"I did the Sears catalog this spring, but it really wasn't much. I was wearing overalls and pretending to be a construction worker. Then I did an ad for Eddie Bauer a few months ago."

"Did you hear that, Mariella?" he said. "We have a model on our staff."

Mariella smiled, pointing to Winter. "We have two."

"If nothing else," Edward said cheerfully, "we have the best-looking campaign staff in the state." He turned to Winter. "I'm going to take Jim on the campaign trail with me for a week or two."

Winter agreed, of course.

"Can you write speeches?" Edward asked me.

I had never written a speech in my life. "Um . . . sure. My major in college was creative writing."

He chuckled, then made the required joke: "Creative writing . . . hah, hah, hah! That's all political speech writing is anyway!"

Everyone roared, clutching their sides, bursting with deliberate laughter.

Later that night, at the Shark's Club in Newport Beach, Chuck, John, Renee, and I met up with some other female staffers from the campaign. I swung by my house and changed into faded Levi's and a tight-fitting white T-shirt.

The bar was classy, with a gigantic aquarium full of miniature sharks and octopuses. Our party of twelve commandeered a long table, which Chuck promptly covered with cocktails. This was Chuck's troupe. I could tell they were all loyal to him, even John and Renee. Every time Mariella's or Winter's name came up, they all cringed. But I think they were pulling punches for my sake. No one knew where I stood. All the girls at the table had mid- or low-level jobs at the campaign—accountants, receptionists, computer consultants, field reps. Chuck had brought most of them with him from Arizona. They were fun-loving girls, professional, moderately good-looking, slightly older than me—not necessarily the kind of women I normally hung out with—but I got on with them famously, especially after I let it be known I was secretly pro-choice.

By midnight empty glasses and bottles had overrun the table, and we were all hammered. Chuck sat at the head of the table directing vodka shots at us like Patton ordering artillery strikes. All the girls loved Chuck. They clung to his arms and smiled at his every move. John and I were talking politics with Renee. At some point, she asked me to dance.

"Why certainly," I said.

Our drunken swaggering started a trend, and soon the dance floor was filled with our campaign staffers. John Griggs perched himself on the go-go stage and mimicked John Travolta as the Bee Gees whipped the yuppy crowd into a frenzy of gyrating hips and badly flailing arms. Chuck and I danced in a grotto of campaign girls. We passed a bottle of rum around the dance floor—twelve Republicans behaving badly. Chuck had dropped a generous tip, so the bouncers let the bottle fly. I strutted my stuff across the lit tile. This was my kind of politics.

By now Renee was dirty dancing me into a lusty froth, activating her hips with intent. She was seven years older than me, but she didn't act or look it. She still swam two miles every morning, and it definitely showed through her short silk dress. Her nipples were hard, and I could feel them tracing up and down my chest. She ran her fingers through my hair and reeled me in. Our bodies slowed down and our mouths came together. She tasted luscious, like rum and Coke mixed with a dash of lust, and her tongue danced circles around mine. I heard the other girls giggling.

At some point, Chuck grabbed me by the arm: "Let's talk." We walked back to the VIP lounge, where two rum and Cokes were waiting for us.

"What's the deal, Chuck?"

He looked different now, more serious.

"I know you're close to Mariella and Winter," he said. "And I don't want to put you in the middle. But have you heard anything recently from them?"

"Like what?"

"Like they might be planning to get rid of me," he said.

"I haven't heard anything."

"But you'd tell me if you did?"

"Of course I would."

"Look, Jim, Mariella is going to destroy this campaign if we don't all stick together. She has no experience in politics. She's telling Edward to spend all his money on fluffy television spots when we don't even have a goddamn field operation in place, not to mention that we have absolutely no money allocated for a get-out-the-vote effort. The list goes on and on. But it's not even that. The bottom line is that the professionals—Bud, Sal, and myself—we aren't able to make the necessary decisions regarding the direction of this campaign. Our hands are tied as long as Mariella continues to grab more power. Do you understand?"

"Sure," I said.

He slapped me on the shoulder. "Good. Now let's get back to the girls. I think Renee's gonna pounce you, sport."

FOUR

A week later I was surfing on my lunch break. I needed a few minutes away from the melodrama of the office. I was still beating the sun out of bed every morning to do the clips, but now Winter had me staying late with her, usually until one or two in the morning. I was living like a gypsy with a cause. My family never saw me, and my friends suspected I was back in Europe. Politics had overrun my life. Mariella had actually installed two hospital beds in an empty office, and we used them often. I loved being near Winter. Sometimes she would sleep in the hospital bed next to me wearing only a bra and panties, and she didn't seem to mind that I saw.

My little brother ran across the tourist-infested beach holding my campaign cellular phone. When I saw him, I ate shit on the wave but caught the next one to shore.

"Your phone's been ringing for the last ten minutes," he said, handing it to me.

A minute later it rang again—Edward.

"Jim, I tried calling everyone else, but I can't seem to get a hold of anyone. A thousand employees and not a single person when you need something simple. Anyway, I need to see a story from the *San Diego Union-Tribune*. I heard that their political reporter blasted me on the editorial page this morning."

"He did," I said. "It's a terrible hit piece, Edward."

"Fax it to me, please. For some reason no one is answering the phones at the office."

"The editorial is on its way."

It was the first time Edward had ever called me on the phone. A proud moment.

When I got to the office, the place looked like it had been evacuated in an air raid. Maybe there was a fire alarm? The receptionist's coffee mug sat on her desk, still steaming. The phones were ringing and ringing, but no one was around to pick them up. What the hell was going on?

As I walked to my office, I ran into Renee. She was scurrying out.

"You better get out of here," she whispered.

"What's going on?"

She mouthed: "Chuck and Mariella are having it out," and slipped out the door.

Shit. Edward was waiting by his hotel's fax machine for the editorial. I had to go in. I wasn't even halfway to my office before I heard the battle raging. Mariella was in Chuck's office, with the door slightly ajar.

"Fuck you, Chuck!" I heard.

"Fuck *you*, Mariella!"

I crept over to my desk and grabbed the *Union-Tribune* piece. I had to make this fast. As quietly as I could, with Chuck's door only ten feet away, I placed the clip on the fax and dialed Edward's number. The damn thing had never screamed so loud as it did right then, echoing through the empty office hallways. But Chuck and Mariella couldn't hear anything over their shouting. Mariella let out an ear-splitting screech, and I heard something crash into a wall. For a moment I thought I might have to break up a fistfight.

"Get the hell out of here, Chuck! You're a drain on my husband, and this campaign! You're completely incompetent!"

"You get the fuck out of here! You don't even have a job here. Do your husband a favor and butt the hell out! And speaking of money, this campaign spent more on hairdressing and travel for you than we did on voter registration last month!"

At that moment, Mariella let out a violent shriek. As soon as I saw the fax was going through, I bolted for the door. But I couldn't help looking over my shoulder. Mariella and Chuck were standing toe-to-toe, fingers pointing, angry spit flying between them. I saw a shattered telephone on the carpet and a hole in the wall above it. I got the hell out of there.

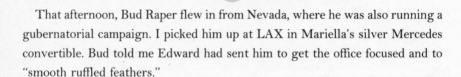

That afternoon, Bud Raper flew in from Nevada, where he was also running a gubernatorial campaign. I picked him up at LAX in Mariella's silver Mercedes convertible. Bud told me Edward had sent him to get the office focused and to "smooth ruffled feathers."

"What the hell's going on in that office?" he asked me.

I was so nervous talking to Bud that I could hardly concentrate on driving. "Chuck and Mariella are at each other's throats," I told him.

"Fuck . . . just what I need."

Bud obviously wanted to stay out of it. He told me the only reason he was working Edward's campaign was for the "shitload of dough" he was being paid. My informant in accounting told me Bud was pulling down $50,000 a month, plus a minimum $500,000 bonus if Edward won. For that amount, I figured he shouldn't be griping.

I got lost on our way back to the campaign, but Bud didn't seem to mind. I had the top down, and he was basking in the autumn sun, gazing out at the ocean and trying to enjoy a tranquil moment. I think Bud was running at least eight major political races around the country. One of his *five* cellular phones rang every few minutes. Bud would cuss out whoever was on the other end, yelling things like, "You tell that fuckin' pussy-ass reporter I'll kick his fuckin' nuts out through his teeth if he runs that bullshit story!" Then he would hang up and let out a long sigh. I was always nervous around Bud. He could build or crush someone's career with a single phone call.

"So, how do you like politics so far, kid?" he asked me.

"I fuckin' love it," I said.

It was always a good idea to swear around Bud. He was from the old school, from a time when politics was dirty as a rule. He loved to portray himself as a bar-brawling, cigar-chomping political gunslinger still kicking ass in the Information Age. My hero.

"I like your style, kid," he said. "Lemme tell you something: forget everything those pansy-ass professors taught you in college. If those sons of bitches knew jack shit about politics, they'd be out here kicking ass with you and me. You always gotta follow your instincts in politics, and always play to win, for *yourself.* Fuck as much media muff as you can. But, hell, you seem to have picked that one up already. Good press coverage is the key; these days it's nearly the whole fuckin' game, aside from paid advertising. After this race, when you get out there on your own, always ask for twice as much money as you think they'll pay. And never, under any circumstances, get sentimental about a candidate. They're all fucked in the head or they wouldn't be in the game to begin with.

"There's only four solid rules you always need to follow if you're gonna kick ass in this life. I call em Bud's Rules: One, never murder anyone. Two, never try heroin. Three, never sleep with another man. And four, whenever you get your opponent on the ground, with his face pressed against the curb, especially when he's begging for your mercy, always stomp down on that motherfucker's neck."

I nodded. "I'll try to remember that."

"You should pay strict attention to rule number three."

"Fuck you," I said, pushing my luck. He loved it, and punched me on the shoulder hard enough to swerve the car. I was immensely proud to be horsing around with Bud Raper; I couldn't wait to tell people about it.

Bud reached into his suit pocket and pulled out an envelope.

"Hey, I got these tickets from a friend who does PR for Sony." He tossed the envelope in my lap. "Why don't you take that reporter you're fucking and some of her friends. God knows someone needs to water the press on this campaign."

Using my knees to steer, I ripped the envelope open.

"Fuck yeah!" I hooted. "Thanks, Bud."

I was holding six front-row tickets to the Eagles reunion concert at Dodger Stadium.

"No problem, kid. Just tell Winter I gave you that night off."

I smiled, squinting into the windshield as we sailed down Highway 1 along the coast. My life was moving almost faster than I could dream up new ways to propel it. I stepped outside my body, floating at a vantage point somewhere over the freeway, and I saw myself racing along in the expensive Mercedes with this mega-political guru taking me under his powerful wing. The image was like throwing gunpowder on a fire.

FIVE

Chuck had pulled me aside again and had given me his version of the postbattle office. According to him, Mariella was dragging the campaign under with her own egotistical, self-promoting agenda, which he claimed had little to do with Edward's long-term good. It was true that Mariella had no experience in politics to speak of, and that she had basically muscled her way into the top decision-making post at the campaign. Chuck was secretly urging the entire campaign staff to rally behind himself and Bud, and to convince Edward that the campaign should be left in the hands of professionals—basically, to put Mariella in her place. The fight wasn't over anything ideological, it was about power and control.

I saw two problems with Chuck's plan. First, Bud didn't seem interested in confronting Mariella. Why should he risk losing his lucrative deal with Edward? More importantly, I didn't believe Edward would ever stand up to Mariella, no matter who was pushing him. He always told people: "Just work with her; she's the smartest person I know, and she *is* my wife."

Now I was about to get Mariella's version of the campaign. She had invited me to Edward's estate in the wealthy beach community of Pacific Palisades for lunch that Saturday. I borrowed my pop's Buick for the two-hour drive from Newport; I was embarrassed to pull up to a mansion in my '89 Ford Probe.

When I pulled onto their street, I couldn't miss the Winstons' house. It was a mansion all right—colossal, with at least forty rooms, white exterior, red roof tiles, balconies, acres of green lawns, magnificent rose gardens, a dozen fancy cars in the driveway, and the most splendid ocean view in all of California. Château de Winston stood out like a brilliant dream on the coastal landscape. I pulled the Buick slowly through the front gate and drove around the circular cobblestone driveway, looking for somewhere to stash it out of view. Now I was even ashamed of the Buick. A valet dressed in a tuxedo ran up to take the car.

"Hello, I am Julio," he said politely. "Mrs. Winston is waiting for you inside, Mr. Asher."

"Just call me Jim," I said, climbing out of the car. "And if you don't mind too much, could you sort of park it out of view?" I asked.

He grinned. "No problem . . . Jim."

I checked myself one last time in the side-view mirror.

"Here goes everything," I mumbled.

A maid met me at the door. "Please be seated in the living room. Mrs. Winston is on the telephone in her office. She will be down soon. Can I get you anything, sir?"

"Oh, thanks, but I'm okay. And it's Jim."

As she escorted me to the living room, I was overwhelmed by the sheer grandeur of the house. An elegant split staircase flowed upward like a parting marble wave from the front door, ducking under a chandelier, and spilling onto a giant ballroom on the second floor. I sat on a couch that faced a wall of windows looking at the ocean. I watched a flock of seagulls frolicking as the waves crashed against the rocks with a fine, clear mist. A rich serenity washed through the window and spilled over me. Everything about that moment was leisure.

Then I heard Mariella's voice.

"Jim, I am so glad you could join me," she said.

I turned around and saw her gliding through the living room. She was dressed exquisitely—if not strangely—in a draping Indian sari made of white silk with gold embroidery. The garment started by wrapping around her naked waist then up and over her shoulder—like something you might see in *National Geographic*. Mariella's hair was impeccable, as usual. I took her hand and kissed it, figuring that's what was appropriate.

"You're so sweet," she purred. "Let's go out to the veranda and take lunch."

Take lunch—I loved that kind of talk! I was used to just *eating* mine. We walked out through the open French doors and sat down at a glass table near the ocean. Two waiters appeared with silver platters. They removed the shiny dome from my plate with some degree of presentation.

"I thought you would enjoy filet mignon," Mariella said.

"Perfect," I said.

She was taking the same thing, but her steak was even bigger.

One of the waiters pointed to a wine cart and asked which I preferred. I didn't know the names of any wines, other than the disreputable Boone's Farm from my college days. I was fairly certain that Boone's was not part of the Winstons' selection, so I pointed to a random bottle: "I'll have that one."

Mariella smirked. "No, sweetheart. That's white zinfandel. You need red wine with steak."

"Oh." Well, at least my face was red.

"We'll have the Mondavi cabernet," she told the waiter.

I wanted to change the subject. "How did you like Samantha's piece on our immigration speech?" I asked.

"Very well done," she said. "Samantha can be a great asset to this campaign. But you must make personal relationships with all the reporters, even in San Francisco and San Diego. You're so good with the media, darling. But please, don't start breaking all the female reporters' hearts until Edward has won the race." She laughed at her own joke.

I wasn't quite comfortable being known only for bedding reporters. True, I liked that people were talking about me, but I wanted to be recognized for all my talents—writing, research, networking, spinning deals. But for now I went along with it; I had to start someplace.

"Jimmy, I feel that this campaign is moving forward toward our goal. Edward is going to change Washington. There is a synergy melding together. I see you and Winter and John creating a positive field of support for Edward. Michelle is also contributing to this. We must reinforce what is working and discard what is not."

I nodded. She was obviously heading somewhere with this.

After lunch, Mariella gave me a tour of the $13 million mansion. As we walked around the third floor, admiring and commenting on paintings and sculptures I knew nothing about, I felt like an impostor. I had grown up in a tiny three-bedroom tract house. My parents didn't move to the beach until I was already overseas in the military. We certainly didn't have maids, racquet-ball courts, two swimming pools, or a movie theater with THX Dolby sound. And still I felt like it all could be pulled out from under me in a breath. So I resolved to soak up as much as possible, hoping I could take the memories with me when I was inevitably kicked back to the poor man's curb.

"Would you like to have a massage?" Mariella asked me.

"Um . . ." Was she talking about giving it to me personally?

"We have a staff of masseuses here at the house. They are so wonderful. Along with meditation, massage is one of the keys to life."

"Okay," I said.

A room on the fourth floor had a sign on the door: MASSAGE SUITE. I changed in the men's gymnasium towel room, retaining my boxer-briefs under the white towel around my waist. With Edward out of town, I felt a little awkward strolling through his house half naked. But what the hell, this was going to be my first "legitimate" massage.

When I opened the door, Mariella was standing nude in the small massage room, apparently waiting for me. She was flanked by two masseuses—one

Asian, the other Nordic. I couldn't help but stare at Mariella's body. Her skin was bronzed and smooth, covered with a barely noticeable but very sexy layer of blond down peach fuzz. Her breasts were large, sagging just slightly, but her waist was thin, her hips sultry. She had that comfortable European nonchalance about her nudity. I didn't.

She grinned at me. "You won't be needing that towel, sweetheart." She motioned to the massagers. "They've seen it all before."

Shit, I wasn't worried about *them!*

Now I really felt like a buffoon. When I took off my towel she would see my underwear. Oh well. I dropped the towel. All three of them smirked at my Calvins. I was scared, but luckily not scared stiff. I pulled off my underwear and stood there lamely. To say I was looking my best at that moment would be a falsity. I was so shriveled with fright, I probably resembled an ambitious mushroom cap, at best. Mariella's eyes drifted methodically down my torso and stalled for what seemed like an hour on my unmentionables.

"I'm ready," I said, trying to get this deal under way.

"Lay on table," one masseuse told me. Her Asian accent dragged.

I leaped facedown onto the white linen massage table. Mariella laid down on the table only two feet away.

"Don't be nervous, sweetheart. You must relax to enjoy the massage. Let the hands put energy back into your body."

"I'll try."

I wasn't even pretending to be relaxed at this point. What if Edward found out? Surely this wasn't normal? Then the masseuse's hands touched me. They were warm and smart, moving skillfully up my legs. I closed my eyes, and my tight muscles melted to butter under those forgiving fingers.

"Jimmy, I've been wanting to talk about the campaign," Mariella said.

"Sure."

"How do you think the campaign is progressing?"

"Well," I said, "I think we're on track. Of course there are some office problems. But in general, I think things are going well."

"Yes . . . I think there are some destructive elements in the office that need to be addressed."

I knew what was happening. I was involved in one of those conversations that would make other employees cringe if they knew it was taking place. This was my opportunity to drop bombs on whomever in the office I wished.

"I think Chuck is bringing a substantial amount of negative energy to Edward's campaign," Mariella continued. "I know he has been talking to you, sweetheart. We need to be careful. And we need to make sure Edward is always our number one priority."

"I agree."

"When Edward wins the Senate race, he'll need a press secretary for the Capitol Hill office. I think you will be perfect for it, Jimmy. It will be a whole new world for you. We are going to shake up the cozy Washington establishment. And Edward always rewards loyalty. But right now, we need to focus on winning this campaign. Any obstacle standing between this moment and the moment when Edward is sworn in as a senator must be eliminated. Do you understand, sweetheart?"

I understood all right. "Yes, I think winning should be the priority, no matter what," I said.

"I'm so glad to hear you say that, sweetheart. Now tell me what Chuck is planning. I know he intends to try something desperate and destructive very soon. You must tell me what he is doing so I can go to Edward and take care of these ugly problems before they begin to affect the campaign adversely."

This was it. I had a decision to make. I *did* know what Chuck was planning. The office was poised for a huge shakeup. The only question was, where would I fall? Chuck had told me his plans in confidence, and I knew it would be wrong to tell Mariella. I don't know what came over me at that moment. I guess I figured I had to choose sides if I was going to survive and benefit from the outcome. I told myself this was a fair fight between two adults, and in fair fights people choose sides. I chose mine.

"Chuck is planning to squeeze you out, Mariella," I said. As the words came out, I started feeling terribly guilty. But they just kept flowing; they had to. "He's going to tell Edward that either you must stay away from the campaign, or he's going to quit."

"An ultimatum," Mariella said. She looked at me as if everything was now clear. "When is he going to do this, sweetheart?"

"On Monday," I said. "Mariella, you can't tell anyone where you got this information."

"Don't worry, honey. Is there anything else that Chuck has been doing?"

I thought back to what Bud had told me—the thing about stomping down on your opponent's neck. Whether I liked it or not, Chuck was now my opponent. I had already jumped off that bridge. I felt terrible, emotionally and physically, but I had to put Chuck out of his misery now.

"He's sleeping with several of the young girls at the office," I lied. "It's awful."

"Oh, that is awful," she said.

I knew that neither of us thought it was awful, but Mariella and I seemed to be making a telepathic pact. We both knew Edward *would* think it was awful. Now Mariella had all the ammo she needed.

"Thank you, Jimmy. You have done a big favor for Edward, and yourself."

———————

I felt like the slimiest, dirtiest, worst-smelling sack of wet dog crap in the world as I drove home from Mariella's house. What had I done? Was I so fast to sacrifice how I felt about myself just to advance my career? I didn't want to see it that way. But it seemed like I had just cast myself as the bad guy in my own movie—the ruthless cutthroat who always gets his before the credits roll. So I kept retreating to the logic that Chuck was a grown man who had chosen this profession and associated himself with this campaign. Politics is a business with great rewards, which necessarily makes it a business of great risks.

During the ride home, I vowed to always make sure I separated things that were perhaps disloyal, or a bit unruly, from things that were truly wrong, like stealing, or cheating, or hurting innocent people. I would never let myself get away from my own ethics. I knew I was a good person inside. I always had been. There were objective ways I concluded this: I liked kids; I was kind to animals; I always pulled my car over to help stranded motorists, even when it would have been easier to just whiz by; and I loved my family and friends. I knew I was good in my own way. Highly ambitious and sometimes reckless, yes, but never malicious without provocation.

Mariella was going to move against Chuck sooner or later anyway. I had simply sized up the situation and made my choice. Now it was time to ride this beast I had unleashed—ride it to glory on the swift legs of treachery and then, maybe, one day reach that place where I could lie back and exhale with relief and delight on the side of a green majestic hill and then renounce the very tricks that had propelled me to that place as better-forgotten missteps along my path to bliss and, perhaps, to honor. That was the plan anyway.

———————

When I got home, my dad was watching TV in the living room. Our house was small but well decorated with country antiques—very homey. I always felt comfortable when I got home, like the outside world couldn't touch me there. The further I delved into the crazy world of politics and money, the more of a sanctuary home became. At home I had family and neighborhood friends who didn't care anything about politics. They were proud of me. But they would have been proud of anything I did as long as it was right and it made me happy. If my parents knew the turmoil I was presently swimming in, I'm sure they would have been concerned. But I always tried to work things out on my own. When I had been terrified of dying on those cold February nights during the Gulf War, standing on the flat, lonely desert ten thousand miles from home, knowing I might die during the next battle, I didn't send home panicked letters to my parents. No. I wrote that I was feeling brave and ready to fight, and sure that I would be perfectly safe. Why worry them?

I dragged myself to the kitchen and mixed up a protein shake. I had to eat healthy because I wasn't exercising much. I was working at the office all day, never leaving—most days I had no idea what the weather was outside, or what girls my surfing buddies in Newport were hooking up with, or anything that would have previously interested me. Politics was my entire existence.

"So, how's it going?" my father asked.

"I'm tired, Pop."

"Come over here and sit down with your old man. You're like a stranger these days. Hey, there's a great special on Discovery about lions and hyenas."

I sat down on the La-Z-Boy and kicked my legs up with a sigh. It was a glorious nature show, with plenty of exciting chases and unscrupulous beasts eating one another. My dad was dressed in his shabby bathrobe. He was a quiet man—a Vietnam vet who had worked faithfully for a freight company for thirty-five years. He had turned down promotions to management for years and years until the company finally stopped offering. I admired my father because he was content with what his life was and never chased in vain what it was not.

"You look beat, Froggy," my pop said. "Like you've been in a fight." Froggy was my nickname as a kid; Jake was Tadpole. It felt good to talk to someone who had known me longer than two months. In politics, I was operating in a world of shallow, split-second relationships. "Is everything okay?" he asked.

"Sure," I said. "But politics is ruthless, Pop." I wanted to say: I'm a ruthless piece of dirty scoundrel garbage, Pop.

"Well," he said, "everyone knows politics can be shady. Next to used-car salesmen and lawyers, politicians are pretty high on the dirtbag list. But it seems like you're really doing well for yourself. You always have control over what kind of man you're going to be, Froggy. Don't ever forget that."

"I know, Pop. Actually, I really like politics. I was worried I'd drift through my twenties and never find what I wanted. This political thing just fell in my lap."

He nodded. If my dad didn't have something important to add, he simply wouldn't say anything. Unheard of in politics.

I went to my bedroom and checked my voice mail. Four messages—pretty good. I could always tell where my life was at any given moment based on simply how many voice mails I received. Tonight I had three messages from friends I now classified as "nonpolitical," and one from Samantha.

"Jimmy, call me at the station if you get this before five," her voice said. "I got your message. Yeah, I'll cover Edward's crime speech tomorrow at the Hyatt. I wouldn't miss a chance to see my favorite boy—you. And I called Holly; she's going to cover the speech for Channel Two. She might even do a little interview with Winston, if he's game. I told her you could probably set it up. Hey, do you want to meet for a cocktail before the event, maybe around eleven-thirty at the hotel's bar? Call me, babe."

I went back downstairs, flopped on the couch, and watched the rest of the nature show with my dad. With all that had happened at the campaign, I wasn't sure who I sympathized with more—the lions or their prey.

SIX

When I walked into the office Tuesday morning I knew it was going to be a long day. Somehow, a feeling of turmoil seemed to radiate from the walls as I walked past the vacant receptionist's desk. People were moping around the office with heads hung low.

I went straight to the kitchen and brewed up a pot of my vile blend. John Griggs wandered in, looking routed.

"Damn, playboy, you look like Satan personally kicked your ass," I said.

"I feel like he did worse than that," John grumbled. He rifled through the kitchen drawers. "Where's the aspirin, man?"

I gave him some Advil from Chuck's private stash over the microwave.

"What's going on around here?" I asked.

He gulped down five. "You missed a helluva night at the Shark's Club."

"On a Monday?"

"Special occasion." His bloodshot eyes fixed on mine, adding gravity to his next words. "Chuck quit last night. We had a big send-off for him."

Shit. That was fast. I quickly threw on my actor's face and, without missing a beat, asked, "What happened?"

"I guess he got fed up with everything." Then he looked around with darting eyes, and whispered: *"Mariella."*

"Damn, that sucks," I said. "So what's gonna happen now?"

"Bud's having a meeting in the conference room in ten minutes."

"Man . . ."

John nodded regretfully. "Half the staff is quitting right now. Chuck wants Renee and me to go with him to Arizona. I think your name came up, too, Jim."

"Are you going?"

"I don't know, man. I mean, I'm loyal to Chuck and everything, but I've got a great job here. You know I just bought that new Jeep and . . ."

Well, at least John would be staying with me.

The next day, I packed up my office supplies and moved to my new space at the campaign: Chuck's old office. Bud Raper took over as acting campaign manager, but he wasn't around much. I had a new job position and, more importantly, I had Mariella solidly in my corner. With Chuck and half the staff gone, I was appointed assistant campaign manager. My new salary was $3,900 a month—more money than I'd ever seen. I guess Mariella didn't trust Bud completely, so she placed me where I could keep an eye on things for her. Along with Winter, she now considered me one of her loyal agents. I didn't like being indebted to her in this way—feeling like she was a pawnbroker holding my integrity in hock—but so far my relationship with Mariella had been extremely lucrative in nearly every respect. I was still the master of my own fate.

All the remaining employees decided to translate my new job title into something less offensive, like "assistant to the campaign manager." And they were right. What did I know about running a campaign? But I didn't care about any of that. I had gone from volunteer clip boy to second in command in three blistering months. I was smoking like a damn six-gun.

I can't really say I had much of a political philosophy at this point. Sure, I called myself a Republican. I didn't like welfare, high taxes, illegal immigration—standard right-wing stuff. But those were mostly reactionary beliefs, not grounded in anything substantial. I didn't like our opponent in the Senate race, Dana Steadfield, that was for sure. She favored strict gun control—banning all guns—and consistently voted to raise taxes and expand welfare. I really wanted Edward to win, and I was glad the election had tightened to a neck-and-neck race as we entered the last month of the campaign. But honestly, at that point, I was mostly caught up in the chase, the glitter, the game, and the prospects of plunder.

As a young white guy from a good family, what else would I be interested in? I didn't care about food stamps, college loans, Medicare, welfare—whenever I came face-to-face with the government I was either standing in a long line at the DMV or handing over my hard-earned property in the form of taxes or speeding tickets. Besides building roads and checking to make sure my hamburger meat was safe, what had the government done for me lately?

I turned to Mariella and Winter, the intellectual ideologues in the office, and they were happy to recruit me into their lofty school of political thought. Mariella gave me books by Edmund Burke, Madison, Bloom, Strauss, Plato, and Olasky. I read them all, and my mind absorbed them with astonishing greed and clarity—almost as if they were my own thoughts just waiting to occur to me. I would be intellectually well armed going into the final months of the campaign.

———————————

A new employee arrived at the office. He took the office next to mine. From the first minute I saw Bill Crutchman, I knew why he was sent to the campaign.

He shook my hand with a sturdy iron presence.

"Hello there, young man," he said.

"Nice to meet you, sir."

His face was leathery, and I noticed muscular forearms under his shirt. His hair was short and lined with stiff comb tracks. I knew right away he was a military man. Crutchman wasn't even in the office ten minutes before he pulled me outside for a talk. We took the elevator down to the first floor without exchanging a word. Crutchman had introduced himself around the office as the new accountant, and no one had seemed to question him. But I knew better. This guy had the distant, glassy eyes of a killer.

We walked onto the patio. Crutchman pulled out a pack of Marlboro red dogs.

"Wanna smoke?" he asked.

"Sure, thanks."

He lit my cigarette, then his own with an old camouflage Zippo.

"So," he puffed with squinted eyes, "you know who I am?"

"Former military?" I said.

"Twenty-seven years. Army."

"Me too. Well, not the twenty-seven years part—"

"I know who you are. James W. Asher. Nineteen Delta Recon Scout. Second Armored Cavalry Regiment, battle of 73 Easting. You were decorated during combat operations in the Iraq and Kuwaiti theaters. Two ARCOMs, three AAMs, one Bronze Star with valor. Secret clearance, six months JTF counter-narcotics . . ."

This guy had been over my confidential service records. No one at the campaign had that information. I had a Secret clearance for a six-month Joint Task Force operation I'd done with the DEA. Secret was one step above Classified and one below Top Secret. No one outside the Pentagon had access to that information—no one.

"How do you know that?" I asked.

"I know everything about everyone in that office up there. Look, I'm gonna talk straight. That's what I do. And what I say stays with you. Understand?"

"Understood."

"Edward sent me here because he's worried about security leaks at the campaign."

I nodded.

"For the past ten years, I've run security for Edward's father's corporation in Silicon Valley. I don't give a damn about politics. I only give a damn about Edward and the family. I'm here because Edward thinks there might be a smear attempt against him. He also suspects there could be a mole at the campaign. That's why I checked the background of every employee. You were my first target, Asher. No political experience to speak of. You just drifted into the office from out of nowhere . . ."

My pulse accelerated. I tried to think if there was anything I had to worry about in my past.

". . . but after looking at that service record of yours, I knew you were okay."

"Oh, thanks." What else could I say? I had a pretty good idea what kind of work this guy had done in the military, but I sure as hell wasn't going to ask.

"We'll have to go out for drinks one of these nights and talk military shop," Crutchman said. He gave me a slow smile. "But right now, let's talk about the other employees in the office."

At least I seemed to be on his good side. I wouldn't want to be on any other.

———————

That afternoon, a new television spot came in from Washington, where our media consultant, Larry Hakney, had his offices. Larry was arguably the best ad man in the business. He had worked on George Bush's infamous Willie Horton ad, so he had a sterling reputation. If you wanted hard-hitting ads Larry Hakney was The Man.

John rushed into my new office. "Check it out, man—a new spot!" He waved the videotape.

"When does it go up?" I asked, following him to the conference room.

"Tomorrow night. It's going into heavy rotation."

Heavy rotation meant they were going to flood California's airwaves with it, as they had done once before, much to Dana Steadfield's chagrin. Our television attack ads were the best ever made—savvy and brutal. Even *Newsweek* and *Time* had written feature stories on how effective the ads were in breaking down Steadfield's image. Of course, Steadfield complained that the ads were mean-spirited, and that she couldn't compete fairly against a $30-million, self-financed media blitz. We all felt very, very sorry for her, of course. Every time one of our attack ads went up, we watched Steadfield slip in the overnight polls.

The commercials were by far the most expensive part of our budget, but none of us at the office were ever involved in making them. They just seemed to drop out of the sky. Advertising was the big leagues—Bud, Edward, and Larry's turf. I was happy at this point just to get an early glimpse of their latest genius.

John popped the cassette in the VCR. Other staffers crowded into the room. We all stood there in the conference room, anxious to see how Hakney would brutalize Senator Steadfield this time. The tape counted down and the commercial rolled. The screen was split—half red, half blue. Hakney had spent weeks searching for the worst possible picture he could find of Senator Steadfield. And he sure as hell found it! But he wasn't finished there. Hakney had secretly fooled around with the image on his Cray supercomputer graphics terminal—adding lines to her face, spiking her eyebrows slightly, bleaching her skin to appear ashen, and generally making her look like a mean, old, estrogen-depleted battle-ax.

For the first ten seconds, only Steadfield's name flashed across the red side of the screen. The smooth-voiced announcer blasted her for riding around in limousines at taxpayer expense. A picture appeared of Steadfield climbing into a limousine in front of the US Capitol—a nice touch, I thought. Then the scene switched to a black-and-white slow-motion video of some Chinese guy handing Steadfield a thick envelope at a dinner party. The announcer's voice ominously said: "Steadfield has taken over eight million dollars in special-interest money . . . Winston won't take a penny."

Then Larry dropped the bomb. When Steadfield's new, modified photograph appeared on the red side of the screen with the words BOUGHT AND PAID FOR underneath it, I exploded with laughter, literally falling to my knees.

"Goddamn!" John shouted. "Steadfield looks like a dead rhino!"

I was howling, and slapping the carpet. Every time I glanced up at the picture, I burst into hysterics. It was the most grisly, wonderful hatchet job I've seen to this day. Steadfield must have ducked under the bedsheets every time it came on TV.

SEVEN

I parked my Probe around the corner—sufficiently out of view—and walked down the palm-lined street to Samantha's house. Tonight was her annual "Gellhorne Hot Tub Smoker." I was ready to get mad loose.

When I walked up the brick path, I saw dozens of people flirting around on the back porch. The hot tub was open, steaming with a red glow. Samantha had rows of varicolored lights installed in the tub, which could flash on and off in hypnotizing patterns. All the partygoers were dressed impressively. The men were sporting the typical Palisades jeans and half-unbuttoned shirts revealing chest hairs, an occasional string of tribal beads, oversize belts, and Italian sport coats; the women were clad in miniskirts, bell-bottoms, and silk blouses that dazzled the eye for their ability to contour and reveal more than may, or may not, have been intended.

I felt a little awkward walking up to this group. Most of them were twenty years older than me. My eyes searched around for Samantha. She was probably somewhere with her new boyfriend, Rick, who was actually a hell of a cool guy. I smiled lamely at everyone, nodding and saying hello with my hands in my pockets. I finally spotted Julia, a CBS News producer whom I'd met through Samantha at a press conference. She looked delicious, wearing a stylish leather miniskirt. Her skin was a rich mocha color and her eyes were a magnificent Caribbean green—very exotic for a black girl.

"Hey, Jim, how are you?" she said.

"Great, how's life in the big network leagues?"

"This election cycle is a killer. I'm producing all the political coverage for the five western states now. In the last two days, I've been to Phoenix, Seattle, Vegas, San Francisco, Portland, and now LA."

"Damn. Where do you live, Julia?"

"LA. Hermosa Beach."

"Well, you'll have to go out to dinner with Winston and me one of these nights," I offered.

"Yeah, I've been meaning to talk to you about that. I've been thinking of doing a network piece on your boss and—"

I cut her off. Not that I didn't want to line up a national piece for Edward, I just didn't want to *look* like I wanted to. I always tried to keep the personal relationship real, then make my pitch subtly. "We can talk politics later," I said. "We're here to get loose. So where's Samantha?"

"Inside," she said, taking my hand. "She's got the mayor bartending."

"You're kidding?"

"With Samantha, I'm never kidding."

Sure enough, Los Angeles Mayor Richard Tarken, draped in a red-and-white apron with the words SAMANTHA'S KITCHEN embroidered across the front, was behind the bar mixing up margaritas with a deft hand, juggling two pitchers like a veteran of the Tijuana bar scene. Samantha was his bar-back, wearing dark sunglasses and passing out beers. Julia and I made our way through the dense crowd and flagged down Samantha.

"Jimmy!" she shouted. "I'm so glad you came." She rushed around the bar and hugged me, planting a nice long kiss on my cheek. "Come back here, we need some help."

Julia took a tray of margaritas from the mayor and walked outside. I followed Samantha behind the bar. The mayor smiled at me with that typical politician's blank, fraudulent smile. I thought he might even slap a campaign button on me.

"Hello, young man," he said.

Samantha hugged him, her arms wrapped all the way around his ample belly. "Dick, this is Jim Asher from the Winston campaign."

I could tell the mayor didn't remember me from Billboard Live. "Oh, that's terrific," he said. "So, Jim, come over here and tell me how the campaign's going." He took off the silly apron, becoming very businesslike, as if suddenly ashamed in the presence of another Republican. "I hear things are looking up for Edward."

"Our overnights are holding steady right now," I said. "We're floating about two points ahead."

"That's great," he said. "It'd be nice to boot Steadfield out of the Senate. She's been good with federal highway money, but she's a beast in terms of water allocation, SSI, and capital gains."

I nodded, feeling quite important to be talking politics with the mayor.

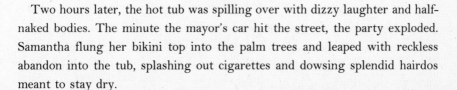

Two hours later, the hot tub was spilling over with dizzy laughter and half-naked bodies. The minute the mayor's car hit the street, the party exploded. Samantha flung her bikini top into the palm trees and leaped with reckless abandon into the tub, splashing out cigarettes and dowsing splendid hairdos meant to stay dry.

"Let's get fucking *crazy!*" she yelled. "And what's with all these clothes?"

With one hand submerged and resting on my thigh, Julia poured a mixture of rum and guava juice into my open mouth. If I was going to get naked, I wouldn't be sober. I closed my eyes and let the juice race down my throat. Samantha's boyfriend, Rick, came outside wearing patched-up Bermuda shorts. I had met him at a party the week before, and we hit it off right from the start.

Some Italian slickster in the tub yelled out, "Five million dollars a year and can't even afford a real bathing suit!"

"Fuck you, Tony," Rick said. "Maybe it's time I took a little more interest in *your* studio's stock profile."

Tony laughed, a little too nervously. Coming from a ruthless corporate-raiding lawyer like Rick, those were words to curdle the blood of any CEO. Rick slipped into the tub between Samantha and me. He pulled a crooked joint from behind his ear and sparked it.

"Hey, Jim, try some of this LaLa," he said, handing it to me.

Samantha was looking at me, urging, "Go ahead, Boo-Boo. We promise not to tell Winston."

Suddenly it seemed like everyone was watching, waiting to see if the outsider Republican was cool or not. The whole scene was like a bad after-school special. I held the joint between my thumb and index finger and took a hit, not really thinking I inhaled much. But when I exhaled, a cloud of thick white smoke drifted ominously up to the stars.

Ten minutes and three hits later, I knew why they called it LaLa. Every time anyone said anything, I thought it was the most strikingly humorous thing I'd ever heard. Then someone else would say something, and it was even funnier, sending me into another round of fits.

With a knowing grin, Rick asked: "You feelin' it, bro?"

I looked around. The trees were hazy now in a warm, poetic way, like an impressionist painting. Laughter swirled through my head, rising in hypnotic swells that calmly tapered to romantic bliss, as if a great conductor in the heavens were manipulating the emotional currents of my mind like the strings of some golden harp beneath his fingertips, and Julia's hand felt almost translucent as it moved across my thigh, and the motion of the water enveloped me . . .

I slapped my own face.

"I'm fucking torqued, man!" I said.

Rick laughed. "Check this out." He flipped a switch, and the red lights in the water disappeared. In their place, a white strobe light flashed, making each movement a still picture until the next flash.

"Just what I needed, Rick!" I grabbed the rum concoction from Julia and guzzled it down. I kissed Julia and ran my hand up between her shapely thighs. Every inhibition in my body was in full retreat. "Rick, tell me how you got to be so fuckin' rich," I blurted out.

"It's simple. I'm an entertainment lawyer. I specialize in buying and selling production companies."

Samantha rubbed his shoulder proudly. "Tell Jimmy about the Castle Film thing, honey."

"Oh, the Castle thing," Rick said. His eyes narrowed, giving him a sly and almost gleeful appearance. Although Rick seemed prone to giggles, he certainly could handle his high rather well. He was able to focus his attention quickly. "Well, basically, here's how it went down," he continued. "After analyzing their profile, I decided to make a run on the Castle Film production company last year. Banks let me use their assets because I have an outstanding track record and they trust my instincts. So, last fall I waited for a dip in the retail value and started buying up huge blocks of Castle stock, ten thousand shares at a time . . ." He paused. "You know you can't repeat any of this, right?"

"Who the fuck am I gonna tell?" I laughed. I was giggling enthusiastically throughout the entire story.

"So I was buying up these shares at thirty bucks a pop until I hit half a mil. Then I floated rumors around town and in New York that I was mounting a hostile takeover. It didn't take long before Castle's share value skyrocketed. When the price hit forty, I dumped everything and walked away with five million in my pocket."

"Brilliant!" I exclaimed, laughing my ass off. "Why am I in politics? So what happens to the companies after you bail out?"

"Who gives a flying fuck what happens to the companies. That's the beauty of it!"

"Rick, you're one twisted cat," I said, still laughing.

EIGHT

After a long day at the office, Bill Crutchman asked me to go out for drinks. An invitation from Crutchman was more like a summons. We drove to the Red Lion hotel in his big Cadillac without speaking a word. Crutchman seemed to like to get wherever he was going, then begin talking—and never in the office. We walked through the lobby and into the bar. The Asian bartender flashed a smile.

"Hello, Mr. Crutchman. How you tonight? You looking very sharp."

"Good, Tran. How's the family?"

"Oh, very good, very good, Mr. Crutchman. Wife make *good* lunch today, hee-hee-hee!"

"The usual," Crutchman said, sitting down.

"And for you friend?"

"He'll have the same. Tran, this is Jim. Jim, Tran."

I said hello. "How do you know him?" I whispered to Crutchman.

"From here. I come to meet ladies at this bar—classy ladies. Tran also happens to be from Danang, a place I spent some time."

"Oh."

A waitress walked by, running her hand over Crutchman's shoulder. "Hey there, handsome."

"Hi, cutie pie."

Crutchman seemed to be a legend at the bar, which was strange, I thought, because he had only been in town for two weeks. Even the drunkards at a nearby table paid homage to Crutchman with a toast. Tran set two drinks in front of us—straight alcohol, no ice.

"What are these?" I asked.

"Double bourbon."

He drank down half of his, then passed me a smoke. Tran was ready with a lighter, but he waited to light Crutchman's first.

"I need your help, Asher."

"Sure, anything."

"It goes without saying . . ."

"Of course."

"You know Edward has been preparing for his big debate against Senator Steadfield on *Meet the Press.*"

"Sure, I've been working on the opposition research."

He raised one eyebrow. "So have Steadfield's people."

"What do you mean?"

He polished off his bourbon. "I found a device during one of my routine sweeps last week." He stared at me for a solid five seconds.

"Shit."

I knew about his periodic countersurveillance sweeps. At first, Crutchman would only do them when the office was empty, but he later let me in on it. I was at the office so much it was hard to get around me, I suppose. One night I saw him going around with a huge electronic device of some sort, scanning all over the place—around phones, ceilings, corners, plants, even inside the lobby bathrooms. Our office was also bugged internally, by Crutchman himself. That's why I watched everything I said, especially on the horn. I wasn't sure whether the information went to Edward and Mariella, or just to Edward. I'm positive Bud didn't know.

Crutchman ordered two more bourbons and lit another smoke.

"So why don't you go public with the information about the bug," I offered. "We could leak it to a friendly reporter. I know someone at Channel—"

He cut me off with a sharp wave of his hand. "Who's talking here?"

"You are, sir."

"Okay then. Now, do you believe for one second that I haven't covered all possible contingencies before determining a course of action?"

"Of course not."

"The reason we can't go public, Asher, is that the Steadfield campaign already uncovered *our* device."

I nodded, surprised.

"What I need is someone placed inside the Steadfield campaign headquarters, to gather information for a few days. Do you understand?"

"Yes."

"You are that person."

I nodded again. Suddenly I felt like I was back in the service, preparing to receive an operations briefing. Actually, I loved the intrigue of it all.

"You managed to slip right into Edward's campaign from out of nowhere," he said. "You're ideal for a job like this. Hell, if they tried to check you out, you're not even a registered Republican. I went through the records."

"Uh, I've been meaning to get around to that."

"You're talking again. Here's the deal. We pull you off the payroll. You fly to San Francisco next Monday. That should give you a few days to get settled into an observation post inside the campaign, preferably in their research office. *Meet the Press* is a week later. Not only do I need you to gather all the information you can on scene, I also need you to drop a new device. Do you think you can handle that?"

"Yes, sir. No problem."

"Through various sources, we've learned that the Steadfield campaign has something big they're preparing to drop on Edward. We need to defuse their 'bomb,' so Edward won't be ambushed during the debate. Understand?"

"Completely."

"You also understand that if anything happens, if you were to become compromised, this campaign would disavow all knowledge of you. We'll simply say that you were fired—a loose cannon acting on his own to redeem himself. And there won't be any paper trails."

That made me uncomfortable, of course. I felt like I was working for the CIA, which I may have been in a certain sense.

"Look, we'll float you some cash—plenty of cash. You'll come out smelling sweeter than a rose's ass if you pull this off. Are you on board, Asher?"

Crutchman was right, I was the perfect person for the job. I'm sure he would not have asked me unless he really needed my help. And I didn't want to think what would happen if I said no—thirty million dollars were on the line. It was all very exciting.

"I'll do it," I said.

Crutchman reached out his hand. "Put 'er there, partner."

NINE

Three days before I was set to leave for San Francisco, I met Edward for the first leg of a statewide tour. This was supposed to be our last day together. The door closed and the pilot gave us a thumbs-up over his shoulder. I was sitting next to Edward in one of the plush swiveling captain's chairs. The armrests were leather, with lots of electronic gizmos at our fingertips. TV. Mini bar. A small coffee table between us. A framed needlepoint Monopoly box cover was decorating one of the walls. As the helicopter lifted off the tarmac, I flattened my nose against the glass and watched the fuel trucks turn into marbles on the sidewalk, impressed by the speed with which we rose. Edward's private helicopter was named *WINCO II*. The Gulfstream jet was *WINCO I*. The chopper banked over the Pacific, and just for a moment I lost my stomach. Then we leveled out and I relaxed a bit. I was surprised how luxurious and quiet the ride was.

"Jim, have you ever been in a helicopter before?" Edward asked.

"Only in the army, but those Black Hawks and Hueys are twenty times louder than this."

"Oh yes. Well, *WINCO II* is equipped with the latest sound-absorption lining and floating bearings. This thing is quieter at two hundred miles an hour than my Lincoln is at sixty."

"I believe it."

"It allows me to get a lot of work done."

"Right."

Edward and I would hit seven cities in twelve hours. The election was only two weeks away. And *Meet the Press*—only eight days away—would be the defining moment of the campaign. If Edward could at least come out even with Steadfield in the debate, we would probably win. He was still leading by three points in the polls. Plus, our ad guy Larry Hakney was cutting new TV spots to blast Steadfield. Edward was buying up so much air time that other advertisers like Pepsi and Burger King complained that they couldn't get their ads up. So far, Edward had spent $30 million on the campaign—the most ever spent on a Senate race. He was planning to spend another $8 million on the final ad barrage, a five-day California media blitzkrieg. Everyone agreed—Steadfield was in deep shit. I was on my way to Washington, DC.

One of the cellular phones chirped. I picked it up.

"Winston for US Senate," I said.

"Is this Mr. Winston?" a man's voice asked.

"No, this is Jim Asher, deputy campaign manager. Can I help you?" I was still immensely proud of my title.

"Andy Murphy from *Newsweek* here," he said. "I'd like to talk to Mr. Winston about the race. Is he available?"

"Just a second, please." I covered the phone. "Edward, it's that Los Angeles reporter from *Newsweek*, Andy Murphy. Do you want to talk to him?"

Edward raised his eyebrows, thinking for a moment. "Do we like him?"

"I think so. He did a good blurb on your new immigration ad last week."

"What does he want to talk about?"

"Andy, what is it you'd like to speak to Mr. Winston about?"

"A new poll is showing the race neck and neck. I just wanted some comments."

I explained it to Edward. He took the phone.

"Hello, this is Edward Winston . . . Oh hello, Andy, nice to talk with you . . . Yes, that is true. Our internal tracking has us ahead of Ms. Steadfield . . . um . . . yes . . . three points . . . that is correct . . . um . . . can you hold on just a moment, Andy? . . . Thank you."

Edward held the phone down. "Jim, he wants to know why we're winning this race."

"Because the polls say we are," I said.

"No. He wants to know *why* we're winning."

"Oh . . . well . . ."

Edward was looking at me like I was supposed to know the answer.

"Well," I replied, "you're ahead because Californians don't like leaders who base policy decisions on the direction of the political winds . . ." Not very elegant so far. Then I remembered a line I had been thinking of. "If political waffling was an Olympic sport, Dana Steadfield would be a celebrated gold medalist. She ran on the death penalty, then flip-flopped and now she opposes it; she ran on cutting taxes, but as soon as she was sworn into office she voted for the largest tax increase in American history. California's voters want a senator with strong convictions, not a wet finger in the wind."

Edward nodded. "That's good." He picked up the phone. "Andy, sorry about that, I had another call . . . yes . . . that's right . . . Well, I think California's voters are fed up with politicians who base policy on the direction of the wind. If political flip-flops were an Olympic sport . . ."

I loved that Edward was repeating my lines smoothly and naturally, as if they were his own. This guy could be a US senator, most likely would be. Who cared that he was just parroting my catch phrases—I figured a millionaire four hundred times over like Edward probably had to rely on experts in every area of his life. I had heard him on the phone with his investment brokers in New York, his real estate buyers in Florida, and his accountants in Washington. Mastering a stable of experts was probably better than trying to master everything himself, I figured.

I looked down at the coastline as the chopper cruised like a gliding bird over the naval docks of Long Beach. I was feeling proud; my political life was now catching up with my dreams.

When we touched down at LAX, a mob of reporters was waiting. The campaign's local field team had a podium set up, and a small but vocal crowd of Republican zealots gathered. The chopper's door opened hydraulically. I felt like a prince as we walked down the steps into the humid and smoggy afternoon sun.

"Good turnout," Edward said.

"I'd say about thirty reporters. More than expected."

Edward waved to the crowd. I walked on his left, something I had learned in the military: walking on your superior's left is a position of respect. I stood off to the side as Edward took the podium. Crutchman had instructed me to keep a low profile, and to stay away from cameras. The crowd of mostly retired people cheered and waved Winston campaign signs like hired extras on a movie set. I spotted Samantha and her cameraman.

"Hey, Boo-Boo," she said. "Looking hot in that suit and tie. *Très* debonair."

"How are you?"

"I'm always the same—fucking awesome."

I smiled and hugged her.

Edward gave his usual stump speech. "This Senate race isn't over, but I can see a light of promise on California's horizon," he proclaimed. The reporters shot questions, the usual stuff, like, "Are you trying to buy the election, Edward? How much have you spent so far, Edward? What makes you qualified to be a senator?"

Edward handled the questions with the usual spin: "I'm not buying the election, I'm investing my money in California's future." That was Bud Raper's line; it was great because it was hard to argue with. Before I walked back to the chopper, Samantha gave me a secret kiss and an invitation for drinks at her house.

"That went well," Edward said. He sat down and buckled his seat belt.

I paged through my notebook. "Next up is Fresno."

"Great, Fresno. A lot of good Republicans in Fresno," he said.

It was around 10 A.M., somewhere over Burbank, when Mariella called on one of the cellulars. Mariella seemed to call Edward at least ten times a day. She was basically running the campaign now. Edward listened quietly, as usual. As I pretended to watch the passing mountains to the west, I glimpsed Edward's face, which seemed slowly to drop as the conversation continued; his expression then turned to measured terror. He gulped and hung up.

"What's wrong?" I asked.

He sank into the seat and covered his face with his hands.

"Edward, what's wrong?"

"Pilot, back to Orange County, immediately," he said.

"Orange County?" the pilot asked.

"On the double, please," Edward said.

I didn't look at him. Maybe someone had died?

Another cell phone rang. Edward motioned not to pick it up. It kept ringing. Then another call came in. Within five minutes, both phones were ringing solidly. Edward picked them up and tried to turn the ringers off, but he couldn't figure it out, so he ripped out the batteries.

I had no idea what was going on, and apparently Edward was not going to tell me.

When we got back to the campaign office, it was literally under siege. Eight cameras were set on tripods outside the campaign building, with dozens of reporters ready to jump us. Edward and I were in the backseat of his Lincoln. The driver pulled up to the curb.

"Jim, you get between me and the reporters," Edward said.

"Okay."

I got out first. The reporters circled the car, smelling blood. I pushed through the cameras and walked to Edward's side of the car. When he stepped out, the reporters mobbed us. They jumped over one another, holding cameras aloft just to get a shot. I threw elbows and fought through the pack as Edward held on to the back of my coat.

"Is it true you employ an illegal alien, Edward?" one of the reporters shouted.

"Edward, tell us about your illegal alien," shouted another. "Aren't you a hypocrite on immigration policy? Aren't you a disgrace, Edward?"

The words hit me slowly, but sank in hard. What was this about an illegal alien? My heart was thumping. One of our campaign staffers was standing guard at the door, keeping reporters out. I shoved a fat cameraman. "Fuck you," he yelled, and he moved toward me. I stomped down on his toe, and pushed him back. The staffer opened the door, and I hustled Edward into the lobby.

When the door closed, I noticed how starkly quiet it was inside. Mariella and Bud met us near the elevator. Bud told me to take the stairs. The three of them looked grave as the elevator's doors shut. I looked at Ralph, the guy guarding the door.

"What the hell is going on here?" I asked.

"You don't know?" Ralph said.

"Something about an illegal alien?"

"It's all over the radio. The *San Francisco Chronicle* is breaking the story in their evening edition. Apparently, Edward and Mariella have an illegal alien working as a chauffeur or something. The media's going crazy over the story. One of these television reporters told me they're going to camp out here tonight."

"Camp out? What the hell! Is it true about the illegal alien?"

"Who knows?" Ralph shrugged. "No one tells me shit, man."

I took the stairs to the office. The doors were locked. I had never even seen them closed during business hours before. The receptionist didn't look me in the eye as I let myself in. Winter's door was locked with a hastily scribbled sign taped to it: KEEP OUT. I went to John Griggs's office. He was wearing dark sunglasses and staring at the wall.

"John, what's going on?"

"Jimbo. Man, this isn't good, not good at all."

"Is it true?"

"Afraid so. Apparently, the *Chronicle* has Edward nailed. His name is Julio. I guess he works—"

"Julio? . . . wait a minute. I know him. I met him at the Pacific Palisades house."

"When did you go to the house?"

"Uh . . . well, I had to drop off some paperwork one day. But the point is, I met this Julio guy. He parked my car."

John shook his head. "We're in big trouble, man."

"How big?" I asked.

"Ever hear of Watergate?"

I walked out to the hallway and ran into Bud Raper. He didn't look happy.

"Do you understand what's going on here, kid?" he asked. "This is a major fuckin' blow. I've seen it before. In less than two hours, we're already tracking a five-point hit in the polls. We'll drop another six or seven by tomorrow morning—bet on it. We're not taking any press calls until we can get a handle on this fuckin' thing. Nobody talks to the press, understand?"

I nodded. "Does this mean we're gonna lose, Bud?"

"It probably does, kid. I can't believe Edward didn't tell me about this Mexican kid he's employed for over two years. Thirty-five million dollars down the fuckin' toilet. What a waste. Edward should've just bought another hotel with the damn money." Bud shook his head. "What was he thinking! I told you these politicians are all fucked in the head, kid." He walked back to the war room and slammed the door.

My spirits were in a quick downward spiral. I saw my press secretary job in Washington vanishing. I had worked so hard, and now it seemed that my fate was being run into the ground by circumstances completely out of my control.

I told John Griggs what Bud said.

"That's bad news," John said. "Bud Raper is never wrong."

"This sucks, man. After all our work, after all our plans. What a stupid fuckin' thing to have happen."

"Yeah, but it's even worse because Edward just endorsed Prop. 187. That's kind of like coming out against cigarettes, then getting caught smoking Camels in the boys' room. The timing couldn't be worse. It's even hard for me not to think of the guy as a hypocrite; imagine what people are going to say who *don't* work for him."

"It must be a mistake, John. Maybe it'll all work out. Maybe it'll blow over if we put a good spin on it?"

John stood up and patted my shoulder on his way out the door. "It's best if you just accept it, Jim. They'll be other races, other fights. Listen, you're part of the game now, buddy."

I walked to Winter's office and knocked on the door. She didn't answer. I peeked in and saw her hunched over her desk, crying. I walked in quietly.

"You okay, Win?" I asked.

She looked up and wiped a shaky hand across her face. Winter always tried to portray herself as a professional woman under consummate control—a masculine competitive drive wrapped in a stunning feminine package. But I knew better. One night, a month before, I had to get some paperwork out of her car. When I opened her trunk, hidden under a stack of clothes, I found a cute, fuzzy little teddy bear. It really changed how I viewed Winter. Under all the fashion model looks and lofty Princeton manners, she was still a sweet little girl inside.

I rested my hand on her back. Her body was firm, tense. I rubbed her shoulders tenderly. Even now, in this turmoil, I was thinking of naughtiness. Shameless am I.

"I'm okay," she mumbled. "I need to be alone."

I kissed the back of her head. "Everything'll be okay, Win."

She squeezed my hand and turned around. "Jimmy, they don't even care."

"Who? Who doesn't care?"

"Bud, and Sal—all the consultants . . . all these people here. Do you know what Bud told me? He said we were going to lose."

"He told me the same thing."

"They don't even care, Jim. They're just in it for the money. It's just another race to them—another notch on their belt."

"I know. That's how they are."

"It's not just a race to me," she said.

"Me either, Win. This is my first race. It means everything to me."

She squeezed my hand harder. I loved being on Winter's side. Maybe I just loved Winter.

"I need a hug," she said. "I need something warm and positive."

She stood up and hugged me. I kissed her cheek. She kissed mine, then kissed closer to my lips. Tingly warmth spread through me. Her soft breasts pressed against my chest. She smelled wonderful—expensive perfume.

"This is the only time this will ever happen," she said.

"What?"

She cupped my chin and kissed me on the lips. I hugged her close and kissed her back. Her fingers ran through my hair. We needed each other right then. The last four months of our lives were crumbling down around us.

eight months later . . .

TEN

Edward Winston lost the Senate race by only thirty thousand votes. I felt terrible. It hit me harder than anyone, like a sledgehammer to the chest; even harder than Edward, I think. The week following the election was slow and miserable. People lingered around the drowsy office collecting their things in cardboard boxes. Movers came and took the furniture away. I felt like an actor whose TV show had just been canceled, forced to watch the crew disassemble the set. Edward, Mariella, Bud, and Winter flew back to the East Coast immediately. Winter landed a speech-writing job for a US senator from Colorado. John Griggs took a job at a think tank in LA. Everyone had connections from previous campaigns. I didn't have anywhere to go.

My parents suggested I pursue law school, especially if I wanted to run for office myself someday. But I didn't want to waste three years; I wanted to keep charging full speed ahead into politics. I loved it, and I was really good at it. But I needed direction. After a long phone conversation, Winter finally convinced me to fly out to Washington, DC. If politics was going to be my life, she told me, where better to go? I packed a duffel bag and caught the red-eye that night.

When I first arrived in DC, I had no idea what to do. All I had were stars in my eyes and a bunch of sandalwood-colored résumés in my hand. It seemed like every Republican alive had flocked to DC after the elections. Even though she was extremely busy, Winter tried to help me find a job, but I had practically no experience to speak of. I checked into a cheap motel, temporarily. I told my parents everything was great—that I was sure to land a terrific job any day. Three weeks later I was still living in that wretched little hole, the Highland Inn. Once my money ran out, I started climbing in through my room's back window late at night. I spent five days ducking the motel owner, a toothless old man named Jerry. One morning he spotted me walking out the front door and chased me halfway to the subway station, yelling: "Get back here, you sumbitch! Where's mu' damn money!"

Eventually, after trying everything else, I broke down and told Winter I was headed for disgrace—with a watery mouth I had been eyeballing the local soup kitchen. Winter told me to "stay put, sweetheart." An hour later Mariella called and invited me to move into the pool house at the Winston's Virginia mansion. From then on, I was rolling. With a single phone call, Bud got me a job writing at the *McHoffman Group*—one of my favorite political TV shows. After only two months, my supervisor quit, and I was promoted to booking guests and producing the show. I seemed to keep landing at the right place, right time. Of course, I was still working sixteen-hour days—a practice I figured I could keep up for at least two more years, or until I got rich. I noticed that other employees at the show were troubled by my work habits. They tried to talk me out of coming in before sunrise and leaving at two in the morning every day. I'm sure they felt they had to keep up. But I knew I was a rare case. I had all these visions of glory in my head and I couldn't stop chasing them.

In politics, television is power. My social life erupted like a geyser when my name got out as a producer at the *McHoffman Group*. I met all the big political players, went to lots of parties. Mariella was becoming the GOP's premier socialite. DC's top power brokers—senators, congressmen, opinion makers, CEOs—flocked to the Winston mansion every weekend for roast duck, champagne, and a chance to say they'd partaken in high conversation while seated on Napoleon Bonaparte's former love seat. Invitations were extremely hard to come by, but since I lived at the house, I was always invited. Mariella and I got on famously. Whenever Edward was working on Wall Street, we would stay up late at night, sometimes with Winter, sipping wine and talking philosophy. Mariella had a sizzly side to her, that's for sure. One night after a few bottles of Crystal, she even pulled out some old modeling photographs, which had been taken before her marriage to Edward. Mariella was sprawled out on the rooftop of a Gothic building, draped seductively over a stone gargoyle, a spooky bolt of lightning frozen in the background, and the only thing she was wearing was a red satin scarf. Of course, I liked Mariella's unpredictable nature; it filled out her personality. Sometimes when Edward was home she would wink at me across the dinner table, and we would sneak outside for a cigarette. I think we were two spirits who actually knew enough to appreciate our paths crossing in the night.

My life at the Winston house was grand, but I soon grew disenchanted with my job. The show's outspoken host, John McHoffman, turned out to be a filthy animal. On television, McHoffman's pugilistic personality was clever and amusing, but in person it was pure poison. Besides, the weather was freezing cold in DC. Who wants to live anywhere that cold if there isn't even good skiing within two hundred miles? Back in California I could surf in the morning, mountain bike for a few hours, then ski Big Bear mountain the same afternoon—all with my shirt off in the spring. DC also disappointed me with its disgracefully trash-littered streets and rampant poverty within spitting distance of the Capitol building itself. The city is strewn with thousands of bums, but I never understood why. They sleep on frosty park benches from which icicles hang, with only the *Washington Post* for a blanket. One day I was walking from the subway to the office, the icy ground piercing through my dress shoes, and the biting cold air freezing the snot in my nose. I stopped and told a bum: "Go south, my brother! Florida, that's where you wanna be!" He gave me a peculiar look and mumbled something about cheese.

The TV job was incredibly stressful—almost to the point of insanity. One employee, James, kept a Japanese rock garden on his desk; whenever McHoffman was really badgering him, James would do some Zen breathing exercises and move the rocks around with his little red rake. I had no such release, and I let the stress eat at me. I wanted to go home. I dreamed of warm sand between my toes and steep waves sweeping me along on my surfboard under the sparkling California sun. I knew I wasn't prepared to conquer DC. Just yet.

When I got back to California, the political landscape was fraught with turmoil. After winning a one-vote majority in the assembly during the last election, the Republicans had failed to seize the speakership. Through trickery, chicanery, and sheer audacity, the longtime Democratic Speaker of the Assembly, Willie Black, had managed to cling to power. I didn't know the details, but the whole thing stank to me, like the shady dealings of some two-bit banana republic.

I flew into LAX. John Griggs met me at the baggage carousel with a jolly grin. He was still working at the public-policy think tank in LA.

"So how was DC, playboy?" he asked.

"Dirty as a dog's ass," I said. "Cold as hell, and nothing but politics. I mean, if I was a professional rock climber, I'd probably love Mount Everest the same way."

"I know whucha' mean. DC is a political animal's Mecca."

We grabbed my bags and walked to the parking lot. The temperature was forty degrees warmer than DC. The smog enveloped me like an old friend. I was happy to be back in miserable, wonderful LA. At my insistence, we took the top down on John's Jeep. He maneuvered through the crowded airport streets onto the freeway. Drivers honked at one another maliciously as the city's skyline looked down half-proudly through the haze. I was home.

"So, tell me about DC," John said.

"DC was cool. McHoffman was a nut. But I don't really feel like talking about him. Shit, I wanna know what's going on *here*. What's up with the assembly?"

"You wouldn't believe it if I told you."

"So—?"

"Well, after the last election, Republicans had enough votes to take the speakership. The Republican leader, Frank Buckman, should have been voted in as speaker but—"

"Who's Frank Buckman?"

"He's the Republican minority leader, from Long Beach. He's fat, half Samoan, walks around with a cane. He was supposedly wounded during the Korean War, which he plays up every election cycle, of course. Anyway, Buckman engineered the whole election victory. The Republicans had enough votes to take the speakership—forty Republicans versus only thirty-nine Democrats—but right before the speakership vote, Willie Black talked one Republican into voting for him, basically swiping the speakership from Buckman and the Republicans."

"Who's the traitor?"

"Bryan Gentry."

"He's my fucking assemblyman in Newport!"

"Yeah, I know. So anyway—"

"Why'd he do it?"

"Who knows? Willie promised him all kinds of goodies, and made him speaker pro tem, with a big office, big budget, and lots of perks."

"What a slimy piece of garbage. What a filthy traitor!"

"I know."

"So what's gonna happen now?"

"Nothing. There's nothing the Republicans can do . . . short of killing Bryan Gentry."

"We could always call Bill Crutchman," I joked.

"Right! So what are you gonna do out here, Jimbo, as far as work?"

"I've got a job lined up with the Statesmen Institute. Ever heard of it?"

"Sure, they're the biggest think tank in California. They're hard-core conservatives. How'd you line that up?"

"Through Mariella. She made a few calls when I told her I wanted to come back here."

"That's cool. It's all who you know, bro. So what's Edward gonna do now?"

"I guess he's decided to run for California governor. I told him it was a good idea."

"Yeah, but you know who has the final say."

I grinned. "Mariella *wants* him to run."

"Then, there you go. Looks like we'll be working for Edward again."

"Shit, we'll be running his campaign this time, buddy. Everyone else bailed out on Edward after the Senate race. But I stayed at his side, lived at his house, kept him up to speed on everything. It'll pay off. You watch."

"Yeah. I should really call him soon. Hey, but you know who else is going to run for governor, don't you?"

"Who?"

"Dale Spencer, the attorney general."

"Shit—he's ugly. He doesn't have a prayer against Edward."

"You can't go just on looks. Spencer's real popular with rank-and-file Republicans."

"That's all fine, but the guy looks like a disgruntled car salesman. Believe me, looks are more than fifty percent of the deal. California's the most media-intensive place on earth. That's why Edward is perfect. Tons of money. Good-looking. He'll blow a fuckin' hole through Spencer."

"The world according to Jim Asher!" John exclaimed. "Dude, in your world, no one could run for office unless they were a millionaire or a Calvin Klein model."

"I'm telling you."

"Well, that race isn't for another year, so don't start measuring drapes for the governor's mansion just yet. Hey, in the meantime, what's up for tonight? It's Friday night and my homey is back in town." He punched my shoulder. "We've gotta get loose tonight, baby—it's mandatory!"

"Samantha is throwing a 'smoker' tonight. Why don't you come along—if you think you're a real playboy, that is. It'd be a great chance for you to meet some reporters."

"Cool."

John dropped me in Newport. My parents listened to all my stories about Washington. It felt great to be home. DC was too immense; it sucked someone like me right up. I knew I needed to be in a smaller pond. Now I was back where I knew things, where I could keep track of people and develop a plan of action. California was ripe for a mover and shaker like me. By my estimation, there were only a handful of smart and savvy people working politics in the state. I was ready to plunge in and test my buoyancy.

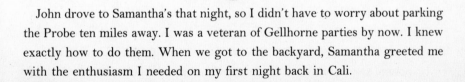

John drove to Samantha's that night, so I didn't have to worry about parking the Probe ten miles away. I was a veteran of Gellhorne parties by now. I knew exactly how to do them. When we got to the backyard, Samantha greeted me with the enthusiasm I needed on my first night back in Cali.

"Jimmy! My little Republican man is back!" She gave me a kiss that made the anxieties of DC vanish, and John blush. "Who's your friend?" she asked.

"Samantha Gellhorne, this is John Griggs. He's a big-time Republican player. We worked together at Winston, and he also worked in the Bush White House." In politics, I had learned, it was always customary to introduce people as being twice as grand as they actually were. It was a pleasant, fraudulent practice.

"Pleasure to meet you, John." She shook his hand. "Jimmy, there're some people you really have to meet, come on."

An hour later, I was planted in a chair near the hot tub, two drinks in hand, chatting with a reporter from the *LA Times* named Greg. He was a cool cat, sporting a goatee and hair just long enough to pull into a ponytail.

"Greg, you wrote a few stories on the Winston campaign, didn't you?" I asked.

"Yeah. I was second-stringing that race for a couple weeks."

"What're you doing now?"

"I've actually been doing some editing, which is kind of a big deal in my circle. But I'll probably be covering the political races next year."

"Great. You know Edward Winston is planning to run for governor."

"Really," he said, scratching his goatee. "How do you know that?"

"I just know. But that's between you and me."

He nodded, knowing it wasn't. I was obviously planting something on him, and we both knew it but didn't have to acknowledge it.

Two young and pretty girls walked up and sat suspiciously near us, glancing over every few seconds. Greg winked at me. "Interns." He waved to them. "Yo, girls, why don't you join us."

They acted surprised for a moment, then slid their chairs over.

"So where do you ladies work?" Greg asked. They said they were interns at Samantha's TV station. One of the girls was very lovely, about twenty, and she was giggling at everything I said. But I really wasn't interested. I left Greg to handle the girls and went inside.

Rick shouted when he saw me. "Jim Asher—get your young ass over here and do some tequila shots with me!"

"Hey, Slick Rick, good to see you, bro." I slapped his back. "Destroyed any companies lately?"

"Matter of fact, I'm working on something hot right now. But never mind that. Sit down. I've got a new bottle of Sauza I brought back from Acapulco."

He poured two shots. We slammed them—then two more. Rick was already drunk before we started, so I figured I was safe to match him. Samantha joined us a few minutes later.

"Jimmy, I invited this girl from NBC for you. Her name's Ellen. I think you'll like her. She's your type."

"Samantha, how do you know what my type is?"

"She's a news producer and she's gorgeous."

I grinned.

"So what are you doing now, Jim?" Rick asked.

"I got a job at some think tank in Riverside."

"*Boring*. You should come work for me in Hollywood—make some real fucking money."

"Edward's gonna run for governor next year," I said. "I'll make plenty of dough on that race."

Samantha's eyes lit up. "Edward's going to run for governor?"

"Yup."

They both smiled. Rick was a Republican—like lots of rich lawyers—and Samantha was drifting that way after twenty years of what I termed her "misguided liberalism."

"Well, cool, looks like we'll be back on the campaign trail together," Samantha said. "Jimmy, let's go find Ellen."

Thirty minutes later I was in the oven. Ellen clawed at the headboard in Samantha's guest room as I took her from behind. She was tall and athletic, with long blond hair that I had wrapped around my hand. She flipped over.

"I wanna look at you while you do me," she said.

"Okay."

"Jim, I shouldn't be doing this. I'm a reporter, and you're—"

"Just wrap your legs around me and hold on."

Ellen shrieked like a wildcat with every move—much louder than was warranted, I thought. Her fingernails raked my back. For some reason, and I don't know why, I looked around. A silhouette was outlined in the open door. I kept going anyway. The shadow moved closer to the bed. Then I felt a third hand run across my shoulder. I turned around. Samantha.

"Hey, sweetheart," she whispered in my ear. "I knew you'd like Ellen."

I could tell from the shadows that the bedroom door was wide open. I stopped. "What if Rick walks in, Samantha?"

"He's passed out. Too much tequila—the story of our lives."

Ellen was unfazed. Her fingernails drove sharply into my hindquarters, making me jolt inside her. Samantha stood there watching silently. Then her hand rubbed my back, moving up and down, and occasionally pushing my hips into Ellen. This went on for several minutes.

"Hurry up and finish with her," Samantha said. "I need to talk to you."

"I can't hurry if you tell me to hurry," I protested. The whole situation was bizarre.

Samantha leaned over my shoulder. "Ellen, can you leave for a minute?"

Ellen gave Samantha a nasty look, then rolled off the bed and gathered her far-flung articles of clothing. A minute later she was gone.

"I'm so glad you're back, Jimmy," Samantha said.

I rolled over, let out a deep sigh, and reached for my underwear, which was dangling from a lamp.

Samantha grabbed me. "Don't . . . I wanna look at you." She rolled me toward her. "I love to look at your ass. It's like marble."

"Yeah," I said, "it's white."

I put my Calvins on.

"I'm feeling down about Rick," she said. "He does this every party now. It's gotten worse since you left for DC."

"What's he doing?"

"He passes out almost every night. It's like he can't operate without drinking."

"That's Rick. He's always been like that since I've known him."

"But now it's not as cute anymore. He's talking about getting married."

"Married?"

"I know," she gasped.

"What are you gonna do, Samantha?"

"I don't know. I'm getting older. He's got a shitload of money. I just don't know."

"Well, you'll always have me," I said.

"Come here, Samantha needs a kissy."

I kissed her but pulled away because I was sweaty and my head was swimming with tequila.

"So, is Edward really going to run?" she asked.

"I think so. I'm trying to get the word out, get some momentum building."

"You know about Dale Spencer, right?"

"Of course."

"He's not very good. I covered both his congressional races in the eighties. I know Dale. Winston can beat him."

"That's what I think, too," I said.

"But Winston has problems. Like the illegal alien thing. That's still going to linger. And most hard-core Republicans don't trust him."

I nodded. "That is a problem for the primaries."

"You guys need to line up all the party bigwigs and endorsements you can get now—before Spencer locks them up. He's moving fast from what I've heard."

When it came to politics, Samantha was always on top of everything. Only a select handful of people will ever posses her level of clarity and natural insight. True political players aren't coached or taught, they are born. In fact, if Samantha wasn't a reporter, she could have cleaned house as a political consultant. Fortunately she always took a keen interest in my career—like I was some experiment of hers. We had a strange relationship of unspoken understanding; we did things for each other that always happened to benefit ourselves in the end.

"You and Winston need to figure out how you're going to get the party's core element on your side," she said.

"I've been thinking about that."

"This think-tank job sounds fine for now, Jimmy. But the real action's in Sacramento. That's where you wanna be, babe."

"So what's your take on this whole assembly speakership thing, Samantha?"

"Basically, your Republican pals got their asses spanked. But I'm surprised that they haven't tried to recall Bryan Gentry yet."

"Recall? Can they do that?"

"Why not?" she shrugged. "I've seen it done before."

"How does a recall work?"

"Basically, a group of Republicans would launch a recall campaign against Bryan Gentry."

"Based on what?"

"Based on the fact that he ran as a Republican, then switched to support a Democrat—Willie Black. It's pretty simple. You get a strong Republican candidate to run against him; then it's basically just like any other special election. If your candidate beats him, Bryan Gentry loses his seat."

"So all we have to do is file for a recall election and find someone to run against Gentry? That doesn't sound very difficult."

"There's some paperwork involved, but it's no big deal. Once Gentry is replaced, the Republicans would have a one-vote majority, and then they could vote in a new Republican speaker. Actually, I think there was some talk about it a few months ago, but a recall campaign takes a lot of money, and right now every Republican in the state is flat broke after the last election."

We both looked at each other. I think Samantha said it first.

"Except Winston!"

Until the sun splashed across the balcony the next morning and John Griggs banged on the door, Samantha and I drank wine, made love, and plotted the future of California.

ELEVEN

My job at the think tank suited me perfectly. I came in at nine every morning and spent my day thinking. The Institute was nonprofit, so the atmosphere was academic—laid back. I even bought a sport coat with suede elbow patches. I had a pleasant little office, a fax, a computer, plenty of supplies, and access to a huge library. The guy in the office next to me, David, was writing a book about China. Another employee named Julia was designing an interactive CD-Rom about the French Revolution. I was the only person on senior staff without a Ph.D., and I was years younger than everyone else. But because I was director of communications—media, writing, talk shows—everyone thought I knew something they didn't. For some reason, everyone thinks media relations is mystical—a strange realm where slick wordsmiths interface with reporters in some unspeakable tango of phrases and intrigue. So as long as I got reporters to show up at the Institute's events, and newspaper editors to print our articles, my boss was happy not to know any more.

Along the way, I was developing a strong political philosophy on my own, albeit a customized one. While I was generally a conservative, I began to lean heavily toward a personal version of libertarianism. I didn't join the Republican Party to pay homage to religious holy rollers or anti-abortion bullies. I believed, as America's founders did, that freedom should be the ultimate goal of government. Humans cannot be happy without freedom, and freedom cannot exist without responsibility. Fortunately, humans enjoy both naturally, if allowed to. I dreamed of a smaller, less intrusive government. In my mind, government should physically protect the weak from the strong, defend the nation from foreign aggression, break up natural monopolies, build roads, fight epidemic diseases, educate children at the local level, and otherwise leave citizens alone to blaze their own trails to happiness.

If a man wants to jump from an airplane at forty thousand feet, suck oxygen down to twenty-five thousand, pop a parasail, glide onto the peak of Mount McKinley, then snowboard at breakneck speed to the bottom, it is his freedom to do so. Feeling his balls suck up into his stomach as he blasts off a fifty-foot ice cliff gives him untold personal bliss, and he is hurting no one. Why should the government take away his happiness? At the same time, the snowboarder's neighbor should not be forced to cover his medical bills when he plummets into a thousand-foot ice ravine. Why should some bloated congressional bureaucrat force an adult to wear a helmet when riding his motorcycle, as if he were a child unable to think for himself? Or steal his property—under the auspices of "Social Security"—from which he will likely never see a dime if he is under thirty? Isn't this grown man capable of opening his own savings account at the bank? No matter what the politicians say, Social Security is nothing short of outright theft, period. What else can forcibly taking a man's property without returning it during his lifetime be called? How fucking arrogant these politicians are!

If a man chooses not to work, that is his freedom. He is at liberty to stroll Florida's beaches or spend months trekking through America's glorious Rocky Mountains. He cannot be forced to work, as in some countries. But he, and only he, is responsible when his stomach grumbles. The government should never take bread and milk from a working stranger's table three thousand miles away to cover for his free choice to roam the hills. Freedom can be unkind to those who ignore its responsibilities, but freedom remains the only hope for human happiness. Most politicians will never understand—or choose selfishly to ignore—this simple and oldest of political truths.

The Republican Party was not a perfect fit for me. When it came to issues like drugs and prostitution, I was on the expanding edge. After long deliberation and many hundreds of philosophy essays and discussions, I favored legalization. Why should some politician in Washington tell an adult how to conduct himself in his own home, in his own bedroom? If he wants to snort blow, that's his choice. He enjoys the rush, the high, the false flash of immortality. But again, he must take responsibility. If he violates another citizen's property rights by force—stealing to fuel his habit—the government must use force to stop him, and lock him up. Sometimes the GOP seemed too narrow to accommodate my free views. What if I had wanted to wear a nose ring to political functions? I would have been ostracized, and out of a job. So I played along. Part of my drive was to change the party—to restore freedom as its subatomic force. I was running with a crowd of like-minded players— young, freedom loving, with the looks, influence, and intelligence to slowly shift the party's direction.

With my salary at $46,000 and no bills to speak of, I had plenty of money. But not nearly enough to support my new lifestyle. I was partying with reporters every weekend now—it was my life, my specialty. And whenever one has a specialty, he is a fool not to capitalize on it. Even though I had a full-time job, politicians were always calling to ask if I would help them drum up media coverage for some lame event or some trivial bill they sponsored. "Help" meant freelance pitching. They paid me at least five hundred dollars to promote each event or bill. Typically, some pimple-faced legislative aide on their staff would have been tasked with cold-calling reporters, asking if they would please be kind enough to cover their boss's event. I didn't need to cold-call; I would just call and ask when the next party was. Who do you think was more successful—me pitching reporters and network producers over piña coladas in a Jacuzzi hanging over the Hollywood Hills, or some faceless Joe on the phone at 7 A.M.?

The money started rolling in. My tiny ten-by-ten office at the Statesmen Institute turned into a one-man public-relations firm. The word was out: "If you need media, call Jim Asher at the Statesmen Institute. He'll go *all the way* for you." The politicians didn't care about my methods, they only cared about results—how many cameras showed up, how many reporters, how many positive articles they could clip out and mail to their fund-raisers, period. I was churning out thirty to fifty memos a day on my fax. The kindly old receptionist lady would ring my phone and say, "Jim, it's that lady reporter . . . again. What are you doing to these girls?"

I think my boss suspected something was up. I always had my door closed, acting quite suspiciously, juggling four phone calls while receiving a fax and E-mailing some editor. For all my boss knew, I could have been running a Central American revolution from my laptop.

Two months into my new job, I got a call from Samantha that changed everything.

"Boo-Boo. Hey, I've got some info. Do you know Brett Alexander?"

"He's an up-and-comer Republican in the assembly, right?"

"Right. Well, I heard he's thinking about launching a recall campaign against Bryan Gentry."

"Great. Does he have any dough?"

"Doubtful. You should make some calls, babe. Look, I've gotta run. I'm working on something big."

"It's not an exposé story about a beautiful scheming reporter and her sexual boy-toy political operative boyfriend, is it?"

She laughed. "God, I hope not! Boyfriend? You're so sweet . . . Hey, you've gotta come up to the house tonight."

"I can't. I've gotta go to some damn fund-raiser."

"Blow it off, Boo-Boo. Those things are small-time. I'm having Paul and Greg over, and some girls from the station. You've *got* to come."

"Why don't I just move in with you, Samantha?"

"I don't think Rick would be into that."

"Nine o'clock?"

"See you then, Boo-Boo."

TWELVE

The next morning, I dragged myself in to the Institute an hour late. As always after a Samantha Gellhorne night, I was hung out to dry. I had a coffeemaker in my office now, so I didn't attract attention with my filthy, quadruple-dark-roast mud brew. Once it was full, I dropped some ice cubes into the pot and let it cool to room temperature. I guzzled the entire pot: I had shit to do.

My fax was overflowing with memos, now falling directly into a scattered pile on the carpet. My desk was cluttered two inches thick with articles I was writing for the Institute's newsletter. I was also in the middle of writing an important speech on race relations for my boss to deliver at UCLA. I dug around my desk and pulled all my pink phone-message slips into one pile, looking for a message from Edward Winston. I finally found it, but it was six days old. I decided I would act like I had never received the message when I called him. "Damn secretary," I would scorn.

I dialed Edward at the Virginia house. He had a Pacific Palisades estate, a New York penthouse, a West Palm mansion, plus the villas in Hawaii, Athens, and Paris. It was difficult to keep track of him, but the Virginia house seemed to be Edward's headquarters for the moment.

I still got nervous every time I called him.

"Hello," the familiar voice answered.

"Oh, hello, Mariella, it's Jim."

"Jimmy, how are you, darling? How is the new job working out?"

"It's wonderful, thanks. But I miss everyone out there."

"We miss you, too, around the house. Cynthia is tugging on my dress right now. She says hello."

Winston had a lovely six-year-old daughter named Cynthia, who I spent a lot of time with when I lived at the house. She loved to go for bike rides and play on the jungle gym in the backyard, but most of her nannies were old ladies who weren't half as fun or adventurous as I was. Cynthia was always delightful company, even though she had once taunted me as being "Dana Steadfield's boyfriend" during the Senate campaign. It was a vicious smear, but I loved her in spite of it.

"Say hello to the rug rat from me," I said.

"Of course. Emmm . . . I've been meaning to talk with you, sweetheart."

Uh, oh—those were famous words.

"I really think Edward needs to get moving on the governor's race. I'm hearing about Dale Spencer every day."

"I agree."

"Has Edward said anything to you about his plans?"

I wondered why *Mariella* was asking *me*. "No, we haven't talked about the race very much lately. Actually, that's why I'm calling."

"Wonderful. I think you need to stay in close contact with Edward, and encourage him. He's working on Wall Street so much now, and he doesn't get a chance to keep up with politics like he should. I think he needs someone full-time out there in California. You would be perfect, sweetheart."

"Well, I can't do it full-time right now, Mariella, but I could probably consult."

"That might be even better, darling. That way you can keep up your media contacts."

"Exactly."

"Okay, let me get Edward for you, hold on. I'll see you soon, sweetheart."

After what seemed like an hour, Edward was on the phone.

"Hello, Jim, how are you?" His voice was kind, as usual.

"Great, and how about you?"

"Oh, just tremendous. I'm trying to earn back all the money I lost on the senate race. Say, I'm coming out there next week. Can we meet for lunch? I want to talk about the next race."

"Sure," I said. "Any time."

"How about"—I heard him flipping through his appointment book—"how about Tuesday?"

"Sounds great."

"Let's meet at my country club. They put on a terrific lunch. Here, let me give you directions . . ."

My blood was really pumping. Becoming a full-fledged consultant to someone like Edward Winston was the dream of every man, woman, and child working in politics.

". . . so, anyway, I'll see you Tuesday," he said. "And why don't you put together a strategy memo and gather up some recent clips on the race. I'm a little behind on my reading."

"No problem. See you Tuesday, Edward."

I hung up and exhaled with a great gust. *That went well,* I told myself. Now I had to come up with a campaign strategy for Edward and put it down on paper before next Tuesday . . . only five days away.

I needed some advice. I phoned Bud Raper in Washington.

"Bud," he barked into the phone.

"Bud, it's Jim Asher."

"Hey there, kid. Balled any hot media muff lately?"

"Nailed a cute field reporter from NBC the other night—a blond, big cans."

"Damn, when am I gonna see some video footage of this shit?"

"I don't want you looking at my ass, Bud."

"Listen here, motherfucker—"

"Just kidding. Hey, Bud, I need some advice. Edward wants me to draw up a strategy memo for his governor's race. What should I do?"

I explained the plan Samantha and I had cooked up. Bud seemed to like it.

"The first thing is to kick that son-of-a-bitch traitor Bryan Gentry out of the assembly. You go after him like he killed your fuckin' dog, you understand. If you can use Winston's dough to take the assembly for Republicans, he'll be the hero of the party. See—Winston can fuck Spencer up in a primary. All you need is a few million in negative TV. But Winston can't win if the whole establishment is behind Dale Spencer. Here's what you've gotta do. You win back the assembly and install your own speaker, maybe this Brett Alexander guy you mentioned, then you make him campaign for Winston. Then start buying off endorsements from every Republican politician in the state with thirty-thousand-dollar campaign contributions."

"Bribes?"

"Contributions."

"Okay . . . but what about Frank Buckman? Won't he become speaker automatically, since he's the Republican leader?"

"No such thing as automatic in this game. Listen, you always gotta step back and look at the big picture—who the fuckin' players really are. Buckman's tight with Spencer; so if Buckman becomes speaker, you won't be able to control him. Fuck Buckman. If he gets in your way, you go straight for his throat, you hear me, kid? No fucking around. You either fight to kill or go home crying. Discredit that fat motherfucker—track him with surveillance, research his finances, catch him with a whore, dig through his fuckin' garbage cans if you have to. You find out what kind of shit he's up to. Remember, everyone's doing something fucked up enough to drop into a thirty-second commercial . . ."

Bud talked for nearly an hour. I was writing notes so fast they resembled hieroglyphics—field operations, media buys, convention maneuvering. I got a crash course on political management 101, directly from the master. Bud would have charged a client at least twenty thousand dollars for the same strategy advice. But as long as I was cool with him, he always helped me out, even when there was no reason to—which I think says a lot about the kind of man he was. Before Bud hung up, he said: "When it comes time to talk money, ask Winston for a shitload of dough—you'll get it."

The rest of the day, all I could think about was next Tuesday—the day I would be crowned a genuine political consultant.

THIRTEEN

Once again, I was back in Pop's Buick, on my way to Pacific Palisades. I really needed to get my act together and buy a new car, I told myself. I was nervous for the entire drive to Edward's country club. How much money should I ask for? Would he like my strategy? Or would he laugh me out of the place for the impostor I was? I knew I only had one shot at this. For the past few days I had been on the phone with everyone who knew anything about California politics. I thought I had a solid proactive plan. Now it was time to put everything to the test.

I pulled up to the country club with my hands gripping the steering wheel nervously. The fat guard at the security shack eyed the Buick skeptically.

"I'm here to meet Edward Winston," I said.

"Oh, yes. Mr. Winston just came through." He smiled. "You must be Mr. Asher?"

"Uh, yes . . . Jim."

He waved me through. I felt royal. I couldn't believe the guard actually knew my name. I was meeting Edward at the golf course clubhouse. I was impressed beyond measure as I cruised up the pancake-smooth black street. A lush, well-groomed golf course wrapped around a private lake filled with swans. Palatial estates sprinkled the rolling green hills. Flower gardens stretched before me at every turn, bursting with fragrance and color. I found the clubhouse and parked the Buick behind a large catering van, out of sight. I methodically removed every last piece of lint from my gray suit, took a deep breath, and walked up the steps to the clubhouse. The lobby was a distinguished-looking hall with hardwood flooring, fine oil paintings, and polished brass fixtures.

The receptionist smiled when she saw me, probably noticing how out of place I was.

"You must be Mr. Asher?" she said.

"Yes . . . Jim."

"Come this way. Mr. Winston is waiting for you in the dining room."

Edward stood up when I walked into the large dining area. He was the only one in the room. He wore a chalk-stripe gray flannel suit, and his smile was welcoming.

"Jim, I'm so pleased you could make it," he said.

I shook his hand and sat down at the table.

"This is a very nice country club," I said.

"Yes. I've been coming here for years. It's a nice place to relax. So, how was the drive?"

"It was great. PCH all the way."

"I love California. During the primary, I saw parts of this wonderful state most Californians don't even know exist."

"It's the best state in the world," I said.

Edward always had a way of listening that made me cautious about what I said—he really seemed to absorb every word, not wanting to miss out on some crucial point that might affect his life dramatically. It was flattering, but a little unnerving. At the same time, I could never tell if anything I said was sinking into his head or not; often he would simply nod. Edward looked slightly thinner now, and a little more wary than during the campaign, but his clothes and hair were impeccable, with slight traces of gray beginning to show near his sideburns, and his shallow blue eyes were full of disarrayed energy that made him seem different and somehow elevated, as if the money itself had actually changed his physiology over the years. But there was always a confused coolness to him, an awkward distance. Not only couldn't I seem to figure him out, but it also occurred to me that Edward Winston had never paused long enough to figure *himself* out, or to understand his own place under the stars. He always seemed like somewhat of a floating soul, adrift and without a definable purpose, which was sad to me.

"So, how's your job at the Statesmen Institute?" he asked.

"It's okay. I'm learning a lot, in terms of political philosophy, and I'm making a lot of media contacts."

"Think tanks are a great training ground for young conservatives. That's why I donate every year to three or four of them, including the Statesmen Institute."

I didn't know he was a donor to the Institute. That explained how I got the job so easily.

"Let's talk about the governor's race," Edward said. "How do you think it's shaping up?"

"Spencer is off and running. He already has several key endorsements, including the police unions. But he doesn't have any money, and he's not good at fund-raising."

Edward nodded.

"I've been thinking about the primary," I continued. "Right now the party is like a feudalistic society. And the key to the crown, as it was then, is the nobility—in this case, the party bigwigs and elected officials . . ." I had the whole stupid speech memorized and rehearsed. "If we get their support, the others will follow. Then we can use your money to smoke Spencer out of the primary."

"Okay . . . how do we do that?"

"Well, I've been thinking. How do we impress the party's hierarchy? How do we get them to believe that you're the man who can win the governor's office and hold on to it? We need to make them see you as a man of action, Edward, a man with a solid plan and the means to execute it. Let me ask you, what is the one area of California politics that's wide open right now? The one problem that's frustrating the party's leaders more than anything else?"

He sat back in his chair and gazed out at the golf course. I could almost see the hamster running on the wheel.

"The assembly?" he suddenly said.

"Exactly!—the assembly. Republicans should be in control of the assembly right now. There's no excuse for the way Frank Buckman got rolled by Willie Black. We have a Republican majority, but the leadership has failed. The assembly has been under Democratic control for twenty-five years. If you were to liberate it, Edward, you could write your own ticket to the governor's mansion. You'd be the hero of the party."

Very slowly, as if the entire next two years were unfurling right there in his lap, Edward grinned. "You're right," he said. "It's an absolute outrage that we don't have the assembly. So . . . what are you suggesting?"

"Well, Frank Buckman is considered a loser by most of the party now. And *you* certainly can't become the speaker. But what if we took the hottest Republican in the assembly, Brett Alexander, and set him up?"

"You mean, set him up to become speaker?"

"Exactly. Every Republican in the state is broke right now. No one has the money to run a recall campaign against Bryan Gentry—except you."

"So what's to keep me from spending a bundle of money, then getting dumped on, like I did with the school voucher campaign last year?"

"I've got a plan for that . . ."

I explained, and Edward agreed it could work.

"Okay," he said. "It sounds like we've decided on a strategy. But you've got a lot of phone calls and business to take care of, Jim. Do you think you can handle all of it on your own?"

"No problem. I'm going on half-time with the Statesmen Institute so I can concentrate on your priorities." Of course, I hadn't discussed that with my boss at the Institute yet, but no matter.

"I'll need you full-time around the conventions and whenever I'm in town," he said.

"Absolutely. And I'll send you update faxes when you're out of town."

"Great. Now, let's talk money. This will be a consulting arrangement, so you'll have to handle your own taxes. How much do you think you'll need?"

Here it goes, I thought. Just before the words came out, I decided to lower the asking price: "Well, I'm making a lot of money now with my consulting. And of course I'll have to drop that . . . and I'm trying to buy a condo. So, I'll need nine thousand a month."

I could barely keep a straight face. I was ready for him to start laughing. But Edward's face was motionless, expressionless; even his eyes gave nothing away. He leaned back in the chair and formed a pensive triangle with his hands in front of his mouth. He was in deep thought. I was in deep panic.

"Here's what I can do," he said. "I'll write you a check for seven every month. And I'll make it ten on convention months, because you'll be working much harder. How does that sound?"

I nearly blasted through the roof! I nearly shouted out with glee! I nearly lost control of my bodily functions.

"That will be sufficient," I said.

"Good." He pulled out a binder-type checkbook. "I'll just get the first check out of the way right now."

———————————————

As soon as I cleared the country club's security shack, I stood up through my open sunroof, steering with my knees, threw my fists into the air triumphantly, and howled, "Fuck yeah! Fuck yeah, baby!" Shivers ran up my spine. "I'm fuckin' loaded!" I picked up the cell phone and called home.

"That's great, sweetheart," my mom said. "Now you can take care of your poor old mother when I retire."

"Of course I'll take care of you," I said.

"Well, you've been working very hard. It was bound to pay off sooner or later. What exactly will you be doing for Mr. Winston?"

"Basically, I'll be his only political employee. So I guess I'll write all his speeches, set him up with meetings, help him choose good causes to donate to, stuff like that. The first thing we're going to do is launch a recall campaign against Bryan Gentry."

"You mean our assemblyman here in Newport?"

"Yeah. The guy's a traitor. He sold out to the Democrats."

"I know a little bit about it. But what does that have to do with Mr. Winston?"

"Well, if Edward helps kick Gentry out of the assembly by financing a recall campaign, he'll be the hero of every Republican in the state. Then we're going to set up a guy named Brett Alexander to become the next speaker of the assembly, and he'll campaign for Edward to become governor."

"What do you mean 'set up'?"

"Uh, well, it's kind of complicated. There are actually a lot of rivalries within the Republican Party itself. But we've got a bunch of good people working on it, not just me."

"Oh, I see. Well, I won't pretend to understand it, but just be careful, Jim. There are a lot of people out there who don't have the same values you were brought up with."

"I know, Mom. Don't worry. It's all part of politics. And I'm sticking with the good people, like Edward."

"He has been very good to you."

"Is Jake around? I wanted to tell him about the new job."

"Sure. Oh, by the way, I wanted to tell you: your father's been watching that friend of yours on TV, Samantha Gell . . ."

"Gellhorne. Samantha Gellhorne at Channel Seven."

"Right. Ever since she called the house asking for you, he's been watching her every night."

"It's an outrage . . . he's a married man!"

My mom laughed. "Okay, I'll go get your brother."

"What's up, bro?" Jake answered.

"You won't believe how much money Winston's paying me, dude."

"How much?"

"Seven a month."

"Seven hundy? That's pretty good."

"Fuck seven hundy. I'm talkin' seven thow . . . seven Gs, baby! Plus ten thousand on convention months—twice a year."

"Holy shit!"

"I know. Hey, do you have school tonight?"

"No. I just have to write a term paper."

"Fuck that, playboy. We're going on a Vegas run tonight."

"Vegas?"

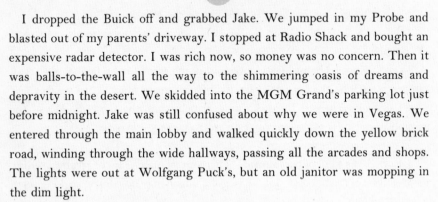

I dropped the Buick off and grabbed Jake. We jumped in my Probe and blasted out of my parents' driveway. I stopped at Radio Shack and bought an expensive radar detector. I was rich now, so money was no concern. Then it was balls-to-the-wall all the way to the shimmering oasis of dreams and depravity in the desert. We skidded into the MGM Grand's parking lot just before midnight. Jake was still confused about why we were in Vegas. We entered through the main lobby and walked quickly down the yellow brick road, winding through the wide hallways, passing all the arcades and shops. The lights were out at Wolfgang Puck's, but an old janitor was mopping in the dim light.

"So what are we doing?" Jake asked again.

"Patience, grasshopper."

I walked to the cashier's cage and plunked down my check from Winston. I cashed the whole thing. The wicked-looking hag behind the counter ran the check through their system, then asked, "Howdya' want this?"

"All in one-hundred-dollar chips," I said.

A minute later we were at a blackjack table—not the five-dollar tables full of disgraced alcoholics and truck drivers where I usually sat. No. Tonight I was at the high-stakes table, where I truly belonged.

"C'mon—what are you doing, man?" my brother finally demanded. "How many chips do you have there?"

"Seven thousand dollars' worth," I said, grinning.

"Jim, don't be stupid. That's a lotta scratch. In an hour you'll be totally broke, or down to almost nothing. These games are stacked against you, man."

"Right," I said. "The longer you play, the more your odds go down. That's why I'm only gonna play one hand."

I sat down and placed my entire rack of chips on the last empty spot at the table.

"You're crazy," Jake said. "I can't even watch this."

But my mind was made up. The $7,000 was just play money. I hadn't been expecting it, so if I lost it, what the hell: I would just pretend I never had it. At least that was the plan.

I was sitting in the last seat to the dealer's left. He flicked out the first card to me. Jack of spades. The dealer went around the table, then dealt himself a queen. I closed my eyes, and took deep breaths. This was it. I was either going to get mildly rich or humiliatingly disgraced in the next ten seconds. If I got rich, I decided I would buy a new car so I wouldn't have to hide the shameful Probe anymore. If I lost, I'd buy a few drinks for my brother and me, then drive home and try to forget I had ever done such a stupid, impulsive thing.

I looked at my brother; he was still shaking his head, looking grave. The dealer went around again and paired my jack with a three of hearts. Shit. My odds had just taken a dramatic downswing. Now I was stuck. I started to feel panicked. I should never have done this, I told myself. I could've bought a ski boat with the money, or taken an around-the-world cruise. The other players at the table were all watching me now. People walking by stopped and gathered around the table when they saw my fat rack of chips. I heard excited whispers pass through the crowd. Should I stick with thirteen and hope the dealer busts? Or hit? I looked at my brother.

"It's up to you," he said. "You came here to gamble. Might as well grab your *cojones.*"

My central nervous system was in a mild state of chaos—my breaths were rapid and shallow, my hands trembling, my eyes blurring. If I lost I would feel like the biggest fool ever, and in front of all these people. "Get a hold of yourself," I mumbled, reminding myself. "It's not even your money. If you lose it, you never had it."

The dealer looked at me like I had just escaped from an institution.

"Here goes nothing," I told my brother. He was bouncing up and down on his toes.

I closed my eyes and dragged my cards across the green felt, motioning for another card. I took a deep breath and held it. Everything seemed to freeze, and for a brief moment I couldn't hear a single noise or feel a single sensation, except gravity pulling down on me. Slowly, hesitantly, I opened my eyes. I looked down at the card the dealer had given me: eight.

"Holy SHIT! Motherfuck ME!" I sprang out of my chair like it was on fire. "Fuck yeah! Twenty-one motherfuckers!"

Everything seemed to ignite in bright flashing lights exploding all around me. My brother caught me before I hit the carpet. I stared up at the casino ceiling and wailed in rapture. Tears of excruciating joy streamed down my cheeks. Jake propped me back into the chair. The crowd around the table was laughing.

The dealer had nineteen and I had $17,500. The way things had been going for me lately, I figured he was lucky to get that.

FOURTEEN

On Monday I had work to do. With the help of my able young college intern, Ashwin, I spent the morning researching and writing an article on property rights for my boss, which would run in *Reason* magazine under his name. I always let Ashwin help me with the work he thought was cool and exciting— writing speeches or articles for magazines. I still remembered what it was like to be new on the political scene, overwhelmed and impressed by anything that seemed quasi-official. I enjoyed seeing the same eagerness in Ashwin. After my lunchtime MET-Rx health shake, I gave Ashwin the afternoon off. I needed to get down to some real Machiavellian political shit.

I called Renee, who was now the governor's chief fund-raiser. Renee and I had the sort of typical instant friendship I was learning to master in politics. To be a real player, you have to keep up dozens of superficial relationships that can be activated on demand by phone.

"Hey, babe," Renee answered. "When are we going out?"

"How 'bout tonight," I said.

"I have a fund-raiser for some jackass congressman."

"Tomorrow?"

"Okay. But that's not why you're calling, is it?"

"I need to meet Brett Alexander. Didn't you work for him?"

"I've worked for everyone, Jim. Fund-raising is a nomadic business. So what do you want with Brett anyway?"

"I wanna find out about this recall campaign I've been hearing about."

"You're not thinking of hooking up with that racket, are you?"

"Why not?"

"For one thing, they don't have any money; and two, Frank Buckman is just going to let Alexander and his cronies work their asses off to recall Gentry, then he'll step in and take the speakership for himself. Buckman's got too much support in Sacramento."

"What's the deal with Buckman? I've never met the guy."

"He's gigantic, and he walks around with a cane because of some war wound or whatever. I guess a lot of people think he's an asshole, especially people who get on his bad side. But no matter what people say, Frank Buckman is a skillful politician."

"What about this Brett Alexander? What kind of guy is he?"

"He's great. You'll like him, Jim. Former prosecutor. He got the death penalty for Richard Ramierez in 1987, then ran for the assembly. Brett's dynamic—young, smart, almost as good-looking as you."

"Hey, take that back!"

"Seriously, Brett Alexander is an up-and-comer, big time. After Buckman and Assembly Whip Pringle, Brett Alexander is probably the number three Republican right now. In fact, he actually turned down the whip job so he could focus on passing his Three Strikes law last year. Brett has oodles of potential, but right now, I think he's getting himself in over his head. Buckman and Spencer don't like him."

"I wanna meet him anyway. Edward Winston wants me to talk to Alexander on his behalf."

"Are you handling Winston's business now?"

"Yup."

"Shit. You're gonna have every Tom and Dick in the state knocking your door down for money."

"Bring 'em on."

"All right, just call Brett's office and tell him I recommended he see you. But honestly, Jim, you don't even need that. You've got Edward's name."

"Thanks, Renee."

"Hey, just be careful. You're stepping into a whole new arena now, Jim. These state-level guys are fucking scoundrels. They thrive on petty little intrigues. Just be careful."

"Of course. I'll see you tomorrow night."

"My place. Eight o'clock, babe."

I called Alexander's office. The receptionist told me to "come on down." Apparently it wasn't very difficult to get an appointment with assemblyman Brett Alexander.

I walked out to the Institute's parking lot. My new vehicle sparkled across the asphalt like a dream, standing proudly above all the other cars. The long era of the Probe had finally come to an end; the shame was no more. I hit the alarm button on my key chain and my new Humvee beeped a greeting. I had driven Humvees during my army days, but this one was different. Solid black glossy paint. Safari rack. Tan leather seats. CD changer. Cell phone. The works. It was a flashy car for a self-fashioned flashy guy. My license plate said it all: SPIN DR.

Nearly every part of my life was a contrivance now. Everything I did was calculated to present an image: brilliant young renegade political consultant. Eccentricity was part of any image-building package. I daydreamed about people trying to figure me out. They would say: *he's a political machine, barely a year in the business and he already handles all of Winston's business, plus he works full-time for a think tank, writes speeches, and sleeps with tons of reporters—the guy's a fuckin' animal!*

Who knows what they were really saying? Probably something like: *he's a scheming little bastard, making up for his deficiencies by driving a flashy car and sleeping with reporters like a three-dollar whore.*

I climbed into the Hummer and drove to the city of Orange. Brett Alexander's office was attached to the Mall of Orange. I had grown up in a small house just down the street, but I never knew the offices were there. I literally had to walk past two giant dumpsters to get to the front door. The receptionist was bubbly. She talked to me about the latest movies for thirty minutes while I waited to see her boss. Finally, her intercom beeped.

"He's ready to see you, Mr. Asher," she said.

"It's Jim."

"Okay, Jim, he's ready to see you."

When I saw Brett Alexander sitting there behind his cheap desk in his ramshackle office, I knew I had a killer politician on my hands. He looked just like me, only a few years older and fifteen pounds heavier. As I watched him stand up to shake my hand, a million thoughts flashed through my head. I was already shaping his image, seeing him ten pounds thinner, and with a nicer suit. If this guy had half a brain, he could be a major political force.

"Jim Asher," he said. We shook hands. "Nice to meet you. I've been hearing things about you." His voice was a perfect political voice—authoritative yet understanding.

"Likewise," I said. "Everyone tells me you're the up-and-comer in California politics."

"California?" he said. "Only for starters."

Ambition! I was about to embark on a potent new friendship.

"I'm here to talk about the recall campaign," I said.

"Great. Only there isn't a recall. We'd love to do it, but we don't have any money—at all." He gestured around his office. "We spent everything last fall just to pass Three Strikes. I can barely cover the rent on this dump."

This guy was a Picasso sitting in a flea market, ready to be dusted off and taken public in a big way.

"I might be able to help with the money," I said.

"Really? You work for Winston, right?"

"Right."

"Well, that'd be great if you could help out. We've put together a plan for the recall, but it's pretty rudimentary."

"Can I see it?"

"You'll have to get with my chief of staff, Francis White. He's got all the polls, voter registration, and mailer information. Do you know Francis?"

"No. I've been in DC for the last eight months. I really need to meet more people out here."

"DC, huh? I'll be there one day," he said. His entire body and every word from his mouth was infused with anxious energy.

"You'd love it," I said. "Pure unadulterated politics."

"Great. We'll have to talk about it someday. Right now let's talk money. How much can you put into a recall?"

"Edward is setting up a statewide 'Republican Victory Fund.' We're starting out with two hundred thousand dollars."

His eyebrows raised. "Damn, that's a lot of money. I think we can get a recall started with that. Does Edward want to be involved in the recall?"

"Definitely." I leaned back in the chair like I owned it.

"Okay, great. Hey, Jim, do you wanna grab some lunch? I'm starving."

"Sure. How about Aroma Italiano?"

"You familiar with this area?"

"I grew up two blocks away, down on Galley Street."

"A local boy. I think I'm gonna like you," he said.

It was beautiful outside, so we left our coats at the office and walked to Aroma Italiano. We both ordered pressed Parmesan chicken sandwiches, the house specialty.

"So, Jim, tell me what the strings are," he said. "No one hands money out for free."

"It's real simple. But this has to be off the record . . ."

He gave me a funny look. "You don't know me very well, Jim. Everything I do is off the record." Brett had a very likeable, midwestern-type ease about him, which I suspected masked a remarkably sharp edge underneath.

"Good," I said. "Then here's the deal. We'll get the recall up and running. I'll work at the campaign. All you have to do is pledge your support for Edward Winston's gubernatorial campaign once you become speaker."

"Speaker? Who said anything about me becoming speaker? I'm not even a part of the Republican leadership."

I looked right at him, unblinking.

He tried to keep his face straight for a few seconds; then he grinned, a smile breaking across his face like he was suddenly seeing a reflection of himself in me. He leaned back, sipped his coffee, and waved down the owner. "Riccardo, this is the best mocha you've ever made! Any chance of getting a couple Baileys shots?"

"For you, my friend, anything," Riccardo said. He disappeared into the back.

Brett was quiet for a minute, but I could see him plotting. His eyes didn't conceal much; he was too raw to have cultivated a political poker face yet. When the shots came, Brett proposed a toast. "Here's to recalling that traitor Bryan Gentry." We clanked glasses. "And to my new friend, Jim Asher." We drank the shots. "But listen," he said, "this isn't going to be a walk in the park. Frank Buckman is a ruthless asshole. He'll try everything he can to derail us. If we win, he'll go for the speakership himself, like the whole recall was his idea."

"Leave Buckman to me and Winston," I said.

"What the hell are you gonna do? You may have DC experience and a boss with a lot of money, but you don't know shit about Sacramento, buddy. Frank Buckman has more clout with the caucus than you think."

"We'll deal with that when the time comes. Do we have a deal, Mr. Speaker?"

He laughed. "It's Brett. And, yeah, I think we have a deal."

We sipped our coffees, looking each other over. We were two of a kind and we both knew it. In my mind, I saw everything unfold—the speakership, the governor's office, and then . . . I looked at Brett. I knew this guy was my ticket to the top, the very top. He might be wallowing in a grimy shack of an office now, but I could already see him in ten years, standing on that blue carpet in the Oval Office, right on top of the golden eagle seal, with me right there at his side.

I drove back to the Statesmen Institute and quit my job, just like that. "I'm going to work on the Bryan Gentry recall campaign," I told my boss. "Then I'll work for the new speaker of the assembly, Brett Alexander."

My boss looked at me like I was insane. But what could he say?

I spent the rest of the day on the phone. Edward was pleased that the plan was moving forward. Samantha was ecstatic.

"I told you, Boo-Boo," she said. "Come over to the house tonight and we'll talk about the recall. Are you running it?"

"I'm not sure," I said. "I think so."

"I'll see you at nine."

I called Bud Raper in Washington.

"How do we win this recall?" I asked him.

"Shit, that's easy," he said. "Direct mail. Don't spend money on TV unless you really need to. Hit that motherfucker with the hardest, dirtiest mail pieces you can dream up. Here, let me give you a number for the best mail guy in California, Don Baker. He's a ruthless son of a bitch. By the time Baker's done with Bryan Gentry, the guy'll be lucky if he's not in the fuckin' slammer."

FIFTEEN

To save money, we set up the recall campaign in some empty office space behind the Blackjack Surfboard Shop in Newport Beach. The office had been a hand-me-down from one Republican campaign to another for years. At least it was free, and the beach was right outside our door. I could literally throw a beer can from my window and hit the pier. And I had a splendid view of all the bikinis passing by. Instead of starched shirts and cramped leather shoes, I wore board shorts and tank tops to the recall office, and I surfed every day on my lunch break.

The only other people in the office were Francis M. H. White, Brett's cousin and current chief of staff, and the receptionist, Missy. In his previous life, before politics, Francis had been a successful private detective in Los Angeles. He was young like me but infinitely more serious. He carried around a clipboard with all the things he needed to do that day numbered and categorized; he would check them off as he did them. He was nerdish-looking, with greasy black hair, a premature belly, and slight acne. Francis wasn't very much fun. His idea of a good time was picking up Asian hookers on Harbor Boulevard, right down the street from Disneyland. He claimed his wife didn't mind him messing around, but I never believed it. Of course, Francis and I did have one thing in common: we both wanted Brett to become speaker, and we were willing to do whatever it took.

Edward stopped by the recall office to check on things whenever he was in California which wasn't very often. He was busy stacking chips on Wall Street. Brett hung out at the office on Fridays, when the legislature was out of session. Brett and I were becoming good friends. I had him jogging every night to lose weight, and I even borrowed a longboard from Blackjack's and taught him how to surf. In return, he taught me the intricacies of state politics.

Because I controlled all of Edward's $200,000, I basically ran the recall campaign. I paid myself five thousand a month, on top of the seven Edward was already paying me. I was living what I considered a Zen political life, and I had even moved into my own apartment, a beachfront two-bedroom only ten minutes from the office.

We hired an opposition researcher to dig up dirt on Bryan Gentry, but he didn't come up with much, aside from his being a damned backstabber. Fortunately, Orange County is Reagan country—the most fervent Republican stronghold in the nation. OC voters don't take kindly to Republican turncoats. Launching a recall campaign turned out to be more complicated than what Samantha had described as "some paperwork." First, we had to file a letter of intent with the voter registrar's office, stating why assemblyman Bryan Gentry should be recalled. After I wrote the letter—in which I had actually called him a "lying traitor"—I mailed it to Gentry himself, as the law prescribed. The only major requirement before the election could actually be called was to gather ten thousand signatures from voters in Gentry's district. At first, ten thousand signatures sounded like a huge amount of work. Normally, a massive volunteer organization would have to be constructed from the ground up, including Republicans from a broad base of coalitions, requiring hundreds of administrative man-hours. But Bud Raper showed me how to get around the system. He put me in touch with a "petition gathering" firm in Los Angeles. For a mere seventy five cents per signature, the firm's army of mercenary employees fanned out through the district and gathered all ten thousand signatures in only six days. The recall was on.

One day Brett invited me over to his house for a barbecue in honor of some judge who had just been appointed by the governor. I decided to go alone because Brett told me there would be single girls at the party. I pulled up in my Humvee. It was the first time I'd been to Brett's house, and I was surprised by its modesty. It was a small tract house, almost identical to the one I had grown up in. The lawn was in need of mowing and the paint was cracking slightly. Brett and Francis were playing one-on-one basketball in his driveway.

"What's up, guys," I said.

Brett looked at the Hummer. "You're going to get in trouble with that thing," he said. "You should buy a less conspicuous car, Jim. Voters don't like political aides who drive sixty-thousand-dollar cars. It tends to make them suspicious."

"They should be," I said, grinning.

"Wanna play?" Brett asked.

"Nah, I suck at basketball."

"Well, go get something to eat then. I spent two hundred bucks at the Price Club, and no one's eating."

I pointed at his belly. "Maybe you should take their example."

"Hey, some of us don't spend our days surfing, buddy."

"And let's get rid of that low-budget seventies haircut," I said, pushing my luck. "If you're gonna be speaker of the California assembly, you should at least look the part."

Brett flipped me off as I walked around to the backyard. I was being serious about the hair and weight—Brett could be the top politician in the state, but I had to persuade him to take himself and his image more seriously. The backyard was crowded with middle-aged politicians and their families. They all looked out of place in casual clothes—butt white skin, socks pulled up to their knees, floppy hats. These people belonged in suits.

Brett's wife, Suzy, recognized me from the office.

"Hello, Jim. Welcome to our humble home. Can I get you anything?" Suzy was the ideal political wife. She looked good when she was dressed up, but not *too* good.

"Have you met our son, Brett Jr.?" she asked.

"Not yet."

The little rascal said hello, and I was pleased because he looked like a great decoration for family-values speeches. He asked if I wanted to play catch. We went onto the grass and tossed a football around. Brett Jr. was a great kid, about six years old, I figured; but what the hell did I know about kids? I could have been off by five years. He asked me how I knew his daddy.

"From work," I said. "I work with your daddy."

"Are you a politician?"

"Not yet. I just help out."

"Are you going with us to the White House?" he asked.

The football hit me square in the teeth. *"What was that?"*

"Daddy's going to the White House."

"Oh, yeah," I chuckled. "Yeah, I'll be going with him."

After twenty minutes of tossing the ball around, I decided to grab a burger. Brett Jr. followed me. There were several groups of people talking in their various circles around the backyard but I didn't recognize any of them. Brett Jr. and I pulled our burgers off the grill and sat down cross-legged on the grass. I was feeling happy, enjoying the warm sun on my shoulders and the smell of fresh grass. Brett's dog, Montezuma, tried to snatch the burger off my plate. I managed to trick him momentarily with a fetch stick . . . and that was the first time I saw her. She was in a group of young women gathered around Brett's wife on the back porch, giggling at me wrestling the filthy brute over my burger. She sat in a folding chair, and the wind blew her long platinum blonde hair calmly around her beautiful face. She wore a breezy white summer dress and I could make out the form of her long, lovely, curving body. Brett and Francis walked out of the house and caught me staring. Brett's eyes drifted down to the girl, then back to me. Brett had recently been lecturing me to get a steady girlfriend and to quit "pimping around."

He grinned. "Jimbo, come over here!"

The dog followed me over to the porch.

Brett threw his arm around me. "Everyone, this is Jim Asher, my latest discovery."

"Everyone, this is Brett Alexander, *my* latest discovery," I wisecracked. "You should really get to know him because he's going to be the next speaker of the California assembly."

His wife looked at him proudly. Brett introduced everyone, but I didn't catch any of their names or care anything about them until he got to the beautiful girl sitting beside his wife.

"Jimbo, this is Rachel West. You two should get to know each other. Rachel works for Minority Leader Frank Buckman. I think you two are about the same age."

She smiled at me, fluttering her long eyelashes. "Very nice to meet you, Jim." Her voice was seductive. Her entire manner was entrancing. She literally had me weak in the legs.

"Nice to meet you, Rachel," I said. "Can I get you a drink or something?"

Everyone looked at me and Rachel—and kept right on looking.

"Sure, I could use some punch. But I'll go with you," she said. We walked to the punch bowl inside. She accidentally brushed against me as we passed through the door, and although the touch lasted only for a split second, it made the hair on my arms stand.

"Did you see how they were all staring at us?" she whispered.

"Yeah."

"They're all married, so their only pleasure in life is trying to get everyone else hitched."

"It's a sad business," I said.

I ladled some punch into a Styrofoam cup and handed it to her. I couldn't keep my eyes from drifting all over her. Her cheekbones were high, and her eyes were a transfixing blue-emerald like the finest colors of the ocean when you look down at it from a plane. Her shoulders were smooth and delicate, her stomach flat under the cotton dress. Her long straight hair was parted down the middle, and it framed the picture of finished beauty. Rachel wasn't cute, she wasn't even pretty—she was a downright drop-dead, head-turning stunner, and she was completely aware of it. My senses livened just to be near her.

"So you work for Frank Buckman?" I asked, trying to play cool.

"I'm his field rep in the district office. The only thing that sucks is the one-hour commute from Corona Del Mar to Long Beach."

"That *is* a long drive. How do you like Buckman? I haven't met him yet."

"Oh, Frank, he's great. I mean, he can be tough on people. But if he likes you, he's a big softy."

"That's the first time I've ever heard him described like that."

"I guess he likes me."

"I'll bet. So, Rachel, how did you get into politics?"

"I don't even know. I was never even interested in politics until like a year ago. I was modeling full-time, but then . . . well, it's a long story. Needless to say, I love politics now. I love the fancy dinners and all the important people I get to meet. I love getting out into the community and all that."

"So what do you do as a field rep?"

"I basically go to community meetings and luncheons representing Frank," she said. "It's mostly just people skills."

"That's cool. I think if you're good with people you can do well in any business."

"Totally."

"Personally, I'm completely caught up in politics. It's all I think about anymore. Hey, do you wanna sit on the couch?"

"That's okay, I'll stand," she said. "I've gotta get going soon anyway."

"Oh."

Without blinking she asked: "So, Jim, do you have a girlfriend?"

"I date."

"Oh. That's good. Well, I should really be going."

"So soon?"

"I've gotta go to some golfing fund-raiser in Irvine. I'm going with Ron Latter; we're sort of involved. Do you know him?"

"Never heard of 'im."

"You will. He's working as a consultant to Frank and a lot of other politicians, like Dale Spencer. He's only twenty-eight, and he already has his own consulting firm. Ron's like the hottest rising star in the party right now."

"I don't know about that."

She looked at me like I was full of shit.

I figured it was time to get out of this. "Well, it was nice to meet you."

"See you later, Jim."

She gave me a warm smile over her shoulder as she walked away. But who was I kidding? This girl was not only way out of my league, she was out of my sport altogether. She probably dated rich guys and professional athletes, guys with money and things to offer. What did I have? A small apartment, a workaholic job, and an oversize war jeep. I had a lot of work to do if I wanted a girl like Rachel.

SIXTEEN

The recall campaign was moving along nicely. We commissioned two polls, and they both came back with good news: Bryan Gentry was in deep shit. He didn't have any money to fight back with, so we hammered him with tons of nasty mail. One mailer showed Gentry embracing Democrat Speaker Willie Black. The black-and-white photo had them laughing like two bank robbers after a heist. Under the photo was the word BETRAYED! It was highly effective, to say the least.

Brett recruited a corporate lawyer he knew from college to run against Gentry. The problem was, two other Republicans had also jumped into the race, uninvited. We got the governor to call them, but neither would agree to drop out of the race. The possibility that the three candidates would split the GOP vote and send our Democrat opponent to Sacramento was starting to loom as a real problem.

The recall election was only three weeks away. There were still three hurdles to overcome in the meantime: the GOP state convention in Palm Springs, getting the two extra GOP candidates to drop out, and Frank Buckman. I was going to the convention with Edward, but I now had a dual role because I was growing very close to Brett. Even though I wasn't on his state payroll, I was handling all of his writing and most of his media affairs.

The convention was held at the luxurious Desert Springs Marriott. I drove out alone and checked in under Edward's American Express gold card—I had my own copy. The convention was in its second day, and the local paper, the *Desert Sun,* ran a story called "Behind the Scenes of the GOP Convention: Where the Real Action Is." Of course that grabbed my attention. But as I read through the "behind-the-scenes story," I realized that it was nothing of the sort. The reporter missed the real story altogether: he claimed that all the action was at the discussion panels and fund-raisers. What a joke. Discussion panels, held in bland little convention rooms on subjects like affirmative action and taxes, are strictly the domain of pimple-faced college nerds and policy wonks. Fund-raisers are where old rich people pay way too much money to hear recycled jokes and anecdotes from politicians who couldn't give a damn about anything they say. The real action is unofficial. Deals and plans that affect the future of the nation are made in the shadows, in cigar smoke–filled limousines and hotel suites, and at bars, behind martini glasses.

Edward wasn't arriving until that evening, so I hung out by the pool talking to reporters all day. Samantha and Holly Martinez showed up, plus Julia and Ellen, and Greg and Paul. We sipped delicious piña coladas and I spun like a twister top for five solid hours about what a dirtbag Bryan Gentry was, what a washed-up fat loser Frank Buckman was, what a fine speaker Brett would make, and how Edward was going to blow the barn doors off Dale Spencer in the governor's primary. Samantha always helped by backing me up. She knew I was carrying water for a lot of different people.

Buckman had his people out spinning as well, including the lovely Rachel West. They were already talking about how well the recall was going and what a great speaker Buckman would make—with minority Whip Pringle as speaker pro tem. The nerve of those fuckers! It was happening just like Renee had predicted. I knew I had to work fast.

I found Renee by the pool and kissed her all the way up her back, then used my teeth to unhook her bikini top.

"Hey, stop that!" she giggled playfully. "This is a family hotel."

"I love the smell of your suntan lotion," I said, kissing the nape of her neck.

"It's coconut-banana."

"It's just as yummy as you are, Renee."

She fastened her bikini and rolled over. "You must want something, Jim."

"Why ever would you say that?"

She grinned. "So—?"

"It's that fat fucker, Frank Buckman. He's doing exactly what you said he would."

"What'd you expect? You guys are doing all the heavy lifting for him. Now all he has to do is twist some arms and he'll be speaker. A lot of people owe that guy favors."

"What's the deal on him?"

"He's got dirt, but you can't really use anything against him."

"Why not?"

"Because he's the Republican minority leader. He'll crush you if you fuck with him, Jim."

"What's the dirt?"

"Where do I begin. Well, he has some of the standard stuff, like two drunk driving convictions, but those were a long time ago, and they're a matter of public record. But here's the juiciest one I know: Buckman's sleeping with his fund-raiser, Donna Krassfield."

"How do you know that?"

"Can't say."

"But isn't Buckman married?"

"Completely married. He's got five kids, a dog, the whole deal."

"What a dirtbag."

"They all are, babe."

"What about Rachel West? You know her?"

"Sure, she works for Buckman."

"What do you think of her?"

"I don't know. She's pretty. Why?"

"No reason. I met her the other day. Are you sure about this Buckman thing?"

"Absolutely positive."

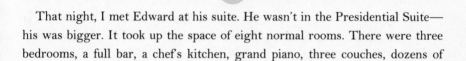

That night, I met Edward at his suite. He wasn't in the Presidential Suite—his was bigger. It took up the space of eight normal rooms. There were three bedrooms, a full bar, a chef's kitchen, grand piano, three couches, dozens of overstuffed chairs, and a classy Japanese butler to boot.

"How are things looking?" Edward asked me. He sat on one of the couches; I was in a chair facing him. The view behind Edward was sublimely pictur-esque—the pool, the golf course, the orange sun setting behind cactus silhouettes in the distant desert.

"Things are good," I said. "But there are a few minor problems."

"Such as?"

"Well, as expected, Frank Buckman is making a push for the speakership. Spencer's out there peddling influence he doesn't even have yet. And we've got two Republican candidates splitting the vote in the recall race—neither will drop out."

"Those don't sound like minor problems to me, Jim."

"Well, put them together and they're not. We'll have to tackle them one at a time."

"Okay, what about Buckman? I know him. He's not going to roll over."

"Well, I think I've got a plan to take care of him. I just need to know that I have your support, Edward."

"As long as it's legal. Is it legal?"

"Yes, it's legal."

"Do I want to know about this?"

I grinned. "Probably not."

"Just make sure it's legal."

Edward had done that before with me, and I had seen him do it with Bud during the Senate race. He didn't want to know about the dirty stuff, which was fine with me.

"What about the recall race?" he asked. "There's no way the GOP can support three candidates. They'll split the vote for sure."

"I know."

We both sat thinking quietly.

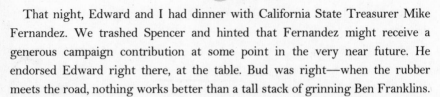

That night, Edward and I had dinner with California State Treasurer Mike Fernandez. We trashed Spencer and hinted that Fernandez might receive a generous campaign contribution at some point in the very near future. He endorsed Edward right there, at the table. Bud was right—when the rubber meets the road, nothing works better than a tall stack of grinning Ben Franklins.

Mariella was arriving in the morning, so Edward went to bed early. He always got nervous before seeing his wife, like they were still teenagers on a first date.

After dinner, I walked to Brett's suite. He answered the door with a worried look.

"Where have you been?" he asked.

"With Edward. We had a dinner with Fernandez."

Francis was hunched over in a chair, looking defeated.

"What's going on?" I asked.

"Buckman and his fucking hack Ron Latter just came by," Brett said.

Francis didn't even raise his head.

"What'd they say?"

"Buckman's making a power play," Brett said. "He offered me the speakership pro tem if I support him. He claims he's already got the votes locked up for the speakership."

"Screw that, Brett. We've worked too hard to let that fat bastard swoop in and snake us now. This speakership is ours."

"It's not that easy, Jim. If he has the votes, he has the votes. He has more clout with the members than I do. If I oppose Buckman and he wins, I'm totally fucked. He'll strip my budget, pull me off committees, and stick me in some closet-size office in the bowels of the capitol. I can't afford to have that happen, Jim. I'd be ruined."

"You'll be ruined if you let that asshole slap you around. Those members don't respect cowardice, they respect strength. They want a leader with brains, and the balls to use them. Make a stand, Brett. If you lose this time, at least they'll know you're a scrapper. You'll still have your dignity. Look, I've been reading a lot of books on evolutionary psychology lately, and I've got some theories . . ."

Brett gave Francis a look like I was losing my mind.

"Hear me out, guys. If you look at behavior in the wild, it's the same as in society; once you strip away all the contrivances, we're actually worse than most beasts—more predictable. It's all about dominance and submission. Everyone is looking to see who the Alpha Male is. If you submit to Buckman, you're admitting he's superior, that he's the Alpha. It's all about appearances and posturing. Buckman is vulnerable right now. It's time to kick him down the dominance chain."

"Did you hear that, Francis?" Brett said, laughing. "We've got Charles Darwin running our recall campaign!"

I ignored the dig. "Edward and I have been talking about this. Let's see if he can do something."

Brett looked up at me. For a moment I thought he might be gaining heart, but his eyes were vacant. I left to find the hotel's bar. The inside of the Marriott was as breathtaking as the pools and landscape outside. A river ran directly through the lobby. A boat took passengers through glass doors on a tour of the entire property. Long ferns draped the balconies inside, and the entire lobby was resplendent with marble and brass.

I found Renee at the bar. Rachel West was sitting with her.

"Hi, Renee, hey Rachel," I said.

They both smiled.

"Rachel, where's your boss?"

She looked around. "He's right over there, behind the piano." She pointed. "But he's with the mayor of Bakersfield. I wouldn't bother him, Jim."

I walked straight over to Buckman. I had seen him before but never talked to him. Besides trying to fuck us on the speakership, Buckman had already endorsed Spencer in the governor's race. So any way I sliced it, he was the enemy. I found him sitting on a couch smoking a cigar and talking to the frail old mayor. Buckman was as fat and sloppy as ever. He had more chins than a Vietnamese Rolodex, and they swung like slabs of pork from his jaw when he spoke.

I interrupted their conversation. Buckman's eyes slowly drifted up to mine. They were fiery eyes, like a bull has in the presence of a matador.

"Jim Asher, right," he said. "I'm busy. Talk to Ron Latter if you need something." He turned back to the mayor like I wasn't there.

"No. We need to talk right now, Mr. Minority Leader," I said. My heart was beating so fast my neck was pulsating.

Buckman stood up and towered over me. He was a giant. "Let's walk over here," he said.

We walked ten feet away, closer to the bar. Rachel gave me a concerned look, but I acted like I didn't see her.

"What the fuck do you want, kid," Buckman said in a gruff voice. He held his wooden cane in his hands, smacking it on his open palm like a weapon.

I used every trick I knew to keep my voice steady and solid. "We want you to back off on the speakership. You already lost once. Brett Alexander is responsible for the recall; he'll take the speakership, as he deserves to."

"I don't have time for you, punk. Why don't you slither back to that pussy-ass boss of yours and rub dickheads together or whatever the fuck you little faggots do in your free time."

"Listen here, you fat fuck—"

"No, you listen here. I'll fucking annihilate you, Jim Asher. You're way out of your league, pal. I'll give you one chance to apologize and then—"

"Fuck you," I said. Adrenaline flooded my body like I was about to get in a fistfight. Maybe I was. "Listen here, you fat Jabba-the-Hut motherfucker. If you don't back off on the speakership, Edward Winston is gonna fuck you up the ass so hard you'll feel it poking your fuckin' eyeballs out!" I was shouting now, and everyone at the bar watched with gaping mouths. "If you try to fuck us on the speakership, Edward's gonna run a Republican against you in your own district. We'll dump five million fuckin' dollars into his campaign just to see you eat the fuckin' shit you've been dealing out for ten years, you lard-ass!"

"You slimy little prick," he said in a lower voice. His eyes were darting around. This was clearly not a conversation he wanted to have in public. "If these people weren't around, I'd drop-kick your pretty-boy little ass and stomp your fucking head in."

"Bring it on, fat boy!" I was acting tough, but the guy outweighed me by a good 150 pounds.

"I don't have time for this," he said, adjusting his belt. "But I'll tell you one thing, pal. You better watch your fucking back. You just fucked with the bull. Get ready for the horns. You'll never work in politics again, you little fucker." He walked away and sat back down.

"That's original!" I shouted.

I went back to the bar, trying to act cool. But my hands were trembling and I knew I looked shaken. What had I just done? I had probably nailed my own career's coffin shut. Rachel's eyes never moved from mine until I sat down next to her on the couch.

"What the hell was that, Jim? Are you crazy?" Renee said. "That guy could make two phone calls and we'd never hear from you again."

"Fuck him," I said. "I'll make a few calls to my Gulf War buddies and we'll see about that."

Rachel was looking at me differently—almost as if she had never seen me before. I was surprised she didn't get up and leave. I had just verbally assaulted her boss, who was still sitting only twenty feet away.

"What was that all about?" Rachel asked.

"It's a long story," I said. "I'll tell you all about it sometime, or I'm sure he will. Do you guys wanna hit some hospitality suites? I need a brew."

"Sure," Renee said. "Let's grab Chuck. He's over at the bar."

The three of us found Chuck and took the elevator to the fourteenth floor, where rumor had it the hospitality suites were jumping. Chuck had moved from Phoenix and was now doing corporate PR work in San Francisco, but he always kept up his political connections. Chuck never did find out that I fucked him during the Winston campaign. It was still hard for me to look him in the eye. We drifted down the hallways. Renee was hanging on my arm, but I was wishing she were Rachel.

Hospitality suites were the key to conventions. Mostly they were hosted by lobbyists or candidates hoping to solicit favor with the party. The drinks and food were always free and I never failed to take advantage. We found a suite hosted by the tobacco industry. They always had the best booze and cigars. I made a direct line for the bar and grabbed three bottles of Samuel Adams, all for myself. I said hello to everyone as I passed through the crowd. I walked onto the large balcony outside and sat down. I needed to think. Rachel was a distraction. I knew I couldn't have her, so why torment myself? The adrenaline from the Buckman encounter was just now working its way out of my bloodstream.

Then I heard Samantha's voice inside. She was looking for me. I really didn't want to see her right now. All I could think about was the Buckman fight. I had been bluffing with the five-million-dollar candidate thing, and he probably knew it. It wasn't much of a threat. But I was new at hard-ball shit.

Samantha and Rick walked onto the balcony.

"Jimmy," she said. "I heard about you and Buckman. Everybody's talking about it. What happened?"

"I threatened him."

Samantha smiled proudly. "And?"

"He said he was gonna ruin me."

"Fuck him. Don't let him scare you, baby. Having enemies is part of the game. This is just another step for you."

"I'm fucked if we don't win the speakership, Samantha. That guy isn't gonna forget."

"Fuck him," Rick said. "You can always come work for me, Jimbo. Don't forget that."

"Thanks, Rick." His offer was starting to sound attractive now.

"I've got some news," Samantha said. "And it's not very good."

"I don't think I can take it right now. Everything is starting to come unraveled. The wheels are coming off."

"Bullshit. Don't think like that. You've gotta remember, you're smarter than these assholes. You can run circles around these guys, Jimmy."

"I guess. So what's the news?"

"Well, I just heard through some reporter friends that the DNC is gonna dump a bunch of money into Bill Cambell's campaign to keep you guys from taking over the assembly."

Bill Cambell was our Democrat opponent in the recall race—our only real threat.

"Just what I needed." I threw up my hands. "So let's talk about that job at your law firm, Rick."

"It's not that big a deal," Samantha tried to assure me. "I've been thinking. All you need to do is run a Democrat opponent of your own to split their vote, too. Orange County can't support two Democrat candidates."

I thought about it. "You're absolutely right. But can we do that?"

"Sure. It's done all the time. But it has to be hush-hush."

"I'll talk to Brett about it."

"Good. Now just remember to keep your head up, Boo-Boo. You'll do it. You and I will show 'em all."

"Thanks. How much money is the DNC gonna give Cambell?"

"I don't know. You're lucky I even found out about it. It's supposed to be a surprise ambush tactic."

"Well, it's not going to be," I said. My mind started working again—scheming.

"We brought the limo out here," Rick said. "Gather up some of your friends. We're gonna hit the strip in style tonight."

"Sounds killer. I need to get loose."

The next morning Brett was banging down my door. The hotel room was hot and stuffy, filled with harsh morning light coming in through vertical blinds. Each loud knock felt like a boot stomp to my temple. I stumbled out of bed, pulled on my boxers, and told whoever the girl was next to me to hide under the covers. I cupped my hand in front of my mouth—my breath was rancid.

"Hold on!" I yelled at the door. I brushed my teeth fast, swabbing my tongue, and answered the door. Brett was dressed in his bathrobe, and his hair was messy. He looked upset.

"What did you say to Buckman last night?" he demanded.

I stepped into the hallway half naked. A maid two doors down turned her head and scurried into the room.

"I told him not to fuck with you," I said. "I told him Winston was gonna smoke his ass if he ran for speaker."

"Isn't that nice," Brett said sarcastically. "He called me this morning and told me to fire you or he was gonna drop everything in his arsenal on me."

"Fuck him. That just means he's afraid. Are you in this thing to win or not, Brett? If not, let me know right now. I just put my ass on the line for you."

"Look, I just don't need any heat from Buckman right now. You don't know how much leverage he has."

"He won't have any leverage when you become speaker and straighten his ass out."

Brett let out a frustrated sigh. If anyone from the party happened to walk by at that moment, they would have been in for quite a spectacle, I thought to myself. The former prosecutor turned assemblyman and his hungover aide plotting the future of the state in their underwear in some random hotel hallway at 6 A.M.

"I've got some other news," I said. "A reporter friend of mine found out that the DNC is going to pour money into Cambell's campaign. I guess they figure the California assembly could be the finger in the dike for next year's national elections."

Brett's expression dropped. "Shit."

"I know. Hey, Brett. Why don't we run a Democrat candidate of our own, to split their vote?"

He stood looking at me for minute. Something flashed behind his eyes. He started counting backward on his fingers. "Shit . . . Dammit . . . I think we may have missed the deadline to register a new candidate. Get Francis on the horn, pronto."

We went into the room. Brett immediately noticed the lump moving under my sheets.

"You can come out," he said, grinning at me and raising his eyebrows.

The girl poked her face out. Fortunately for me, she was very attractive. She held the sheets across her chest and reached for her bra lying on the carpet. But her large, perfect breasts fell out into the open when she leaned over. I caught Brett looking.

A minute later, Brett tracked down Francis on his cell phone.

"Hey, Francis. Did we miss the deadline to register a candidate in the recall race?" he asked, "Right . . . Exactly . . . That's right, a Democrat . . . Great, meet me down in the lobby right now." He hung up and turned to me. "The deadline is Monday. We still have time."

"Thank God," I said. "You know any Democrats who might run?"

He grinned. "Not off the top of my head."

SEVENTEEN

The following Monday was insane. Brett had finally found Mitch Fine, a friend of his wife's brother, who was a registered Democrat. Mitch reluctantly agreed to run against our Democrat opponent, Bill Cambell—to take votes away from him. The connection was just loose enough not to be traceable. But we didn't talk him into it until 1:30 P.M. We spent the remainder of the day frantically trying to gather the fifty Democrat signatures required to register Mitch on the ballot. After we got the petition forms, Brett told us to go into the mall, but we were only able to get twenty signatures there. People were reluctant to sign for some reason, and nearly everyone we asked was Republican. The voter registrar's office closed at 5:00 P.M., so we were running around frantic trying to make the deadline.

Francis drove his Dodge Stealth turbo at high speed. We hit every liquor store and fast-food joint along the route to Mitch's house—"Where better to find Democrats?" Francis joked. We pulled into a Target shopping center at 4:25 P.M. We still needed fifteen signatures. I ran up to an old lady pushing a shopping cart.

"Will you please sign this?" I asked. "It's a petition to put Mitch Fine on the ballot. Are you a Democrat?"

"Yes I am," she said.

Hallelujah! "Okay, great. Will you sign here on the dotted line."

"I'm voting for Bill Cambell," she said.

"Listen here—"

She lifted her nose and walked away.

"Stubborn old . . ."

Francis ran up completely out of breath. "I found a senior citizens' group at McDonald's. We have all the signatures!"

We sprinted to the Stealth. Francis hit the throttle like Luke Duke and we peeled rubber all the way to the street. He checked his watch. "I don't think we're gonna make it, Jim."

"We'll make it."

The speedometer pegged 130 miles per hour as we blasted down the freeway, swerving around cars like they were traffic cones. Brett seemed to call at least every two minutes. "Are you guys gonna make it?" he would ask.

"We're trying," I would say.

Mitch was standing on his front lawn when we pulled up; I had phoned ahead. I swung the door open and leaned the seat forward. Mitch jumped into the back.

"Where do I sign?" he asked. He seemed excited to be a part of some big, sneaky political maneuver.

I passed him the clipboard and a pen. "Sign at the bottom of both."

"Is this legal?" he asked.

I looked at Francis. He winked back at me. "If anyone asks, just tell them you gathered the signatures yourself," Francis told Mitch. "We do it all the time."

Mitch signed the sheets and we streaked away from the curb, leaving two long rubber marks and a cloud of smoke.

"They close in four minutes," Francis said.

I looked at my watch. The damn thing was blazing off the seconds. Our worst fear was to get pulled over by the police, or to get in an accident. Then we'd miss the deadline for sure. Still, Francis pushed it as fast as he could. We blew through stop signs like they weren't even there, screeching around corners so fast we almost flipped. Then I spotted the registrar's office ahead.

"One minute to go," I said.

"My watch says thirty seconds," Francis said.

"Do you set yours fast?"

"Fuck . . . I used to, but not anymore."

"Me either—damn it!"

Francis hit the driveway ramp at fifty, smacking his front spoiler on the concrete. The Stealth lifted into the air and we landed sideways with a jerk. He floored it through the parking lot, then hit the brakes and slid up to the curb like a stunt driver.

"Run," he said. "Run! Hold the doors open!"

I leaped out and ran for the office. I jumped down an entire flight of stairs, knocking over two bicycles at the bottom. Now I could see the doors. I sprinted as fast as I could. My dress shoes were slapping the concrete and my suit jacket flew behind me like a cape.

"I gotta quit smoking!" I gasped.

Then I saw an old lady locking the doors of the registrar's office.

"Hold up!" I shouted, waving my arms. "Hold up, lady!"

I actually slammed against the glass door just as she clicked the lock shut.

"Let me in," I said. "I've got a candidate registration form on its way. He'll be here any second—"

"Too late," she said.

I looked at my watch. Shit. I was screwed. Then I thought of something. I snatched the pager off my belt and read the face: 4:59.12 P.M. I held the pager up to the glass.

"We've still got fifty seconds," I said, showing her.

She shook her head.

"Look, it's not even five yet!"

She opened the door. "I'm sorry, young man." She pointed to her antique watch. "I've got five oh one. You're too late."

"That thing is wrong," I said. "This pager is synchronized through satellites with an atomic clock in New York."

"I don't care about atomic clocks," she said. She started to pull the door shut, but I stuck my hand into the jamb.

"I'll call the attorney general," I threatened. "This is completely illegal."

That seemed to wake her up.

Francis and Mitch ran up exhausted. "What's going on?" Francis gasped.

"Everything's fine," I said, looking at the lady.

Mitch handed her the petitions through the door. The lady looked the forms over suspiciously, then looked Francis and me over. "As long as the signatures are valid," she said. "Okay, I'll take these in." Then she looked directly at Francis. "Don't I know you from somewhere, young man?"

"No," Francis said, turning away. He grabbed Mitch's arm. "Let's get outa' here."

When we hit the parking lot, Francis and I both shouted and slapped high fives.

"We did it!" Francis hollered. "Now all we have to worry about is Frank Buckman."

EIGHTEEN

One week until the recall election and we still had three Republican candidates splitting the vote. The Democrat Bill Cambell was running television spots with his DNC money—lots of them. Things weren't looking so good. The district was 65 percent Republican, but if Cambell got every single Democrat vote we could not beat him.

Edward called and told me: "You better not mess this up, Jim. I don't want to spend two hundred thousand dollars to elect a Democrat to the assembly. I'd be the laughingstock."

I assured Edward that everything was under control, but I knew it wasn't. Brett showed up early that Friday. Francis and I were busy dreaming up ways to get the other Republicans to drop out. Pipe bombs were my quasi-facetious suggestion.

Brett walked in carrying a poll binder. "I just got this from Barnie," he said. Barnie was our pollster—the best in California.

"How does it look?" Francis asked.

"Not good. Cambell's three points up." Brett opened the binder. "We're easily beating the other GOP candidates, but Mitch isn't even showing up on the Democrat side; he's not even a blip on the radar screen."

"He doesn't have any name ID," Francis said. "We should've known that was going to be a problem."

"Hey, what if we ran ads for Mitch Fine?" Brett suggested. "Negative ones against Cambell, with a Mitch Fine tag line to boost his name ID."

Francis and I looked at each other.

"That's a great idea," I said. "That way we pump Mitch up and knock Cambell down at the same time. But is it legal?"

"Yeah, it's legal," Francis said. "But it's not ethical. If we spend money from our campaign on a Democrat candidate, it's going to be a huge scandal, all over the newspapers."

"You're right," Brett said. "And we can't get money from Edward. They'd easily trace it back to him."

"Could we launder it?" I asked. "Through a third party?"

"That's illegal for sure," Brett said.

We all thought the dilemma over.

"I think I know where I can get two or three hundred thousand," Brett said. "I've been saving it for a pinch . . . and I guess this would qualify as one."

"From where?" I asked.

"I'll tell you all about it," he said. "Let me make a few calls first."

While Brett called around I grabbed a cell phone and walked down to the beach. I sat under the cool shade of the pier and called Samantha.

"What's going on, Boo-Boo?" she asked.

"Did you ever find out how much the DNC was giving Cambell?"

"Oh, yeah. I did—two hundred thousand."

"Shit. That's a lot of money," I said.

"It is. Any new polls?"

"Just got a new one. We're down three. We've tried everything to get these two candidates to drop out. They're sucking up all our votes."

"You can still win with them in the race—it'll just be harder. What about that Democrat you guys registered?"

"Nothing. He didn't even show up on this new poll. But I think we're gonna dump some dough into his campaign pretty soon."

"Perfect," Samantha said. "Be careful though, Jimmy. Taking over the assembly is a big deal. They'll be a lot of people watching you, believe me."

"I know."

"Our friend is throwing a yacht party on Friday. You've gotta come."

"Whose yacht?"

"A buddy of Rick's."

"Samantha, I swear, we're in the wrong damn business. We need to pack our stuff and move to Wall Street. You and me. We'd run the place."

"We probably would, babe. But right now, focus on this race. You'll have those Wall Street dogs eating out of your hand if you guys take the assembly. Believe me. There's more power in that capitol building than you think."

I walked back to the recall office. Brett told me to go home and put on a suit; we were driving to San Diego.

"For what?" I asked.

"You're about to get a lesson in fund-raising," he said.

Two hours later we pulled up to the Del Prado horse racetrack in San Diego.

"I wanted you to meet this guy," Brett told me as we parked the car.

"Who?"

"His name is Mike Burke. He manages this racetrack, but he's also involved with the lobbying PAC for the entire horse-racing industry. He's a great guy, one of us."

"One of us" was a euphemism for: he's a conservative Republican with a libertarian bent as unscrupulous as we are. It often meant he partied too.

"This guy is kind of a cloak-and-dagger type, but you'll be okay because you're with me. Remember, all this is off the record, Jimbo."

"You don't know me very well, Brett. Everything I do is always off the record with me."

We walked under the hot sun to the racetrack. A security guard escorted us to the office complex attached to the towering stands. Mike Burke met us in the lobby. His hair and clothes were sporty, like a yacht racer or a polo player. His office walls were covered with racing memorabilia—plaques, photos, saddles, victory cups. Brett and I took chairs. Mike actually locked his door before he sat down behind his desk.

"Good to see you, Brett," he said.

"Likewise. Hey, this is my new guy, Jim Asher."

Mike looked me over. I could tell he was an oozing snake under his clean-cut facade—one of those guys you knew had broken all the dirty banging records at his fraternity. "Great. Then let's get down to brass tacks. You want three hundred Gs, right?"

"Right. But not for my campaign," Brett said. "I need you to put it into a Democrat's account."

Mike grinned. "That's an odd request."

"I told you about our dilemma. We need to split the Democrat vote. Everything else is in place."

"Buckman?" Mike asked.

"Taken care of," Brett lied.

I couldn't believe Brett was discussing this stuff with some racetrack hoodlum, especially our strategy against Buckman. These were sensitive issues; or at least I thought they were.

"Well, I don't have a problem with the three hundred thousand," Mike said. "You just get me an account number and I'll transfer it right away."

"Great," Brett said.

"Now, let's talk about that slot bill I've been telling you about," Mike said. Brett squirmed in his chair. "Sure."

Mike's voice seemed to shift. "As you know, we've been trying to get a bill through the assembly for years that would open up racetracks for slot machines. It would be a tremendous boon not only for our industry, but also for the cities and municipalities surrounding the tracks, not to mention the state tax rolls."

Brett nodded.

"Willie Black has been blocking the bill for years," Mike continued. "But with him out of the picture and you as speaker, Brett, I'm sure we could count on you to see the bill through committee and get it passed on the floor. After all, gambling is gambling, right?"

"Sure," Brett said. His voice rang with traces of defeat. I knew exactly what was going on here. This Mike character didn't even attempt to sugarcoat what he was doing.

I looked at Brett, but he didn't look back. After a short pause, he said: "Okay, I'll carry the bill for you."

Mike was pleased. He walked us downstairs. Along the way he pulled Brett aside. I don't know what they talked about, but I'm sure it wasn't good. Brett and I walked through the parking lot without speaking. I felt awful. I couldn't believe what I had just seen. It was so damn obvious. They weren't even skirting around the edges. They were trading money for legislation, plain and simple. It was disgusting to see Brett prostitute himself like that.

He pulled onto the freeway. "Well, we got the money," he said.

I didn't answer.

"Look, Jim. Not everyone is rich like Edward Winston. The rest of us have to compromise sometimes. You've never seen this side of politics; you're accustomed to having all the money you need just a gold card's swipe away. In the real world of politics, things aren't always that easy. You have to learn these things if you're going to get ahead. This speakership is just the beginning. You can't always count on Edward Winston's money."

"Brett, I know what I saw back there. You just sold a bill for money, straight up. That's not only unethical, it's fucking illegal, man. You could get yourself in a lot of trouble over something like that."

"No one's getting in trouble, Jim. Look, there's no connection between the money and the legislation. We just happen to have simultaneous overlapping interests."

"'Simultaneous overlapping interests'? Who do you think you're talking to here? That kinda shit is below you. I'd rather see you holding a tin cup begging at the mall than pulling shit like that."

"Hey, maybe you don't have what it takes after all," Brett said. "Maybe I misjudged you."

"Hey, fuck you, Brett. That shit won't work on me."

He told me to fuck off. For the next hour we didn't talk. I was mad, but mostly disappointed. I thought I liked the dirty stuff, but I didn't like what Brett had just done. If he had come to me and said he wanted to sponsor a bill introducing slot machines at racetracks, I would have thought he was whacked in the head. What kind of bill was that? It wasn't that I necessarily opposed the idea. Shit, I liked gambling. I just didn't like the way Brett had been pimped into supporting it. Legislation—writing laws—was still virgin territory in my mind. Legislation was the backbone of democracy, and controlling the legislative process was the bottom-line reason we were doing everything we could to get elected, not the other way around.

All along I had been telling myself there were limits to what I was willing to do in politics. I didn't know exactly what they were, but there had to be lines I wouldn't cross, no matter what the reward. Sleeping with reporters and bending ethical rules to win the speakership was one thing. Even planting a Democrat was justifiable in my mind. Mitch was indeed a registered Democrat, and we weren't forcing people to vote for him. But selling legislation, betraying the fundamental American ideal, was different. I didn't understand completely what I was feeling. If I had tried to figure it out on paper, I probably would have concluded that I was a hypocrite. But my mind seemed to be automatically drawing boundaries for myself, and I was actually glad to have the feelings. Reason is not nearly as powerful as instinct, and never as true.

When we got back to the office I needed to clear my head. I decided to get working on the campaign. I had to come to terms with my own feelings before I could judge my friend. I concluded that Brett had the same ideas of right and wrong as I did, only that he was painting over them for a supposedly higher ideal. I knew he was a good man inside.

The dirty money was already in Mitch's account when I logged on with my laptop. A few minutes later, I was on the phone with Larry Hakney, the advertising wizard from the Winston campaign. I described our situation.

"How soon can you have something up?" I asked him.

"How much money are we talking here?"

"I can transfer two hundred and fifty thousand into your account right now. But we also want some full-page ads in the *Orange County Register* and *LA Times.*"

"No problem. E-mail me the correct names of the players and some script suggestions. I just got a new fiber-optic system here at the office; I can have your television spots up by tomorrow morning. The newspapers'll take a day or two."

"Great. I want the full-pagers to run for the three days just prior to the election."

"No problem. My secretary will call and tell you when they're going up."

At nine o'clock the next morning, we watched Mitch Fine's first attack ad air on Channel 13. It was a ruthless smear against Bill Cambell, labeling him "The

Democrat Who Loves Welfare." It made me laugh my ass off. But Hakney must have warmed up his video equipment in hell for the next ad. Cambell—a former judge—opposed the death penalty. The ad's tag line was absolutely without shame: "Bill Cambell lets killers live, after victims die." I howled for five minutes!

Mitch complained that the commercial was "a little too rough." But Brett assured him that at this level of politics, it was normal. For the next five days, Bill Cambell was the scourge of Orange County television. I couldn't turn on a TV without seeing one of Hakney's groin-kicking assaults. Hakney was a modern-day mercenary—an image assassin for hire. We heard rumors that Cambell left town with his family at some point during our negative barrage. I would have.

NINETEEN

I couldn't sleep the night before the recall election—like Christmas Eve when I was a kid. I took three melatonin tablets, but to no avail. All I could think of was winning the speakership. I visualized Brett being sworn in, with me at his side. I pictured us walking through the capitol building triumphantly, everyone bowing down to our brilliance. We would take over Sacramento. Even the governor would pay homage to the new boys in town: Brett, Jim, and Francis. I pictured all the pageantry that awaited us. It was a pleasing, sleepless night.

For election day, Edward rented us the Presidential Suite at the Newport Hilton. We invited everyone in Republican politics. But no invitations were necessary. The word was out on the streets. Revolution was in the air. A new poll came in that morning—it would be close, but we had a slight edge. Mitch Fine's commercials had taken the wind out of Cambell's sails. The governor, suddenly excited about the prospects of dealing with a friendly assembly, gave his entire staff the day off to help us get the vote out. Every GOPer in the state flew into town. We spent the day roaming the district neighborhoods urging Republicans to vote.

At five o'clock, I drove with Brett and Francis to the Hilton. Our suite was already flooded with people. The governor was in the bedroom on the phone. Edward and Mariella were holding court in the living room. I looked around, picking out faces. Mayor Tarken. John Griggs. Renee.

Brett and I went straight to the computer terminal in the dining room. Through the phone lines we were wired directly to the voter registrar's office. We could monitor the election results minute by minute, vote by vote. I was surprised to see Bud Raper sitting in the crowd of consultants around the computer.

"Bud, what are you doing here?" I asked.

"Hey, kid. Hell, I wasn't gonna miss this. I started my political career here in the California assembly. I used to chase skirts with Willie Black when we were both just a couple of no-good punks dreaming about politics. In fact, I worked for the last Republican speaker. Damn, that was twenty-five fuckin' years ago!"

"How're we looking?" Brett asked.

Bud puffed on his cigar and said through the smoke: "We're barely ahead, but they haven't counted the richer neighborhoods or the absentee ballots. Don't call your bookie yet, but get your money handy."

Brett smiled and sat down beside Bud. I wasn't sure if they had ever met. Brett was fresh on the scene, at least nationally. But if we pulled off this coup, everyone in the country would know his name. We would make CNN News for sure, I figured.

Samantha and Rick showed up at six o'clock, with a camera crew in tow. I felt a little strange watching Samantha file her on-air reports from the suite. After all, the whole recall campaign had basically been her idea. Somehow she managed to appear completely impartial on camera—amazing. Buckman showed up with his entourage a few minutes after Samantha. Rachel West was with him, looking breathtaking in a white silk dress. One of the thin straps kept slipping off her shoulder, supposedly by accident, which really got me going. I soon found myself standing directly in Buckman's path.

"Hi, Rachel," I said, ignoring Buckman. I hugged her and ran my hand down her bare back, where Buckman could see it.

Buckman gave me a dirty look. "Let's go, Rachel," he said. "I want you to meet the governor . . . you'll be working with his staff a lot more now." He looked down at me. "Thanks for all your work, kid. Come visit us in the speaker's office sometime. Just make sure you call first."

"Yeah, whatever." I wanted to kick him in his fat nuts.

Rachel pretended the whole conversation was missing her. She handed me a letter as they walked away. "Here, Jim, this is from Dale Spencer's office."

The letter said Spencer couldn't make it but that he wished us luck—pure bullshit.

Winter showed up around seven. She flew in with her new boss, billionaire Fred Torman, on his private Gulfstream jet. They were on their way to Tokyo, where Torman would address their parliament on trade issues. Winter was becoming a big-time corporate speechwriter in New York, making tons of money and dating millionaires. Even though I was doing well enough in California politics, I felt like I could never keep up with her. My dream woman, it seemed, would always stay just that. I spent the next hour with Mariella, Edward, Winter, and Torman. We sat at the dining table sipping port. It was nice to catch up in such a monumental setting.

Besides writing speeches for Torman, Winter was lining herself up for the next presidential race. Stan Williams was the obvious front-runner for the GOP nomination, and Winter happened to be very close to him from her days at the Bush White House. If Williams ran for president, Winter would be his chief speechwriter, and she'd certainly go to the White House if he won. I shared that dream—the White House—so I loved to hear her talk about it.

At eight, Edward and Mariella had to leave. I was wishing I could take Winter outside for a walk, to get her alone, but the situation never quite seemed to present itself. Fortunately, Torman turned out to be a great guy. He was the first person I'd ever met who was richer than Edward. He dressed in khakis and a casual shirt, cussed, drank, smoked, and joked. He loved talking politics. And he seemed fond of Winter, almost like a father. At least she was in good hands.

"Jim, when are you going to come out and visit us in Washington or New York?" Winter asked.

"I wish I could. I've just been so busy with everything out here."

Torman opened a new bottle of port and topped off all three glasses. I watched out of the corner of my eye—a billionaire filling my glass!

"So, Jim, Winter tells me you wrote for the *McHoffman Group?*" Torman asked.

"Just for a few months," I said.

"I love that damn show. It must have been a blast working with that McHoffman character."

"Yeah, you could say that."

"I'd like to meet the guy," he said. "I love the way he shouts at his panelists: 'Wrong!' What a showman!"

"Jim, you'll have to tell Freddie some of your *McHoffman Group* stories sometime," Winter prompted.

"Sure." But I didn't want Torman to think I bad-mouthed former employers.

"Well, Jim," Torman said. "Winter speaks very highly of you—she says you're the Luke Skywalker of Republican politics. If you'd ever like to come join us on the East Side, just let me know. Our jets are constantly running back and forth between coasts, and we can put you up at one of my places in the city."

"Wow, thanks, Mr. Torman. I'd love that."

"It's Freddie to my friends."

By ten o'clock the absentee ballots started rolling in. Winter and Freddie left for the airport, but not before she gave me a peck on the lips in the hallway. Winter always kept me in wonder. Back in the suite, I moved over with Brett, Samantha, Rick, and Francis on the sofas. Samantha and Brett got along well, which was a relief; Brett didn't know all that Samantha had done for him. I loved being the invisible bridge. Buckman was kissing the governor's ass in the bedroom. Bud Raper came over and sat with us. He set a new bottle of Glenfiddich whiskey on the coffee table.

"This was Winston Churchill's favorite," Bud told us. "He drank a tall glass every morning, one at lunch, and two before he wrote every night. This is for you, Alexander. If you can take the speakership, you'll be needing it, pal."

Brett thanked him. My bottle of Alizé was making its way around our circle and I was feeling it. Rachel and Renee sat down with us, and we all listened to Bud's stories for the next magical hour. He spoke passionately about the glory days. "Back then, we didn't have fax machines. We wrote a press release, then we had to peddle our fuckin' bicycles around to the news bureaus. These young punks like Jim have it easy. You're all soft in the bellies these days."

I informed Bud that if he wished to compare abs, I was game. That comment earned me his middle finger. I knew it was damn impressive to be trading jibes with Bud Raper in front of the girls. Rachel was sitting right next to me, actually brushing against my leg. I loved being so close to her. Rachel was more of an immediate desire than Winter. Aesthetically she was younger and more beautiful—more realistic for me. Rachel and I were a perfect match on paper; I wanted to find out how we'd be on sheets.

Samantha's cell phone rang at 11:25 P.M. She hung up and shouted: "Turn on *Headline News*, somebody! They're running a story on the recall!"

We hadn't seen any cameras from *Headline*, but I knew they were doing a story because they had called earlier for comments. Renee turned on the television. Buckman and the governor came out from the bedroom. Everyone gathered around the screen. The anchorwoman came on. A familiar map of California popped up behind her.

"Hello, this is Lynn Vaughn, *Headline News*," she said. "CNN is now officially predicting that a Republican recall campaign in California has succeeded in ousting a so-called GOP turncoat, Bryan Gentry . . ."

The room exploded. Brett shouted triumphantly, spilling his drink everywhere. I nearly collapsed. Renee hugged me, actually holding me up. Samantha was ready to burst out of her skin. She ran out of the room with Rick—a second later I heard a joyous shriek in the hallway. Brett, Francis, and I hugged in a circle. The room was bouncing.

". . . For the first time in twenty-five years, the California assembly will apparently fall under Republican control," the anchorwoman continued. We didn't get much national coverage, so we all listened. "Early reports indicate that a speakership vote will take place as early as next Monday. GOP Assembly Minority Leader Frank Buckman is expected to become California's first Republican speaker in twenty-five years . . ."

A photo of Buckman appeared on the screen. My heart dropped. The room became suspiciously quiet. Brett turned to me, shocked. I looked at the TV again. That fat bastard must have set it up with CNN ahead of time; he was trying to snake us in the media reports. I don't know exactly what happened at that moment. Something fell off of me, and with it fell ten thousand years of civility. Something lurking in the shadows of my DNA emerged—something thousands of laws and billions of nurturing women have not yet driven from my gender. I lunged across the room, blowing past Brett and Francis. Buckman swung his cane at me like a baseball bat just as my fist crashed into his jaw. I hit him hard and his big head snapped back, and I hit him again in the temple. Time seemed to slow my motions, but the pace quickened when Buckman grabbed my jacket and slammed me to the carpet, right at the governor's feet. He fell on top of me with the weight of a couch—I was pinned. My fists were flying but not really landing. Then I felt a hard thud on top of my head. I was in a headlock. I could see everyone panicking around us. The governor reached down and pulled on Buckman's coat, but he was too big to move. I pulled his head close so he couldn't get leverage or space to hit me. I started kneeing his fat-layered ribs and punching his temple with my free hand, but this was turning into an embarrassment.

That's when I saw Renee run up. She kicked Buckman square in the teeth. Thank God for Renee! I squirmed out from the headlock and punched the back of his head. Buckman flipped onto his stomach. I didn't like having a woman fight my battles, but at least it got me on top. I punched the flab rolls on the back of his neck as hard as I could. Brett and Francis finally pulled me off Buckman, and I was actually happy to let them. But I acted like I didn't want the fight to end, pulling forward and throwing out taunts. Buckman got up to his feet. The room was in chaos. All the women were shrieking and crying as people were trying to stand between us. Buckman's face was furious. If he had had a gun he would have blown my head off. We cursed each other for a minute, then the room began to calm. Buckman demanded that I leave. I demanded that he return his cane to the prop department. Everyone seemed to agree with him.

I knew I had just added to the legend I was creating around myself. I think I knew it before I attacked him. But at the same time, I was genuinely pissed off because I knew Buckman had tried to cuckold us by calling CNN. As I watched Buckman collect himself I had feelings of hatred and war. I loved seeing the dark blood on his shirt. I gloated over the fact that one of his aides had to loan him a handkerchief for his bleeding nose. I even enjoyed wiping the blood from my own lip. My right hand was broken, and I loved that too.

The people in the room didn't know how to react. Rachel looked at me strangely, both amazed and confused, but I couldn't read her thoughts exactly. Everyone probably thought I was drunk and crazy and they were probably right. I had to get out of there. Brett patted my back and told me to lay low until tomorrow. Samantha formed a phone with her hand—*call me*. Renee and John Griggs drove me to the local emergency room, but I didn't have health insurance. I was basically self-employed and I had forgotten to sign up for a plan. So I used Edward's American Express and paid the $2,800 outright. That night I stayed at Renee's. It was an even longer sleepless night than the one before. I had declared war and now I had to wage it or fold my tent.

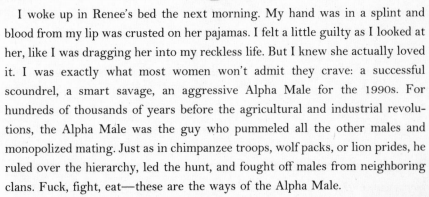

I woke up in Renee's bed the next morning. My hand was in a splint and blood from my lip was crusted on her pajamas. I felt a little guilty as I looked at her, like I was dragging her into my reckless life. But I knew she actually loved it. I was exactly what most women won't admit they crave: a successful scoundrel, a smart savage, an aggressive Alpha Male for the 1990s. For hundreds of thousands of years before the agricultural and industrial revolutions, the Alpha Male was the guy who pummeled all the other males and monopolized mating. Just as in chimpanzee troops, wolf packs, or lion prides, he ruled over the hierarchy, led the hunt, and fought off males from neighboring clans. Fuck, fight, eat—these are the ways of the Alpha Male.

Of course, the old system made selecting a mate simple for women: the guy on the ground with a black eye slithered away, while the guy strutting around victoriously with bloody fists was guaranteed some action in the teepee that night, thus assuring that the strongest genes were passed on to the next generation. Aggressiveness, handsomeness, agility, cunning, intelligence, natural leadership, and a healthy athletic body—traits of the Alpha Male. Today's women, who often settle for a convenient *provider*—husbands of good education and a caring nature—often find themselves desperately unsatisfied; their bodies scream out for a strong dominant male to take them, to ravage them, to make them feel safe. These are the women who devour volumes of "romance" novels with pictures of blatant Alpha Males on the cover; these are the women whose beds I kept landing in.

I understood how to play the game. That's why I now lived my life as an Alpha Male. I ate Alpha Male food—filet mignon. I drove an Alpha Male car—the Hummer. I had an Alpha Male physique—muscular and athletic. Whenever I had time to think over decisions in my life, I always asked myself: "What would an Alpha Male do?" But most of the time I acted on instinct, like assaulting Frank Buckman. Something in my design automatically clenched my fists and launched me at him. Buckman had challenged my group—practically spit in our faces; he had to be confronted, and nobody else seemed willing to step up at the time. Alpha Males never back down, ever, or they are no longer Alpha, by definition. That is what I had been trying to tell Brett. But in a time of laws and courts, being a well-rounded Neo–Alpha Male also required judgment, I knew. I had skirted the limits of civil tolerance with my attack on Buckman. I had to slow down my reactions and try to control myself better in the future. I needed to consciously remember to balance my drive with more rational, intelligent thought before I accidentally ruined everything for myself.

Renee rolled over and started kissing my neck. She climbed onto my lap and pulled her top down. I was starting to really care for Renee—not as a girlfriend—I just appreciated her in my life. We never acknowledged any sort of relationship, but that was the way we both wanted it. If we woke up naked together, we simply went out for breakfast and didn't dwell on it. It was what it was.

After Renee left for work, I checked my voice mail. Eleven messages. A few congratulated me; most were threats from Buckman supporters. I tried to put them out of my mind. But I really might have stepped over the boundaries this time. Maybe I wouldn't have attacked Buckman if I hadn't been drinking? I had no idea how people were going to react. Fuck it, I told myself. It was done. All I could do was concentrate on the present and the future. Brett left a message telling me not to come into the office, but to meet him the following night at Aroma Italiano. That worried me. I knew I either had to capitalize on this Buckman situation or it would capitalize on me. I worked the phones for the next three hours, spinning like a mad dog. I tried to lock up support for what I had done, and for Brett's right to the speakership.

"Everyone's talking about your brawl," John told me in an excited voice over the phone. "Even in DC!"

"How's it playing?" I asked.

"Okay, I guess. It looks like you're loyal to Brett, and everyone respects loyalty. Some people are saying you're crazy, which of course I already know is true. But I think, bottom line, most people want Brett to become speaker. He earned it. That's what they're saying, anyway."

"That's all I want them to say."

A reporter from the *Register* called about the fight, but I asked her to drop the story. She was a friend and owed me a favor, so she did. Underground stories are one thing; media stories are vastly more difficult to manage. They can quickly take on a life of their own.

That night I drove alone to Samantha's house. From there, Samantha sat on my lap in the Diablo as Rick drove to San Pedro, where the yacht party was set to embark. The vessel was named the *Catharsis*. It was the largest yacht I'd ever seen, except in movies—129 feet of regal splendor. We walked onto the front deck and met the owner, Steve Butcher, the CEO of Rick's law firm.

"I heard about you and Frank Buckman," Steve said as he shook my hand.

"I told him about it," Rick said, like a proud uncle.

"Wonderful," I said.

Carrying fifty well-appointed guests, the yacht pulled into the harbor. There were three off-white leather couches sitting on the open deck, apparently only taken out for parties. I sat on a couch with Samantha and some stockbrokers. We were cruising to Newport and back, about a five-hour pleasure voyage. It didn't take long before Samantha and I turned our waiter into a rumrunner. By the time we hit the open ocean I was starting to get loose and enjoy the cool salty breeze and the soothing motion of the deck. I needed to forget about Frank Buckman.

An hour later, six of us were sloshing around in the shallow Jacuzzi on the ship's upper deck, right outside Steve's private room. Steve was the only one with a bathing suit, so the rest of us were either in our underwear or naked. Jazz music played on the bedroom's stereo and we drank Dom Pérignon straight from the bottle. I was doing most of my thinking and scheming at parties these days. Hell, half my life was spent at parties. Rick, Samantha, and I were on a ceaseless quest to find the ultimate backdrop for our lives. This yacht was pretty close. But it was hard to enjoy it fully; I couldn't get the speakership out of my mind. Rumors were circulating that Buckman was going to press assault charges against me. But I didn't believe he wanted to relive the scene in a courtroom; not with an ego like his.

"What's wrong, Jimmy?" Samantha asked me. "You seem distracted."

"It's just this whole Buckman thing."

"You're getting good spin—what's the problem?"

"Francis says Buckman has the votes for the speakership."

"Is he sure?"

"That's what he says."

"Well, it's not over yet, Boo-Boo. You have to convince everyone that he doesn't have the votes. Those fucking politicians up there will vote for whoever they think has the momentum. Once a few break to your side, they all will."

"I don't know shit about those guys, Samantha; I don't know shit about Sacramento. Francis and Brett have been trying everything, making promises they can't even keep. It's hopeless. Buckman has the momentum, and the speakership vote is this Monday."

Samantha gazed off across the deck. The moonlight shimmered like specks of silver off the ocean. She looked beautiful, yet tired, her mind a million miles away.

"Well, it looks like you'll have to get Buckman to drop out," she finally said.

"Shit, don't you think I've tried? I've threatened him. I even punched him. He's only more determined now. And if he wins, I'll be lucky to get a job licking toilets at the capitol."

"You've gotta quit talking like that, Boo-Boo. You're a winner. Look how far you've come already. You almost single-handedly won the first Republican assembly in twenty-five years. That's the stuff of legends, babe. Listen, doesn't Buckman have dirt? I've been hearing shit about that guy for years."

"Yeah—he's got dirt, but nothing official."

"Unofficial dirt is the best kind. What's he got?"

"Sleeping with his fund-raiser. He's married."

"Perfect," Samantha said, smiling. "How do you know?"

"Through a friend. It's solid. But it's not like I have pictures or anything."

"You don't need pictures, honey. Listen, here's what we'll do . . ."

As Samantha explained her plan, I started to feel better.

TWENTY

Sunday evening, and the speakership vote was only fifteen hours away. Buckman's people were working overtime to keep the votes they had. At the same time, Brett and Francis were trying to steal those votes; they twisted every arm they could grab and promised the world to any member who would break away from Buckman. They offered big offices, prime committee assignments, anything and everything. I picked off two members by offering campaign money from Edward. But we were still fifteen votes short—an almost impossible margin to make up.

At eight o'clock that night I hooked up with Samantha at the infamous Viper Room on Sunset. We were meeting Greg from the *LA Times*—the hip reporter with a goatee and ponytail I had met during the Winston campaign. I wasn't as close to Greg as I was to Samantha, so I was nervous about letting him in on our plan. But I was desperate, and he was our last hope.

Greg showed up late, looking like a movie star in a black leather jacket. Samantha had already filled him in on our plan. Like me, Greg seemed a little reluctant, but he was willing to play along, probably because this was his chance to manipulate the political game he usually had to watch from the sidelines. I gave Greg all the information I had on Buckman. He took notes—names, places, dates. We walked out to Samantha's Jaguar in the rain. Greg and Samantha sat in front, Samantha in the driver's seat. I was in back, leaning forward between the two seats. Samantha turned on the hands-free cellular and dialed Buckman's house in Long Beach. The phone rang through the car's stereo system—loud and crystal clear.

"Hello, Buckman residence," his wife answered in a sweet practiced manner.

"Hello, this is Greg Michaelson from the *LA Times*. May I speak to Mr. Buckman, please?"

I was biting off what was left of my fingernails. My knees were bouncing up and down. Everything was riding on what Greg would say.

"This is Frank Buckman," he answered in a friendly voice. Even Buckman knew enough to be nice to reporters.

"Frank, this is Greg Michaelson, *LA Times*."

"Hi, Greg . . . I know you from the convention last year. You did a piece on that congressional race in Riverside."

"That's right," Greg said.

"So what story are you working on now?" Buckman asked. "Are you coming to Sacramento tomorrow for the big speakership vote? I'd be happy to give you a one-on-one. I've already got the votes locked up."

"That's what I've heard," Greg said. "Actually, Dave Spetzer's going to cover that vote from our Sacramento bureau. I'm working on more of a bio piece on you. Who Frank Buckman is, where he came from, that sort of thing."

"Terrific," Buckman said. "Do you have one of my press kits? I could fax you some clips and bio stuff right now if you're near a machine."

Greg glanced nervously at Samantha, like he was about to jump off a skyscraper.

"Actually, I've already got that stuff," Greg said. "I need to ask you about a woman named Donna Krassfield."

The car filled with silence.

Finally, the phone rustled on Buckman's end, and he said: "She's my fund-raiser. What about her?"

"Well, I'm following a story that was brought to me by a Republican fund-raiser in Orange County. I have some questions about your relationship with Ms. Krassfield . . ."

"Such as?" Buckman's voice was strictly defense now.

"Is it true that you've been conducting a surreptitious affair for the last two years with Donna Krassfield, a woman under your employment, despite the fact that you're a married man?" Greg's face pulled back in a cringe as he asked the question. I couldn't believe how hard he was lowering the boom on Buckman.

"Those are vicious rumors spread by my opponents, nothing more," Buckman huffed. "And I resent that you would call my house peddling such garbage, Mr. Michaelson."

"I'm only doing my job," Greg said. "So, if I told you I had two reliable witnesses who saw you spending the night in Ms. Krassfield's hotel suite in Palm Springs, would you refute those allegations, Mr. Buckman?"

"Of course I would!"

"Where did you stay for the two nights of that convention, Mr. Buckman? You didn't check into a room at the Marriott."

"Uh . . . ," he stammered. "I stayed at a nearby hotel. But that's none of your concern. Do you have a serious agenda for this conversation or not? It's late. I've got a big day tomorrow."

"I checked every hotel in the Palm Springs area," Greg lied. "None of them have records of your stay."

I could just see that fat bastard chewing his fist on the other end.

"I don't have time for this. Who's your editor? Does he know you're out chasing filth, Mr. Michaelson?"

"No, he doesn't. In fact, I haven't even decided whether I'm going to pursue this story, to be honest," Greg said. "But it *is* a legitimate story. I have more than three sources. The speakership of the California assembly is a high-profile statewide public office, Mr. Buckman. To tell you the truth, I wouldn't even be interested in this story if you were just an assemblyman. But the speakership is a public trust, and these allegations seem to throw your character and credibility directly into question."

Buckman was breathing heavily, and I could tell he was cupping the phone to shield the conversation from someone else in the room. Samantha watched the conversation like a boxing coach, spurring Greg on with hand gestures.

"So what are you saying here, Mr. Michaelson?" Buckman asked after a long pause.

"What I'm saying is, I'll sleep on this tonight and see what happens tomorrow. I've already got the body of the piece written. I just have to fill in some blanks, get some comments. I'm not going to run the piece yet, because, like I said, if you weren't speaker it wouldn't be much of a story."

"You son of a bitch," Buckman fumed in a hushed voice.

"My number's in the book," Greg said. *"LA Times.* It's up to you now, Mr. Buckman. By the way, do you think I could get comments from your wife, please? You know, just in case I decide to go with the story?"

Buckman slammed the phone down just before I burst out laughing.

"Goddamn, Greg!" I hooted. "You're a ruthless motherfucker! I always knew reporters were smarter than politicians!"

Samantha was cracking up, slapping the steering wheel. "I think you rattled his cage, Greg!"

Greg leaned back in the seat and closed his eyes, running a hand across his forehead. The corners of his mouth slowly curled into a guilty grin. "Well, do you think he bought it?"

"We'll find out in a few hours," Samantha said. "Thanks, Greg. You're a killer, babe."

We three snakes slithered back into the Viper Room. I bought drinks all night on Edward's Gold Card.

TWENTY-ONE

Samantha dropped me at LAX at five o'clock that morning. I was wearing one of Rick's $3,000 Armani suits.

"I'll have it dry-cleaned before I give it back," I told her.

"You know what, why don't you just keep it, Boo-Boo. Rick's got a hundred suits. And it looks so *damn* good on you!"

"Thanks."

I kissed her and said good-bye. She stood up in the open Lamborghini and shouted "Good luck, Boo-Boo!"

I bought a round-trip ticket to Sacramento, then slept bolt upright in a lobby chair for an hour until my flight departed. On the plane I sat next to a fat salesman who kept needing to hit the can. I asked the flight attendant if I could have a whole pot of coffee for myself. "I need it dark enough to set off the plane's oil lights," I told her. She looked at my bloodshot eyes and agreed. I flipped my laptop open and got to work. I had to write an acceptance speech for Brett. I already had a first draft, but it wasn't very good. I was having trouble writing the speech because I wasn't convinced Brett would ever give it.

Think positive, Jim, I told myself. I knew that the way I perceived things affected how they would turn out. Simply being positive, confident, and happy in the mind kept the cycle turning in my favor. I knew the formula, I just had to stick to it. Usually, if I could visualize something in my head, dream about it all the time and actually see it happening, I could make it so. Whether it was seeing myself standing on top of Mount Whitney before I started up the trail or sitting behind the wheel of a new car before I owned it—the object was irrelevant, the method was consistent.

I deleted the entire speech and started with a blank page. I closed my eyes and pictured Brett standing behind the glorious podium of the assembly. I visualized what the cheering crowd would want to hear, what would inspire them, what would *move* them. And the words came. By the time the wheels hit the runway in Sacramento, the speech was *finito*.

I had never seen the state capitol before my taxi dropped me at the bottom of its long marble steps. The building was a palace. Sprawling grounds covered with chestnut trees, park benches, and squirrels scampering around on the grass. Rich classical architecture with deep windowsills. A white marble dome with the state flag rustling in the morning breeze. I stood gazing at the building with feelings of reverence. By the end of the day, I thought to myself, I would either be running the place, or running out of it.

I went inside. The lobby was awe inspiring. The dome's stained-glass port windows filled the air with rich distinguished colors, and the cut marble floors displayed the state seal and various mosaics of California's entrepreneurial history—covered wagons, Native Americans, the gold rush. I found Brett's office on the directory and walked upstairs. The splendor of the lobby contrasted sharply with the dumpster I found Brett's office to be, even worse than his district office in Orange. There was a tacky open reception room, and a mean, shabby little broom closet masqueraded as Brett's office. The Democrats who controlled office assignments in the capitol had dealt Brett a public disgracing. I met the secretary, whom I'd spoken to a million times before on the phone. A strange feeling of confused intensity permeated the office. I grabbed some coffee and squeezed into Brett's office. I found him with Francis, working the phones, with a running tally of votes on the chalkboard.

"So, how you feeling, slugger?" Brett asked me.

"Great. How do things look?"

"Not good," Francis said. His eyes were swollen and red: he hadn't shaved for days. "We're short by seven votes, but even the ones we have could break off any minute."

Brett walked over and sat on the edge of his desk, facing me. "We're thinking of pulling the plug, Jimbo. It's not too late for me to take the speakership pro tem."

"Forget that shit," I said. "You can win this, Brett. You've got a chance to give a speech to the members. You can persuade them. You're a great speaker."

"Words aren't shit next to solid votes."

"Look, I found out last night that Buckman has some *serious* problems."

"Like what?" Brett asked.

"Dirt problems—women."

"How do you know?"

"I just know."

He stared at me. He looked back at Francis, but Francis only shrugged. Then his eyes searched mine, trying to detect the potential impact of what I knew without asking, trying to draw energy and assurance from me. I kept my face solid as a rock; I had to appear confident all the way through. "Is it enough, Jim?" he finally asked.

I wasn't sure, but what did I have to lose. "It's enough."

He let out a quick sigh, and life came back into his face. A glimpse of hope sprang into his body, and he punched his palm. "Okay, Jim. I pray you're right." He turned to Francis. "We're gonna do this thing. Fuck it!"

After I begged him for an hour, Greg left a message for Buckman's wife on their home phone at 9:30 A.M., asking for an interview. We knew she was in Sacramento for the vote, but we hoped Buckman would check his messages. It was the last thing I could do. Everything was up to Brett now.

Brett's lawyer friend was sworn in as an assemblyman that morning. Republicans were now a real majority in the California assembly for the first time since I was born. After taking over the Rules Committee, Republicans set the speakership vote for high noon. I talked to Mariella, Edward, Winter, and Bud on the phone. But talk was all I could do. Renee and Rachel were in Sacramento for the vote. Rachel looked sexy in her stylish business suit—like she was just waiting to tear it off. The girls told me not to worry if Brett lost. Rachel said I'd done a good job on the recall campaign, no matter what the outcome, and that she thought Buckman would probably forgive me if I apologized for attacking him. But those words meant nothing to me. Only the speakership mattered.

Francis got floor passes for all my friends. We stood at the back of the large assembly chamber next to the reporters. Samantha was stuck covering a murder trial, so she couldn't make it. But she told me to call her immediately after the vote. At high noon Willie Black called the session to order by pounding his gavel. All the assembly members took their seats, except one: Bryan Gentry had not been seen since the recall. The speakership vote was major political drama in California; seventy reporters crowded into a space designed for twelve, and dozens of white news vans with satellite dishes swarmed the parking lot outside. Willie gave a short speech. Since the Republican whip had decided not to run, Buckman and Brett were the only nominees for speaker. They would each give a ten-minute speech, then the members would cast open votes.

Buckman was up first. He waddled to the podium; members shook his hand and slapped his back as he crossed the floor. My heart was fluttering. Renee held my sweaty, shaky hand. Rachel stood with Buckman's staff only a few feet away. Francis was pacing in the corner, staring down at the carpet. His ever-present cell phone was clutched in his hand, but now it only looked like an empty prop—completely useless.

Willie introduced Buckman and stepped aside.

"Thank you, Mr. Speaker," Buckman said, his voice echoing throughout the chamber. "Distinguished members and guests. I never thought this day would come. It's been twenty-five years since this legislative body last was under Republican control. Today is perhaps the proudest day of my life . . ."

Buckman was an eloquent speaker despite his burly appearance, and obviously a skilled tactician.

"For twelve years I have served under this roof, in this house. Twelve hard years. Twelve long years. Twelve sometimes wonderful, sometimes bitter years. But twelve years I wouldn't trade for the world. The happiest part of this day is that the voters of California will finally receive what they voted for—what they demanded—in last year's election: change. Citizens are fed up with business as usual, and frankly, so am I. Californians want their leaders to be accountable, as we should be. The voters also made something else clear. By electing a record number of freshmen, they told us they want new faces in government—people from the real world, from the business community. The concerns of California's voters have always been my own paramount concerns. I believe that once any of us are in this building too long, we tend to get sucked into the internal workings, and we lose our roots in the communities.

"During the founding of this great nation, a couple of pretty smart fellows named Thomas Jefferson and Ben Franklin established a rule. Anyone who served as a US ambassador to a foreign nation was limited to seven years in office. The fear was that the ambassadors would assimilate with their host country and 'go native.' Well, I believe they were right. We are all just ambassadors here, ambassadors from the districts we represent. And if we're here too long, we can go native too. That's why I've decided to make a change. After long and careful consideration, and talking it over with my family, I've decided it's time I move on—to Washington."

I nearly shouted when I heard those words. Reporters started buzzing. Francis's knees buckled and he fell to the floor in the corner. Renee squeezed my hand and smiled. Brett sank down in his chair, his hands covering his face in disbelief. At first my back tingled and I shivered, then my whole body flooded in a rush of emotion.

"We got the motherfucker," I mumbled with clenched teeth and fists. *"We got him."*

"Thanks to a recommendation from our fine and gracious governor, next year I will be taking a position as acting vice chairman of the federal Department of Veterans Affairs, where I will continue fighting for the interests of my fellow veterans. So that leaves only one question: who will carry on our agenda here in the assembly? And I think there's no finer man, and certainly no fresher face, than Brett Alexander."

Now I shouted. *"Woooouuuwww!* Brett!" I jumped in the air, throwing punches wildly. Every muscle in my body flexed and veins popped up on my arms. I closed my eyes, dropping to one knee. *"Yes! Yes!"* For just that brief moment, I could have taken on the whole world. I was unstoppable, I could have flown, I could have punched through a brick wall . . . Everyone looked at me, most of them smiling. Winning this speakership meant more to me than anything else in my life. This was the culmination of my dreams. The hair on my neck stood up proudly.

After Buckman's speech, Brett took the podium. The room erupted with wild applause and catcalls. All the Republicans chanted "Brett! Brett! Brett!"—even the ones who had promised their votes to Buckman. Fucking sheep.

"Thank you very much," Brett said in a humble voice. "Thank you, Mr. Buckman and Speaker Black." Brett's wife had flown up with him "just in case." She was standing in front of me, and I could tell by the way her shoulders were violently shaking that she was crying. Brett's son was at her side. "I really don't know what to say here," Brett continued. He pulled my speech out of his coat pocket, unfolded it, and started reading. "Last year Republicans in Congress fired the first shots of revolution against big government. This year we're bringing the battle home to the Golden State . . ."

Listening to Brett read my words, feeling the energy in the air, watching the proud faces around me—it was all too much. By the time Brett got to the Lincoln quotes in the speech, thin tears were streaming down my cheeks. A lump in my throat kept down the boiling emotions, the raw ecstasy. After the speech, which ended on a Reagan quote, the members cast their votes. Brett Alexander, my friend and boss, was the new speaker of the California assembly, instantly one of the world's most powerful men.

I scooped Brett Jr. onto my shoulders, grabbed his wife's trembling hand, and raced up to the podium. Suzy was crying, but with a huge smile locked on her face. As I watched them hug and kiss, I knew this was the biggest moment in their lives, and mine. Brett took his son off my shoulders.

"Can you believe it, champ?" he asked.

"I'm super-duper proud of you, Daddy."

Tears welled in Brett's eyes. At the age of thirty-six he had everything. I envied him, in a positive way. How awesome it must be, I thought. Brett handed the ankle-biter over to his wife and hugged me with one arm while shaking my hand with the other. "Thanks, Jimbo," he said. "I wouldn't be here if it wasn't for you. I don't know what to say."

"This is all I need," I said. "This is what I've wanted. I'll never forget this moment, man."

Brett smiled. "What's this 'man' stuff? It's Mr. Speaker to you, punk."

I punched his arm and whispered: "Fuck you, Mr. Speaker."

Brett threw his arm around my shoulder, and we walked out of the chamber with his family and Francis. We didn't know where we were going, but the whole world was open to us.

PART 3

five months later . . .

TWENTY-TWO

The power hit me fast and hard, like a thirty-foot wave at the Pipeline. Brett appointed me as his deputy chief of staff and head speechwriter. Willie Black had paid his top lieutenants upwards of $120,000. But because we were going to "change business as usual," Brett set a salary cap of $99,000. That's what Francis was paid as chief of staff. Because I was so young, Brett was afraid the media might cringe at those numbers, so he paid me $87,000. But there was a catch. I was only a 90-percent-time employee, which meant I could still take outside consulting money, especially from Edward. State employees are forbidden to conduct political business on state time, but I got around that, too. If someone caught me doing political work for Brett or Edward, I would simply tell them I was on my 10 percent time. How could they dispute me? Brilliant.

I was given an impressive office with fine oil paintings on the walls and a back door leading directly into the capitol dome. I had a smart and classy secretary named Nancy, interns, generous travel and expense budgets, and a state vehicle: a new Lincoln Town Car. I rented a town house a few blocks from the capitol and also kept my apartment in Huntington Beach. Edward was happy to have me well placed in Sacramento; he was now paying me $3,000 a month to handle his affairs and speech writing.

I was wired to the teeth with electronics—cell phone with three area codes and unlimited talk time, pager, desktop computer, laptop, my own home page, four E-mail accounts, digital cellular data modem, and a brand-new experimental satellite phone no bigger than an old-school cellular phone. If my small office at the Statesmen Institute had been a one-man PR firm, I was now a walking PR conglomerate. I could write a speech on my laptop on an airplane, E-mail it over the Satcom to Winter in New York for editing, have it zapped back, edit again, and fax it to Edward in Washington—all from the comfort of my airplane seat while sipping cuba libres and flirting with the flight attendant.

Brett handled his new power like he was born to wield it. With control over legislation and state spending, he was arguably the most powerful politician in the nation's most powerful state. As speaker, he controlled billions of dollars directly, and billions more through regulations. Even the governor had to kiss up whenever he wanted something. Brett had the most incredible office one could possibly imagine. Willie Black had spent $8 million to refurbish it, but I'm sure it was spectacular long before that. The office was the centerpiece of the entire capitol building, larger than three Oval Offices, with carved wood paneling, chandeliers, antique furniture and rugs, long flowing velvet drapes, and a sixty-foot ceiling.

On Brett's first day as speaker, we ran around the capitol discovering areas Republicans hadn't seen for more than two decades. I actually had the key to the capitol building dangling on my Coors Light key chain! Brett, Francis, and I climbed through the empty dome and found our way to the top using a rusty ladder. We swung from the flagpole in our suits and ties and took pictures of one another. We didn't stop smiling the entire day. That night we stayed up until dawn drinking Scotch and smoking stogies in Brett's office. We were like kids with Disneyland all to ourselves for a night. We toasted at least two dozen times and laughed the night away planning the future of the state.

At the office, I was getting thirty voice mails a day. I spent my weekends partying in Southern California with Samantha and the gang, then caught the 5 A.M. flight every Monday morning and kicked ass around the capitol all week. Brett was the perfect boss. He loved my speeches and gave me all the freedom I needed. He also kept his promise and started campaigning for Edward as soon as he became speaker. Edward and I were already gearing up for the governor's race—putting together a prospective campaign staff, media strategy, and recruiting endorsements. But that race was still nine months away.

I usually finished my wheeling and dealing at the office by six, then a limo full of business executives or lobbyists would whisk Brett, Francis, and me away for the evening. We spent our nights being wined and dined by millionaires and CEOs. Our restaurant of choice was Morton's Steakhouse, and our typical dinner bill was $600, but we never picked up the tab. I was living on coffee by day and filet mignon by night. I saw Renee and Samantha on the weekends, but in Sacramento I didn't have time for girls. I was too busy experimenting with my new power. Soon enough, I figured, the women would start flowing like the $200 bottles of port I was guzzling at Morton's every night.

Brett was on a roll as we prepared for the spring GOP state convention in San Francisco. Through hard work and thousands of spin hours, Brett had become the darling of the California media. He was young and handsome, smart and ambitious. He understood that media relations is the most important factor in politics. Brett had been on the cover of every statewide magazine, and I was now writing a weekly editorial column under his name for the LA Times. I loved writing for Brett because the pieces always got published. I would find an issue—crime, welfare, whatever—and pop off about it on my laptop. Sometimes

Brett wouldn't even read them until they were printed. He was too busy, and he trusted me.

———————

Presently, I was maneuvering my Lincoln into the basement parking lot of the capitol. I knew I looked silly driving the big, awkward boat. The CHP officers waved me through, saying, "Good morning, Mr. Asher." I threw out a joke to the boys and parked the car, then took the elevator to the cafeteria level. I bought two large coffees, dumped ice into one and slammed it, then with my hot cup in hand I strolled downstairs to the speaker's office. Like the security officers, the three receptionists always called me "Mr. Asher." I felt guilty in the face of their politeness because I was the youngest person in the office, even younger than most of our interns. I told everyone to call me Jim, but they wouldn't have it.

First up every morning was our communications meeting at seven. The press secretary, Gerald, and the communications director, Janice, headed up the meeting with me. We had twelve employees on the communications staff, covering all media venues—radio, advertising, Internet, research. We all sat in a circle in the middle of the communications lobby. I usually drank coffee and listened. I didn't get pleasure from bossing people around, so I let others do it.

"So, what's in the news this morning?" Gerald said, starting the meeting.

Janice said: "Well, the *San Diego Union-Tribune* ran a story on Brett's tax-cut bill. The reporter, Jerry Gerger, was pretty fair, but he called our economic forecast numbers 'questionable.'"

"'*Questionable*'?" Gerald repeated, mocking outrage. "Where did those forecast numbers come from?"

Everyone looked at one another, shrugging cluelessly.

"I guess we should call the Rev and Tax guys downstairs to find out," Janice suggested.

"Don't worry," I said. "We got those economic numbers from the governor's office. They're rock solid."

"Are you sure?" Janice asked.

I stared directly at her. The room got quiet. "Look, I'll call Gerger at the *Union* and set him straight, okay."

"Okay then," Gerald said. "What about the *LA Times?* Did anyone else catch that awful piece on public housing reform?"

My cell phone rang—just in time. I walked out of the meeting and talked in the hallway. After I got off the phone I went down to Brett's office. The communications meeting would probably go on for another hour at least.

Mostly those meetings were a chance for people to pretend they knew something. Brett's secretary smiled and buzzed me through his security door. As usual, a dozen important-looking people were waiting in his lobby. Brett was alone at his desk answering E-mails. He received more than a hundred E-mails a day, and answered all of them personally, sometimes sitting at his keyboard until two in the morning. It was just another one of the little things I liked about him.

"Good morning, Brett."

"Hey, Jimbo," he said. "Here, take some of these." He handed me a stack of phone message slips.

"Man, you're getting more popular every day." I took the slips and sat down on his leather couch, shuffling through to find the important ones. "Hey, that guy from Intel called," I said. "Garret Johnson."

"Where do we know him from?" Brett asked.

"From that dinner party in Anaheim two weeks ago. Remember? He runs the Intel plant in San Jose, wants you to take a tour of their facility, check out some new virtual reality technology."

Brett nodded. "Set it up."

Even though there was a regular phone right next to the couch, I took out my cell phone and dialed Intel. "Hello, Garret Johnson, please . . . Yes, this is Jim Asher with speaker Alexander . . ." I continued flipping through the slips, making two piles—ones to call back, others for the shredder. "Hey, Garret, how are you? Yeah, Brett really enjoyed our dinner as well . . . Sure, I'll tell him . . . he's right here with me. So, anyway, what can we do for you? . . . okay . . . Terrific, sure . . . okay, then . . . By the way, you wouldn't mind if we brought along a few reporters and cameras, would you? . . . Free publicity for both of us . . . Of course . . . No problem, we'll only invite the well-behaved ones, ha-ha-ha . . . Fantastic . . . We'll talk." I hung up and smiled at Brett. "Hey, Intel is gonna send a private jet for us whenever we can squeeze the tour into your schedule."

"Beautiful," Brett said. "So, are we ready for the convention?"

"Ready to roll."

"Jim, this convention is huge for us. This is where we make our mark. Oh, by the way, you know about the welfare vote this morning, right?"

"Sure. It's going to pass, right?"

Brett nodded.

Francis walked in. "The meeting's ready to start, Mr. Speaker."

We walked to Brett's conference room for the daily senior staff meeting. Brett's senior staff consisted of attorneys and bureaucrats from every area of government—agriculture, tax, regulation, water, sanitation, land use, welfare, whatever. And the senior staff was even worse than the communications staff, infinitely more petty. I always felt like I was walking into a viper pit at these meetings. Everyone wanted a piece of Brett. He distrusted most of them; actually, he barely knew most of them. It seemed like we got a new employee every day.

Francis started the meeting:

"This morning we have a very important vote on the speaker's welfare bill." All sixteen people around the table nodded. "We've already polled the members, and we have the necessary votes to pass it." Francis turned to the press secretary, Gerald. "What do we have planned on the media side? This bill will probably attract a lot of attention."

"Well," Gerald said, "Jim has written a positive press release, which is ready to be faxed out this morning. Also, we're recording the speaker's floor speech, which will be available to radio and TV stations."

"Good," Francis said.

Like me, Brett usually kept quiet during these meetings. It was mostly hot air blowing around anyway. We saved our energy for the important work, behind closed doors, after hours.

Brett's chief policy analyst, Todd Graham, suddenly spoke up: "Is a press release going to be enough? I mean, shouldn't we be capitalizing on this welfare cut? Voters are fed up with welfare. Maybe we should hold a press conference?"

Todd was in charge of Brett's policy issues. He considered himself to be brilliant and masculine, but he was only half as smart as he imagined, which placed him barely above average, and he was out of shape from sitting on his fat, feminine ass too much, bossing people around. The press conference idea was batted around for a few minutes. Then it actually seemed to be gathering steam. I thought it was a terrible idea. Todd started pushing, saying things like: "So, what time should we hold the conference, and where?"

I wanted to speak up, but didn't. As everyone began planning the press conference, Brett nudged my foot under the table, raising his eyebrows. I shook my head almost imperceptibly. Then Brett said:

"Jim, what do you think of a press conference?"

Everyone shut up and looked at me. Todd tried to stare me down, as if to say, *You better not fuck with my idea.* Outside of that guarded, unrealistic environment, I would have dominated Todd, put him in his place. But I had to play along for now.

"Uh, well," I said, "I don't think it's a good idea."

Todd gave me a death stare. People started looking back and forth at each other.

"Why not?" Brett asked.

"Well, I don't think we want to come out swinging on straight welfare cuts. This bill simply reduces the dollar amount of payments by ten percent, it isn't a reform bill at all. Now, Brett's other bill, AB107, which we vote on two weeks from now, is a better bill to make a media splash with because—"

"What are you talking about?" Todd broke in. "Most voters favor cutting welfare, and this is a big cut. You're way off base, Asher. So, like I was saying—"

"Actually," I interrupted. "most voters favor 'reforming' or 'replacing' the system, if you read the polling data carefully. I'd be happy to go over the numbers with you sometime, Todd. The problem with Republicans is that we always come off looking mean-spirited. If we hold a big press conference to brag about slashing welfare payments, what do you think reporters are going to say? They'll call Brett cruel and heartless, leaving innocent children to starve in the streets, et cetera. That's the way the media is."

"But you can't change that," someone said.

"True. But we can work around it. Why don't we wait for the next bill, which reforms the system by requiring work and ending payments for additional children. Along with reducing payments, the new bill will also encourage fathers to be responsible, and will make assistance temporary instead of a lifelong trap. Let's at least have something constructive to say when we hold a press conference. It's all about what the spin on the streets will be."

"That sounds like a bunch of puffed-up liberal crap," Todd said.

At this point, I stood up.

But Brett waved me down. "Hold on now. I think Jim is right," he said. "When we talk about ending welfare, we always need to speak in compassionate terms, like 'rebuilding lives' and 'restoring dignity,' otherwise we look like a bunch of cold-blooded Republicans, as usual."

Todd huffed. "But, Mr. Speaker, today's bill will be popular with people who—"

"That's enough," Brett said. "Next item for discussion . . ."

I really hated office politics, even when I was right. It was truly the worst part of the job. Campaigns were so much better because everyone shared a sense of unified purpose and thrived on camaraderie and late-night adrenaline. But once the power came, so came the vultures. Sad reality. I couldn't wait for the state convention, my playground.

TWENTY-THREE

Once we got the speakership, our top priority immediately became holding on to it. Unfortunately, governing usually takes a backseat to maintaining power, and is often only seen as a means to this end.

Conventions are political, so I couldn't use my state travel budget. Edward got me a fancy suite at the convention hotel, the San Francisco Sheraton. This whole weekend was on his dime. We had work to do on his campaign. Originally, when I first met Brett, I saw him as a tool to get Edward in the governor's mansion. But with every passing day I considered Brett more and more as my ticket to the big time. He was better-looking and smarter than Edward, without an illegal alien fiasco hanging over his head, and his political instincts were unrivaled. The guy was a natural. But for now I had to concentrate on Edward's campaign. Once he was governor, I would be an unstoppable force. With direct influence over the governor and speaker I would be, presumably, the most powerful man in state politics. Then I could start getting serious about my ultimate goal: the White House.

Not only was I writing Brett's and Edward's speeches for the convention, I was also filling in for the governor's speechwriter, who had been in a horrific car wreck the week before. I had already finished Brett's speech, and Edward's was half done. The governor personally talked the speech over with me; he seemed as nervous about me writing it as I was. His chief of staff, Bob Slater, gave me a folder full of his old speeches—they were all great. I was afraid I would turn in a lump of shit and the governor would reject it. I spent most of the first day locked in my hotel suite, chained to my laptop. But I couldn't concentrate on writing. I deleted my first draft of the speech. Maybe I could write better if I had a few drinks.

Edward was arriving from DC the next day, and Brett had fund-raising dinners all night, so I was free to do some playboying. This was the first time I would be together with everyone from the party since we had seized the speakership. I took my laptop down to the lobby bar, found a quiet chair in the corner, ordered a cuba libre, and started banging away. Soft piano music played in the background. I had two pages written before John Griggs walked up.

"What's up, G?" he said.

"Nada. Just writing the governor's speech."

"Man, you're keeping busy. I miss the old Jim Asher. The guy who did nothing but drink beer, chase girls, and mooch free food at conventions. What are you trying to do, take over the state?"

I grinned. "I'm running myself ragged, though, man. I was writing Edward's speech on the plane this morning. I still have to write Brett's column before Sunday. And I've got this damn party to plan . . . I don't know shit about planning parties."

"Don't worry. It'll pay off, man. Look how far you've come already. When you first started, you were clipping articles for pocket change. Remember, I know where you came from, buddy. Hard work pays off. You made yourself useful—now you're indispensable."

"Nobody is indispensable. Hey, check it out real quick, will ya?"

John skimmed through the speech.

"It's okay . . . Not as good as some of your other speeches. Is this thing about Robin Hood correct?"

"Yeah. That's my favorite part of the speech. The Jefferson Institute just published that study. It's weird, everyone thinks taxes were cruel and oppressive during the time of Robin Hood, but actually they're much higher now as a percentage of income. We just don't see it because it's all electronic these days—credit cards, checks, automatic deductions. But I'll tell you what, if the IRS showed up on doorsteps once a year demanding forty percent of people's income, things would change real quick."

"Can you imagine?" John said. "'Okay, Mr. Jones, that will be twenty-six thousand dollars please. Cash or check? Oh, I see . . . you don't have the money, eh? Well then, I guess we'll need the keys to your new BMW, please, and of course we'll have to take all your furniture, including that nice sofa over there, and by the way, how many pairs of shoes do you own?'"

"I think I'll put that into the speech. This Robin Hood bit is all I've got so far."

"Go ahead. Just tell the Gov it was my idea. Direct all credit to John Griggs, please."

Renee walked up with some girls from the governor's office. I could feel the night starting to gather steam. With two drinks in hand, I printed the speech on my Canon portable and tucked it into my coat pocket.

"Are you boys ready to get loose?" Renee asked.

I copied the speech on a disk and left my laptop with the bartender. I didn't feel like running upstairs, killing my buzz. Renee's girlfriends were cute, and fresh out of college. They seemed nervous and guarded around us. I offered my arm to a cute blond and she took it. We walked upstairs with Renee hanging on my other arm.

"Hey, Renee, is Rachel West here?" I asked.

"She's around somewhere. I saw her walking with Buckman and Spencer. All these horny old politicians just want to stare at her ass all day. Why do you ask?"

"Just wondering."

I had been thinking about Rachel a lot lately, daydreaming about her. I'd seen her several times in the last few months, but always at some stuffy fund-raiser or dinner party, and always with Frank Buckman. She seemed slightly more interested in me since we won the speakership. In the back of my mind I didn't like the fact that she only started warming up after I got a powerful new job, but I tried to convince myself that she liked me for who I was, and that my job was only a bonus in her mind. In any case, I was hot for her.

We found hospitality suites at every turn of the head. First we hit the Coors suite and tanked up, then the fast-food industry suite and chowed down.

"I heard the tobacco suite is going off," John said.

The tobacco hospitality suite was in the Presidential Suite. The place was packed. We had to sign in at the door. I wrote: *JIM ASHER—SPEAKER ALEXANDER, WINSTON, GOVERNOR.* What a proud entry! I looked for Rachel's name, but it wasn't on the list. I headed for the bar.

"Two Cadillac margaritas," I told the bartender.

"Coming right up, sir."

Whoever invented hospitality suites ranks in my mind with the greatness of Galileo, Darwin, Einstein, Heisenberg, and both the Wright brothers combined. I walked around. I hated mingling; all the conversations seemed so contrived. Everyone was always looking around when they talked to one another, like they were searching for someone better to be seen with. I didn't like small talk; I liked talking one-on-one politics with power brokers. That's where the real shit gets done. Average people bored me; their level of thought and conversation was too elementary, too recycled. I had already been through all those conversations in my own mind, probably when I was in junior high. I knew all their arguments inside and out, backward and forward, so why bother?

A smartly dressed guy walked up and introduced himself.

"Jim Asher?" he asked, shaking my hand.

"Yeah."

"I'm David Shnurg."

"Shnurg?" I said.

"I know. I was born with it."

His name was stupid, but this guy was a real smoothie. He looked like an amalgam of network anchors.

"Who do you work for, David?"

"Well, this is my party. I'm with the tobacco lobby."

"Oh. Great. I love these suites you guys put on."

"Thanks. So you work for Speaker Alexander and Winston, right?"

"Yup."

"I met you at the speaker's office last month."

"That's right . . ." I didn't remember him. We had a hundred lobbyists a day coming through Brett's office. They all wanted something.

"Your boss is doing a great job. He's been terrific to the tobacco industry."

"Brett is pro-business. He doesn't believe in overbearing government regulations, for any industry."

He looked at my empty glass. "Go for another drink?"

"Sure."

We both got cuba libres and hung out on the balcony.

I pulled out my Marlboro Reds. "Want one?"

"Hell no. That shit'll kill you." He smiled.

"You tobacco guys are fuckin' ruthless! . . . I admire that."

"Let me tell you, it's not easy spinning for the cigarette industry. It's like doing public relations work for Saddam Hussein."

"I think I'd be good at it. I like a challenge."

"Well, if you ever want to get out of politics you can come work for us anytime." He handed me his card.

"Thanks. I'll keep that in mind."

"Hey, we've got a bill I've been wanting to talk to the speaker about . . ."

I had been waiting for that—the pitch. "Send us a memo," I said. "Something in writing. I'll see what I can do."

"Actually, I was thinking of something less formal. Maybe dinner at Morton's?"

"Well, you certainly did your homework. Morton's is our favorite restaurant. I might be able to set something up."

"Thanks a lot, Jim. It's so hard to get through to your office. It's like trying to get a meeting with the damn Pope."

"Brett's really busy."

"I believe it." I think David caught me ogling a woman at the end of the balcony. "So what are your plans for the night, Jim?"

"Hospitality suites for another hour, then some friends and I are talking about driving into the city."

"San Francisco is a great town," he said. "You know, I've got a car I'm not using if you and your friends would like to borrow it for the night."

"What kind of car?"

He grinned. "What kind would you like?"

"Hmm . . . How 'bout a limo?"

"Done. I'll arrange it with the concierge."

"This is just between friends, right?" I said. "Otherwise I'd have to report it to the state as a contribution or a gift. And no promises on anything—especially the legislative stuff. There's no connection between the limo and politics, got it?"

"Don't worry, Jim." He slapped my back. "We do it all the time."

"Here's my card. We're having a big party at the nightclub tomorrow night. Why don't you join us. We'll pick up your drinks and dinner."

"Sounds fantastic," he said.

I found Renee and John by the piano.

"Hey, guys, guess what? I got us a limo for the night."

"Wow. How'd you pull that off?" John asked.

"Industry secret. Let's go hit some other suites. The limo will be ready at ten-thirty."

We found the Native American suite. They always had plenty of goodies. Their agenda was to open up gambling on reservations. I wouldn't have cared if their agenda was taking back all the land we snaked from them a century ago—I was there for free drinks. Our entourage was growing. We met up with people from the Winston campaign, more college girls, legislative staffers, all kinds of political partyers, all wanting to go with us in the limo. Everyone asked about my new job. An attractive coed pulled me aside.

"Can the speaker come talk to my Young Republicans group?" she asked.

"Why not." I gave her my card. "Call my secretary, Nancy. She'll set it up for you." She gave me a moist kiss on the cheek and slipped her phone number into my coat pocket.

At ten-fifteen we went down to the lobby. The limo was ready to go—a gleaming white Lincoln stretch. Meanwhile, all the college girls were running around trying to find fake IDs. I waited eagerly near the front door with John. Suddenly someone covered my eyes from behind. The hands were delicate and smelled sweet. I turned around. Rachel. She looked glamorous in a short skirt and business jacket. Her two friends were also knockouts. I kissed both her cheeks, like a European.

"Hey there, handsome," she said.

"Hi, Rachel."

"What are you boys doing tonight?" She held on to my arm softly, squeezing ever so gently. She knew the right buttons to push. It flashed through my mind that Rachel had probably been mastering the advantage of her beauty since she was a little girl.

"We're going into town to hit the bars. That's our car out there." I pointed.

"Neat. Can we come play?"

John was eyeballing her friends shamelessly.

"Sure. But it might be a little crowded." I pointed to the college girls.

"We don't need them, Jim. How about just the five of us?"

"Um . . ." Rachel was so damn beautiful. "Okay, but we've gotta bring Renee. She's been with us all night."

"Great. I love Renee."

The way Rachel was looking at me—I could have collapsed right there. Actually, I could have thrown her onto the marble floor right there and indulged my wicked, wicked ways.

She smiled seductively, then leaned in and whispered: "Jim, I want you all night." She turned and strutted away like a runway model, smiling over her shoulder. "Was that *bad?*" she said in a kittenish voice.

"No . . . that was good," I shouted.

"I'll be right back. Don't go anywhere."

John looked at me. "What the *hell* was that?"

"You don't wanna know."

"Fucking Jim Asher, playboy extraordinaire! *Unbelievable.*"

I couldn't believe it either. I was going to sleep with Rachel tonight. It had been my dream since I first saw her. It could not have been better if someone had come up to me and said: "I'll give you a million dollars by midnight." Rachel was everything I wanted. Everything else about the night became absolutely unimportant. Every second between now and when I got her back to my suite was just the clock ticking.

I told the college girls to beat it. The limo driver said he hadn't had time to get beer. So John, Renee, and I ran up to the bar and ordered eight Coors Lights each. We did a shot of tequila for good measure. The night was beginning to blur and bend around me entrancingly. I told myself not to drink too much, for obvious reasons. We ran down the lobby stairs. My hands and suit pockets were stuffed full of beer bottles. I dove into the limo. Rachel and the girls were already inside fiddling with the stereo.

I shouted to the driver, "Let's hit it, old sport!"

The girls had invited an older guy to come with us. He was sitting in the forward seat near the driver's partition. I recognized him immediately: Dale

Spencer's campaign chairman, William Hamilton. He was a rich businessman and a former state Republican Party chairman. I didn't think I liked him.

One of the girls introduced us. "Jim Asher, this is William Hamilton."

I nodded.

"Thanks for inviting me, Jim," he said. "Those conventions are full of pretentious bastards. It's nice to get out and party with some good company."

Now I liked him. I tossed him a beer from my pocket. One of the blonds was hanging all over him. At sixtysomething, this guy was soaking up her attention like the Mojave eats August rain. Let the old guy have fun, I told myself. Meanwhile John was already hooking up with the redhead girl, kissing her while his hand crept successfully up her thigh.

Rachel slid across the leather seat and snuggled up to me. Her hand slipped under my coat and up my back. "I've wanted you ever since I saw you, Jim," she whispered.

"Me too. Well, I didn't want me, I wanted—"

"Shhh." She grabbed my belt. "Let's just have fun, then we'll be bad later."

I cranked up my nigga Tupac on the stereo and stood up through the open sunroof. The wind was pushing cold against me, brisk and fast, as the roadside blurred. Suddenly it felt as if my whole life had been leading up to this very moment. And I was unsure about it all. "Is this who I am now?" I mumbled to myself. I looked down at the long car, at my expensive suit, at Rachel's hand on my slacks. "I guess this is what you wanted. This is what it's all about, right?" I gazed up at the stars. "This is life, Jim. This is your life, man—the way you wanted it." I told myself I should get used to getting the things I wanted. I was now the master of my own reality. I was at the top of a mountain, and it was time to breathe in deep. I felt satisfied, but something else, too. Even as I tipped my beer up and grinned at the scene below me in the limo, something impossible to discern yet seemingly imperative to my well-being was nagging at my subconscious . . .

The moment passed. We partied all the way into town. At some point along the way, I pulled out the governor's speech. The girls were impressed that I actually had it with me. I took out my editing pen. We came up with some clever lines, which actually made it into the final speech. The governor's toupee would have blasted clear off his head if he had seen us. We were hammered and laughing at the top of our lungs, but I didn't care. I felt absolutely untouchable. I could do anything.

We stopped at a popular dance club called Johnny Love's. The place was going off. Beautiful people everywhere. Girls were making out with girls, guys with guys. "Fucking San Francisco," John mumbled to me, smiling almost bashfully. But I wasn't paying attention. All I could think about was getting Rachel back to my suite. Just have a good time and play it cool, I told myself. If you act anxious, she'll notice. Think Alpha Male, Jim—supreme confidence. I decided to act like I was barely interested.

I danced with Renee for a few minutes. Rachel had a cold beer waiting for me when I got back. She pulled me aside.

"Don't you like me, Jim?" she asked.

"Yeah, sure."

She kissed me with her mouth open, her tongue tracing my lips. "That's to get you ready for tonight."

I felt high, like I could wave my hand and anything I wanted would happen. "Rachel, I'm gonna fuck you all night."

She smiled. "I know you are."

I prayed I could actually deliver on that statement. I found Renee by the bar.

"Looks like Rachel's all over you," Renee said.

"I know."

"Strange how she likes you all of a sudden, now that you have your new job and everything."

"I know, Renee. Just let me enjoy it."

She shook her head.

The limo dropped us at the hotel at 2 AM. Rachel and I literally ran to my suite. She carried her high heels for speed. I slammed the door behind us and threw her onto my bed.

"Slow down," she said. "I'm not going anywhere."

I turned a lamp on. I wanted to see her. She stood up and kissed me. I ran my hands up and down her back, feeling her firm body. She turned around, pressing her back against me, and placed my hands on her perfect breasts. Her body tugged at me and drew me in. I kissed her neck while slipping her jacket off. She was wearing only a black lace bra under the coat. Slowly, Rachel bent over the bed and lifted her skirt up behind her. I reached down and unhooked her bra, luckily on the first attempt. She pulled her lace panties down around her knees.

"Do me slow at first," she said.

I flung off my jacket. She was so gorgeous, so perfect, the view of her back was so picturesque, it wouldn't have mattered how drunk I was—I had to make this happen. Then slowly, very slowly, I was inside her. My hands slid over the arch of her back, around her muscled sides, over her breasts, then I held her hips as I moved inside her. Ecstasy spread throughout me, making me close my eyes.

"Do me harder now," she said. She rested her face on the bed, lifting her hips and clawing at the comforter. Rachel's body was like an Ansel Adams photo, sloping, smooth, like nature offering its version of ultimate grace and beauty to my eyes. I ran my hands down her long hair, pulling gently. She liked it and arched her back. "Pull harder, Jim." I tugged. She pushed against me, then threw her head back with her mouth open, panting, moaning, driving me on. I flipped her over. She wrapped her legs around me, her feet sliding up and down my back. Her eyes closed and her face filled with rapture.

"You feel so good inside me," she said. "Jim, will you promise me something?"

"Sure."

"Promise me we'll do this again."

"I promise."

She used her hands to stop my motion. "Jim, you like to play rough, don't you?"

"Rough?"

"Have you ever done . . . bondage?"

That word *bondage* set me back for a moment. "I'm not into being tied up, if that's what you're asking."

"No, silly. I want *you* to tie *me* up. Sometimes it's the only way I can get off."

"Oh, sure."

She pulled off one of her black thigh-high stockings and handed it to me. She flipped onto her stomach and crossed her wrists behind her back. It seemed a little weird, but I was always up for something new. I used the stockings to tie her hands together. Then I bent her over the pillow. She cried out, she loved it, especially when I pushed her face into the mattress. I turned her around and lifted her off the bed, making love to her standing up. Her arms dangled behind her back, my arms under her legs holding her up.

"Fuck me hard," she said.

I slammed her against the wall, hitting a light switch and knocking a painting off the wall. It shattered on the floor. I went fucking crazy. Her back slid up and down the wallpaper. "Oh, Jim, don't stop. Fuck me. Oh my *God!*"

My body shuddered.

"Come on my stomach, Jim." I set her down on the bed, pinning her hands under her back. "Jim, are you gonna come? Please come on my stomach—I wanna feel it."

I looked at Rachel—I was having everything I thought I ever wanted from this life. Or was it having me?

Afterward, I rested my head on Rachel's soft breasts, lying still for a few minutes. With my eyes closed, only the sound of her heart assured me she wasn't just a dream. I kissed her forehead, then her lips. I couldn't be so close to her without being drawn in. I rolled her onto her side and made love to her again, for a long time. After the third time, we were both completely exhausted, sprawled out on the bed with slick bodies and breathing hard. I have never been so utterly depleted or content in my life.

"Jim, you're so wonderful," Rachel said. "You're so right for me." She wrapped herself around me like we had been lovers for years. After a few minutes I grabbed a beer from the fridge and walked out onto the thirty-story balcony naked. I didn't care who saw. I heard Rachel climb into bed. I was glad she was staying the night. I sat in the chair and sipped my brew, gazing down at the twinkling city lights. I couldn't really believe any of it. My life had taken on a life of its own. I started wondering where the boundaries were. I kept going faster and faster, yet nothing was there to slow me down. Then something more unsettling occurred to me: I wondered if I would ever want to stop?

TWENTY-FOUR

The phone woke me. My head was throbbing, and my eyes were puffy slits. I reached across Rachel for the phone.

"Asher!" an angry voice said. "Where the fuck have you been?"

"Who the fuck is this?"

"Bob Slater, governor's chief of staff."

"Oh . . . sorry, sir." Shit, I had forgotten about the speech! "Um, I've been working all night on the speech."

"The governor was looking for you last night. We heard you went downtown, drinking."

"No. I was working at the business center."

"The fucking business center closed at six o'clock yesterday, Asher. We checked. Why the fuck are you lying to me? The governor is going crazy over this speech. Andy Murphy from *Newsweek* is covering it. That fucking speech better be done, and it better be good."

"Uh . . . I'm just putting the finishing touches on it."

"The governor wants to see what you've got, right now."

"Um . . ."

"That means now!"

"I've just gotta print it up real quick."

He slammed the phone down.

Rachel rolled over and whispered in a dreamy voice, "Make love to me again, Jim."

"Rachel, I'm really sorry, but get out. I'm totally fucked. I forgot about the governor's fuckin' speech."

"What?"

"I have to write a twenty-minute speech in three minutes, right now."

"Jesus Christ, Jim."

"Look, I don't have time. I'll see you tonight, okay."

She started rounding up her clothes, pouting.

I went to get my laptop. But it wasn't on my desk. It wasn't on the floor. Then I remembered—"Oh, shit. It's at the bar!" I threw on a T-shirt and boxers and ran to the elevator, leaving Rachel in the room. A minute later the elevator still hadn't come. "Fuck!" I ran down the stairwell. The lobby was already bustling with hundreds of Republican delegates all decked out in campaign shirts, hats, and buttons. I jogged past the front desk as casually as possible, given my appearance. I spotted the governor having breakfast at the restaurant. I did a quick about-face and ran the long way around to the bar. I interrupted the bartender: "I left a laptop here last night. I need it right now."

He looked at me like I was disturbing him, then took his time searching behind the bar. "I don't see any laptop back here," he said.

"It's under that blender right there. I saw the guy put it there last night."

"You can look if you want, pal."

I leaned over the bar, my feet dangling in the air. The laptop was gone.

"You might check the lost and found," he said. "But they don't open until nine."

The governor's speech *started* at nine. "Fuck."

Everyone at the bar was watching me panic. Then I remembered the backup floppy disk. It was in my coat. I sprinted back upstairs. When I got to my door, I almost collapsed. I forgot my damn card-key! Rachel was gone. The door was locked. I ran down the empty carpeted hallways until I finally saw a maid's cart. I rushed in the room. She was scrubbing the sink.

"Hello, I need to get in my room. Can you let me in, please?"

"Oh . . . No unda-stand."

"Fuck . . . My room. Can you let me into my room."

She shrugged.

I pointed to her keys. "My *casa*. I need to get in my *casa*." Clearly, I didn't speak Spanish. "I need something out of my casa."

"Open door?"

"*Sí* . . . Yes, please . . . *Gracias*."

I've never seen anyone walk as slow as this maid. Her stubby little legs only covered five inches per step. I wanted to throw her over my shoulder and dash down the hallway. The governor was going to kill me. My reputation would be ruined. I was feeling guilty and panicked because my lifestyle had never affected my work this directly before. The damn speech wasn't even close to being finished. And I was severely hungover. My stomach felt queasy. After what seemed like twenty minutes we got to my door. I ran in and rifled through my coat, throwing things everywhere. I found the disk, and the printed speech, which was scribbled with our late-night limousine edits. But I didn't have a computer. Every second felt like five minutes. My pulse pounded through my head. The business center! I could use the computer there, if it was free. I threw on jeans and sandals. No time for hygiene. My phone rang. Probably

Slater calling to ask where the speech was. I grabbed my card-key and a stack of policy journals and sprinted downstairs.

An old lady was using the only PC in the business center.

"Would you mind if I used this real quick?" I asked her.

"I'm trying to finish this luncheon flier," she said.

"This is very important. I have to print the governor's speech," I pleaded. I was prepared to kung-fu her old ass out of the chair.

She looked me over skeptically. "The governor, eh? Well, I suppose . . . as long as you're quick, young man." She saved her stupid flier and stood up, hovering right behind me as I sat down. I grabbed a *National Review* from my stack of magazines. The main point of the speech was supposed to be property rights. I had two pages done; I needed six more. As I worked, I kept picturing the governor and his staff panicking, wondering where I was. The *National Review* was a year old, but the entire magazine was dedicated to property-rights issues. Perfect. I started borrowing good lines and phrases, trying to mix them up and paraphrase. The old lady watched me the whole time with her arms crossed.

I typed frantically for ten minutes. The speech was full of mistakes. I had lifted phrases and sentences before—every political writer does to some extent, because there are only so many clever things that can be said in this universe— but normally I was careful to change the sentences and words around by at least 30 percent, the unofficial rule. I didn't have time for that now.

I didn't notice Bob Slater until he tapped on my shoulder.

"Is this damn thing done yet?" he asked. "The governor wants to see it right this second."

"Almost," I said. "Just three more minutes. I'm finishing the last paragraph."

"Let's go. The governor's pulling his hair out." He sat down in the lobby where he could see me.

My shaky fingers blazed across the keyboard. For some reason, my brain kicked into high gear. I banged out the seventh page. Now I needed a good ending—something uplifting. The last paragraph of a speech is the most important because the audience takes it with them. With Slater watching me anxiously, I tore through all the magazines until I found a great quote by Winston Churchill. I typed in the entire paragraph. It fit into the speech perfectly. I tried to change the paragraph around so it wouldn't be recognizable—plagiarism can destroy a writing career faster than anything else. But it was an obscure quote from a letter Churchill had written long after the war, and the phrases were so perfect I couldn't find a single word I wanted to change—

like trying to edit the Gettysburg Address. I left the passage basically word for word and ran the spellcheck. I felt bad, but who other than me sat around reading Churchill letters from four decades ago? I would never do it again, I swore to myself. Slater snatched the pages one at a time as they rolled off the printer. I saved the speech and handed him the floppy disk.

"Is it good?" he asked.

"I think so. Maybe a few typos."

"Damn it, Asher." He looked me over, shaking his head. "You're a damn wreck. You can't see the governor like this. Go get cleaned up. He wants you there for the speech. Why, I have no idea."

"Yes, sir. Is he mad at me?"

"Furious."

———————

I needed a jump start, so I took a shower that was cold enough to shrivel a polar bear's nuts. Refreshed, I threw on a suit and went down to watch the speech. Dozens of reporters were gathered on the press stage, and an audience of hundreds sat in neat rows of folding chairs. I grabbed a tall Bloody Mary and started spinning. As usual, the governor's people had passed out copies of his speech to reporters. Of course, this time it made me very nervous. Sal Puchman, who had been a senior consultant at the Winston campaign, was the bright center of spin on the press stage. Dozens of reporters circled him, writing down all his witticisms. But I was now the number two guy. Reporters were getting to know my name. It's hard to say when the spotlight first caught a piece of me, but somewhere along the way I had moved out from behind the curtain. I knew all the best information, the latest gossip. I talked at least six hours a day on the phone, and I knew almost everything in California politics—I was in the middle of most of it.

A reporter named Jean from the *Orange County Register* wanted comments on Edward's campaign.

"It's going great," I told her. "Spencer is on the run."

"On the run? From what?" she asked.

"Well, from his shameful record, of course. When he was a congressman, Dale Spencer voted for no less than two hundred and twenty tax increases. And now he claims he'll cut taxes in an election year? Go figure."

She scribbled it down. "Great, Jim. By the way, I got a funny quote from Frank Buckman earlier this morning. I'm going to use it in this piece. Do you want a chance to respond?"

"Sure. What's the line?"

"Well, Buckman says he was at a function with Edward and Mariella last month. Basically, he's saying that Edward is a puppet for Mariella's ambitions. Here's Buckman's line: 'It is not entirely clear to me whether Edward can speak while Mariella is drinking water.'"

Damn. That *was* a good line. I actually laughed. But now I had to step up. Battling someone in print is the ultimate test of a spin doctor's skills. This was my chance to school Buckman. I thought as quickly as I could. Puppet? No. Maybe a fat joke? No. Water? Drinking? Drinking! That was it. I remembered something Renee had told me.

"Doesn't Buckman have like two driving-under-the-influence convictions?" I asked the reporter.

"I think so."

"Okay. Here's the quote: 'I find it curious, considering his shameful driving record, that Mr. Buckman is making jokes about drinking.'"

The reporter smiled. "Are you sure you want to say that?"

"Print it."

"Okay. Thanks, Jim."

"I'll see you at Edward's party tonight?"

"I'll be there," she said.

I could hardly wait to see the quote in the paper the next morning.

Slater stood beside me as the governor took the podium for his speech. It would be the first time a politician read my words from an electronic TelePrompTer.

"Thank you," the governor said. The crowd was alive, electric. "The founders of this nation started with a simple precept—a set of philosophical values set forth with simple elegance in the Declaration of Independence and the Constitution . . ."

I usually lip-synched along with my speeches, but I didn't know this one. I told myself I needed to quit drinking. I really should stop partying so hard. Sometimes it seemed to free my spirit and unlock my creativity—it tore down the inhibitions that blocked me, but now alcohol was beginning to stalk me from a closer, less comfortable distance.

"The speech is a little dry," Slater said.

"I know. I'm really sorry. I think I need to focus harder on my work."

"I should say so."

When the governor got to the Robin Hood part, a buzz spread through the crowd.

"*That's* very good," Slater said.

"The governor can use it for his other stuff if he wants to," I offered.

Slater nodded.

The Churchill quote silenced the room, and when it was over I heard a reporter say: "That was pretty good. Who wrote this one?" Nobody noticed the plagiarized words. The governor was all smiles and handshakes coming down into the audience. The angel was still on my shoulder.

———————

That afternoon I picked up Edward at the airport. I could have used the gold card to rent a car, but I still had the limo. Shnurg, the tobacco PR man, had left me a voice mail saying I could use it all weekend. Who was I to argue?

Edward was in a good mood coming off the plane.

"Hello, Jim," he said. "How is the convention coming along?"

"It's busy," I said. "Lots of political maneuvering."

"Are we all set for the speech and the party?"

"Locked and cocked," I said. "I've got your speech in the car."

"Great. Let's go. Oh, by the way, my daughter made this for you."

He handed me a crayon drawing from his leather satchel. It was a picture of a grotesque-looking stick figure with my name scribbled under it. There were hearts and stars around me and the words I MISS YOU, JIMMY across the top.

"What a hatchet job," I said. "I've got three arms here!"

Edward chuckled. "Cynthia really likes you, Jim. She says she's going to marry you when she grows up."

"Wow—does that mean I'll get all your money, Edward?"

"If you don't spend it all first."

We went downstairs, picked up Edward's luggage, and climbed into the limo.

"Jim, I notice you're looking a little rough around the edges," Edward said as we pulled away from the curb.

"I was up late writing the governor's speech," I said—which was true, in a way.

"I hope you didn't give him any of my good lines."

"Never. You're always *numero uno*, Edward."

TWENTY-FIVE

For weeks Edward and I had been talking about throwing an event at this convention. We needed to impress the Republican Party and win them over. We thought about a yacht outing on the Bay, but Edward said it was "too much." Eventually I talked him into throwing a real party at the hotel's nightclub, the Bohemian Room. I arranged to rent the entire place for the night. The Bohemian was more than just a hotel bar—it attracted clubbers from all around San Francisco. I spent the afternoon getting things ready. I told Rachel to move her stuff into my room; I didn't want her to disappear. She helped me recruit some college volunteers to pass out party fliers. I was terrified that the bar would be empty and Edward would look stupid. When he first came to power, Adolf Hitler would rent tiny rooms for his meetings. If he expected two hundred people to show up, he would rent a hall that accommodated one hundred. It was always better to be overcrowded than the other way around.

In planning the event, I had another trick in mind. Rachel informed me that Dale Spencer was holding a party at exactly the same time on Saturday night. Spencer's soiree had a Hawaiian theme, complete with leis, roast pig, and an Elvis impersonator. How lame.

At eight o'clock the Bohemian Room started filling up with Republicans. Edward was going to make his grand entrance at nine, so I had to get the place packed before then. The bar had printed up a thousand FREE DRINK tickets, which I passed out at the door. But by eight-thirty, the bar was only half full.

I found John Griggs talking to Rachel.

"Hey, where is everyone?" I asked them. "Edward is coming down in half an hour and the place is empty. He's gonna kill me!"

"Everyone's over at Spencer's Hawaiian party," John said. "He's giving out two free drinks."

"Yeah, I'm supposed to be over there with Frank right now," Rachel said.

"Forget that."

"Jim, he *is* my boss."

"Just hold on a sec. I'll be right back."

I stormed off and found the bar manager in his office.

"Hey, is there any way to get more people in here?" I asked him.

"Not really. I mean, you rented the place. We're turning away our regular customers at the door."

"Screw that. Let 'em in. Let everyone in. Hey, do you have any more of those free drink tickets?"

He grinned. "We happened to have printed two thousand extra, just in case."

"Fork 'em over," I commanded.

Ten minutes later I had an army of beautiful coeds passing out thousands of free drink tickets at Spencer's party. By nine, the Bohemian was overflowing and Spencer's stupid Hawaiian party was deserted. Eventually Spencer and Buckman even showed up at our party. I gave Spencer a handful of drink tickets as a show of good sportsmanship. Brett and Francis had a fat stack of tickets themselves, and were clearly enjoying the party. Everyone was looking for me, asking for more tickets. I felt like the God of cocktails. Some college guy asked me for tickets while I was talking to Rachel.

"Gimme ten push-ups, sport," I told him. "One ticket per push-up."

The wretched bastard dropped down and knocked out fifty! I was having a blast.

When Edward finally walked into the bar he was all smiles.

"This is marvelous," he said. "Great idea, Jim. But isn't this rock-and-roll band a little too loud?"

"Not at all—people love it, Edward."

"Okay. I guess they seem to be enjoying themselves, and that is the idea."

A few minutes later, Brett got up on the stage and stopped the band. He took the microphone from the lead singer. "Hello," his voice boomed through the club. "Everyone gather around, please." Most of the crowd moved onto the dance floor around the stage. When the speaker spoke, people listened. "Is this a party, or is this a party!" Brett shouted. The crowd roared. "Let's bring up the man responsible for all the fun, the next governor of California, Edward Winston!"

John Griggs started chanting: "Winston! Winston!" The crowd soon joined in.

Edward was beaming as he climbed onstage. "Thank you, Mr. Speaker." With all the cheering I could hardly hear him. Spencer and Buckman were sulking in the corner, trying to ignore the hoopla by talking amongst themselves. Spencer's new campaign manager, Ron Latter, looked pissed when I caught his eye. Apparently Rachel had dumped him only a week before.

"Is everyone enjoying themselves?" Edward asked. Hands flew up and cheers roared out. "Well, you'll enjoy this even more: I'm opening up the bar for the rest of the night. All the drinks are on me!"

The place went berserk.

"I didn't know he was going to do that," I shouted above the roar to Rachel. "He *can* think for himself, Jim," she said.

Dressed in a pinstriped designer suit, with thousand-dollar Italian dress shoes and platinum cuff links, Edward looked somewhat silly standing next to the grimy, drugged-out band members, but the crowd was loving him. "I won't take up too much of your time," he continued. "I expect to see all of you in the months ahead as we gear up to win the governor's race. Along with Speaker Alexander, we're going to change California. We're going to take back the Golden State from all these misguided liberals. And, if I'm elected, I promise no taxes, no speeding tickets, and, for good measure, no more homework!"

The crowd erupted. Edward *did* have his moments. Brett and Edward held their hands aloft in triumph. The band kicked in. The walls shook. Everyone was shouting and dancing, balloons dropping from the ceiling.

A minute later, Ron Latter stormed up to me.

"Hi, Rachel," he said.

She played him cold. "Ron."

"Asher, I wanna talk to you."

"Well, how about a formal introduction first," I said. "I'm Jim Ahser."

"Forget that shit."

I told Rachel to give me a minute, then I pulled Latter aside.

"You better watch how the fuck you talk to me, pal," I said.

"That was a fucked-up stunt you pulled on us," he said. "That Hawaiian party cost a lot of money to throw, and the Elvis guy—"

"Fuck Elvis! Listen, pal, if you can't stand the heat—"

"That was the lowest—"

"If you think tonight was bad, wait till we start airing our attack ads on your new boss. Then you'll see *real* humiliation. We're gonna trash Spencer with millions of dollars' worth of TV ads. Edward's already buying up huge blocks of commercial airtime around the primary. You tell Spencer to grab onto the handrails; we're about to take him for a fucking ride. By the time we're finished, Dale Spencer is gonna look like the slimiest, dirtiest, most incompetent politician who ever slithered his way through this state. When it's all over, he'll be lucky if he's not in jail."

"Yeah right—he's the fucking attorney general."

"Well, then maybe he'll have to arrest himself."

"Fuck you, Jim Asher. This shit's gonna catch up to you one day. I only hope I'm around to spit on you when you fall." He turned and walked away.

Sore loser, I thought. I found Brett near the dance floor. As usual he was surrounded by hangers-on.

"Thanks, Brett. That was great," I said.

"Hey, it's the least I could do for Edward."

"He appreciates it. By the way, we're going into town tonight. Wanna come?"

"I don't know. Is my speech finished?"

"You've got it, right?"

"Yeah. But I haven't read it yet. Is it good?"

"I think so. I put a lot of Reagan quotes in it."

"Good. I love Reagan quotes. They always get the crowd pumped."

"So, you're going with us then?"

"Yeah, okay. I might as well see how you single guys live. But my speech is at noon, so we can't stay out too late."

"What's the problem, old man, can't keep up?"

"You never knew me in my college days. At Stanford they used to call me Banzai Brett."

"Okay, Banzai Brett. We'll see about that."

He grinned.

Rachel couldn't believe it when I told her. "We're going out partying with the speaker of the assembly?" she asked.

"Yup."

"Who else is going?"

"We can't bring too many people, otherwise Brett will feel uncomfortable. Why don't you invite Natalie." Natalie was her attractive blond friend who worked as a freelance lobbyist. She had also just modeled in a big ad campaign for Mossimo.

"Jim, Brett is like our boss," Rachel said. "I mean, he's our boss's boss."

"Will Nat go?"

"What do you think? Of course she'll go."

We found Natalie talking to some older guy near the bar. Rachel whispered in her ear. The bar was getting ready to close.

"I'll be right back," I told the girls. I found the manager and asked how much Edward owed for the night. After some frantic calculations, he handed me the bill.

"Damn!" I said. "Eleven thousand dollars. What a bunch of alcoholics!"

Edward was sitting at a table talking to a reporter. I was almost embarrassed by the huge tab.

"Here's the bill," I said, handing it to him.

He glanced at the slip. "Okay, just use the gold card."

"Just like that?"

"Why not? There's no limit on that card."

"Oh. Well, okay. I'm taking off, Edward. I have some work to do with Brett."

"Have fun. And by the way, great party, Jim."

"Thanks."

"I'll see you at my suite tomorrow morning to go over my speech."

"I'll be there."

I felt strange giving the bar manager the gold card. But a minute later he handed me a receipt. The $11,000 didn't even register on Edward's face. It was less than pocket change to him. During the Senate campaign I had once seen him write a four-million-dollar check for advertising like he was buying a home stereo. But it never seemed normal to me, no matter how many times I saw it. With mischief in my heart, I looked at the gold card. I could use it to buy a private jet and a desert island, then take off and live like a retired pirate with Rachel. But then Edward would send Bill Crutchman after me. I put the card back in my wallet.

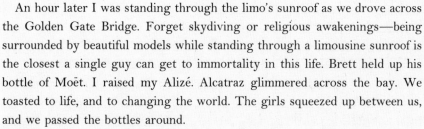

An hour later I was standing through the limo's sunroof as we drove across the Golden Gate Bridge. Forget skydiving or religious awakenings—being surrounded by beautiful models while standing through a limousine sunroof is the closest a single guy can get to immortality in this life. Brett held up his bottle of Moët. I raised my Alizé. Alcatraz glimmered across the bay. We toasted to life, and to changing the world. The girls squeezed up between us, and we passed the bottles around.

"Here's to the greatest speaker this state's ever seen," I declared.

"And to his Machiavellian speechwriter," Brett said, slapping my shoulder.

The girls were loving it. I could see it in their faces. I ducked into the car and turned up Notorious BIG full blast on the stereo. With a fresh bottle of champagne, I rejoined the party. The driver had instructions to "cruise all night"—no destination. Natalie grabbed Brett's hands, and they danced waist high in the chilly night air. Natalie's long hair blew in Brett's face, so they turned around. Rachel started kissing my neck, then my mouth. The stereo was thumping. I boogied to Biggie. Rachel's skirt came up and my hands glided over her G-string.

Brett looked down, then up at me, as if to say, *What the hell am I doing here?*

"Let's get loose, Banzai Brett!" I shouted. I threw my empty bottle from the car and it shattered on the Golden Gate.

"Banzai Brett?" Natalie said.

"An old college name," he said.

"I like that," Natalie said. "I'm getting cold, Mr. Speaker."

They ducked into the car. Rachel started to follow, but I grabbed her arm.

"Jim, he's married. I know his wife. I baby-sit his son, for Christ's sake."

"He's not gonna do anything. Shit, he's the speaker of the assembly. She'll be fine."

I went to kiss her, but she stopped me. "I just hope Natalie doesn't get hurt."

Oh shit—here we go, I thought. "What does that mean?"

"It means that she likes him, obviously."

"Well, we're just having fun here. He *is* married."

"Jim, try to think of how she feels for a minute. That's the speaker of the assembly down there."

"Brett's a good guy. Listen, let's stop talking and do what we came to do."

I took a swig and we kissed with wet, dry champagne mouths. I was becoming comfortable with this new conservative bohemian existence. Another day, another crazy shining night. After ten minutes the wind started getting chilly and I started getting drunk. When I ducked into the warm car, Natalie was on top of Brett with her blouse around her waist. From my angle, her breasts looked large and full on the sides.

I started to go back up through the sunroof, but Brett shouted: "Jim—pass me a brew from the cooler."

When I finally saw his face, Brett looked aroused, but uncomfortable—out of his element. I tossed him a Coors. Natalie leaned in against his chest, running her fingers through his hair, ignoring me and Rachel. After a few long seconds Brett pulled back. I could tell he was trying to have a good time without doing anything to feel *really* guilty about. I was a little concerned; we were all plastered at this point. Maybe I was putting him into a situation he didn't want to be in? Of course, he was responsible for his own actions. We were all walking a thin line of morality here. But we knew what we were doing. I turned off the cabin lights.

TWENTY-SIX

Brett woke me up at four in the morning, poking my shoulder. Rachel and I were on my couch. Brett and Natalie had crashed in the bedroom of my suite.

"I've gotta' get out of here," Brett whispered with a trace of hysteria in his voice.

"Huh? . . . What's going on?" I asked, still basically asleep.

Brett fumbled around my desk in the darkness. "Where's my planner? . . . Damn, I think I lost my schedule . . ." As my eyes slowly adjusted to the dim city light coming in through the window, I could start to make out Brett. His hair was going in every direction, his shirt was half buttoned and untucked. When I thought of him standing so prestigiously every day in his suit at the assembly speaker's podium, I couldn't help but chuckle to myself. Everyone in this world is a damn faker!

"Ah, geez, where did that schedule go . . ."

"It's probably in the limo," I whispered, trying not to wake Rachel. "Don't worry, I'll get it for you later. You've got the speech at ten."

"But I might have something before then."

I was still a little punchy, so it was really hard to hold back the giggles. "You'll be okay. Here, put this on so you won't be recognized." I tossed him a crumpled baseball cap from my suitcase. I was trying desperately to stifle the laughter.

Brett put the cap on and knelt down next to me. "These girls will keep quiet, right?" he said.

"Of course. They know the drill."

Brett shook his head, sighing. "I don't know how you keep up this pace, Jim. Okay, nine o'clock sharp for breakfast."

"You got it, boss."

He stumbled across the room, smacking his knee on a chair. "*Aww . . . damn!*" He was still buzzed. When Brett opened the door, light rushed in around his silhouette. He looked up and down the hallway—all clear. With the baseball cap on slightly sideways, like a rapper, and his shirt still untucked, shoelaces dangling, Brett looked comical. I prayed he wouldn't run into anyone we knew on the way to his room.

Rachel and I moved into my bedroom and slept on the bed with Nat—all three of us naked, me in the middle. Pure bliss. I got up at six and wrote for a few hours, downing two pots of java. At eight o'clock I ordered breakfast for the young ladies and took an arctic shower. I had two speeches to worry about today. Somehow I had pulled the governor's speech out of my ass, but I knew I had to work hard for the rest of the day. Having fun was one thing, but if I didn't work hard I knew all of it would go away. The limos, the gadgets, the girls—they all would disappear if I didn't have my job.

———————

I talked Brett through his speech at breakfast. He didn't have time to keep up with every issue every day. I did. I followed all the policy journals, read the latest books. Mariella had been coaching me on how to take Brett national. She told me to pick one issue and hammer at it relentlessly in the national media. I chose welfare because I thought it was the most misguided and destructive government policy. I read every article and book I could find on the subject. I visited welfare offices and interviewed administrators. I even drove to South Central and pounded forty-ouncers on the curb with some cool but frustrated recipients; by the end of the day I was playing street football with my shirt off and very much enjoying my little "policy research field trip." But I did take the work seriously; it provided me an intellectual outlet. Mariella introduced me to the country's foremost welfare experts—Marvin Olasky, Robert Rector, and Eloise Anderson. I took part in national reform seminars and discussion groups. Soon I began to formulate my own theories and solutions. I wrote editorials on restructuring the entire welfare system—some of which were published under Brett's name in prestigious national journals and newspapers. I wanted Brett to be the nation's foremost welfare reformer—a hero for working Americans, and a liberator of those trapped in the despair of government dependency. Sometimes it was difficult keeping Brett up to speed with what he was supposedly writing. Several times Brett got caught on a television show debating his "theories" without having any idea what they were. I always apologized when that happened, but Brett would say, "It's my fault, I should be paying more attention to my articles."

I knew Brett's welfare speech would get the convention crowd's blood pumping. And it did. All the applause lines hit like laser-guided missiles. The biggest cheers came when Brett said: "Let's put all these welfare recipients back to work. No more free apartments. No more free money. No more sitting around watching talk shows and playing Nintendo. Federal welfare has stolen our citizens' dignity and robbed them of their work ethic. It's time we treated adults like human beings with souls rather than mindless children. No work, no money!"

I had to talk him into the Nintendo line, so I was glad when it worked.

After Edward gave his speech, my work at the convention was done. Brett was the most popular politician in the state. Edward had broadsided Spencer— humiliated him—and stolen the momentum in the governor's race. Political momentum is not something you can put your hands on, but when you've got it, you know it. Things were progressing according to plan. I spent the rest of the day in my suite making love to Rachel.

TWENTY-SEVEN

The legislature was out of session and I had the week off—my first vacation in nearly two years. I was at home in Huntington Beach when Samantha called with big news. She and Rick were getting married. They were buying a $6 million mansion in Bel Air, and they wanted me to come to their housewarming party.

"I'll be there," I said.

"Listen, Boo-Boo, this doesn't mean we can't be together."

"I'm happy for you. You know I like Rick."

"I'll see you Saturday."

I *was* happy for Samantha. She needed some stability in her life. I was surprised she had survived this long. She partied all night and worked like an animal all day—every day. I would go out with her until four in the morning, only to see her chasing some corrupt politician early the next morning on television. I had no idea how she did it. But she was getting older. I didn't want her to grow old alone. I certainly wouldn't be around by then.

I picked up Rachel at her apartment in Corona Del Mar, where she lived with two other hot girls. We drove to my favorite haunt, the Newport Sea Landing. From our table on the outside terrace we had a perfect view of all the blue and green lights shimmering around the white yachts on the harbor. I ordered two Papa Dobles, a tropical daiquiri invented by Ernest Hemingway. The Sea Landing was the only restaurant in California that served real Papas, with the original El Floridita recipe from Cuba.

Rachel sipped hers. "This is too strong," she said.

"Hemingway liked 'em strong."

"I'm not Hemingway, Jim."

I ordered the most expensive cabernet on the list. The bottle was $160. But money was only filler in my wallet. I was making far more than I needed. I hadn't cashed a state paycheck in weeks—they were piling up in my desk drawer in Sacramento.

"You know, Rachel, I used to scrape money just to buy fast food two years ago."

She nodded and mumbled a completely empty, "Wow."

"When I was a kid, I got three dollars a week allowance," I said. "My neighborhood buddies all got the same amount; I think our parents must have worked out a price-fixing agreement or something. Anyway, we would get our allowances on Fridays, then we would throw our suggestions on how to spend the money in a hat. Someone would pick a suggestion, and that's how we spent the three bucks—usually at the movies or McDonald's. It was a huge, involved production how we spent those three dollars. Now I spend money like it's nothing. I don't even think about dropping three hundred on dinner when I could cook something at home for a few bucks."

"That's the way life goes. You get older, you get richer," she said.

"Yeah, but not for everyone. A lot of people don't even give a damn about money, like they're happier without it."

"Whatever wets their whistle, but personally, I think people should achieve things in their lives. I want to have a big house and a good-looking husband and maybe kids. I never want to turn into one of these average suburban-incarcerated slam hound wives. I think people should set goals."

"For some people, happiness is its own goal."

"That's what I'm saying."

I drank my Papa and ordered another.

"Jim, you should really let me take you out shopping. We can hit Guess, Calvin Klein, Armani, Versace. You need to spruce up that wardrobe of yours. You're a player now."

"I dress pretty good."

"I'm not saying that. I'd just like to go out shopping with my boyfriend."

"Boyfriend?"

"You heard me, *buddy*."

I smiled. "Can we use your dad's credit card?"

"What?"

"For the shopping."

"*Jim!* You're rich. You're like twenty times richer than me."

"But I'm not richer than your dad. Besides, I'm saving to buy a new car soon."

"Really . . . like what?"

"Like maybe a Ferrari."

"Jim, are you retarded? Brett would totally kill you if you pulled up to the office in a Ferrari. He already gives you shit about that Hummer. Imagine a Ferrari."

"It's my money. Brett can't tell me how to spend my own paycheck."

"Okay, we'll see about that. Why don't you get a Porsche? A convertible."

"I've always wanted a Ferrari since I can remember."

"Well . . . then get a Ferrari. I'll ride around with you. We'll be the perfect glamorous Republican couple. Maybe we could even get into the celebrity photo section of *George*. Did I ever tell you how happy I am with you?"

"I'm happy too."

"Jim, are you going to do things to me tonight?"

"Very bad things."

"Goodie," she giggled.

"Hey, I was meaning to ask you. What has Buckman said about you dating me? Isn't he pissed?"

"Well, I haven't exactly told him yet. I mean, he knows we're friends." She was quiet for a minute, picking at her oysters and occasionally glancing up at me. "Um, Jim, I've been meaning to tell you something. But I'm a little embarrassed."

"What? You can tell me anything."

"Well, I guess you'll find out sooner or later. I was just afraid to tell you before because you're, like, Mr. Conservative-head speechwriter man and all that think-tank stuff . . ."

"What is it?"

"I'm into girls."

"Say again?"

"I like girls."

"Oh."

"Are you mad at me?"

"Um, no. Actually, I was expecting something different, that's all."

"I don't know. I have this friend who works as a cocktail waitress at Cowboy Boogie. Oh my God, Jim, she is *so* beautiful. Long, tan legs—she has like the perfect body."

"So you're sleeping with her?"

"I haven't since we started seeing each other."

I nodded.

"I just thought you should know."

"It doesn't bother me. So how'd you get into that?"

"I'm not even sure. It's not like I woke up and all of a sudden I wanted to be with a girl. I guess when I was in high school I thought my best friend was really pretty."

"So you slept with her?"

"No. But I thought about it."

"Who knows about this?"

"Not very many people."

"You've gotta be careful, Rachel, with your job and everything."

"I know. People are weird. They're so fake, especially people in this party. What does it matter to them, you know? You should've seen my dad when he found out . . . *oh my God.*"

"You told your dad?"

"I didn't actually *tell* him."

"What . . . he caught you in the act?"

"Kind of."

I had to hear this.

"It happened when I was in high school . . . he found a vibrator under my bed."

"A vibrator doesn't prove anything."

"Yeah, but he also found a *Penthouse* magazine right next to the vibrator."

"Oh . . ."

"He totally *freaked.*"

"I guess so. Did he yell at you?"

"No. He didn't know what to say. He didn't talk to me for like six days."

"Wow."

"So it doesn't bother you, Jim, really?"

"Not at all."

"Good. I'm so relieved. Maybe you can meet Jill."

"Jill?"

"My girlfriend at Cowboy Boogie."

"Sure." Visions of three breakfast trays danced wondrously before my eyes.

"Her husband, Ted, has been trying to get Jill to bring me into their bed."

"Absolutely not," I said.

"I don't want to."

"No way."

"Do you wanna meet Jill tonight? I think she's working till two."

"Cowboy Boogie is in Anaheim, right?"

She nodded, sipping her wine.

"What are we sitting around here for?" I whipped out my wallet. "Waiter, check please!"

TWENTY-EIGHT

The next morning I ordered out for breakfast. "Bring it on three separate trays," I told the delivery guy at the restaurant. Jill looked lovely with her head cuddled on Rachel's tan breasts. I didn't wake them; I just wanted to stare at them all day. The phone rang. I took it on the balcony.

"Jim Asher."

"Jim, it's Greg, from the *Times*."

"Hey, what's up."

"Got some bad news, buddy. You might not want to hear this."

I swallowed. "Go ahead."

"Our reporter in Sacramento, Dave Spetzer, called me this morning, asked if I knew you."

"Shit, is this about the Buckman thing?"

"No—thank God. Something about the governor plagiarizing Churchill . . . ?"

A rock swelled in my throat.

"He says you wrote the governor's speech for the GOP convention; is that right?"

"Uh . . . yeah."

"Well, apparently, someone in the crowd—some old retired guy—recognized a quote in the speech. Dave checked it out, and he says it's a straight rip-off."

"So what's he gonna do?"

"I guess he's writing a feature story. I shouldn't even be telling you this. You could get in big trouble over something like this, Jim. Remember what happened to Joe Biden over plagiarizing."

"Has Spetzer talked to the governor's people yet?"

"I don't know. Maybe."

I had to think fast. I started talking even before the lie was fully formed in my head: "Well, Spetzer's got it all wrong. That quote at the end of the speech *was* Churchill; the governor just skipped over a line that credited Churchill."

"What?"

"Well, I put a line in right before the quote: 'As Winston Churchill once said . . .' But the governor skipped over it. That's all."

"Jim, Spetzer's got the text of the speech."

Oh fuck. Now panic set in. "Oh, I know . . . I know what must have happened. I must have forgotten to save that line before I gave it to the governor's people. They printed the speech from that disk. It's just a misunderstanding."

"I suggest you call him right away in that case."

"What kinda guy is Spetzer? I don't know him."

"He's a reporter. He's gonna go after this if he smells a story."

"Can you talk to him?"

"Not really. And he can't know I talked to you. But he *is* friends with Samantha; they went to school together at UCLA."

"Okay. Thanks, Greg. I owe you, man."

"No problem."

I called Samantha.

"Boo-Boo. How's my little gigolo man?"

"Not good." I explained the situation.

"Well, Jim. I don't know what to say. Reporters cover stories. I doubt Dave's gonna drop this just because I ask him to."

"Can you at least try? I'm totally fucked here, Samantha."

"You can't let this kind of shit happen, Jimmy. You've gotta separate the partying from the work. I've been doing it for twenty years."

"I know, but I'm not as good as you are yet."

"Okay . . . So you're lying about this line that the governor supposedly skipped over, right?"

"Right. I claimed I added the line just before I printed the speech, but didn't save it on the disk, which was used to print copies for reporters."

"Okay. It seems to me there's only one way to handle it: you have to make sure the original copy isn't around anymore, the one you printed for the governor before saving the speech to the disk."

"Right. That's the only proof. All the other copies were printed from the disk."

"Do you have someone in the governor's office? Someone who could find out what happened to the original?"

Thank God for Renee, again. "Yeah, I do. I have someone close to the governor."

"Call whoever it is, then call me back."

"Thanks, Samantha."

"You need to take better care of yourself, Boo-Boo."

"I know."

I called Renee.

"Babe, what's shaking?"

"Hey, Renee, I need a favor. But it's gotta be quiet."

"I know all your secrets, Jim."

"Yeah right. Anyway, you remember that speech I wrote for the governor?"

"Sure."

"What happened to it?"

"He liked it."

"No. What happened to the actual speech he read from, the text?"

"Oh . . . I think he keeps them in a file somewhere."

"The originals?"

"Yeah, the ones with ink marks all over them, right?"

"Exactly. Can you get the original copy of my speech?"

"Get?"

"Steal. Destroy."

"What's going on, Jim?"

"I can't go into it. I made a mistake. And now I'm gonna get fucked if I don't destroy that copy."

"Jim, maybe you need to slow down a little. I'll see what I can do, okay. I think I saw the folder last night in the press office. But you realize I could get fired for this."

"I know. I owe you. Anything you want."

"How about a night of sex . . . a long night?"

"You got it."

"Two nights of sex." Now her voice was playful. "Plus, I want you to do me in that Hummer of yours, on the freeway."

"Done."

"I'm so bad."

"I'm worse."

I hung up feeling better. Renee always followed through. That's why she was the best fund-raiser in the state. If the speech was still around, she would find it. I sat on the balcony with the lower part of my legs drenched in the warm sun. Right as I was lapsing into a dreamy half-sleep stage, I got an unexpected call from Washington.

"So how's my blond-haired California boy-wonderful?" Winter said.

"Pretty good. I miss you, Win."

"I've got some big news on this presidential race. Guess who just got hired as Stan Williams's chief consultant?"

"Who?"

"The one and only Bud Raper, your mentor."

"Shit. That's awesome! Is it for sure?"

"For sure."

"I love this life. I love you, Winter! Can I marry you—pretty please?"

"Stop it, Jim. So you know what this means, right?"

"I *do* know what this means."

"Okay, you need to fly out here pronto. I'll set you up with everyone. Maybe you can hop a lift on one of Freddie's Gulfstreams . . ."

Just then Rachel walked out in a nightgown. I smiled and kept talking.

"Thanks, Win. I'll call you tonight and let you know. I can't wait to tell Brett about this."

"Bye, bye."

When I hung up, Rachel asked who I was talking to. She looked upset when I said it was Winter.

"You're both models. Maybe you'd like each other," I suggested.

"She's stuck-up, Jim. She thinks she's *all that* because she wrote for Bush and went to Princeton."

"She's actually very nice."

"To *you* she's very nice."

"Look, you know how I feel about you. How many guys can say they have a smart, successful girlfriend who's also amazingly beautiful. You're an elegant dream floating before my eyes, Rachel."

"You're so *sweet*."

"Don't ever use that word," I said, grinning. "I've gotta get going. I have a big day with Brett."

"What're you naughty boys up to today?"

"Jet skiing. One of my buddies who's a lobbyist with Yamaha set us up with wave-runners for the day."

"You guys are so bad."

"We're just havin' fun. We never make promises about legislation, ever."

"Let's do it again before you go, Jim." She kissed me and rubbed my zipper. "Jill really liked you last night. Can we do it again?"

"How can I say no to two lovely girls like you."

"Can we videotape it again?" she asked.

"You're really into this taping thing, huh?"

"I don't know . . . it just totally turns me on."

TWENTY-NINE

I was thinking about the Churchill mess the whole drive to Brett's house. But there was nothing I could do until I heard from Renee. I hated waiting for anything. All I could do was put it out of my mind.

Brett Jr. was playing street football in the late morning sun with his neighborhood buddies. I played quarterback for his side while his dad finished up some phone calls. I told the boys stories about playing desert football during the Gulf War.

"We used to play at night, before the ground war started," I told them.

"But how did you see the ball if it was dark?" one of them asked.

"We wore night-vision goggles. We all had our own pair, and each one cost eight thousand dollars."

A chorus of "wows!" rose from the boys. I love talking to kids. For the short duration of their attention span they are infinitely interested in what you have to say, especially if it's about blowing people up, or anything else along those lines.

Brett walked out wearing swim trunks and a T-shirt.

"Damn—you better work on tanning those legs!" I joked, putting on my sunglasses. The boys roared with laughter.

"Hey, punk, some of us have real jobs, remember?" He held his right leg out, modeling it. "I'm not *that* white."

"Yes, Mr. Speaker. You're really tan—tanner than a Spaniard. Let's get going. We're gonna be late."

"You're driving. Do you know how to get there?"

"Dana Point, right?"

"Come to think of it, why don't I drive. I've never driven a Humvee before."

"Sure." I tossed him my keys. "Now, be careful. This is a real man's car."

"I've been driving since you were finger painting, chump."

Brett sat in the driver's seat. I had to show him where the emergency brake was.

"This thing's a beast, Jimbo. What kind of gas mileage you get?"

"It's disgraceful. Something like eight miles a gallon."

He stomped the gas pedal, and the engine shook the vehicle. The boys jumped up and down and waved as we drove off.

"This is cool," he said. "You'll have to loan me this thing sometime. I'd love to take the family camping in this sucker."

"Sure. You can buy it if you want. I'm getting something new."

"Like what? You just got this monster."

"I've been looking at sports cars. Maybe a Porsche, maybe a Ferrari."

Brett slowed the car and glared at me. "No way. No Porsche, and definitely no Ferrari. Are you trying to get us in trouble?"

"Just a thought."

"Get rid of it."

"All right." *Damn.*

"Hey, I've been wanting to talk to you about this situation with Natalie and Rachel," he said.

"Is she giving you problems or something?"

"Not really. But she has called the office a few times—the Sacramento office. She uses a fake name, but I think my secretary's getting suspicious."

"Tell her not to call."

"That's where I was hoping you might help. This is delicate, Jim. If she gets bent out of shape, she could be a huge liability. Know what I mean?"

"Yeah . . . I'll have Rachel straighten her out."

"Do you really think we can trust these girls?"

"Sure. I mean, why would Natalie want to be caught up in a scandal? Her career would be ruined too. We could just deny it, anyway. Nothing really happened. It's not like you nailed her."

"Still . . . if the press got a hold of the story—"

"Don't sweat it, boss."

Brett mashed down on the gas pedal. The Hummer hit seventy as we merged onto the 405. The day was perfect. My arm was dangling in the warm air. We listened to Bob Marley on the CD player, bobbing our heads and singing along. I was surprised that Brett knew the lyrics to "Redemption Song."

"What a glorious day," I said.

"This is what Southern California's all about," Brett declared. "You know, I grew up just south of the Oregon border, near Lake Shasta. I didn't move down here until my senior year of high school. What a difference. It was freezing up there. My first car was an old Plymouth I got from my grandpa. I used to take it out on the frozen lakes and do spinouts all day with my buddies. We would drink beer and drive as fast as we could, then crank the wheel. That sucker would slide for half a mile sometimes."

"Cool."

"Yeah, until it went through the ice one day. I didn't get a new car for two years. I had to bum rides off my buddies. My grandpa wanted to kill me."

"It still sounds fun."

"It was a blast, to tell the truth. But So Cal is my home now."

Just then, I noticed blue and red flashing lights in the side-view mirror. I looked at the speedometer. Brett was doing eighty.

"Shit, there's a cop behind us," I said.

"Damn! Just what I need." Brett pulled onto the shoulder. "Shit, where's my wallet?" he said. "I hope I brought it."

"You didn't bring your wallet?"

"I didn't think I was going to be driving."

The cop swaggered up and leaned in the open window. "License and registration."

I pulled the registration from the glove box. Brett dug through his gym bag in the backseat.

"Sorry, officer," he said. "It's hard to tell how fast you're going in this thing."

The cop's face was like stone.

"Um, I don't seem to have my license on me, officer," Brett said. "I do have a license, but I didn't bring it with me because—"

"What's your name and license number?" The cop took out his ticket book and pen.

"Um, I'm Brett Alexander, my license number is CA J3676221."

The cop's eyes moved up to Brett when he heard the name. "Just a moment." He strutted back to his patrol car.

"Think he knows who you are?" I asked.

"I don't know. He looked at me kinda strange. But I can't just bring it up myself."

"Bring it up. He'll probably let you go."

"I'm not gonna bring it up. That looks like I'm trying to throw my weight around. People don't like that."

"I would."

"That's why you're not the speaker, and I am."

After a few minutes, the cop walked back up to the car. "Do you know how fast you were going, Mr. Alexander?"

"Seventy?" Brett shrugged.

"More like eighty. I could cite you for reckless driving. That carries up to five days in prison."

"I'm really sorry. It'll never happen again, officer," Brett said.

"Well, just watch your speed from now on. This will be a warning, because I'm in a good mood."

"Thank you, officer. I'll be more careful in the future."

"Have a nice day. And by the way, you're doing a great job, Mr. Speaker." The cop flashed us a smile and strode away.

"Shit . . . that guy really had us going!" I said.

"Whew," exhaled Brett, shaking his head and smiling. "I always wondered what would happen if I got pulled over."

We both laughed. Brett pulled onto the freeway, very slowly.

My buddy Mark was waiting for us at the Dana Point harbor with a trailer full of new wave-runners. He gave us free hats and T-shirts, a box lunch in a waterproof bag, and said we could use the runners as long as we wanted. As he backed the trailer into the water, Brett and I changed into wet suits and climbed on. The water was warmer than I'd felt in years.

"We're getting a warm drift up from Mexico," Mark told us. "Have a blast, Mr. Speaker."

I pulled the top part of my wet suit down. The sun was warm on my chest and shoulders. We pulled into the harbor. As soon as we passed the five-mile-per-hour buoys, I gunned the throttle. A thick shaft of water shot out from behind the runner. I headed straight for nearby Doheney Beach. It was a weekday, so there weren't many surfers. I raced up behind a wave and dropped down its face just before it broke; then I pulled a sharp turn that sent a glorious spraying arc into the air.

Brett cruised up. "These things are a blast!" He was excited. "Watch this." He hit the gas and did a quick spin, blasting me with a wall of water. "Ha! This is great!"

"Hey, Brett, let's head out to that boat way out there," I said, pointing to a giant oil tanker anchored at sea.

"I don't know. That's pretty far."

"Come on." I hit the throttle and nailed Brett with a giant blast, knocking him off his runner. He climbed back on and followed me out to sea. Seagulls darted by, some landing in the water ahead of us. I tried to race them, but they were too fast, so I attempted to run them over instead. It took twenty minutes to reach the tanker, but what a glorious twenty minutes! The breeze pushed against me like the warm hand of God as we skipped over the choppy whitecaps at full speed.

The tanker was enormous, practically a city on water. A rusty anchor chain with links thicker than my waist stretched down into the water. I pulled up to the front of the ship. It towered over me like a floating skyscraper. The submerged hull was white and it made the otherwise dark blue water look clear and turquoise around it. Brett pulled up cautiously. His mouth was wide open as he gazed up.

"This thing is huge!"

"Let's ride around it," I said.

"Okay, but be careful. If this thing drifts, it'll crush us. Can you imagine the newspaper headlines on that!"

We cruised around the side of the ship slowly. Because of its shape we were actually under the ship's sides, in its shadows. When we got to the back we could see the giant propellers under us. They looked murky, eerie and dangerous, like they could easily chop us to bits. The ship's Filipino crew watched from the aft deck. They were hanging over the rails and eating sandwiches. Brett tried to pull some fancy tricks, but he wiped out and the Filipinos howled at him.

"Let's eat lunch," he said.

We cruised to the other side of the ship. With the engines off for the first time since we had set out, the sea was suddenly calm and tranquil. I ate my sandwich and enjoyed the serenity. The clear sun sparkled crisply off the water's surface, causing me to squint. I pulled a bottle of red wine from the dry box. I had forgotten to ask for a corkscrew, so I pushed the cork into the bottle and took a long swig. Brett started drifting away. I motored over to him and tied us together.

"Great idea," he said, eyeballing my wine.

I pulled out another bottle and tossed it to him.

"This is perfect," Brett said. He took a long swig and laid back on the seat. The cushions were made for three riders, so we had plenty of room to stretch out and enjoy the sun.

"This is truly heaven," I declared. I pulled off my wet suit and sprawled out in my swim trunks. The fresh sun made my legs tingle. I sipped my wine and tossed bread crumbs to the seagulls. At some point I drifted asleep.

I dreamed I was playing football with Brett Jr. and his friends on the White House lawn—spectators watching us from outside the iron gates, wishing they could play; the lawn perfectly groomed like a golf fairway; me making dazzling catches, then walking inside; the Marine guards all smiled when I told a joke, completely out of character, and after I took care of some business in my plush office, I went to the Lincoln Bedroom and jumped up and down on the bed with a young girl I did not recognize and we fell on the bed with old Abe looking down at us, then I covered his eyes with her pink bra and then . . . someone was calling my name, a shadowy dark figure—a reporter, wanting to know why the president had plagiarized Churchill, but I couldn't think of a good lie; I was caught this time, and I started to panic—I had to get out of the White House and talk to someone, but there was no way out, except the window, and then I heard the reporter coming toward me down the hall, and then . . .

"Hey, look how far we drifted," Brett said, waking me up.

We were a mile from the boat, farther out to sea.

"Shit," I said. "I just had the weirdest fucking dream." I let out a deep gust, incredibly relieved.

We finished off the wine.

"Hey, Brett, I've got some big news I've been waiting to tell you."

"Shoot."

"Guess who's handling the Stan Williams presidential campaign?"

"I dunno, who?"

"The illustrious Bud Raper."

"Really? Wow. That is good news. Is it confirmed?"

"It's all set. From what Winter Hallman tells me, he's already running the show."

"Fantastic. I think Bud likes me."

"I know he does. You know what this means, right?"

"The VP slot," Brett said with raised eyebrows.

"That's right. I think we've got a real shot at it."

"Well, hold on now. It's great that Bud's running the campaign and all, but I really don't think I have the credentials."

"Like Dan Quayle did!"

He smiled. "You've got a good point there. But at least Quayle was a senator."

"It doesn't matter. You've got a master's in economics, a bachelor's in international relations, and a law degree with an outstanding record as a prosecutor. You're the speaker of the California assembly—which is about the same or better than being a senator from Indiana. You're a nationwide leader on state's rights and the battle to reform welfare. Your numbers are higher than any other politician in California. And this state is crucial to any presidential candidate. Our fifty-four electoral votes are the key. Williams already has Texas locked up; he needs California. All we have to do is convince him and Bud that you can deliver this state. Plus, Williams is an old man—you could bring some youth and vitality to the ticket, Brett."

Brett stared at me. He looked out across the ocean, then up at the sky, pondering. "Do you really think so? I mean, do you *really* think so?"

"I really think so. We've got Winter and Bud pulling for you at the campaign, plus Mariella with her column. We've got a few other heavies who will carry water for you, Brett. The only question is: do you want it? Do you want to be vice president?"

"Who wouldn't?" he said. "Since I was a kid I've been dreaming about the White House. In fact, if you look in my sixth-grade yearbook, I wrote as my goal: 'President of the United States.' Of course, so did five other kids. But yes, the answer is yes. Might as well give it a shot."

"Yes!" I shouted. Only the birds could hear us. "Yes! We're gonna do it, Brett. I've been planning it for months. The fucking White House, baby!"

THIRTY

"Pass me a forty, *nigga.*"

John grabbed a Mickey's from the backseat of my Hummer, cracked the cap, and handed it to me.

"Man, I love the bass in this thing," he said.

I twisted the cap off, cranked up the stereo, and guzzled. Snoop Dogg blasted and thumped through my four twenty-inch woofers. We were cruising up PCH, bobbing our heads, me smoking a red dog and driving. John loved doing anything with an element of California exclusivity. Anything we could do in California that couldn't be done somewhere else is what he wanted to be doing. "You won't find 'em doing this back in DC," he loved to say.

"I hope there's some hotties at this party tonight," John said.

"There will be. I'm gonna go Alpha Male on these chicks tonight."

John laughed. "You're a dog." He lit a fat Cohiba. "So, how's the governor's race shaping up?"

"Good. I want to bring you on as issues director."

"I did that last time, on the Senate race."

"I don't know what to tell you, John. Edward wants me doing all the communications."

"Hmm."

I sipped the forty, flicking ashes out the window. I felt bad having to tell John he couldn't be press secretary. He really wanted the slot. It was also awkward because John had been my first boss in politics.

"I might be able to get you on as deputy campaign manager," I suggested. Edward really needed someone with field operations experience, but I had to tell John something.

"Deputy campaign manager sounds pretty good," he said.

We clanked forties. I switched the CD changer to the Geto Boys. I listened to the kind of music Republican politicians scorned for publicity. The woofers thumped through me, invigorating me, making me want to tip the forty up with each deep, rhythmic boom. I hung a right off Sunset and drove into Bel Air. Samantha had told me her new house was "gargantuan," but I didn't fully understand until I pulled up to the front gate. The house was solid white and bigger than five of her old houses put together. The corners were all rounded and everything sloped, ending with entire walls of glass. It looked like a giant spacecraft on the edge of a hill.

Rick met me at the door. "Jimbo! How's it hangin', playboy."

"This place is strong, Rick."

"Thanks. I've been looking at it for months. I was worried about the foundation because there was a mudslide here a few years ago, but I got a great price, and I've got insurance, so fuck it."

I wanted to ask how much, but I decided to wait until Rick was hammered— he would definitely tell me then. Samantha and Holly Martinez, a hot anchorwoman from one of the local affiliates, were cooking something in the kitchen.

"Jimmy, get over here and give me some hugs and kisses," Samantha said. She was in a good mood. "I'm making my famous Gellhorne meatballs. Go check out the house, Boo-Boo, it's unbelievable. We've got three bars!"

"Three bars! Just what you need, Samantha."

Samantha pulled me aside. Her face became serious, something I had never really seen. "I talked to Spetzer today," she whispered. "I told him about the missing line from the speech."

"What'd he say?"

"He said he was going to check it out. I guess he's going to call over to the governor's on Monday."

"I've got someone searching for the draft. I'm pretty sure she'll find it."

"Good. You've really gotta be more careful, babe." She kissed my cheek.

It was strange: no matter how I looked or sounded, Samantha never asked me how I was. She would ask what I was up to, or how things were going, never how I was doing, physically or mentally. I guess she assumed everyone was like her—invincible. I hugged Holly and performed the smooth European kiss. Her body was drawing stares in a short skirt and halter top, her tan stomach showing with visible muscles. I introduced John. He couldn't pull his eyes off Holly. I elbowed him.

"I'll show you guys around," Holly said. "Come on. You won't believe it." She led us through the huge living room. Besides a few scattered boxes, the place was pretty much moved into. We walked into a long atrium corridor made completely of glass—a hundred feet long. I looked up and saw the stars. At the end of the glass hallway we walked into a huge room. The far wall was also made completely of glass, looking down on a magnificent blue-lit swimming pool. A gigantic white couch sat in the center of the room, the biggest couch I'd ever seen. A dozen overstuffed chairs were casually placed around the room. Jukebox. Pool table. Projection TV. Ten-speaker stereo. A giant clay coffee table covered with flickering candles and bottles of wine sat in front of the couch.

"This is the party room," Holly said. "It's the centerpiece of the house, at least as far as Rick and Samantha are concerned."

"How many rooms?" John asked.

"Samantha doesn't even know. She thinks there's around twelve or thirteen."

John was flabbergasted. "She doesn't know how many rooms in her own house?"

"If you knew Samantha, it wouldn't surprise you," Holly said.

Rick walked in with two guys I didn't recognize.

"Hey, Jimbo. Can I recruit your Hummer for a little mission?"

"Sure, what?"

"I've gotta get some stuff from the old house. I figured, what the hell, I've got a bunch of guys here to help out, anyway."

"So that's the scam, eh?"

We drove to the old house and filled the Hummer with boxes. We drank beers as we went, so the round trip took almost two hours. By the time we got back, the party was straight going off. The long driveway was bumper to bumper with Mercedes, Jags, Ferraris. We unloaded the boxes and went inside to get loose. The surround-sound stereo shook the walls in the party room. Good-looking girls were everywhere. I perched myself behind the bar and talked to everyone. Rick and I did shots. He introduced me to some actor.

"So what have you done?" I asked the actor.

He gave me a strange look. "Lots of stuff."

"Like what? Anything I would've seen?"

"Well, geez. Yeah, I've done *Frasier, Hercules, Melrose Place,* lots of stuff."

"Cool."

He walked away.

"What's wrong with that guy?" I asked Rick.

"Actors are assholes. Don't sweat 'um."

"Whatever."

A girl walked up and introduced herself. She was a heavenly brunette, and her body was more than compelling.

"Samantha told me to hook up with you," she said nonchalantly.

I decided to go Alpha Male on her. "Is that right?" I said. "Well, I guess we better go upstairs and fuck then."

"Okay—you go upstairs and hold your breath." She stood on her toes and kissed me full on the mouth. Then she walked behind the bar and poured herself a straight vodka. Nothing shocked me at Samantha's anymore.

"What do you do?" I asked her.

"I'm a publicist."

"Any famous clients?"

She started counting on her fingers: "Let's see . . . Chevy Chase, Judd Nelson, Will Smith, Mario Van Peebles . . . need I go on?"

"Those guys are all tools."

"Tools?"

"You know, dorks. Especially that cocky asswipe Will Smith—I'll slap his ears straight if I ever see him."

She giggled nervously, not sure what the hell I was talking about.

"Listen, I've been looking for a woman like you all night," I said.

"Really?"

"Yeah, I need a publicist."

"You don't seem to have any discernible talents."

"All discernment will take place upstairs."

She scowled.

"Seriously, I'm trying to find a publicist for my friend."

"Depends on who your friend is."

"He's the speaker of the California assembly, Brett Alexander."

"Oh—I saw him on TV last weekend. Some political thing or whatever. He's *cute.*"

"I'll tell him you said so. Do you think you could do anything for him?"

She thought it over. "Maybe. I mean, it's not like he's the president or anything. But he *is* a babe. Here's my card. Call me Monday. The best thing to do is start with radio promos, then some cameos. Is he doing radio promos?"

"Not really. But we are doing tons of interviews. Every time Brett has a free minute I'm shoving a cellular in his face for talk radio."

"That's fine, but promos are better. You know: 'This is Brett Alexander, and you're counting down the top twenty hits with Casey Kasem.' That sort of thing."

"Sounds good to me."

"Well, I might be able to work up some buzz around him. Does he know how to act?"

"He's a fucking politician."

She laughed.

"Hey, what's your name?"

"Cindy. Cindy Johnson."

"Cindy, would you like to test out Samantha's new hot tub?"

"I barely know Samantha."

I turned to Rick. "Is it all right, man?"

"Of course," he said. "We'll probably all be out there by the end of the night." He handed me a six-pack of Pacificos from the refrigerator. "Don't kill yourself, sport."

I put my arm around Cindy and walked outside.

"I don't have a bathing suit," she said.

"No problemo. Samantha would probably kick you out if she saw you wearing one anyway." I moved my arm around her waist, assuming the sale. "By the way, you should know: Brett's probably going to be the vice presidential candidate."

"Really? Now you're talkin'."

I scooped her into my arms, threw her over my shoulder, lifted up her skirt, and spanked her playfully—she giggled. I carried her down the steps to the pool.

"Don't even think about it," she said.

I walked right up to the edge of the pool and dangled her over the water. "I don't know if Samantha heated this thing up yet or not."

She slapped my back. "I'll kill you. Not in my clothes!"

"You better take 'em off then."

"Put me down and I will. I promise."

"Are those expensive shoes you're wearing?"

"Yes, yes they are."

"Damn shame. Good thing mine aren't."

With Cindy over my shoulder, I leaped into the pool. When I splashed in, my heart froze. The freezing water pierced my brain. I shot onto the deck like a missile, leaving Cindy shrieking and splashing. She climbed out drenched and shaking. Her hair was matted, her makeup running.

"You asshole!"

"I hate it when my shoes slosh around," I said, kicking them off, then peeling off my shirt. "You better pray that Jacuzzi works."

She didn't have much of a choice. "I'm totally soaked. You are the most crass, arrogant, self-absorbed—"

"Hey, it works!" I turned on the bubbles in the Jacuzzi. "Are you finished, or do you wanna go back into the pool?"

"You are *such* a jerk." She started undressing. "Did you even think about towels?"

I grabbed a Pacifico and climbed into the Jacuzzi. The hot water sent shivers through my body and prickled my skin. "Ahh . . . this is heaven."

As soon as her clothes were off, Cindy eased into the water. Her breasts were perfect, with tan chiseled nipples. She straddled my leg. Her hand moved up my sides, over my stomach, across my chest.

"Man, you must work out all the time," she said. She squeezed my arm and kept squeezing, as if she had never felt an arm before. "How do you get like this?"

I pulled her against me and kissed her. She moved onto my lap and guided me inside her. *"Eeewhh,"* she moaned. "That feels so good." She wrapped her arms around my shoulders and started moving up and down, side to side, rotating her hips and kissing my neck. The water made her feel gritty, so I lifted her and sat on the cold concrete edge. The air was chilly, so we gripped each other close. We were in clear view of the party room, but that only made it more exhilarating.

"Don't come inside me," she whispered.

"Why not? Aren't you on the pill or whatever?"

"Of course I am. But I just get, well, I get nervous. I mean, I don't even know your name."

"It's Jim. And don't worry, I'm a Republican."

She leaned in and pressed her cheek against mine, gasping.

THIRTY-ONE

After the Jacuzzi I changed into some of Rick's clothes and rejoined the party. Cindy was acting weird, hanging out in the laundry room watching her clothes dry. I figured she felt guilty. No worries for me, though—I still had her card.

John Griggs was in filthy heaven hanging out in the crowded party room. He toasted me when I walked in.

"Jimbo, you're a porn star," he said. "Maybe we should call you Jimbone. We all watched that little scene in the Jacuzzi."

"How'd I look?"

"Shit—you think I was looking at *you?*"

"So, how do you like this place?"

"Killer, absolutely killer. My friends back in DC wouldn't believe it. I was just talking to Kevin Costner's agent."

"That's always the way it is when you hang around Samantha—one surreal scene after another."

"Dude, thanks for inviting me."

"Sure. What's it worth if you can't share it with friends. But you're doing good for yourself." I slapped his shoulder. "After two or three of these, you can just show up on your own."

"Cheers, brother! Here's to being amoral Republicans."

We clanked bottles. I lit a bone. "That's a joke."

"What?"

"Morality."

"Attention, everyone," John mock shouted. "Jim Asher says morality is dead . . . story at eleven."

"Actually, it was never alive."

"You better not let people hear you talk like that. Most politicians don't hire pagans as speechwriters."

"I don't care." I felt the rumblings of a philosophical storm coming on. "Morality is just a contrivance of genetic wisdom. It's a self-preservation mechanism of natural selection. What masquerades as 'morality' is nothing more than a trumped-up set of base instincts, like hunger or lust. In a collective sense, we feel good when we do 'moral' things because it increases our chances of survival as a species. If we felt good about killing each other in cold blood we'd all be dead pretty soon. So most of our genes are programmed to avoid things like incest and murder—things that would wipe us out. It's like religion. All religions follow a basic set of innate natural laws—don't kill, don't steal, do unto others, that sort of thing. The reason they've all been so similar, over all these thousands of years, is that human nature and the behavioral codes required to sustain it haven't changed. What passes for morality in this century is nothing more than an arbitrary stab in the shadows against our other, darker instincts, the ones we needed to hunt icy plains of Europe ten thousand years ago. That's what Nietzsche says."

"Nietzsche was a fucking nut."

"Name one genius who wasn't."

"True. But if you listen to yourself, Jim, you're saying morality *is* real. Just like hunger is real."

"Survival is real. Morality is deader than Moses. Religion has always been an elaborate, illusory framework, supposedly for self-preservation. Fuck religion." John broke into a grin when I said that. "Hey, listen, I don't feel a stitch of guilt for saying that. Fuck no! Why should I? Religion is a plague on humanity—it's the academy of our ignorance. Nothing has caused more destruction, death, and torture. Who do you think is going to set off the next nuclear bomb? I'll tell you who—some fuckin' Muslim fanatic nut who knows it's his *religious duty* to murder thousands of fellow human beings in cold blood just because they believe in a slightly different set of myths. You tell me how that can be good for our race!" I slammed my beer, feeling increasingly indignant. "Look. If some idiot wants to sit in the privacy of his own house or church and conjure up absurd fairy tales to help allay his fears of death, let him do it. But how dare he impose his fuckin' fables on me! I'm sick of it!"

"Hey, I agree. I don't get the whole religion thing either. I mean, how arrogant people are to believe that *their* version of God is the right one. Why should some white guy in Rhode Island be so sure that Christianity is right? If he was born in a different geographical region, he would probably be just as certain that Buddhism was the absolute cosmic truth. It's so damn arbitrary. If he was born in Africa he would be willing to lay down his life in the faith that crocodiles were gods, or whatever. It's all ridiculous."

"The thing that kills me is that all these people are duped into believing it. Shit, every president of the United States has been religious. In other words, a human being with the power to destroy every other human being on earth, a man with the ability to wipe out our entire existence, adheres to some ludicrous set of parables and myths, and makes his decisions based on them? That's fucking crazy!"

"I think Bush was truly into religion, but Clinton just pretends, to get votes."

"God, I hope so!" I grabbed another beer. "But you see, if religion is bunk, then what should I base my ethics on? Actually, the Bible contains the only universal ethic humanity requires: the Golden Rule. If you strip away all the bullshit, it comes down to treating others as you would want to be treated."

"Unless you're a sadomasochist, of course," John said, toasting.

"Good point. But you see, I shouldn't feel guilty when I sleep around. I'm not married to Rachel. We don't have kids because she's on the pill. When I'm married I'll be a good husband. When I have kids I'll be a good father. Those are my duties; and unlike most people, I understand why they're my duties. But until then, it doesn't matter. I've simply moved my own thinking ahead to keep pace with science."

"But what if Rachel found out? It's not 'right' to hurt people."

"She won't find out. See, I have my own version of 'morality.' It's called 'reality.' All human behavior, if you think long and hard about it, has its roots in self-interest. Because I understand reality going into the game, I'm actually a much better contributor to the human race. That's why I live for right here, right now—for the pleasure, the excitement, the love, the friendship, the fear, the rush, the challenge, the fuckin' thrill of discovery, man. I'm pursuing my own existence, chasing my own version of happiness, driving it, because existence, in all its glory and despair, is all I have, or will ever have."

John drank some beer. "So, dude, speaking of outsmarting nature, where'd you stash the rubber?" he asked.

"Whada'you mean?"

"The rubber. You did use a rubber on that publicist chick, right?"

"I don't use rubbers with chicks like that."

He shook his head. "You sound like a guy on an AIDS commercial—the suddenly aware guy who just found out he's got AIDS."

"You've been watching too much TV, John. The truth is, and you'll never hear this on TV, but good-looking, straight rich people don't use rubbers, man. We don't need 'um."

"What kind of theory is that?"

"The truth. I bet if you did a study, I'd be proven right."

"Maybe. By the way, remind me not to share beers with you anymore."

"Fuck you."

John smirked and walked over to the bar. I sat on the couch and drank my beer, watching all the conversations and exaggerated hand gestures. Sometimes I liked to sit back and just absorb. All night I had been trying not to think about the Churchill quote, but it lurked in my mind, and no amount of sex or drinking could run it out of me. I took out my phone and called voice mail. Renee's was the fourth message:

> "Babe, I've got some news about this speech thing. But I guess you'll have to call me to find out. Report to Renee's house tomorrow night at eight o'clock sharp for duty. You've got some business to take care of, Jim."

What a relief. Jim Asher, bailed out again. Everyone was always bailing me out. Winter once told me it was because I had "a lot of positive energy" and "supportive nature" around me. I wasn't sure about that. I liked to pretend it was the angel on my shoulder. All my friends and family knew about the angel. My whole life I'd been landing right in the middle of one radiant flash of human theatrics after another, usually coming out on wings. I had always sensed that something exceptional was definitely going on with me. If I did have an angel, she had certainly been with me during the worst night battles of the Gulf War.

Samantha walked up and sat on the back of the couch, letting herself topple over—her legs dangling over the backrest, her head on my thigh.

"Having fun, Jimmy?"

"Always." I poured some Crystal in her open mouth. "I'm off the hook on this speech thing."

"See—Samantha takes care of her Boo-Boo. Let's go upstairs. I have something to show you."

I had a pretty good idea what it was. Holding hands we walked up a spiral staircase. We got lost on the third floor. The place was like a carnival funhouse—you never knew where a hallway would lead. There were balconies, bathrooms, bedrooms, game rooms, sitting rooms.

"I think it's up these stairs," she said.

We walked up a dark staircase, searching around and giggling in the darkness. When we found the light switch, we were standing in a strange bedroom—round, with curved walls and a huge glass dome ceiling. The glass was slightly clouded, but I could still see the stars. In the center of the room was a perfectly round bed.

"Lay down on it," Samantha said enthusiastically.

I jumped on. She hit several switches on the wall, and the bed started rotating like a carousel.

"What the hell?" I rolled over and gazed at the glass canopy. My head was already spinning. I closed my eyes. I felt Samantha climb on as the bed slowed down slightly. "Where's Rick?" I asked.

"Passed out on the couch in the living room. He won't budge. I tried to get someone to carry him up to our room, but he just keeps shouting: 'I love this house, I love this fucking house!'"

"Fuckin' Rick," I said.

"See what I mean, though? He's always pulling this crap."

"I'm sorry. I don't mean to laugh." I rolled over and kissed her. Samantha pulled a joint from her shirt pocket and sparked it. We smoked it so fast the entire joint was an ember.

"Will you make me moan, Jimmy?"

The line had excited me the first time I heard it; now it sounded empty, almost pathetic. "Samantha, I would, but I just nailed some chick in the Jacuzzi."

"I know . . . I watched."

"Sorry."

"I guess you're just outgrowing old Samantha. I mean, I can't do much for you anymore."

"What're you talking about?"

"Now that you're going national with Brett, I'm not very useful to you. I'm just a lowly LA reporter."

"Why are you talking like this? Is something wrong?"

"I don't know, Jimmy. Everything's wrong. This house, it's just a show. My life's a fucking joke. I'm getting ready to marry an alcoholic who ruins people's lives for money. I spend my days dredging through the same old recycled scandals and corruption. After a few years, just the faces of the dirtbags change. And what do I have to show for it? . . . Five thousand hangovers and a numb heart. I don't have children, and now it's probably too late. Look how I treat my body." Thin tears trickled down her cheeks. I wiped them with my thumb as she spoke. "I don't know . . . I probably shouldn't be dumping all this on you, Jimmy. I'm sure you don't want to hear about it . . . I'm sorry . . . I guess you'll find out when you get to this point yourself. Nothing really changes, Boo-Boo, just the backdrops. Sometimes I feel like everything's pointless. We're just gliding through this life and none of it's real. See that wall over there? It's just dirt. Every cell in your body will be replaced by a new one within seven years. My doctor told me that. But the point is, we're not even real. Just fancy dirt, so why care about anything?"

"Samantha, you know better than that. We *are* real. Nothing is more real than we are. There's an entire universe of reality inside both of us. Look, I think about this shit a lot. We have to grab hold of our own existence and run with it, now. Grab everything that fills us. As long as it doesn't harm others. Politics happens to fill me up, and traveling, and reading, and making love. Life's about discovering and doing, trying to find your own meaning. And that's a glorious fucking thing! The best part is, the quest always doubles back on itself and becomes a three-dimensional universe without an end—your own truth, your own eternity." I puffed more Buddha. I was fascinating myself. "We don't need to fear death, Samantha, not at all; we only need to worship life. We don't have to lie to ourselves anymore, we don't need to cower in dark corners alone, slowly terrified of facing the unknown, paralyzed by our solitary anxieties over death. Fuck death! Death is dead—it can't stand up to the light, the pure bright shining white light of truth, Samantha! Listen, I've discovered something amazing, something that sent a chill up my spine when it struck me the other day. See, we're all baby universes, each of us is a singularity beginning and ending with our own consciousness, and the space-time of our existence wraps around into a sort of continuous loop—like a black hole, or the universe before and after the big bang . . . What happens outside of our personal universe is absolutely irrelevant, it has nothing to do with our existence, just like the space-time before the big bang, when the laws of physics completely broke down. Life creates our singular universe, and it ends with life—there is literally no time or space for death . . . Do you understand what I'm saying here, Samantha? *Do* you? We're all immortal. Every one of us is a self-contained, immortal universe; most people just don't know it yet."

Samantha took a long drag off the joint, her watery eyes focusing on the stars. "I guess I believe that," she said. "But most of the time I feel like I'm just grasping at thin air."

I dusted off the joint, totally keyed now. "I read something once that Hawking wrote: try to think of our lives from the sun's perspective," I said. "The sun won't run out of hydrogen for five billion years. That's a long time. When the sun looks down on us, our lives must look like tiny flashes on this planet: a speck of light appears, then flickers out in a breath. That's why we've got to cram everything into that speck. This is it. This right now is that speck."

Samantha let out a long, deep sigh. "Maybe we just think too much. I don't know. I miss having you around though, Jimmy."

"Look, about what you said earlier. I don't like you because you're useful to me, Samantha. I like you because you're smart and fun and we talk about things like this that I don't talk to other people about. And you're pretty."

She smiled and kissed me. After all those complicated thoughts and words, *pretty* was all she really needed.

"So how's the VP thing going?" she asked.

"Good, I guess. I'm trying to convince Brett that he's qualified. But I don't know. What do you think?"

"He's definitely qualified. The only question is whether he's positioned."

"He's only the speaker of the assembly."

"The speaker of the *California* assembly. Look at someone like Geraldine Ferraro—she was just a stupid congresswoman before Mondale picked her. California speaker is better than congresswoman."

"I never looked at it that way."

"You just need to concentrate on getting Brett lined up. You guys should be in DC every weekend. If you guys really want the VP slot, you can't think about anything else. You've got to live and breathe it, sleep with it, drive with it, eat it, fuck it." Samantha was like me. No matter how she was feeling, good or bad, she came alive when she talked politics. "California. That's your angle. You need to pump Brett up and show the boys in Washington he can carry this state."

"That's what we've been talking about." The whole room was spinning now, so I got up and turned the bed off, accidentally turning off the lights. "But how do we do that? How do we convince them Brett can carry the state?"

"Oh, that's easy. Here's what you do. First, you—"

I pounced on top of Samantha and kissed her. "I love you, Samantha. Have I ever told you that?"

"I love you, too." She ran her hands over my face gently. "Speaking of galaxies—you're the brightest part of mine. You make life fun for me again, Boo-Boo. I hope we'll always have each other."

"We will. Remember, we're immortal."

"Come on, take Rick's dumb shorts off and do scandalous things to me. Samantha needs her Jimmy tonight."

THIRTY-TWO

"I can't believe I let you talk me into this," Brett said.

"It's part of the package," I said. "A very important part."

"Jim, I like you better when you're sitting in your office writing speeches for me."

"Quit complaining," I said. "Let's go. Pick up the pace, Mr. Speaker."

Half-naked Rollerbladers whizzed by us. Brett eyed them with envy. We hadn't even hit the two-mile mark yet, but Brett was already huffing. He hated jogging. Especially on a hot day like this. But he had already lost ten pounds and was looking much better—his baby fat gone, his face more defined and masculine.

"Next, you're gonna want me to get plastic surgery," he gasped.

"Funny you should mention that."

He slowed down and gave me a dirty look.

"Just kidding," I said. "Let's go, get motivated, old sport!" Brett was really struggling. "Hey, Brett, we've gotta talk about this VP thing. I've got some ideas."

"Shoot."

"Winter tells me Williams is going to make his VP choice by the end of this month, only three weeks away."

"Damn. Why so quick?"

"No idea. But that means we have to move fast."

Brett was starting to suck wind. "Okay. Set up . . . a meeting with Raper."

"That's not a problem." I started jogging backward, causing Brett to frown. "I think we need to bring something to the table with us."

"Like what?" he asked.

"Polls. We need impressive poll numbers to show Bud. He doesn't fuck around, Brett, he goes by the numbers. That guy lives by electoral vote counts and demographics. We need hard numbers to convince him that you can carry the state and contribute to the ticket."

"Contribute what?"

"Young low-propensity voters and women. Winter thinks we might be able to convince Bud if we can show him solid numbers."

"My numbers . . . are good," he huffed.

"They need to be *great*. Williams is looking at governors and senators with huge name IDs."

"Tax-cut pledge? That's usually good . . . for a five-point spike."

"We need a fifteen-point spike, Brett. We need a TV ad campaign."

"Where do you . . . sit around . . . and dream this shit up? It's not even . . . election season."

"Who gives a fuck. You can run positive ads now—unanswered. How often can you do that?"

"You want to run . . . positive ads for me . . . now? And you think that . . . will pump up my numbers . . . and that will convince Raper . . . and Williams?"

"Exactly."

"You're crazy. People will think . . . we're totally nuts."

"Fuck 'em."

"I don't know. We've got no money . . . in the bank. Zero."

"I figure we need a ten-day ad barrage. That's about four hundred thousand dollars. Is there anywhere we can get that kinda dough?"

"I don't know."

"I don't know either," I said.

"Edward? Think he'd give it to us?"

"What's he got to gain? Edward only gives money when he gets something back, something tangible." Just then, something slammed into the back of my knees. My legs came out from under me and I flew backward onto my ass. Some clown on a skateboard was squirming underneath me.

"Sorry, bro," he said.

Brett looked down at me in great delight. "Serves you right, Mr. Fitness!"

I gave the skateboarder a dirty look and brushed the sand off myself. "So, are we on for these TV spots, Mr. Vice President?"

"Okay. But on two conditions."

"Anything," I said.

"First, we need to find the money."

"I'll call everyone I know."

"Yeah, I will too."

"What's the second condition?"

"No more jogging today."

Rachel was basically living at my apartment in Huntington now. She was on the phone when I walked in. My phone bill grew by six pages the first month she moved in. But I figured it was all part of the entire, beautiful package.

"I'll call you later." She hung up and smiled at me. "Jim, you're all sweaty. I like you like that."

She hugged me. I was really beginning to adore Rachel. Once I got past her airhead impersonation, her aloof manner, her nonchalant attitude, then her wary but caring temperament, all of her various self-conjured exoskeletons, Rachel was actually soft like a southern twilight, and smarter than most people believed. Rachel was often the victim of her own image building. Of course, the bisexual thing had surprised me, but it didn't cancel out the possibility I could marry her someday. Same with the bondage. I wondered why they didn't bother me? As usual, I went to science and philosophy books. My conclusion: I didn't mind her sleeping with girls because girls didn't pose a threat to my genetic line. Girls can't get girls pregnant. And the fact that she liked being tied up probably had to do with the glossed-over shift of modern societal roles—an instinctual but crude regression toward a state of nature. Rachel had no way of controlling such things. Sometimes I thought it was dangerous to base my life on science books. But they seemed right.

Rachel grabbed a towel and walked down to the beach. She knew I had work to do. My extra bedroom was a political lair. State maps with targeted districts marked in erasable ink covered my walls, next to posters of John Lennon, Errol Flynn, Hemingway, Eazy-E, Socrates, Jim Morrison, Twain, Camus, Darwin, Lincoln, Kerouac—strange denfellows. I sat down at my computer and pounded out Edward's column, then E-mailed it to the *Los Angeles Times*. With the column out of the way, I called Edward. I liked having something positive to report before hitting him up for cash. I tracked him down at the New York penthouse.

"Oh, hello, Jim," he answered. "How's everything? Am I governor yet?"

"Not yet, but we're on our way. I just finished your column."

"What's it on?"

"Community policing. There are some great new programs in Oakland, which I used as models in the column."

"Fantastic. Will you fax me a copy, please."

"Sure." I closed my eyes and got ready to pop the question. "Um, Edward. I was wondering—"

"You need money."

"Yes. We're trying to get Brett lined up for this VP slot."

"Mariella told me all about it. I think it's an excellent idea. I really like Brett."

"Well, the problem is, we need some money to run positive TV spots here in California, to pump up Brett's poll numbers so we have something to show Bud."

"That sounds like a good idea."

Yes! Whenever Edward said something was a good idea, I knew I was getting the dough.

"Thanks, Edward. We need about four hundred thousand."

"Look, Jim. I'm sorry, but I can't do it this time."

My face dropped. "Excuse me?"

"Not this time. That's my decision. We have a governor's race to worry about. Don't let yourself get too sidetracked. I hate to say it, goshdarnit, but the VP slot is just pie in the sky. Remember, Brett is only one part of *our* plan. I need you committed to the governor's race."

"I know. But it's only this one last time, Edward. Then I promise I'll focus like a laser on the governor's race."

"You have my decision."

A lump came to my throat. I knew he would never change his mind now. I had to control the damage. "No problem, Edward. We'll get the money somewhere else. So, like I was saying, the column runs Tuesday. I'll fax you a draft right now. Then next week you have the police officers' breakfast in LA. I'm working on the speech for that. It'll probably have a lot of this community policing stuff and . . ."

I was talking, but I hardly knew what was coming out. It was the first time Edward had ever turned me down for money. Initially it stung. Then when I hung up I felt hollow, like a kid sent to bed without dinner. But I had no right to expect the money. I walked into my bedroom and slouched over on my bed, face in my hands. I looked at the photograph of Edward and me on the wall. We were standing with Ronald Reagan in his Century City office. The Gipper had been dazed and confused that day, but it was still a magical moment for Edward and me. I told myself I shouldn't have asked for the money. Now Edward probably thought I was using him, like everyone else did. I felt terrible. In the grand scheme, this was only a slight setback, but somehow this rejection stripped away some of my personal momentum. And personal momentum is what I thrived on. I vowed I would never ask Edward for money again. Unless it directly benefited him.

I took a bath and thought things over. I was walking so many tightropes, a stumble was bound to happen. Concentrate, Jim. Remember what Samantha said about the vice presidential slot—live it, breathe it, eat it. I had to pull myself together and come up with another plan. But where could I get $400,000?

I called Brett with the bad news.

"Well, it was only a matter of time," he said. "I told you we can't always count on Edward's money. You're with me now. We'll figure it out. Don't run yourself ragged. It's Sunday—go spend some time with your family, Jim."

"You're right. Thanks, Brett."

I wallowed on my bed, trying to think. I needed advice. Normally I would have called Bud in Washington. But this time Bud was the target of my scheming. I couldn't ask him how to trick himself. I was on my own. All of a sudden things were looking more complicated. I had always loved being in the middle of everything. Bud, Winter, Brett, Edward, Mariella, Samantha—all these dynamic forces were interwoven through me in one way or another. Indeed, I was now the center of a powerful political cosmos. But sometimes the center can seem like the farthest, loneliest place—especially when the orbiting forces begin to diverge or collide. In a sense I was now racing against myself. And the stakes were raised all the way up.

THIRTY-THREE

I flew up to Sacramento Sunday night. When I got to my town house, I called Winter in Washington. She said she would try persuading her boss, Stan Williams, that Brett would be the best running mate for him. My job was to convince Bud. The presidential race was already up and running. A week before, Bud had appointed Brett as Williams's state chairman in California, which pissed off the governor because he was also angling for the VP slot. Every aspiring Republican in the nation was chomping at the same bit.

I was at the state capitol by sunrise; I was operating on DC time now. I spent the entire day dialing 202. I arranged a meeting with Bud for two weeks out, right before Williams would make his decision. That gave us fourteen days to get Brett lined up. I asked Renee if she knew where I could get $400,000. She laughed. "Every Republican in the state is rolling pennies, Jim."

That night, Brett and I went to a fund-raising dinner for the Statesmen Institute, my old think tank. It was black tie, so I bought a tux on my lunch break. I spent the entire dinner spinning reporters with VP buzz. I wanted newspapers to report that Brett was under serious consideration. "You didn't hear it from me," I would tell a reporter, "but we've been getting calls from the Williams campaign." Then I would pretend like I wasn't allowed to tell the rest, until, of course, they talked me into it. "Bud Raper's been feeling us out for the VP slot. But, listen, that's *way* off the record." It's a tricky game, starting a rumor, but two or three casual, well-placed comments to a columnist can usually get the mill churning.

A major tobacco company had sponsored the fund-raising event; they passed out free cigars at the end of the dinner. I grabbed a whole box.

Some guy walked up and shook my hand. "Jim Asher?"

"Yep."

"David Shnurg, remember me?"

How could I forget that name. "Right, the tobacco guy."

"That doesn't have a pleasant ring to it, but yeah. We're sponsoring this event tonight."

"Well, thanks for the stogies then." I showed him the box.

"I have a whole case in my rental car if you want them."

"That would be a gift. I can't accept gifts."

He grinned. "Like the limo?"

"Right."

David's eyes seemed different now, more focused and intent. "Morton's tomorrow night?" he asked.

"I'll talk to Brett."

"Great. Well, what are you guys up to tonight? I'm in town for a few days."

"I'm writing a speech on taxes," I said.

"That must be infinitely interesting work, speech writing."

"It's an infinite pain in the ass. Take this speech I'm writing, for example. What the fuck do I know about taxes? I go to H&R Block. And I'm supposed to write a groundbreaking speech on the future of state tax policies? What a joke."

"Well, you're probably learning a lot."

"That's true. I can tell you all about the state's water system. I can write a thesis on sanitation policy, or air quality management—shit like that."

David smiled. "What do you say to hitting Morton's tonight? I'm starving."

I thought about another long, dreary night at my keyboard. "Yeah, sure, why not. What the hell, I can write that speech tomorrow. Morton's it is!"

We found Brett. I introduced him to David. Ten minutes later we were at Morton's. Normally we ignored whoever was taking us to dinner and just talked freely amongst ourselves, but tonight we really couldn't talk about the VP stuff—it was too sensitive.

At some point, Brett said he recognized David.

"Yeah, probably from *60 Minutes*," David said. "I was on three weeks ago."

"That's right," Brett said. "That's where I know your face from."

"You were on *60 Minutes*?" I asked.

"It was a nightmare," he said, shifting into storytelling mode. "Mike Wallace hammered me about nicotine content. I'm not a medical doctor. It was worse than the Spanish Inquisition. Let me tell you, it's no fun representing the tobacco industry on *60 Minutes*."

Brett chuckled. "What did you expect?"

"Oh, I knew it was gonna be hell, but my firm gave me a two-hundred-thousand-dollar bonus to do the interview. I was only on camera for a few minutes, so it worked out to something like thirteen thousand dollars a second."

"Good work if you can find it," I said.

"Yeah, it is. But I had to go on national TV and claim cigarettes aren't addictive. To tell the truth, I felt like a snake oil salesman, only worse. I almost didn't do it."

At least David owned up to being a lying scoundrel. I despised people who claim to believe their own spin. A good spin doctor decides what he's willing to do, then separates his work from reality. There's nothing worse than a supposedly self-righteous spin doctor who tries to spin other spin doctors, because a real spin doctor can't be spun.

After dinner we walked back to Brett's office. David was noticeably impressed. Brett grabbed his shabby blue trench coat and a bottle of gin from his secret bar. "Let's go out on the deck," he said. Right outside his office door Brett had a colossal private balcony, twenty feet deep, more than a hundred feet long, lined with thick marble columns stretching all the way up to the dome. The lights of downtown Sacramento glimmered below. I loved sitting on that mighty balcony, recalling all of the times Brett and I had discussed the future while the city slept below us.

We pulled out stogies. Brett poured gin into three Styrofoam cups.

"We need to get some real glasses," I said. "These cups are a disgrace to the office."

"They're fine," Brett said.

"You guys do this a lot?" David asked.

"Once in a while," I said.

The air was cold enough to see your breath. I sipped the gin. It tasted like paint thinner. I never understood how people can enjoy sipping straight alcohol. I figured they were all faking it, like I was. But David was clearly enjoying himself.

"So, David," Brett said. "What's the pitch tonight?"

"Oh—thanks, I really didn't want to bring it up myself." David sat up in his chair and leaned forward, elbows on his knees. "We've got a bill drafted. It's pretty straightforward. Basically, it involves the Tobacco Taxpayer Initiative anticigarette campaign. We believe it's unfair for state money to be used against our industry."

"We've had antismoking ads for years," Brett said.

"True, but this initiative is different. Take their most recent TV ad. They have a fat, greedy tobacco executive plotting how to get kids hooked on cigarettes, laughing and counting stacks of money. Have you guys seen that one? It's outrageous."

"Okay, that one is a little harsh," Brett said, chuckling.

"They're all a little harsh," David said. "It's not fair to use taxpayer money to slander a particular industry. These ads go after the motives of the tobacco companies."

"You're going to sit here and tell me tobacco execs aren't ruthless, greedy, scheming sons of bitches?" Brett said.

"We both know they are. I'm not here to bullshit you, Mr. Speaker. I'm only saying that these ads are mean-spirited and they unfairly single out our industry."

"They're extremely popular with the public," Brett said. "And effective."

"That doesn't make them right."

Brett looked at me. I didn't know what to think.

"What does your bill do?" I asked.

"The language is very simple," David said. "It says that no state money can be used to specifically slander the tobacco industry. It doesn't affect smoking health-awareness campaigns, only ads that attack the industry."

"I don't know," Brett said. "The people of California voted for that initiative, and it's their tax money. Of course, it's ironic that we're out here smoking stogies and talking about this, but cigarettes are different. They're a public-health hazard. If any other product was found to carry the same health risks as cigarettes, it would be pulled off the shelves immediately. Smoking costs this state nearly three billion dollars in direct health-care expenditures every year. Now, if this was a libertarian society, and taxpayers weren't forced to cover one another's health costs, then I would take your side, David. Philosophically, you're in the right. But unfortunately, we don't live in a libertarian state . . ."

Everyone was quiet for a minute. I'd seen Brett turn down a thousand bills. What was one more? I sipped my gin fraudulently, trying to blow rings with cigar smoke.

"David, how much has your PAC given to Republican candidates in California this year?" Brett suddenly asked.

"Oh, I'd say at least four or five hundred thousand."

Brett took a casual swig of gin and said, "We need four right now. Can you do it?"

David sat back and puffed his cigar with narrowed eyes. "Probably. I guess we're due for a contribution."

I looked at Brett, aghast: *What are you doing?*

"When can we get the money?" Brett asked. "We're trying to put up some ads in a hurry."

"I'll have to bring it to my board and everything, but I imagine I could transfer the funds in a few days."

"Two days?"

"Sure," David said. "By the way, I'll send the bill draft to your office tomorrow. Just have your legislative guys look it over so it can go straight to committee."

"Look, I can cram it through committee after we scrub the language, and I can probably get it to a floor vote within a week or so, but it's going to take some serious arm twisting on the senate side. I'll have to cash in some favors I've been saving."

"No you won't," David said. "We've already got the senate locked up."

"You've got the senate?"

David nodded, confident and cool.

"What about the governor?"

"That'll be our problem, Mr. Speaker."

Brett leaned back in his chair, obviously surprised. Apparently David knew what the hell he was doing. He was claiming support in the Democrat-controlled senate, and implying that the governor was already greased too. Impressive, I thought. But then, tobacco companies had crates of ready cash.

"Well, shit, okay then," Brett said.

David finished his drink and said he had to go.

"Just knock on the CHP door to get out in the basement," Brett shouted to him on his way out.

Brett turned to me, clenching his fist in the air, bearing his teeth with a mock devilish grin. "*Yes!* Four hundred thousand dollars!"

"What the fuck was that, Brett?"

He filled his cup and took a conscience-dulling swig. "Don't start, Jim."

"You're goddamn right I'm gonna start!"

"You said it yourself—we need the money. We're trying to change the country. We can't do it from here. Jim, you want the White House as much as I do. It's just this one last time, okay?"

"That's what you said with the racetrack thing. Where's it gonna stop, Brett? We worked so hard to get you elected, then you sat out here tonight and pimped the authority of your office. The truth is, this won't stop, will it?"

"Don't act like a fucking crusader on me here. It doesn't work for you, Jim. This is just part of your selective morality. I don't have time for it."

"You're right, I'm not a crusader. And I don't have morals. I make my choices based on universal ethics. And this feels wrong, period. I don't ask much of you, Brett. But selling legislation for money is dead wrong. Don't you understand that?"

"Look, we can use the money, VP slot or no VP slot. We've got another election cycle coming up and—"

"If you pull this shit, I'm leaving."

"You won't leave."

"Fuck you."

"No, fuck you. You won't sit here in my office and talk to me like some fucking punk. I'm your fucking boss."

"No! My boss is like me. He's here for a reason. He's here to change things, like our welfare bill. Like this fucking crime bill we just passed, or prison reform. We have to have a reason why we're doing all this. People trust us. Think of the guys we went to high school with, or the guys in our neighborhoods. They're out in the world now, trying to raise families, trying to do the right thing. They trusted you when they voted for you, Brett. We're supposed to be on their side, man."

"Nothing really changes. You haven't been up here long enough to see it."

"That's the problem—you have."

"Maybe, but I've also been on the other side, too. I've seen everything, and that's exactly why I know that there's nothing I can do to change the rules now—I'm too far into the game. Look, I know how smart you are, Jim. Just relax and see what happens, okay."

"I'll tell you what. If you can convince me that you would have thought this tobacco bill up in your own head because you believe it's the right thing to do, then I'll support you. If not, you're just another disappointment in my life."

I left him sitting on the balcony alone, grabbed my laptop from his desk, and walked to the elevators. I could hardly see straight. My heart was fluttering. My legs wobbled. "What the fuck are you doing?" I mumbled to myself in the elevator. "You can't walk out on this now. You're just getting started." The elevator doors opened to the basement parking lot. My Lincoln was the only car in the building. I stopped in the doorway. The doors tried to close but bounced off me, then bounced off me again. The little safety chime began to ring, but my eyes were fixed on the concrete under my feet. I felt dizzy, paralyzed, confused.

"Fuck it."

I pushed the button for the third floor and walked back to Brett's office. He was still on the balcony, hunched over in his chair, the collar flipped up on his trench coat. I could only see the top of his hair. He drank a swig straight from the bottle—the picture of defeat.

"When are you gonna get a real coat?" I said.

"Please, sit down, Jim."

He passed me the bottle. We said nothing until it was finished and our eyes were watery.

"I'm sorry, man," he said. "Maybe I *have* been up here too long."

I lit a smoke.

"Sometimes I don't even know why I'm up here doing any of this," he said.

"Yes you do. It's for the same reasons you put your life and family at risk to prosecute murderers."

"Just this one last time," he said.

"Damn it, Brett. It's not right."

"Jesus . . . what the hell is right?"

"What feels right is right. That's it."

"But we can do so much that *is* right once we're set."

"We are set. Look around you."

"You just don't get it, Jim. You rode Edward's bank account to get here. I've been here for too many years in this damn building. You're just seeing a tiny sliver."

"You rode Edward's money, too. You wouldn't be here without it."

"Eventually I would have."

"And eventually you'll be in the White House. I knew that the first day we met. But you'll never make it if you keep up this mentality. You're above this petty money shit. You're destined for everything you want, Brett." I stood up and paced along the stone railing. "If you won't look at this from an ethical perspective, look at it from a legal one. We don't know this David guy. Shit, he could be FBI for all we know. Why risk everything?"

"Because I'll never get the VP slot without the numbers. You said it yourself. Look, I've been getting a lot of phone calls from Washington, Jim. I'm actually beginning to think this VP thing could happen."

"And I agree. But what's the power worth if we have to sell it to keep it? It's not even power anymore, it's something else."

"Jim, you only want power so you can bone these little hussies and drive a Ferrari and write my speeches on a five thousand-dollar laptop and—"

"That's right. That's a legitimate use of power. Why do you think all these fucking guys are in politics? The bottom line is sex, it's always sex, even in business or Hollywood or war. I won't apologize for my fucking nature."

"No. Power is its own thing. The women and the dinners and the fancy luxuries, they're all just symptoms of power."

"Whatever. I just know this tobacco thing is wrong."

"What about that shit you pulled on Buckman with that reporter?"

"What shit?"

"You know exactly what I'm talking about."

"No, I don't."

"Play stupid if you want. Buckman knows. It's not that hard to put two and two together, Jim. Do you think you're invisible? Buckman's seen you messing around with Samantha at conventions. And anyone who's been around politics as long as Buckman knows that Samantha Gellhorne is close friends with that Greg Michaelson guy from the *Times*. Buckman knows. A lot of people know, Jim."

I was stunned. How long had Brett known? I had been meaning to tell him about it at some point, but now I looked like a sneaky liar. I wondered who else knew? "Look, that was totally different from the tobacco money. Buckman brought it on himself. He cheated on his wife. I didn't break any laws."

"You conspired with two journalists to alter the outcome of a high-level state election. You might even be guilty of blackmail, Jim. You're just lucky Buckman can't go public, for obvious reasons. So don't bring the law into this."

Was he right? Had I broken the law? I had never taken the time to find out. I knew the phone call to Buckman was shady, but I didn't think it was illegal. Besides, Buckman was violating his duty of marriage. I had simply called him on it. I didn't know what to think now. I had to get off the subject.

"We can get the money from somewhere else," I said. "We don't need dirty tobacco money."

"Where?"

"Hell, I don't know. I'm drunk. We'll find it. We can borrow it."

"Banks don't lend money to politicians, ever."

"I realize that."

"We've got the money now. Let's move forward. I promise on my life this will be the last time. I promise."

"Shit, Brett."

"Come on, Jim. Stand with me on this."

"I don't know."

"I need you on my side. We're going all the way to the top. Me and you. Whada'you say, Jimbo?"

THIRTY-FOUR

I needed a damn drink. I had a few cans of Foster's in my office for late-night speech writing, but I really wanted to be at a bar. I walked through the empty capitol, my shoes squeaking on the marble floors, echoing off the walls, which were covered with historical paintings and glass-encased artifacts. I passed by the attorney general's office. The building was dim and quiet.

I walked across the street to the Hyatt and took the elevator to the sixteenth floor. The bar, Sid's, was busy for a Monday night, full of lobbyists and politicians doing their dishonorable deeds. The capitol dome was directly outside the window at eye level; it looked close enough to touch. I spotted an assemblyman I knew, Gordon Wolfe. He was short and wore cowboy boots with his suit. I liked Gordon because he was the only bachelor in the assembly. He was chairman of the Revenue and Tax Committee, a very powerful slot.

"Jim, what's up, man," he said.

"Nada."

"What's the speaker up to?"

"Just chillin' in his office. What's new with you?"

"Did you get my memo on the tax-cut bill?"

"Yeah. Haven't read it yet. I've been so busy."

"Hey, no problem. Do you think you could write an op-ed for the *Union-Tribune* when you get a chance? I can have my chief of staff send you all the materials."

"Sure. Just put a packet together—clips, statistics, rhetoric. Maybe I can write it next week. I've been running myself into the ground, Gordy. I'm drinking fifteen cups of fucking coffee a day, never sleeping. The only time I ever eat is at fund-raisers. Fuck, I can't even remember the last time I slept for more than four hours at one stretch."

"You're an animal, Jim."

"I don't know how long I can keep up this pace, though. Maybe six more months, I figure, then I've got to slow down."

"Just pace yourself."

"I can't. It seems like there's always something big going down."

"Well, at least you're still young. Wanna drink?"

"Sure." I pulled a recipe card out of my wallet. "Give this to the bartender."

"What's this?"

"It's called a Papa. Order me three, will ya'?"

"Three? Everything all right, Jim?"

"Yeah."

We sat down at the bar. I took off my jacket and pulled some slack on my tie. The bartender did a shitty job on the Papas, so I drank them rapid-fire.

"These are great," Gordon said.

I didn't feel like going into the drink's history. I ordered two more and fired up a smoke.

"So, who are you banging these days, Jimbo?"

"That chick you saw me with at the convention, Rachel."

"She's smokin'!" He slapped my shoulder. "She got any friends?"

"Yeah. I'll come up to Santa Barbara, and we can all go out."

"Perfect. I just bought a new convertible BMW. Women love those cars."

We toasted, to nothing. I saw a girl looking at me from across the oval bar.

"Who's that girl over there?" I pointed.

"Oh, her. She's a lobbyist. I think she works for Arco, or one of the oil companies."

"Hottie."

"Hell yeah she's hot. She was in my office a few weeks ago pushing this energy tax credit bill. Man, she walked in wearing a short skirt . . . her ass was literally hanging out of the thing."

"That's smart. If I had a lobbying firm, I'd hire nothing but hot babes in miniskirts."

"So go talk to her, man. You want me to introduce you?"

"Yeah. Go tell her I wanna fuck her."

He practically blushed. "I'm an assemblyman."

"Okay, then tell her I want to make love to her all night on the capitol lawn."

Gordon laughed with an unnatural tension in his face. He walked around the bar. I tried to look busy as he pitched the girl; I smoked my cigarette, played with my watch, then fiddled with my pager. I slammed my fourth Papa. I was starting to get that watery mouth and powerful warmth that rises from your stomach and rises to your head. I glanced up. Gordon had the girl smiling. Her arms were thin coming out of a black cocktail dress, and her lips were full, her bottom lip pouty. I ordered a shot of tequila to speed up the process.

The girl walked up and sat on the stool beside me. She had sexy peach fuzz sideburns like a Spanish girl and tiny gold Mayan sun earrings. Her skin was tan and glowing smooth.

"Gordon told me to introduce myself," she said.

I handed her a fresh Papa. "Wanna fuck?"

"Excuse me?"

"Do . . . you . . . want . . . to . . . fuck?"

I always knew Papas were cold—they sometimes gave me freezer-head when I drank them too fast—but I had never felt one on my face before. The frost slid down my neck and chest. I squinted and wiped the drink away from my eyes. A sharp slap rocked my head, and I fell backward off the bar stool and crashed to the floor, my head smacking the hard tile. I looked up and saw my shoes leaning against the stool. The girl poured what was left of her drink directly onto my crotch and stormed off. People on bar stools were looking down at me, shocked.

Gordon rushed up. "What happened?" He helped me up.

"Fuckin' bitch . . ." I shook my head, trying to collect myself. The whole bar was looking at me now. I hadn't noticed him before, but that fat bastard Frank Buckman was pointing from his crowded table, laughing. Some were amused, others were shaking their heads pitifully.

"What's that chick's problem?" I mumbled.

"What the hell did you say, Jimbo?" Gordon asked.

"Nothing. I didn't say shit."

"You must've said something."

"Forget it." I ordered a straight Hennessy.

"Hey, Jim, why don't you let me call you a cab? You don't look so good, buddy."

"I'm fine."

I grabbed my glass and walked to the bathroom. My eyebrow had a thin cut above it and blood was coagulating in a droplet. I slammed my Hennessy and pressed a damp paper towel on the cut. "Damn rings!" I cleaned the sticky mess off my clothes the best I could and went back to the bar, trying to look nonchalant. I would laugh it off.

"Your shirt's all blue," Gordon said. "You should probably head home, man."

"I'm fine. Bartender, 'nother Papa please!"

He looked at me twice before mixing the drink. "You want a Band-Aid, pal?" he asked.

"No thanks. Just keep the Papas coming, sport."

I felt a hand on my shoulder. I turned around. Natalie. I hadn't seen her since the limousine extravaganza with Brett. Gordon winked and walked away.

"Hey, good-looking, how are you," I said.

"Great. How are *you?*" Natalie asked, looking concerned. I caught her eyes fixating on the cut above my eye.

"I'm fine. What are you doing in Sacramento?"

"My client has a bill going through Ag Committee. What was that scene all about, Jim?"

"Some chick asked me to fuck her, and I said no. She just went crazy."

"What a complete *psycho*," Natalie said.

"No kidding."

"So how's everything with you and Rachel?"

"Fine. She's kinda living with me."

"That's what she said."

Natalie was all dressed up. She looked beautiful, her blond hair pulled into a bun, with thin wisps dangling down her cheeks.

"So where's your guy?" she asked.

"Over at the capitol."

I handed Natalie a Papa.

"You guys are usually joined at the hip."

"We had a little argument."

"About what?"

"Fund-raising. But everything's fine now, I guess."

"I read your welfare piece in the *Times*."

"Like it?"

"Pretty good. I really need help with my writing, Jim. I'm filling in for our press secretary now. I loathe writing. I hated it in college and I hate it now."

"Let me know if I can help."

"Thanks, that's sweet."

"Don't use that word."

"Okay, Mr. Macho-head. You know, you're cute when you're all messed up."

I watched the bottom of my glass appear as I drained another Papa.

"So, does Brett talk about San Francisco?" she asked.

"Sometimes."

"What does he say?"

"He thinks you're hot. But he's married."

"Obviously."

"*I* think you're hot."

"Is that right. What would Rachel say?"

"She would prob'ly say I'm a dog," I slurred.

"Everyone knows that Jim Asher's a dog. Believe me, I've heard all the freaky shit they say about you."

I grabbed the small of her neck and pulled her to me. Her lips pursed when I tried to kiss her, and she pulled back. I held her firm and then she opened her mouth and kissed me. Her hand slid over to my knee.

"Jim, what are you doing?"

"I've always wanted to do that."

"Rachel's my best friend."

I kissed her again. After a few counts she let herself go. Her hand slowly rubbed the stubble on my face. "I've wanted this too, Jim."

"Let's do a shot. Bartender! Four tequilas with lime and salt."

"But, Jim, I have to work early tomorrow."

"Bartender, make that six shots!"

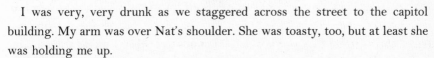

I was very, very drunk as we staggered across the street to the capitol building. My arm was over Nat's shoulder. She was toasty, too, but at least she was holding me up.

"How are we gonna get in?" Natalie asked.

"I'm Jim fucking Asher—that's how we're gonna get in goddammit! That's how!" I knew I was barely intelligible.

We stopped at the automatic glass doors on the side of the building. I waved to the security camera bolted on the wall. The intercom crackled and a CHP officer's voice said: "What can I do for you?"

"Jim Asher, with the speaker."

Normally they let me right in. But I had never showed up in the middle of the night with a drunk girl in a cocktail dress before.

"What are you doing?" the officer asked.

"Gotta get some paperwork from my office," I shouted at the camera.

The doors opened automatically. We walked in.

"I told you, babe. All these CHP guys know me."

I thought Natalie seemed impressed.

"Have you ever been in Brett's office?" I asked.

"No. But I've seen pictures of it in the *Cal Journal*."

"It's fuckin' awesome."

"Are you gonna get in trouble for this, Jim?"

"Fuck no. These fuckers can't touch me. They can't fuckin' see me."

"You're drunk."

We stumbled through the dark lobby. It was all a glorious blur. I shouted "Hello!" and it echoed off the dome and tile floors. Natalie giggled. We caught the elevator to Brett's office. He always locked his door at night, so we walked through the conference room door, which was hardly ever locked, and then through the adjoining door into Brett's office.

"Wow," Natalie said. "This office is unbelievable."

I grabbed a bottle of Captain Morgan from Brett's bar and drank.

Natalie sat down behind Brett's huge mahogany desk, rubbing her hands over the armrests. "Ooh. I feel so powerful," she said.

"Sometimes I come in here late at night and just sit behind his desk and put my feet up on it."

I handed her the bottle. Drink, I said. I could hardly form sentences without thinking them out ahead of time, and even that was hard. Everything around me seemed fake and superficial, deceptive, like nothing mattered—my life had no consequences anymore, no meaning, so I grabbed Natalie and threw her onto Brett's desk, knocking over his picture of Brett Jr., and as it shattered I smacked it across the room. Then I tried to rip her panties off, but they didn't rip, so I pulled them off and they were stretched out of shape when I tossed them on the floor, but she lifted her hips and pulled her dress over her head and then her naked legs were open to me and I pounded the desk in a rage as I fucked her and I felt like dying because my life was nothing—an empty fucking nothing . . .

THIRTY-FIVE

I hadn't spoken to Brett for five days, since he had discovered me all fucked up in his office that fateful morning. I hadn't talked to a single person in politics. I was still on the state payroll, but I didn't dare go there. I didn't know what to do. I figured rumors were spreading about me—talk moves fast in political circles. I hadn't seen Rachel. She was in Sacramento with Buckman. How would I tell her? What would I be worth without my job? I sat around my quiet, miserable apartment drinking vodka and watching talk shows.

I kept thinking about Brett. I thought of flying back to Sacramento. Maybe I could salvage my life. But what did I have worth salvaging? I had no honor, no purpose. What is life without meaning? It is nothing and not worth struggling over. But I had to go to Sacramento sooner or later. I had my town house. My state car was sitting at the airport. I thought about calling Brett, but the longer I waited, the more embarrassed I grew—I was digging a deep hole for myself. The White House seemed too far away now.

I called my brother and asked if he wanted to go camping.

"Sorry. I can't. I've got school. Are you all right, bro?" he asked. "What's happening with you?"

"Just taking a little time off."

"People have been calling Mom's house. Why aren't you answering your phone?"

My call-waiting beeped. "Hold on, Jake . . . Just a sec."

I pushed the flash button.

"Jim Asher."

"Jimmy, it's Winter."

"Hi, Winter, let me dump my other call . . . Okay, I'm back. So what's goin' on?" I tried to sound upbeat.

"Bud wants to see you," Winter said.

"Brett and I have a meeting with him next week."

"He wants to see you *now.*"

"Is it good?"

"I can't tell you exactly what it is, Jim. But it is good."

My heart raced and my breathing came fast. "Is it the VP slot, Winter? Tell me, tell me!"

"Bud would kill me if I told you."

"Okay, I'll catch the red-eye tonight."

"That won't do you much good."

"Why not?"

"Bud's in Honduras, on vacation."

"*Honduras?* Who vacations in Honduras?"

"You. He wants you to come down to his plantation on the Bay Islands of Honduras."

"What the hell does Bud Raper grow on a plantation—politicians?"

"Funny. Actually, from the pictures I've seen, it's quite beautiful, Jim. I wish I could go; this presidential race is getting hectic."

"I can't go to Honduras."

"Why not?"

"I don't know."

"Jim, trust me on this. Go to Honduras and see Bud. I'll give you a hint: it's something you've been dreaming about your whole life."

I started feeling better immediately.

"Good luck, sweet boy. I'll see you in Washington real soon."

She hung up.

I closed my eyes and screamed, "Yes!" In the last twenty seconds my life had completely turned around. I was going to Honduras. I was back in the game.

THIRTY-SIX

I stepped from the modern airliner onto rusty movable airport stairs. We had just landed in La Ceiba city on the Caribbean coast of Honduras. The air was warm and humid, but in a welcoming way. I was sweating before I hit the tarmac. The airport was nothing more than a strip of asphalt in the jungle, and the main terminal looked like a forgotten warehouse. I made my way inside. It was ten degrees hotter in the terminal. All the signs and instructions were in Spanish, which I didn't understand. The building was crammed with bodies. Sweaty people kept rubbing up against me. I was already drenched in my own sweat, so I really didn't mind. I soon learned that the standard rules governing human behavior while standing in line simply do not apply in Honduras. There was plenty of shoving and jockeying for position—every tourist for himself.

I finally reached the Honduran Customs officer. He was fat, with craters on his face and neck. He grunted something in Spanish. I shrugged.

"No hablo Español," I said.

Then I noticed a change in his eyes. I handed him my passport. He had barely glanced up at anyone else in line before stamping their passports. But now he was taking a keen interest in me. He looked at my passport photo, then back at me, then back at the photo.

"You have paperwork?" he asked.

"What paperwork?" I had been watching him the whole time, and nobody else had presented any paperwork other than their passports. "Here's my paperwork," I said, handing him the passport again.

"Paperwork! Paperwork!" he demanded. He was getting angry. The sweaty people behind me started grumbling and pushing against my back.

"Okay, here's my paperwork." I handed him all the IDs, tickets, reservation stubs—all the shit I had in my pockets.

"No paperwork!" he shouted across the terminal to another fat guy working at the metal detector. The second guard nodded; I swore I saw him wink. "Go over there."

I walked across the terminal and put on my innocent, stupid-American face. "Here's all my paperwork," I offered.

"No. No. You need paperwork," he said. He pulled a crumpled slip of paper from his pocket and wrote my passport number on it. "Sign here," he said, handing me the fraudulent-looking scrap. "And that will be twenty American dollars."

"Twenty dollars! For what?"

"Paperwork." He pointed to the piece of paper. "You need paperwork."

"Fuck it!" I didn't want to spend the night in a filthy jail cell. I forked over the twenty, and I was free to go.

I exchanged a few hundred-dollar traveler's checks for Honduran lempiras at the counter. The exchange rate was astounding—something like 1:2,100—so I was practically as rich as Edward. I bought a bottle of red Chilean wine at an airport shop. The girl at the counter opened it for me right there, and I took a long swig. When I stepped out the airport's front door I was mobbed by thirty eager cabdrivers. Where did I want to go? How long was I staying? Did I want a girl? Or two? They all knew the best hotel for me. I grabbed the youngest guy from the crowd: "Let's go."

"*Hola,*" he said as we walked to the parking lot. His blue cab was his regular car, too; I could tell he just took the yellow cab sign off when he wasn't working.

"What's up," I replied, fishing to see if he knew English.

"*Nada,* man, just workin'."

"I'm going to the Hotel Partenon Beach," I told him. "You know that one?"

"*Sí.*"

He punched it and went racing out of the parking lot. We were flying around corners at high speed, wheels screeching, and he was singing along passionately with the salsa music on his tape deck. All of a sudden we came up fast on a bicycle rider. The cabby didn't even try to swerve. We hit the guy just hard enough to send him and his bike careening straight into a curb. He went flying over the handlebars and landed on his back in front of a bus stop.

"Oh shit!" I screamed. "Aren't you going to stop?"

"No, man," the cabby said. "He'll be all right."

The guy on the bike got up and flipped us off as we sped away. Right then and there I threw life's rules out the window—I had no further use for them in this place.

I was quite pleased with the hotel when I arrived. It was an old and distinguished-looking establishment with Mediterranean whitewashed walls and Spanish tile. I checked in. The clerk at the front desk was plump, soft-faced, and ridiculously feminine—not what I expected. He sashayed around behind the counter, obviously relishing his role as a privileged Honduran. The room cost only sixteen dollars, so I was in a good mood. A young Honduran boy with a charming smile and messy hair wanted to help with my bags, but I only had my backpack, already on my back.

"No thanks," I told him.

But the boy was persistent; he really wanted to carry the bag. After a few more times of telling him no, I handed him the backpack, which held everything I needed for a week. Laptop. Clothes. Boots. Books. Toiletries. Altogether it must have weighed fifty pounds. When I handed the backpack to the boy, it hit the tiles like a sack of concrete. I could tell he was embarrassed. But he wasn't going out like a chump. He summoned all the strength in his little sixty-pound body and swung the bag over his shoulder. I was impressed, and he could see it in my eyes. He waddled alongside me with the bag scraping the ground. When we got to the stairs, I lifted the bag lightly from behind, so as not to damage his pride. The room was impressive. Large bed. A deep, round white tile bathtub. Nice desk. Satellite TV.

I gave the boy some Honduran money—a couple of dollars, I think—but at that point I wasn't sure. There's a learning curve with foreign currency, and on your first day in a new country you're at the bottom. The boy sat with me on the room's balcony under the hot sun and we shared the Chilean wine. He took long, impressive swigs. But soon the boy went back to work and I was drinking the wine by myself, gazing out across the white sand at the turquoise Caribbean waters. The wind was warm and relaxing. Sitting in that laid-back wooden chair, so far from the political turmoil that was my life, I felt a wonderful serenity wash over my body and flow through my mind. Letting go of my demons calmed me.

After the wine I decided I couldn't pass up the chance to swim in those marvelous waters on my first day in Central America. I also had a buzz and thought the water might snap me up. Bud was meeting me at the hotel's bar that night. Then we would both catch a single-engine plane over to the Bay Island of Roatán. I couldn't wait to see him, and to get the good news that was sure to turn my life around. I went down to the beach and dove in the waves. The water was much warmer than I expected—warmer than most heated swimming pools. I swam out past the gentle waves and floated on my back. The sun felt like heaven as it sprinkled down warm on my face and chest and the salty sea held me up like a strong grandfather. Suddenly, a scary thought jumped into my head: I wonder if there are sharks out here? I hadn't bothered to ask anyone. I tried to tell myself I was being paranoid, but the paranoia kept creeping back. "It's perfectly safe out here," I reassured myself. After all, I hadn't read about any sharks in my travel book, and those books are full of horror stories. But then again, why was I the only person swimming? The few people who were at the beach were sitting on shore. That's when I started seeing dark shadows in the water. I panicked and swam back to shore faster than a speedboat. I felt a little embarrassed with myself as I crawled onto the sand. But what the hell, I figured. Mother Day was already tucking the sun in for bed, and Father Night was sprucing his hair and splashing on cologne. I was ready to get loose, Central American style.

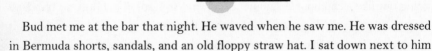

Bud met me at the bar that night. He waved when he saw me. He was dressed in Bermuda shorts, sandals, and an old floppy straw hat. I sat down next to him at the bar.

"Hey, kid. You made it."

"Man, it's good to see a familiar face, Bud."

"So whad'ya think of Honduras?" he asked.

"I had no idea Honduras was like this. When I thought of Honduras, I thought of guerrilla warfare and grass huts—shit like that."

"Wait till you see my place on Roatán. Makes this place look like fuckin' Mexico City. You know how to scuba dive, kid?"

"NAUI certified."

"Roatán has the best diving you'll ever find. We've got the second-longest reef in the world right off my front porch. The longest is the Great Barrier in Australia, but fuck Australia. You can't get a bottle of beer for ten cents down under. We've got white sand beaches, waterfalls, fuckin' monkeys swinging from palm trees."

"What are we waiting for?"

"There's only one flight a day since the storm last month. And I needed to come over here to the mainland for supplies anyway. Those local islander sons of bitches try to rake old Bud over the fuckin' coals for a decent bottle of whiskey. So I buy it here. Got two cases at the store—case of whiskey, case of rum. That should hold me over at least a month. Last year I made a run on a case of whiskey in one week, but I vowed never to do it again."

"Impressive." I pulled a videotape out of my fanny pack and handed it to Bud.

"What's this?"

"You got a machine on that island?"

"I've got all that shit, tough guy. Satellite. Big screen. Fuckin' stereo surround-sound. I come down here to relax. So what's this tape?" He read the label. "Rachel, huh?" He grinned. "You little bastard. You finally came through for old Bud." He slapped my back. "Is she hot?"

"She's a fuckin' bikini model."

"Hot damn! Let's pick up one more case of whiskey, kid. This is gonna be a long week. And we've got business to talk—presidential business."

THIRTY-SEVEN

The tiny airplane taking me and Bud to the Bay Islands was frightening. The flight only cost eighteen dollars. When the pilot spun the propeller with his own hands, I considered swimming. But I swallowed my fear and climbed in. The pilot sat right beside us on a bench seat. The engine roared, and the plane shook violently. I started scribbling down my will. But soon the plane lifted over the Caribbean and the view replaced my anxiety with wondrous awe— tropical jungles ran to the edge of the emerald sea, a twisting strip of white sand floating under a cloud of coastal mist. I was living now, really *living*. I had to wait until we got to his house before Bud would tell me the good news, but I was already feeling like a new man.

Bud's houseboy, Pedro, picked us up at the airport in a new Land Cruiser. I rode in the back, taking in the sights. Roatán was not only a world removed from mainland Honduras, it was a world removed from everything. Dirt roads cut through magical rain forest peaks, then swept along the sea. There were few noticeable telephones, clocks, or cares. My head was hanging out the window, enjoying the breeze like a blissful dog. I saw large, rainbow-colored parrots perched casually in the trees. "I thought they only lived in pet stores," I told Bud.

Bud's plantation took up the entire southern tip of Roatán Island. He told me he could walk from one side of the island to the other in twenty minutes—"Ten if there's a señorita waiting on the other side." After I settled into my large guest room, we had lunch at the rustic little restaurant on the beach.

"I let this German couple run their restaurant on my property," Bud said. "They look after the place when I'm in the States. Great couple. You've never seen anyone who can drink beer like that bastard Nicholas. He's used to the German stuff, says American beer is 'piss ale.' I'll have 'em up to the house tonight. Great couple."

"So you actually grow coconuts here?"

"I don't make shit as far as money, but what the hell. It provides jobs for these local sons of bitches, keeps 'em from robbing me. I only hire the skinny bastards to work here, though. If they show up with no shirts and ribs poking out, they're hired."

I laughed. "Why's that?"

"They're better tree climbers. I've got this one bastard who can race up a tree so fast he makes the monkeys howl. All my coconuts are handpicked. And all my maids are handpicked, too."

"Man, I saw one of those girls. Really cute."

"The local girls are this island's best natural resource. You know, this cove right here used to be a pirate hideout."

"Is that right?"

"This whole island was swarming with fuckin' pirates two hundred years ago. After they'd make a big haul, they'd retire here on Roatán, then take up with a local girl. That's why their skin's so light. I'll take you diving off Key Point this afternoon. There's a sunken Portuguese clipper down there."

"Do you think there's any treasure around here?" I asked.

"Legend says that Captain Morgan's loot from his raid on Panama in 1671 is buried on the island somewhere. I don't know if I believe that shit, but I've got these sons of bitches digging on their days off. Keeps 'em from drinking all my whiskey."

"So, Bud, why'd you bring me down here? I know it wasn't to talk about coconuts and pirates."

"Patience, patience. We'll make a run on that whiskey tonight and talk shop. But right now, let's go diving. It's the only sport an old bastard like me can do anymore. The only problem is, with this fat belly of mine I have to strap on thirty pounds of dive weights to keep from floating to the surface. Old age is a son of a bitch!"

That night we got toasty with the Germans and watched my video. The Germans loved it. Bud loved it even more. I told him he could keep the tape. He could not have been happier if I'd handed him the deed to Rockefeller Center. I think the Germans must have gotten bored stuck on the island all the time. It was only the two of them, and the occasional tourists at their restaurant. Mostly they had each other. I gave the Papa recipe to Bud's maids and they fixed us drinks all night. Bud proclaimed it "the best fuckin' drink" he ever tasted. At midnight the Germans went to their bungalow and the maids joined us for more drinks on the porch. We watched the ocean waves crashing gently under the moonlight. It was warm out, and Bud had turned on the ceiling fan above the porch. I loved having my shirt off at night. We smoked Cubans and had a raucous time.

"So, you're wondering why I dragged your ass down here, aren't you?" Bud asked.

"You could say that."

"Here, have another." He poured me a drink from the pitcher. "Whad'you call these suckers?"

"Papas. Come on, Bud. Tell me."

"You really want to know, don't you?" he teased.

"Fuck you." I laughed.

Bud enjoyed fucking with my head, but I couldn't take it anymore. I had to know about the VP slot. If we got it, everything would be straight with Brett and my life would be great again. But Bud wasn't ready to say anything yet, so I started talking to the cuter, younger maid. Her name was Maria, and she spoke Island English, which sounded like melodic reggae in her sugary soft voice. I grabbed some Salva Vida beers and walked with Maria down to the old dock in the cove. Under a tapestry of stars we sat with our legs dangling over the salty planks.

"How old are you, Maria?"

"Seventeen," she said.

Her eyes were warm and emerald green like the water had been under the afternoon sun. I kissed her softly. Her breath had a sweet smell like a baby's. She trembled when my hand touched her cheek. She leaned in and hugged me, her face against my chest. I ran my hand over her long hair, looking out at the moon over the dark edge of the ocean.

Bud walked up.

"Maria, will you get us something to eat, please? I need to talk to Jim."

Maria hugged me for a long time, like she didn't want to let go, but then went inside.

Bud sat on the dock next to me and sipped his drink, flicking cigar ashes into the surf. "I was just fucking with you, kid. I'm an asshole sometimes."

"I'm fine. Maria is beautiful."

He grinned. "She's a virgin."

"Really? How do you know that?"

"Her sister told me. But let's talk politics." He took another drink. "Winter tells me it's always been your dream to work at the White House."

"Ever since I can remember."

"I want you to work for me."

"What?"

"I want you to work at the presidential campaign."

"I thought this was about Brett getting the VP slot?"

"Shit, kid. Brett Alexander has about as much chance of getting that VP slot as I have of climbing one of these fuckin' coconut trees. I want you to come on board the campaign with us in Washington. I've never seen anyone who handles these fuckin' reporters like you. We could use you on the team."

"But I'm running Edward's race now. And Brett. Oh, man, Brett's gonna be—"

"You're not hearing me, kid. I wanna take you to the White House. I'm offering you the press secretary slot on the presidential trail, probably the most important job. You'll travel with Williams and write some of his speeches. He saw Alexander's welfare speech in Washington and loved it. He wants to meet you in DC next week."

I couldn't believe it. "What would I tell Edward?"

"Fuck Edward. I can only pay you sixty or seventy, but I can guarantee you an office at the White House if we go—not the Old Executive offices attached to the White House; your office will be inside, near the president. You and Winter will head up our communications office. This is the big time, kid. Fuck that statewide shit. You'll hit three hundred cities in eight weeks. You'll meet more high rollers in one afternoon than you've met in your whole fuckin' life. And then, well, the White House. What can I say. So, you want the spot?"

"Fuckin A right I do! Fuck yeah, the WHITE HOUSE, MOTHERFUCK-ERS!" I stood up and jumped off the dock, splashing into the warm waves. I leaped up and down, slapping my hands on the water and howling at the monkeys.

Bud almost fell off the dock laughing. "Enthusiasm!" he shouted down to me. "I like that. Hey, you're stepping into a whole new fuckin' world, kid. You won't believe the shit you're gonna see."

I pushed off in the water and floated on my back, smiling. I didn't care about anything in the wide universe. No one could touch me or see me or know what it was to be me. I closed my eyes, and the saltwater tasted better than champagne. I was going to the White House!

Maria came out with a big plate of garlic fried shrimp and four frosty beers.

"Please, sit down," Bud told her. "I was just going inside."

I swam to the dock and climbed up the slippery side. "Thanks, Bud. I don't know what to say."

"Just get us some good fuckin' media coverage."

"You got it! Hey, Bud, you got a phone around here?"

"The only regular phone is in town. That's why I love this place—gets me away from all that shit. But I've got a satellite phone in my office for emergencies."

"I just need to check my messages."

"Whatever. It's seven bucks a minute for satellite time, so don't dictate a fuckin' speech or anything. Maria can show you how to use it. I'm crashing out." Bud grabbed Maria's sister from the porch and disappeared inside.

"I will get the telephone," Maria said. "You are too wet with your clothes, *Jeem.*"

I took my shorts off and laid back on the dock in my wet Calvins. Maria brought the phone out and set it down next to me. It looked like a high-tech black shoe box. She flipped the top open and aimed it at the stars. A green keypad lit up.

"Wow," I said. "This is neat."

"Bud, he lets the people use it sometimes for emergency, like when the bad storm came."

"That's nice. How does this sucker work?"

She gave me the handset. "Dial your numbers here."

A minute later I had the AT&T operator, crystal clear, like she was whispering in my ear. I called my voice mail center. With GTE message consolidation, all my voice mails—office, home, pager, cell phone—forwarded automatically to one number. I had eleven messages. Brett's was the third:

> "Jim, it's Brett. Look, we need to talk. I don't know where you're at, but I wanted to tell you I turned down the money. I killed the tobacco bill in committee. Those bastards are pissed at me, especially David. Call the office, man."

I smiled and replayed the message twice before saving it. I shut the phone down. Everything was perfect now.

"Do you know I'm going to the White House?" I asked Maria.

"You go with Bud?"

"Yessiree."

"That's good."

"Yeah, that's good. Would you like to go swimming with me?"

"At this late time?"

"Why not. It's warm out, the stars are shining for us . . ."

"But I have no swimming clothes, *Jeem.*"

I grinned.

six days later . . .

THIRTY-EIGHT

When my plane touched down at LAX all I could think of was the White House, and my meeting with Stan Williams in four days. I had so many people to tell. My family would be incredibly proud. My friends would be envious, and maybe I could even help a few of them get on with the Williams campaign. This presidential race was my ticket out of all the dirty drama in California. I was excited to be working with Bud and Winter again, especially Winter. We would be locked in the world's biggest political battle—together again. Winter and I could fall in love, then run President Williams's communications office as a dynamic team. I could finally put my writing and networking skills to a legitimate national test, without whoring myself. My shady dealings were over; I didn't need that shit anymore. I felt like a new and cleaner Jim, rising from the ashes.

I waited in the Customs line with a mob from a Korean Air flight. They were nearly as pushy as the Hondurans. Normally I would have fired up my cell phone as soon as I hit US airspace, but I figured a cell phone wouldn't do much good in Honduras, so I had left it in my Hummer. I finally got through the line. I only had my backpack, so I whizzed past the hordes of Koreans with their teetering suitcase carts, and I headed straight for the pay phones. I couldn't wait to check my voice mails. I always loved checking voice mail after being away for a while. Sometimes a long afternoon produced a slew of eight or nine messages. Imagine a whole week! I figured I'd also have bundles of letters and E-mail when I got to the office.

I had spent the flight finalizing how to break the news to Brett and Edward. I figured they would be disappointed at first, but eventually they would understand. Once I got to the White House I could be a tremendous asset to both of them. I might even be able to help Brett land a cabinet slot, something he badly wanted.

I found a wall of pay phones and dialed my mailbox.

"Please enter your access code," the voice said.

I'd had the same code since I was a horny teenager: 69–69.

"Thank you," the voice said. "You have one hundred twelve voice mail messages . . ."

I almost hit the floor. "One hundred and twelve messages—*holy shit!*"

"To check your new messages, press one, to check your previously saved messages—"

The word must be out, I said to myself. Jim Asher's goin' to the White House, baby! Time to rock and roll.

I pressed one.

"First message, sent on May first at 2:21 P.M. . . . 'Hey sexy, it's Renee, call me. Let's go out this weekend.'" I erased it. "Next message, sent on May first at 4:37 P.M. . . . 'Jimbo, it's John, call me, homey—let's hit Frank's party in Hollywood on Friday. Later.'" Erased. "Jim, it's Rachel. I bought something special for you, but you have to make love to me first before you can have your treat. I miss you. I've just been so busy working in Sacramento. Sorry I haven't called. And guess what . . . I love you." Saved. "Jim, it's Francis, call me, we've gotta talk about this DC trip and—" Erased. I figured this would take an hour. I started saving messages as soon as I recognized the voice. Party at Samantha's. Party in San Diego. Dinner invitation from a lobbyist. An editor from the *Times* asking where Edward's column was. "Shit, I forgot about the column," I mumbled.

Then I heard a voice I didn't recognize. "Jim Asher, listen carefully . . ." The voice was distorted, creepy—with heavy background noise. "You are under federal investigation. Your phone lines are tapped—all of them. You've been under police surveillance for weeks. Erase all your messages, dump all your E-mail, and destroy your computer files—immediately! Right now. This is not a joke, Jim . . ."

My heart dropped into my stomach. I couldn't swallow. Everything stood still around me. My vision narrowed, focusing only on the phone and the white stucco wall with chipped paint.

"'. . . I won't call again,'" the voice said. "'Get a lawyer—fast—and don't talk to anyone. You're in deep shit and if you don't want to get deeper, keep your mouth closed.' To save this message, press two, to listen to it again, press one . . ."

My head was spinning. I started to panic. The Korean guy on the phone next to me gave me a concerned look as I grabbed the phone stall to hold myself up. This must be a joke. It must be John Griggs with a Radio Shack voice synthesizer, I told myself. But it didn't sound like a joke. It sounded like words surfacing from a nightmare. I closed my eyes and tried to slow my breathing down. Deep breaths, Jim, in through the mouth, out through the nose. The Korean guy kept talking but watched me the whole time. Just check your other messages, Jim. That will prove it's a joke. Then you can kill John for fucking with your head. I locked my knees and straightened out my clothes. I saved the message and played the next.

"Sent on May first at 4:46 P.M. . . . 'Jim, you've got a serious fucking problem. A *serious* problem. Erase your messages, RIGHT NOW. Don't talk to anyone—NO ONE . . .'" It was Francis's voice, muffled. I could tell he was on a pay phone. "'Erase everything and get a good lawyer the minute you hear this. This shit is going down fast. Stay away from everyone . . .'"

I collapsed to my knees in the middle of the airport and I knew my life would never be the same.

THIRTY-NINE

I hit the freeway in a daze. I couldn't comprehend the events taking place around me—the traffic noises swirled through my head with those of the radio and the wind coming through my window. I had to concentrate to keep from hitting the other cars, but I couldn't. I hit the hazard lights and skidded onto the gravel shoulder, scraping my front fender along the concrete rail. The passing cars made me wince as they thundered by. I closed my eyes.

I had to talk to somebody. I called John Griggs on the cell phone, but I got his answering machine. I called Renee.

"Jim, where the *hell* are you?" she said in a panicked voice.

"I don't know, Renee. I'm fucking freaking out here."

"Calm down, Jim. You can't call here. Get a lawyer right now. Hang up and call a lawyer."

"What the fuck is going on?"

"They're saying you fled the country, Jim. Where are you?"

"What? What are the fucking charges? Is this about the horse-racing thing, because—"

"Jim, where are you?"

"LA . . . somewhere in LA."

"Haven't you read the papers?"

The lump in my throat constricted my voice. "No—I've been out of the country on business. What the fuck is happening, Renee?"

"I can't talk to you, Jim. I'm sorry. Really sorry." She hung up.

The car was dead silent except for the passing traffic. The sun glared through my dusty windshield. I felt like crying, but I couldn't. I started the Hummer and drove slowly to the next off ramp. Cars swerved around me, honking. I pulled up to a 7-Eleven and stumbled inside. The Arab clerk stared at me like a car accident. I found the newspapers. The *Times*'s headline buckled my legs: "SCANDAL ROCKS SPEAKER'S OFFICE: TOP AIDE COPS PLEA, 2nd AIDE STILL 'AT LARGE' SAYS DA." The color photo was of Francis walking out of a courthouse, fighting off a swarm of reporters and cameras. I set the paper down and closed my eyes.

By the time I got back to Huntington Beach my nerves were fissured. I walked upstairs to my apartment like I was walking to my own funeral. My door was locked. I almost expected to see yellow crime-scene tape. My keys rattled nervously as I opened the door. The living room was perfect, exactly as I'd left it. I walked cautiously to my bedroom. Untouched. I opened the closet door. The rack was empty where Rachel's clothes had been. I looked down. Empty carpet where her shoes usually were. I rushed to the bathroom. Her toothbrush and her army of shampoos were gone. My soap and hairbrush were knocked on the floor, like she had cleared out in a hurry.

I searched the rest of the house and found nothing out of place. I tossed my backpack on the floor and sat down, hunched over the edge of my bed. I couldn't believe any of it. This was not supposed to happen right now, right when everything was falling into place. I still didn't know what the whole thing was about, but I was pretty sure it had to do with the horse track. That deal had been haunting me for months.

I had to get my act together. I called Rachel's apartment.

One of her roommates answered.

"May I speak to Rachel, please."

"Yeah, just a minute."

"Hello," Rachel answered.

"Rachel, it's Jim."

She was quiet.

"Rachel?"

After a long pause I heard the receiver clank against plastic. The line went dead.

"What the fuck?"

I dialed again. The phone rang. And rang again. Two rings later the answering machine picked up. "Hi, this is Erin, Rachel, and Beth, we're out having fun right now . . ."

Everything stopped. My body flushed with desperate adrenaline. I couldn't believe she hung up. I thought about calling back. I had to do something else, fast, before it really hit me. I called John Griggs on his cell phone.

"Jim, where the hell are you?" he said. "The whole state is out looking for you, man. The cops have been calling my office—"

"What the fuck is going on, John?"

"You don't know?"

"I've been in Honduras for a week."

"The papers say you fled to Central America."

"Fled? That's complete *bullshit!*"

"Where are you?"

"I'm home—in Huntington—at my fuckin' apartment."

"Look, Jim. Get a lawyer. Everyone told me not to talk to you. I think your phones are tapped."

"Who told you not to talk to me?"

"Jim, I really can't talk to you because—"

"Don't gimme that fuckin' shit! Tell me what's happening right now, John!"

"You really don't know what this is about?"

"NO, for the second time."

"I'll tell you, but don't say anything in response. They could use it against you in court, or against me. The Orange County DA is charging you guys with rigging the recall election."

"*What?*"

"The DA says you registered a Democrat to split the vote. Something illegal. I don't even understand it completely myself, but—"

"That's bullshit. He signed those—"

"Shut up, Jim. I've gotta go."

"Wait, wait—"

John hung up.

I was boiling into a slow rage but also slightly relieved now. All along I'd been thinking it was over the racetrack bribe. The Mitch Fine race was really nothing in comparison. We hadn't done anything illegal, had we? We *did* gather the signatures without Mitch as a witness, which Francis said was technically wrong, but how bad could the penalty be for that? And this business about "fleeing" the country was nonsense, and I could prove it. I felt better. Now I wanted to read all the newspaper stories. But I had to clean things up first. If the DA didn't know about the racetrack bribe, I sure as hell didn't want him to find out by digging through my personal files.

I tried to think of everything incriminating in my political life. There was plenty. But most of my deals had been made in conversation. No one ever puts a political deal to paper. That would be suicide. My laptop and my Sacramento desktop computers were clean. I never used them for sensitive political business. The only thing I had to worry about was my journal, which I kept on my home PC. I had seen plenty of political scandals and trials where a diary sent an otherwise untouchable politician to the grave. I always thought those people were stupid. Who would keep a political diary and tell everyone about it? That's just inviting trouble. No. I was smart about my diary. Only a few of my closest friends knew about it, and the file was well hidden on my PC. I figured I would use the journal to write my memoirs at the end of my long and illustrious career at the White House. Now I had to erase the file or stash a disk somewhere.

I turned on my PC in the den and waited for Windows 95 to boot up. I tried to think where I could hide the disk if I copied it. Maybe I could bury it somewhere? Or stash it at my parents' house? I hadn't even talked to my parents yet. I wondered what they must be thinking right now. Their son was being disgraced in the newspapers every day. I hadn't told them I was going to Honduras; I hadn't told anyone except Winter. It was supposed to be a big surprise when I came back with the good news. I had to call them, soon.

I clicked on Microsoft Word and found my journal file. It was camouflaged as a Document Template titled "Elegant Memo." If anyone searched the files superficially they would only see a standard template next to all the others. I was not, however, a computer whiz. Like most people, I knew how to work computers but I didn't know how computers worked. I copied the journal onto a floppy disk, then deleted the file from the hard drive. I checked the File Manager, but the journal was still in the Recycle bin. I erased it again. Then I remembered: when I was at the Statesmen Institute, I had once lost a column I was writing for Edward. Our computer consultant, Josh, had somehow been able to resurrect it from my hard drive. I didn't understand how he did it, only that I got the file back. Josh told me that no file was ever *really* erased. I started to worry. I read my Windows manual, but I couldn't understand it. "Fuckin computers," I growled. I had to remove that file. The journal contained detailed accounts of every shady, filthy, low-down deal I'd ever spun. It was sitting center-mast on my hard drive like a land mine ready to blow my life to shreds. I had to call someone and ask how to remove the file completely. I searched for Josh's phone number, but then I remembered it was in my Sacramento office. The more I thought about what was on the disk, the more I thought I was insane to keep a copy—like a person in a horror movie who decides to go search the dark, eerie barn. "Fuck that," I told myself. "I'm not retarded." My garbage disposal made quick work of the floppy disk. I grabbed a bottle of Jack Daniel's and fiddled with the hard drive for an hour, then gave up frustrated.

I needed to talk to a friend. Samantha. She could always cheer me up; she could always bail me out. I called the station. She was out. I found her at home.

"Samantha, it's Jim."

"Jim, where the hell are you?"

"I'm at home in Huntington."

"I can't talk. We can't talk. I'm sorry. Don't call me."

For the fourth time in two hours I heard the phone go dead. I didn't understand why everyone was acting this way. What was the big deal? I grabbed the JD and drank. I had to think. I concluded that I should erase the file, then call a lawyer. I knew plenty of lawyers but they all worked for Brett or Edward. I was scared to call my parents. Suddenly they were all I had. Everything else had melted away in the last two hours. How could so much fade so fast? Maybe it was all fake to begin with; maybe my whole life and everyone around me were like a Hollywood set—fancy building fronts held up by rickety two-by-fours. It was a disillusioning thought.

I didn't want to call Washington only to be hung up on again. I was too embarrassed to call Winter, Edward, or Bud. What would I say? The whiskey started to dull things. I drank long swigs from the warm bottle and smoked red dogs. I wanted to flush the whole day down the toilet, along with my whole damned life. Maybe everything would just go away if I ignored it.

My pistol popped into my head. I had to at least look at it. I walked over to my closet and took the Glock out of my fanny pack. I shouldn't be near a gun now, I told myself weakly. But it kept pulling on me. It wouldn't leave me alone. The pistol felt cold and terrible in my hand—heavy and very real. I pulled back the receiver and inserted a full clip. I let the receiver snap forward, chambering a round. I took another swig of whiskey. My hand moved on its own. I pictured the hollow-point bullet shattering through my front teeth, expanding to three times its initial diameter as it ripped through my brain tissue and blew out the back of my skull, splattering brain and bone fragments onto the wall behind me. My hand rubbed the barrel across my lips, my thumb settling onto the trigger. I closed my eyes. My body was shaking in a sick fever. One more little push, Jim. Then your truth will be over, your universe complete. Just do it. Push the goddamn trigger. Push the goddamn fuckin' trigger! I opened my eyes and looked down at the black gun in my trembling hands. This is stupid, I told myself. Two years from now you'll be looking back on this like it was nothing, Jim. I grabbed the JD in one hand, the Glock in the other, and I got filthy drunk.

FORTY

Something loud awoke me. I looked out my window; the sun was setting over the beach. Something pounded on my door. The pistol was lying on my chest. I stashed it under the pillow, then stood up and nearly fell over, my head reeling. I staggered to my front door and looked through the peephole.

"Who is it?" I yelled.

"County Sheriffs—open the door!"

My heart exploded. A gang of angry men in dark clothes was getting ready to knock my door down with a battering ram. "SHIT." I froze. My body started twitching. "My journal," I mumbled, "they'll find my fucking journal!"

"Open the door, we have a search warrant!"

I had to say something. "Where's your identification?" I shouted.

"Smith and Wesson is our fucking identification!" one of them shouted.

"Oh F-u-c-k." With unthinking speed I reached up and pulled down the bookshelf standing next to me. It crashed down, blocking the door, books scattering around my feet. I ran to the den and kicked the monitor clear off my computer, the screen shattering as it smashed against the wall. I heard something banging hard against the door. I picked up the computer and ripped the cords away from the desk. Adrenaline flooded my body as I threw the computer terminal to the carpet and stomped on it brutally, only denting the metal casing. I heard angry shouts from the living room. They were already coming through my door. I panicked and threw the computer against the wall hard enough to shake the floor under my feet. The casing came off. I kicked the frame against the wall, then picked it up and ran to the bathroom and smashed it on the tile and tore it apart with my hands. Now I heard them inside the house. I had to find the hard drive. I tore the components out but I couldn't find the hard drive—I didn't even know what it looked like . . .

"Sheriff's department—FREEZE!" I heard from the living room.

I didn't look up. I stomped down on the circuits with the heels of my boots again and again and again. Rage overwhelmed me and terror wrestled control of my central nervous system. I picked up the mangled frame and pounded it hard against the bathtub, shattering the circuit boards, ripping apart the insides, pieces flying everywhere. Then something heavy and hard blew me against the tile wall, smashing the side of my face into the shower knob. I saw the wall and then I saw black.

When I woke up, I was on my back looking at my white ceiling. My wrists were handcuffed on my lap and my head was brutally numb. A dozen men were ravaging my apartment, tearing out heating ducts and dismembering kitchen cabinets. A man was ripping my sofa apart with a slip-blade knife. The officers wore dark-blue windbreakers with the word SHERIFF printed in yellow on the back. They looked terrifying. I closed my eyes, trying to retreat into myself. There was nothing else I could do. It was all worse than a nightmare. All I could think of was my family. Did they know what was happening? I hoped they didn't. But I needed help.

A dozen reporters mobbed me with cameras and microphones as I was carried hog-tied by four sheriffs to a waiting squad car. Now I understood why criminals try to hide their faces. I tucked my chin against my chest and closed my eyes. Painful, ripping humiliation filled me—utter shame that reached to my very soul and pulled my spirit down with strong arms until I could not push against the embarrassing pain any longer.

I was taken to the Costa Mesa police station and given a Breathalyzer. My handcuffs were removed, leaving purple indentations with red specks on my wrists. I was seated on a folding chair and told to wait. I was suddenly very alone. I needed to vomit, but I held it in. I thought about running for the door. But where would I run? All the doors were locked. I decided to say nothing from this moment forward. I would not incriminate myself. My head hurt like I had just stepped off a spinning amusement park ride. After ten minutes, I was escorted to a desk protected by inch-thick bulletproof glass. A female officer sat on the other side filling out paperwork. A big deputy stood with me. He told me to remove all my jewelry. I had a bead necklace a girlfriend in Germany had given me years ago. I told the deputy it had never come off and that it had "religious significance." He shoved me against the wall and ripped it off my neck. Beads spilled everywhere, rolling around on the linoleum floor. Now he was pissed.

"I'm gonna have to clean this shit up," he told me.

I removed my watch and placed it in a tray on the counter. He patted me down.

"Got any weapons?" he asked.

"No."

"Drugs?"

"No."

"Pipes or syringes?"

"I'm a fuckin' Republican. I work for the—"

"Shut the fuck up and answer the question."

"No needles or guns or pipes."

He kicked my feet apart and frisked my shorts.

"Unbutton your pants and pull 'em down around your knees," he said.

"What're you, a faggot or something?" I said.

His elbow crashed into the back of my neck like a sledgehammer, snapping my head forward, smashing my face into the wall. Blood streamed from my nose, trickling warm down my chest. "Fuck you, MOTHERFUCKER!" I shouted. My words echoed through the hallways. He hit me harder this time.

I was searched in the most humiliating fashion imaginable and literally thrown into a mean little concrete cell with cold, white-painted brick walls. I shouted to the guards that I wanted to make a phone call. After a few dazed minutes I noticed a pay phone right there in my cell, bolted to the wall near the steel toilet. I picked up the handset and got a dial tone. I called my parents' house.

"Mom, I'm in jail." Those words hurt me more than any words I've ever spoken.

"Oh, sweetheart. Your father and brother are at the police station right now, trying to get you out. We saw what happened on the news."

"Mom, what's happening to me?"

"I don't know, sweetheart. Just sit tight. Your father is there for you."

Her voice made everything come to the surface. *"Mom."*

"I know, baby. I know. Be strong."

"I just want it to be over, Mom. I didn't do anything"

"Everything is all right. Try to stay calm."

My mom was crying now. I couldn't take it.

"I've gotta go, Mom."

"Just hang on. Your bail is a hundred and thirty thousand dollars, Jim. They say you're a 'flight risk.' Your father is trying to mortgage the house, but the bank is closed and we don't know what to do."

My heart crumbled. "Don't mortgage the house, Mom. Please don't mortgage the house. I have money. I can sell the Hummer and cash my checks . . . please don't let Dad do that."

"Your grandfather is driving up from San Diego. His law firm is going to represent you."

"I don't want Grandpa involved. I don't want him dredging through the sordid details of my life."

"He has other lawyers at the firm—good lawyers. Just sit tight, sweetheart."

"Mom, promise me Dad won't mortgage the house. I'd rather rot in this nightmare. Maybe it'll do me some good."

"Just try to relax. Remember, Jim, we love you. We all love you. Don't do anything rash."

I hung up. After staring at the wall for a few minutes, I sulked over to the bed and lay down on the grimy mattress with no sheets. I wrapped myself up in a fetal curl and draped the tiny green wool blanket over me. My cold feet stuck out the bottom.

Over the next three hours, various criminals were hustled by my cell, but no one spoke to me or told me anything. I didn't even know what time it was. I was experiencing information deprivation, and I was soon longing for any contact at all, even another ass whipping from the deputy. Now I had nothing but my own mind to terrorize myself with.

A deputy finally opened my door. "Come with me."

I followed him down the empty hallways to a holding tank. There were dozens of hard-looking criminals sitting and leaning against the walls. Unlike my holding cell, this room had actual bars. The iron door slid open with a clank, and I was shoved into the cell. Now I was officially behind bars. Everyone glared at me, looking angry, fierce. I was one of the only white people in the cell. I told myself I had to act tough. I'd seen plenty of jail movies—I had to act confident and carry myself with vigor, like I could shank someone if they fucked with me. An empty space in the corner became my new home. I had nothing now. No property. No privilege. No dignity. I sat next to a black guy who looked like a drug dealer. At least he didn't look like a killer, like some of the others. A Mexican wearing a red bandanna mad-dogged me like he wanted to rip my throat out. I felt so far from what my life was; I felt like an outsider among these savages. But maybe I was one of them all along and only my wits had conned me into the upper echelons of life. Maybe this was what I truly was—a criminal, a motherfucking menace. I said nothing and looked at no one.

An hour later three deputies opened the cell and told us to pair off. I figured I would hook up with the black guy next to me. Out of absolutely nowhere, a grubby little white guy walked across the cell and said, "You're with me." He looked like a speed freak, with tattoos and tangled hair. He acted like we had to be partners because we were both white. I went along with it. The deputies cuffed us together and marched us outside to a bus.

"Where are we going?" I asked my cuff-mate.

"Courthouse," he said. "See the judge."

"The judge? I haven't even seen a lawyer."

He looked at me like I was an amateur. We boarded the bus. There were bars on the windows. A marshal with a shotgun stood behind the driver. The engine started. I thought back to all the times I had passed a prison bus on the freeway. The men on those buses always looked like animals to me—not human. Now some guy driving along to work would look up and see *me* through the bars. I didn't believe I deserved this. Another marshal with a shotgun walked onto the bus. He looked at us and shouted: "Is there a James Asher on this bus?"

I stood up, yanking my partner's cuff accidentally. "I'm James Asher!"

"You made bail," he said. The other prisoners eyed me with open envy. The marshal opened the cuffs, chained my partner to the seat, and said: "Let's go— move your ass! I don't have all day here!"

I was out of jail, for the time being, anyway. I met my dad and brother in front of the police station. They managed to give me a smile through sad, shattered faces.

I didn't want to talk about the case, so I said, "I told Mom I didn't want you to bail me out, Pop."

"I didn't," he said. "Someone else bailed you out."

"Who?"

"The name was withheld. That's all they would tell me."

I rode back to my parents' house with my dad. I couldn't go to my apartment. In fact, I never wanted to go back there. Neither my father nor brother asked me anything on the way home, and I appreciated the silence. The whole time I was wondering about who bailed me out? I decided it must have been Edward. He's the only one I knew with that kind of ready cash. Edward's money had bailed me out before, carried me over obstacles that would otherwise have tripped me up.

When we got home, my grandfather was with my mom in the living room drinking tea. I hugged everyone and walked solemnly upstairs to my old bedroom. I looked at my war medals on the wall and my high school wrestling trophies. Where did that Jim Asher go? That Jim Asher didn't have money or influence, but he had something more—a simple kind of honor and happiness. I wished I could go back to him.

My grandpa knocked on the door. "Can I come in, Jim?"

"Sure."

He poked his head through the door. "Let's go for a walk, champ."

The living room was empty. We walked out to the beach. My grandpa knew I loved walking along the surf. He put his big arm around me and it made me feel better.

"Jim, I spoke over the phone with the district attorney today."

"Grandpa, I don't even know what the charges against me are."

We sat down on the brick wall between the boardwalk and sand.

"You're in a pretty big mess here, champ," he said. "You might even call it a quagmire. Here's what we're looking at. The sheriff has filed obstruction of justice charges—because of the scene with your computer. But I think I can get that dropped. The DA intends to prosecute you on two misdemeanor counts and one felony. The first two counts are violations of the state election code—falsifying nomination petitions and filing false petitions. The third count is the problem, Jim. The DA is considering felony conspiracy charges."

"Conspiracy? What is that?"

"It means that you conspired with one or more persons to falsify and file those petitions—a very serious charge."

"What are the penalties for those kind of charges?"

"The first two can be bargained down to a few months in prison, at the most. You may just get probation. Conspiracy, on the other hand, carries a much stiffer penalty."

I closed my eyes and braced myself mentally and physically. "How stiff?"

"Six to fifteen years in a state correctional facility."

"*Fifteen?* Grandpa, I can't do fifteen years in jail. I'll be old."

He pursed his lips at that. "Now, hold on, Jim. I'm not finished here. There's a catch. The DA isn't really interested in sending a young political aide to prison. That is not a popular thing with voters, especially on violations as technical as these. What he really wants is your boss, Speaker Alexander. Now, I don't know exactly what you've been wrapped up in, Jim. But the DA seems to think you know something incriminating that could put Alexander away. He'll only discuss the details with you in person. Now, I can go with you to his office tomorrow morning—"

"I think I've gotta do this alone, Grandpa. For the last two years everyone's been bailing me out of one thing after another. Either the money saves me, or the power. Someone's always catching me right before I hit the gutter. I've missed everything life's been trying to teach me. I think I need to save *myself* for once. I just want to stand up like a man one more time, if that's all I ever do, Grandpa."

"Well, it's good you figured it out now rather than ten years down the road. Some people never learn that lesson, Jim. They go through their whole lives trying to beat fate, but really they're just beating up themselves. You've still got everything ahead of you, your whole life." He patted my back with his big, comforting hand. "But listen, don't commit to anything with the DA. Don't agree to any deals until we've had a chance to talk it over."

I decided to unleash the only ace in my sleeve. "Hey, I was meaning to ask you—those sheriffs never read me my Miranda rights when they arrested me. Can't I get off on a technicality like that?"

"Normally, yes. A violation of Miranda rights is grounds for dismissal, but in your case it does not apply, unfortunately."

"Why not?"

"Because your blood-alcohol level was point two-one—well beyond legally drunk. The law does not require officers to read your Miranda rights if you are suspected of intoxication."

There went my last hope.

When we got back to the house my mom was sitting in the living room going through old family albums. "I'm sorry about all of this," she said. "We had no idea any of this was happening to you." She pointed to a picture of me in grade school, receiving a blue ribbon for a book report I had written about endangered California condors. "Your father and I always knew you would do great things, Jim. You were always special. Even when I was carrying you, I knew you were my special gift to the world. It hurts to see this happening to my baby."

"It's my own fault, Mom. I got in over my head. I felt like I could handle everything on my own. I mean, I had my own money and my own—"

"You always need your family. Look at me; I still ask your grandma for advice all the time. You can't go through life alone, Jim."

"I know, but that's exactly what I was doing. Thanks for being here for me. Without you and dad I wouldn't have anything. I'm sorry for all the embarrassment I've caused the family."

"You're never an embarrassment to me, Jim. I'm just happy to have my boy back in one piece. By the way, I have to show you something." She took me out to the garage. "We had everything sent here." She pointed to a stack of boxes against the wall.

"What are those?"

"They're from your office at the capitol—all your books and papers and things. We had them shipped here. And we got this fax yesterday."

She handed me a fax, from the Assembly Rules Committee:

> *Dear Mr. Asher,*
> *Your at-will employment with the State of California Assembly has been*
> *terminated as of May 2 . . . If you wish to retain health coverage, you may*
> *extend your current plan . . .*

My mom hugged me and said she was going to bed. The fax said my last paycheck was in the mail and that I must return my cellular phone and laptop "immediately." Everything would start crashing down around me now. I figured I was fired from the Winston campaign, but I didn't have the guts to call Edward. I didn't want politics in my life anymore.

FORTY-ONE

My mom woke me up. Someone was at the front door for me. The police again? I threw on shorts and went to the door. Standing on the porch was John Griggs.

"Jim, can we talk?"

"Sure." I was surprised but glad to see him. "What are you doing down here?"

"I felt like shit when I had to hang up on you yesterday. I drove down right after work last night, but when I got to your apartment the neighbors told me what happened with the police and everything. Man, I'm really sorry."

"It's not your fault. Shit, I don't even know what the hell's happening to me."

"I took the day off today. Just came here from Brett Alexander's office."

"You talked to Brett today!"

"Yeah." John glanced over his shoulder at the street. "Is there somewhere we can talk?"

"Yeah, sure."

We walked down to the beach and climbed up an empty lifeguard tower, sitting on its edge with our legs dangling.

"What did Brett say?" I asked anxiously.

"He gave me this note for you . . . I didn't read it." He handed me a crumpled paper from his pocket.

Jim, meet me under the Huntington pier on Saturday at midnight.

Brett didn't sign the note. I felt better, though. At least I was going to see him.

"So, are you all right?" John asked. "I heard you were shackled when the cops hauled you in."

"It's a long story. I'm kind of screwed up right now, to tell the truth. I have to see the DA tomorrow. I guess all the shit is finally catching up to me."

"Damn. Jim, it's really hard for me to tell you this, especially now. You're my best friend out here. But there're some things you've got to know before you see the DA."

"Like what?"

John sighed, shaking his head. "It looks like you're going down by yourself.

I've been talking to a lot of people, and everyone's pointing the finger at you. Edward is dropping out of the governor's race. I guess the DA called him a few days before the story broke. I don't know what was said, but it must not have been good. Edward is distancing himself from you in a big way; he says he's dropping out of politics for good."

"Shit. Now I'm bringing down everyone. I wish I would never've gotten into politics."

"It gets worse, Jim. Apparently, all your so-called friends are talking to the DA. They're selling you out."

"Who? Who's selling me out?"

"I can't say for sure, but I know Rachel West gave a long deposition against you. The DA is telling reporters that her testimony is extremely damaging— that it's going to bring you down hard, and probably Alexander, too."

"Rachel? Rachel is testifying against me? No way . . . I don't believe that."

"Believe it. You've gotta know what's coming down on you. I've got something else to tell you, but I don't know if you want to hear it right now."

"What? Just tell me. I've already lost my girlfriend, ruined the governor's race. I'm under FBI surveillance. My apartment is trashed, my bank accounts are frozen. I've been dragged in front of cameras and tossed in jail, slandered by fucking newspapers. The speakership is going down in flames. My whole career is over. I'm probably going to the slammer for fifteen years. My life is ruined. Just pour it on, man. Just fuckin' *hit me with it!"*

"I'm sorry. I've been hearing rumors since you first started going out, but I didn't think it was my place to tell you. Look, there's no easy way to say it, man. Rachel's been sleeping with Frank Buckman."

I felt my whole body sink, and flush hot with blood. I gulped. "Rachel and *Buckman?"*

"It's true, Jim. Brett's known for a while, too. I think Renee knew."

"You've got to be *fucking kidding me!* There's no way Rachel was sleeping with that fat lard-ass while she was sleeping with me. No way."

"I know how hard it is." Neither of us spoke for a minute. I was paralyzed by humiliation and outrage. All I could do was stare at the ocean, but I couldn't see through my rage. "But, hey," John finally said, "I thought you and Rachel had an 'open' relationship, or whatever?"

"Sort of, I guess. But this is totally different. This changes everything. That bitch was playing me all along, working both sides. John, you don't even realize the talks Rachel and I had. That *whore!"*

I was cursing Rachel, but inside I was cursing myself. Betrayal is a complex and slippery emotion, full of danger. I had to slow down my mind, take stock of facts, of reality, and think in logical terms, or this would overrun me. Before he could see the tears, I told John I had to go and jumped off the tower to the sand below. I disappeared down the beach in a daze.

———————

Later that night I was totally fucked up, drunk, desperate, sitting alone shivering on the cold beach with twelve empty bottles of Rhino beer in the sand next to me. I needed more alcohol, anything to make me forget. I got up, tottering, and stumbled across the sand toward the Newport pier. It was a weeknight, so the streetlights shone down on empty roads and parking lots. I walked into a bar called Blackie's. The place was deserted except for a trashy alcoholic lady with smeared lipstick sitting in the corner. All I had on were shorts and a sweaty T-shirt; my bare feet were black from wandering around all day. A rough-looking bouncer eyed me suspiciously as I sat on a bar stool.

"Bartender, three shots of whiskey," I said.

He glanced over at the bouncer, raising his eyebrows.

"I don't think so, buddy," he said.

"Give 'em to me!" I demanded.

The bouncer moved closer behind me.

"Are you okay, friend?" the bartender asked.

"Just give me some beer, okay," I said. "The goddamn stores are all closed."

"That's because it's almost two in the morning. I can't serve alcohol after one-thirty, it's the law. You got somewhere you can go?"

"Listen—here's twenty dollars, just fork over some beers and I'll go."

"Sorry." He turned and went back to wiping down the counters, ignoring me.

I spotted a bottle of vodka right behind the bar in front of me. I waited a minute and glanced back. The bouncer was busy picking up ashtrays and bottles by the pool table. Without another thought I stood up on the stool's foot pegs and reached over for the bottle, keeping my eyes on the bartender. Just as I grabbed it I felt a hard tug on my hair, yanking my head back sharply. I dropped the bottle and swung around to hit the bouncer, but my hand stopped in midair, and my head smashed down onto my knee. The pain was excruciating as my head was yanked down again, slamming me to the ground. He dragged me to the door on all fours, kicking and swinging my fists. Once we were outside, he finally let go. I stood up, ready to kill, but I was shocked and I stumbled backward when I saw it was Bill Crutchman standing there, not the bouncer. His leathery face was full of fire.

I backed up against the wall. The bartender closed the door, locked it, and pulled down the blinds, leaving me to Crutchman.

"You think that was bad?" Crutchman growled.

"What . . . ?"

"Shut the fuck up!" He grabbed my T-shirt and shoved me back. I swung hard for his face, but the next thing I knew his elbow drove into my throat, pinning me against the wall, blocking my windpipe. I gasped for air . . .

"Stand up like a fucking man!" he yelled. He slapped me hard, jarring my brain. "Get your shit together, soldier. You're a goddamn disaster! Stand up straight for Christ's sake! Do you hear me!"

I stood frozen, reeling from the smack. "What are you—"

He raised his hand again. "Look at you. Is this what you've come to—trying to steal alcohol from some dive bar. Is this what you learned in the war, how to be a damn coward, and a loser. Is it? Stand up straight, I said!"

I stiffened upright.

"I'm here to finish off this mess," Crutchman said, reaching slowly into his trench coat pocket.

I was petrified, my limbs trembling fiercely.

Crutchman pulled out a cigarette. "Asher, I'm going to give you the second chance most people never get in this life." He lit it and puffed deeply three times, his cold eyes tracking mine. "Duty is how men like me survive," he said. "I gave my word to Edward's father many years ago that I would protect the family, and that's a duty I'll take to my grave. It's called honor, Jim. Edward doesn't know that I bailed you out of prison yesterday, and he *never will*, understand." He handed me a smoke and lit it, then brushed sand off my shoulder. "Now, look, you have a clear chance to straighten out your life, to do the right thing. So quit feeling fucking sorry for yourself."

I had never seen it in him before, but as the tension went out of Crutchman's stern face, standing there like an oak in the chilly night air, I noticed something different in his steel gray eyes, strong and decent, something that can only be described as an old soldier's compassion.

FORTY-TWO

The next morning I went alone to see the DA, Robert Maltese. I'd met him several times. Maltese was a Republican, but he had never seemed to like me. He was what we called a "straighty" Republican, and I think he spotted my vile propensities the first time we met. I waited nervously in his lobby. Staff workers walked by trying to glance at me casually. They wanted to see the outlaw Republican fugitive they'd been reading about.

I was escorted into the DA's office by a young aide who told me: "Keep your head up, man. You guys have friends—even in here." I don't know who he was, but I will never forget those words; they lifted my spirit right out of the gutter.

The DA was short and bald; he had the eyebrows of a hawk, if a hawk had eyebrows. He was born serious. I reached out, but he didn't shake my hand. I sat down in the chair. His walls were covered with thousands of lawbooks. The bound leather volumes were intimidating, and the DA seemed to draw power from them.

"Jim Asher," he said. "I've heard a lot of shit about you, pal."

I was frightened because I had no idea what this guy knew. Did he know about the racetrack bribe? His face revealed nothing.

"You've got yourself in a serious jam here. Has your lawyer explained the charges against you?"

"Two misdemeanor counts regarding the petitions filed for Mitch Fine in the recall election."

"I'm sure your *grandfather* also mentioned the felony conspiracy charge I'm considering against you—and the grueling penalties that charge can carry."

Grueling? He was trying to scare me. "Yes, he did mention that."

"Well, you have some decisions to make, serious decisions."

"What decisions?"

"I'm wondering. What kind of man do you consider yourself to be, Asher?"

"A good one."

He raised his eyebrows. "Really?" He grabbed a file from his desk and started reading, protruding his bottom lip and shaking his head at certain sections. "Hmm . . . this doesn't look good." He took out a pen and started marking the file. "Not good at all. By the way, do you like gambling, Asher?"

"Gambling? Uh . . . sometimes."

"Betting?"

"I suppose, occasionally."

"I see. I enjoy a little gambling myself. Mostly just office pools. Monday Night Football, that sort of thing. What about limousines. You like limousines?"

I didn't know where he was leading with this. "Sure. Who doesn't?"

"Right, right, of course . . . stupid question." He continued marking the file intently, not looking up at me. "I remember the first time I rode in a limo. Spring of '68, prom night. Jennifer, that was the name of my date—a real dog. Of course I was no prom king myself. Were you prom king, Asher? You probably were. But not me. I was happy just to get a date, even if her nickname was 'Alpo.' See, it really didn't matter though, not once I turned her around and lifted up that prom dress—you know what I'm saying, don't you? But I can honestly tell you, I've never woken up with a whore."

Maltese set down the folder and walked over to the coffeemaker. He took his time pouring himself a cup, then sat back down without offering me one.

"How does it feel?" he asked.

"What?"

"Fucking a whore."

"I wouldn't know."

"Oh, but I think you would."

I tried to ignore his provocation. I wanted to get to the bottom line, to find out what he knew.

"I never got beautiful girls back then. Hell, I still don't. But I'll be damned if the most beautiful woman in Orange County didn't stroll right into my office the other day. This woman was a knockout; a perfect ten! But it's always the same old story. She didn't want me. She wanted to fuck someone else, some other guy. This girl, this absolute beauty, she wanted to fuck you, Asher. I couldn't believe it. And let me tell you, she *really* wanted to fuck you, pal, ha-ha! Imagine that! Women are always drawn to dirtbags, aren't they."

I wanted to lunge across the desk and rip his fucking throat out.

He grinned with a cruel expression. "You're used to getting what you want, aren't you? Just look at your rise in politics. Someone looking at you from the outside—and I'm just playing devil's advocate here—they might suspect you of foul play. In less than two years, you went from clipping newspaper articles to pulling off a statewide upset in the assembly. You went from sixteen thousand a year to over a hundred grand in less than nineteen months. That's amazing. Did I get that right? It's so impressive, really. How did you do it?"

"Hard work."

"Right—hard work. And you're a smart guy. Real smart. Have you ever been to the Viper Room with a television reporter named Samantha Gellhorne?"

I felt my face go pale and my body drain. I kept my expression from changing and tried not to gulp."

"That's okay, you don't have to answer just yet, Asher. So, what kind of phone call did you place from the parking lot, from Miss Gellhorne's cellular phone?"

Suddenly gravity seemed to increase, pulling me into the chair, my head getting dizzy. "I . . . I . . . excuse me." My throat was too constricted to speak.

"Oh, you don't look so good all of a sudden. Are you okay? You must have been out last night drinking again, huh?"

I couldn't answer.

"Well, anyway, here's some of what I know. The really good stuff I'm saving for court. First of all, you blackmailed Frank Buckman into dropping out of the speaker's race. I've got some cellular phone records, and I'm looking into further conspiracy charges on that. Second, you conspired to put Mitch Fine on the Democrat ticket to alter the outcome of a recall election with statewide ramifications. Your good buddy Francis M. H. White has already testified under oath that you were involved in the planning and execution of that false candidacy."

"Francis testified to *what?*"

"He sold you down the river, pal, like the piece of fucking human feces you are."

"Fuck you!"

He stood up. "Get the fuck out of this office right now! You're going to jail for a long time, you little douche bag." Angry spit flew from the edges of his mouth. "Get the fuck out!"

"I'm sorry," I said, suddenly afraid. "I'm sorry. I'm under a lot of stress right now."

"Listen, let me tell you something, you little piece of shit. I don't like you. I'd love to send you to a tiny, dark cement cell for the rest of your fucked-up miserable existence." He sat back down. "Do we understand each other, punk?"

I nodded. I was practically delirious but trying to hold myself together. My shirt was soaked through with sweat.

"As I was about to say. I know all about you. I've been watching you for more than a year now. You, James W. Asher, are a black cancer on the institution of democracy, and I intend to carve you out like the malignant disease you are to this state. Do you understand *that?*"

I nodded.

"Here's what else I know. Your 'girlfriend' has been in here telling me all kinds of interesting things about you and Speaker Alexander. You remember Rachel West, don't you?"

"She's not my girlfriend."

"Oh, that's right. I think everyone knows about *that*. Must be extremely embarrassing. Let me rephrase myself. That little *whore* you were living with has given a blistering deposition against you. Funny thing is, I didn't even have to subpoena her. She came in and volunteered the information."

This asshole was pushing me too fucking hard. My fists were clenched so tight I thought I would break a finger.

"Ms. West told us all about the journal on your computer. But don't worry. We're going to recover that file. You have my word on it. I have an army of computer experts reconstructing the hard drive. It may take some time, but we'll get that journal. She also told me some other things, involving you and Speaker Alexander—things I'm almost embarrassed to repeat. Have you ever met a girl named Natalie Hodgeson?"

He knew about the limo. "That doesn't have anything to do with this case," I said, struggling to keep my voice steady.

"True. Where's my head? That's a whole different subject. Still, I wonder if any reporters would be interested in breaking the biggest sex scandal in California's political history? Dirty money, sex, debauchery, corruption—this story has it all. I'll try to make damn sure it doesn't leak from this office. Let's cross our fingers and hope that doesn't happen." He grinned, revealing a sinister gap between his front teeth. "Asher, do you know what makes me even angrier than a fuckin' little rat weasel like you?"

I kept my face like a stone.

"A bigger rat, a bigger cancer on this state, like Brett Alexander—my former illustrious colleague. Your boss is going down, pal—in a flaming fuckin' fireball. He's violated the sacred trust of his office, from the very first day, with a flagrancy so vile and despicable it churns my fucking gut to even think about it. It makes me sick to remember when he used to work in this very office. But right now, the only question is how long are you going to jail for, Asher? If I wanted to, I could send your ass to the state penitentiary for the next two decades. Think about that. While your buddies are out fucking and getting rich, you'll be whacking your monkey in a concrete tomb. And a good-looking guy like you . . . I don't have to tell you how popular you'll be with the boys in the shower room."

I almost lost it. My whole body was shaking, ready to spring at him.

"Now . . . let's talk about the Del Prado racetrack and a man named Mike Burke," he said. "I've got a receptionist who can place you in Burke's office with Brett Alexander approximately two hours before an enormous sum of money was transferred from Burke's PAC to Mitch Fine's campaign account. You wouldn't happen to remember anything about that would you, Mr. Asher? Remember, you've got to be careful what you tell women in bed, ha-ha-ha!"

The DA leaned back in his high leather chair and calmly offered me a plea-bargain deal that ripped my soul into tiny dead scraps.

FORTY-THREE

Saturday was a difficult day. The day I *should* have been in Washington meeting Stan Williams, getting ready to join the biggest campaign in the world, then to the White House. These days my dreams were slightly less inspiring—like staying out of jail. My grandpa recommended that I take the plea bargain, but then I would have to testify against Brett and Mike in a federal bribery trial. If I did that, the DA told me he would drop all charges and I would be free to live my life. But Brett would go to jail for a long time. I thought about his son. What would he do without Brett? He had a responsibility to his family. What kind of man would I be if I turned in my friend just to save my own ass? That was the wrong motivation. If I wanted to turn Brett in because I thought the racetrack deal was wrong, it should have been completely unrelated to my own fate. I could pretend the two things were separate, but I would always know the truth. And the truth can ruin a man. I couldn't betray my own feelings. In my eyes, Brett had redeemed himself the minute he turned down the tobacco money. How could I hide from myself?

But I wasn't prepared to spend the next twenty years locked up in prison and the remainder of my days a marked felon. I would rather flee the country. The sheriffs were keeping close tabs on me, and they had confiscated my passport. But I could always slip across the Mexican border, then catch a bus south. I thought of those magical white sand beaches in Roatán. But how would I ever support myself or establish a life? I would never see my family. I would forever be running. *That* was not my fate.

This was the first real decision I would ever have to make. But maybe my decision was already made, I thought. Maybe my whole life was predetermined from the moment I was born and I was just along for the ride. Sometimes I felt that way. Like Rachel. When she asked me to sleep with her that night in San Francisco, how could I have said no? Of course I could have, but my instincts insisted I sleep with her—practically demanded it. Maybe all human behavior is determined by the laws of nature, like the planets and the stars and geological patterns. The laws of nature and physics can predict the orbits of planets, tides, weather—they can predict through dazzling mathematical calculations what will happen when a uranium atom reaches critical mass. Maybe the laws of nature control every thought and decision of our lives? Maybe like the planets and atoms, these laws can predict the electrical activity of our brains and we really don't control our own actions? If that was true, my decision was already made and I only had to sit back and see what happened.

But then I thought about it some more. If a set of laws, a complex mathematical formula, could predict our actions, then we could eventually calculate and discover our own futures, and if that were true, we could alter our futures and thus the prediction would unravel itself. Then I thought of the uncertainty principle, and that blew up everything. I thought so hard my brain bogged down, but I couldn't work around the paradox. I decided I *was* free to make my own decisions. Man must be free, must be responsible—we *must* survive. I felt better. No, we are not beasts enslaved to our base instincts and evolutionary programming. We are free souls whose actions determine our existence, not the other way around. We are incandescent beings bound by nothing but the contrived restraints of our own minds, luminous spirits streaking across the dusk sky like brilliant comets racing to meet our own event horizons, the edge of forever, and a man like me must scorch the heavens with all possible intensity so bright that the world will squint against me, and when like all flames I whisper into darkness, an amber blur, a ghostly lingering image, will be forever etched in the curved retina of space-time, and then, only then, will I reach the simplest meaning and beauty the universe knows. That is my destiny.

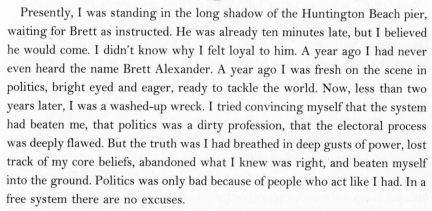

Presently, I was standing in the long shadow of the Huntington Beach pier, waiting for Brett as instructed. He was already ten minutes late, but I believed he would come. I didn't know why I felt loyal to him. A year ago I had never even heard the name Brett Alexander. A year ago I was fresh on the scene in politics, bright eyed and eager, ready to tackle the world. Now, less than two years later, I was a washed-up wreck. I tried convincing myself that the system had beaten me, that politics was a dirty profession, that the electoral process was deeply flawed. But the truth was I had breathed in deep gusts of power, lost track of my core beliefs, abandoned what I knew was right, and beaten myself into the ground. Politics was only bad because of people who act like I had. In a free system there are no excuses.

Growing up, I had always dreamed of glory and honor. I wanted to be a knight, a hero. As a kid I was always full of clean energy, thirsting for adventure and excitement and friendship, fantasizing I would marry the pretty little girl around the corner named Shannon. I would never have imagined myself as a hard-drinking, hard-smoking, petty political criminal ditched by a tramp girlfriend and facing fifteen years in prison for incorrectly filing paperwork. But that's what I was. The boy would have been disappointed in the man.

Brett walked up in a tan trench coat. I hadn't seen him since the meltdown in Sacramento. It seemed like a year ago.

He smiled.

"Well, I finally got rid of that old blue coat you always said was 'disgraceful' to my office," he said, pointing at the new one.

"Fancy."

"How are you, Jim?"

"Been better."

"I'm sorry, man—about everything."

"So am I."

"Brett Jr. says hi. He wants to know when you're going to take him to the zoo to see Samson the bear, like you promised him."

"When I get out of the slammer, I guess."

Brett shook his head. "So what's the DA offering?"

"Blanket immunity."

"In return for . . . ?"

"You."

His shoulders dropped and he turned away from me. "That's what I figured."

"Brett, why did Francis fucking sell me out?"

"I don't know. I really don't. I haven't talked to him since they raided our office. I think what he did is bullshit, Jim. Real men don't turn on friends. Francis was offered immunity to testify against you. The DA is setting you up. He also granted immunity to Mitch Fine, just to put you in a corner. Maltese knows you're the only person who can nail me. You're the only one who was in that office in Del Prado. Mike Burke would never testify against me. He has no reason to."

"You know about that?"

"I've still got friends in the DA's office. Probably more friends than Maltese himself, and I haven't worked in that office for a long time. That tells you what kind of person he is. Maltese is using you to screw me. He thinks if he can scare you, you'll deliver me on a silver platter, and he'll come out looking like a hero. By the way, apparently they couldn't retrieve anything off your computer. Maltese had half of Silicon Valley tearing that thing apart, but the hard drive was cracked to pieces."

"Who told you that?"

"Friends."

I wiped a heavy hand across my forehead. "What a relief. So why is the DA doing this?"

"Ambition—what else. He wants to run for attorney general next year. Maltese thinks this is part of building his reputation. The guy's a menace to the legal system."

"Is he friends with Buckman?"

"Close friends. A lot of people in this state owe their careers to Buckman; Maltese is one of them. Look, Jim, I'm not going to tell you what you should do. You're a grown man and you have a decision to make—a serious decision. I have faith in you. I would never have been your friend and trusted you with so much if I didn't think you were a *certain type* of man." The emphasis wasn't lost on me.

"What are you going to do, Brett?"

"This is between you and me."

"You don't know me very well."

He allowed a grin. "The governor has agreed to grant me a pardon if the DA moves on the conspiracy charges. But that won't happen unless you testify—no one else can corroborate the conspiracy part. But if the racetrack thing comes down on me, there won't be any pardon. I'll go to jail on federal charges, with no chance of parole. If that happens, I'll have to deal with it one day at a time— try to secure my family. But in any case, I've decided to step down as speaker next week. Pardon or no pardon, I've gotta step down. It's just gone too far. The capitol is in chaos. My son can't play in the front yard because of all these damn reporters. Giving up this speakership is the hardest thing I'll ever do. My political career is finished, the only thing I've ever wanted to do with my life . . ."

I shook my head in disgust, maybe self disgust. I couldn't believe any of it. "Do you know about Rachel West?"

He nodded. "That's the other reason I've got to step down. If the San Francisco story leaks, my marriage is over. My family is all I have left."

"If it comes out, I'll testify for you. Nothing really happened."

"Thanks, Jimbo. But honestly, I don't think your testimony would help. You've got to understand—it's all over. You're damaged goods, like me. And I'm sorry I didn't tell you about Rachel and Buckman sooner. I figured you knew what you were getting into with her."

"I should have."

"Look, I can always go to work for my dad's car dealership. I can always survive. And so can you. Maybe the governor could cut you a pardon. Not right away, of course . . ."

"No pardons. I don't want anyone bailing me out this time."

He rested his hand on my shoulder. "That's up to you."

"I want to know how all this happened. What *happened*, Brett? Everything was going so good."

"I'll tell you, but you won't like it."

"Go ahead."

"It's Buckman. The guy's been wanting to nail your ass since that night you slugged him. And then taking Rachel away from him, and that stunt you pulled with the reporters . . . well. Anyway, Buckman found out we planted Mitch as a Dem—which wasn't too hard to figure out; a lot of Republicans knew. Buckman handed everything over to Warren Watts at the *LA Times*. From there, it was pretty simple. Watts obtained copies of the petitions and started checking out the names, one by one. He went down the list and visited everyone who signed those petitions. Watts showed them a photo of Mitch and asked if he had gathered the signatures himself. When everyone said that two frantic young guys—not fitting Mitch's description—had gathered their signatures, the whole thing blew up on us."

"That fat motherfucker. I'll kill Buckman when this is all over. You don't sell out an entire Republican assembly over personal grudges, that fat piece of shit!" I didn't want to tell Brett, but now I knew it was Rachel who had tipped Buckman about the petitions. A month or two before, I had gotten drunk and stoned with her at a party and bragged the whole story of how I had won the assembly. I trusted her.

"Brett, what was all of it worth?"

"What do you mean?"

"Were we doing the right thing? What were we doing all that time, in all those meetings, the legislation, the money? It seems like it was all for nothing."

"Don't ever think like that. We did what we thought we were supposed to do. We wanted to change things. And we did help people. Look at all the work we did on welfare, and taxes. Don't ever think we didn't make a difference. We were fighting for what we believe in."

"Yeah, maybe, but now the Democrats are going to win back the assembly and overturn everything we did on the first day. It all comes out to be just a pointless, stupid game."

"It *is* a game. We played, and we lost. This time."

"I just want it to be over now."

"Me too," he nodded. "So, what's the DA holding over your head, Jim?"

"The two election code violations—"

"Those are nothing."

"I know. But the conspiracy charge is the killer. I could go to jail for fifteen years."

Brett's eyes moved away from mine. "Conspiracy?" he mumbled. His mouth hung slightly open as he looked down and watched the crashing waves. When I caught his eye, something struck me—a faint idea of what he was thinking, and it quickly began to crystallize in my own mind.

"The DA isn't pressing conspiracy charges against Francis or Mitch, right?" Brett said.

"Right. Francis and Mitch testified that me and someone else—presumably you—engineered the whole thing, but they wouldn't testify on the record against you."

"Of course not. And Maltese . . . he already granted immunity to both of them in exchange for testimony against you."

"Right."

"So he can't force them to testify against me."

"Right."

"And those depositions only mention you, right?"

"Right."

"Do me a favor, Jim."

"Sure."

"Don't tell anyone about me resigning. I'm not going to do it just yet. I have an idea."

My whole life changed right then, my whole future brightened.

FORTY-FOUR

Brett drew me a crude map to the DA's house in Westminster. I pulled the Hummer into his driveway and stormed up to the door. It was almost two in the morning. All the lights were out in the house. I pounded on the front door. With Brett's legal coaching, I wasn't afraid of the DA anymore. A minute later the yellow porch light came on and Maltese cracked open the door, wearing a robe. His small amount of hair was ruffled.

"What the fuck do you want, Asher? What are you doing here?"

"We need to talk."

"Come to the office Monday. You don't come to my home and wake me up . . . How did you get—"

"I'm ready to talk about Brett Alexander."

His hawk eyebrows spiked. "Really?" He opened the screen door and stepped onto the porch. "Talk."

"First of all, let me tell you what I know—"

"Make this fast," he said. He looked around the neighborhood. His feet were bare and he wiggled his toes on the cold porch, his yellow toenails scratching the wood.

"Like I was saying. Here's what I know. First, you don't have anything on Brett Alexander unless I give it to you."

"Wrong. I can press charges on the petition violations."

"Maybe. But you'll never prove anything. Neither of us will testify against each other, and even if you could get him on some bullshit charge like that, the governor has already agreed to pardon him."

"Who told you that—fucking Alexander, right?"

"Don't worry who told me. You know the governor. You know he'll do it. And if you press misdemeanor charges against a sitting speaker and lose, well, your career will be over."

"I don't give a fuck what the governor does. I've still got the horse track bribery case. I've got phone records, bank records, a receptionist who saw the meeting take place."

"But you don't have anyone inside that meeting, to tie everything together. All you have is circumstantial evidence. Do you think Mike Burke is going to testify, to incriminate himself? Fuck no. You don't have shit on him. He knows

I'm not going to give up Alexander. He's already been assured of that. You don't have anything to muscle him around with."

"I guess you're forgetting about the conspiracy charges I'm considering against you. Or have you decided that you want to go to jail for the next fifteen years?"

"Fuck you, and fuck your fifteen years! That was a lie from the first time it left your fuckin' mouth."

His face turned red and twitched. "I'll see you at the grand jury hearing on Thursday," he said. "You just ruined your life, pal. You just hung yourself. Give my greetings to Alexander when you both get to the fucking slammer."

He turned and walked to the door, but I grabbed his arm and spun him around. He slammed his forearm down hard on my wrist and knocked it away. He pushed up his bathrobe sleeves and raised his fists, like an old-time boxer. It was an extremely difficult invitation to decline, but I controlled myself and said: "You don't have a fuckin' conspiracy case against me and you know it."

"What the fuck are you talking about, punk?"

"You've already granted immunity to Francis White and Mitch Fine to testify against me. They said I was involved in the planning, but their depositions don't mention Alexander. So that leaves me with one question: how did I have a one-person conspiracy? By definition, and by law, a conspiracy is something that takes place between two or more persons. You are either incredibly stupid, or you've been bluffing me because you think I'm incredibly stupid. In either case, your conspiracy case died the day you granted immunity to the only two people who could prove it."

He stepped back. I saw his Adam's apple move. "Don't think you're going to get out of this, pal. I've still got Brett Alexander."

"You don't have a motherfucking thing!" I shouted.

"Fuck you!"

"No, fuck you!"

We stood squared off, glaring each other down.

two weeks later . . .

FINAL CHAPTER

I woke up and drank a cold glass of pineapple-banana-orange juice. The clear morning sun said the day would be hot but the sand was cool on my feet as I walked across the beach. The seagulls were already busy with their day's work; I envied the simplicity of their lives. I paddled out past the break and sat straddling my board in the glassy green water.

It was all a blur to me now—the last two years in politics were just a mad, scorching spin down the autobahn of life with plenty of spectacles along the way. But it was a part of me now only in my thoughts, and even those weren't absolutely real, only phantom electrical patterns in my brain, so I decided to treat them as such and live a good life. After all this time, after all my science books and grand philosophical deliberations, I finally realized that the only meaning we can know is what we see and feel, and the highest goal attainable is perhaps the simplest—happiness. We are nothing more than what we think, having spent our lives being what we thought. A storm in the South Pacific pushed long-breaking swells at me, and I surfed for two magical hours.

Bud Raper called my parents' house at 9 A.M. My brother got me out of the water. I raced to the house.

"Bud?"

"Hey, kid. You did the right thing," he told me. "You did what a fuckin' man is supposed to do. You stuck with your friend and you told the world to go fuck itself."

"I guess. Thanks, Bud. Thanks for calling. It means more to me than you'll ever know."

"Believe me, kid—I know. I'm still watching that videotape. By the way, when do I meet this Rachel broad?"

"We don't talk anymore."

"Fuck her anyway. Maria couldn't stop talking about you after you left the house. Goddamn, I wish I was a young bastard again. Just for *one* fuckin' day. The things I would do to these girls! Keep your fuckin' chin up, kid. I want you to come down to the house on Roatán after this presidential race is over. I'm gonna set up an English-language newspaper for those Islander sons of bitches down there. I could use a good editor to get things rolling."

"I can't think of anything more perfect, Bud. Tell Maria I'll be there. And thanks."

"Remember. Fuck all these bastards. You live the life you wanna live and let 'em say whatever the fuck they wanna say. If they knew a goddamn thing, they'd be out here kickin' life's ass with us, kid. Never forget that. And remember Bud's Rule number three—you'll be needing it."

I told him to fuck off. He laughed and hung up. I walked with my brother out to the driveway. He asked if he could drive the Hummer.

"Absolutely." I tossed him the keys.

We took side streets to avoid the late-morning traffic.

"So, Brett stepped down yesterday, huh?" my brother asked.

"Yeah. He's a free man. The DA dropped all charges against him. But he can never work in politics again, like me. The whole thing's a shame."

"Hey, you never told me what the second part of your plea bargain was. Why is it such a big secret?"

"I'll show you when we get there," I said.

My brother pulled the Hummer up to the curb. There was only one reporter with a camera waiting for me. I was expecting a mob. The reporter was Samantha. I got out of the Hummer and grabbed my backpack from the backseat. I unzipped it and pulled out a laptop, showing my brother. "This is the second part of the plea bargain," I said. "I get to keep it with me."

He grinned and shook my hand. Samantha came over. She was the only person I wanted to see at that moment. I had already made my peace with everyone else who still mattered.

"What's with the camera?" I asked.

"Oh, the camera. There's not even a videotape in it. It's just in case other reporters showed up."

"Why didn't they?"

"They did. I told 'em to hit the road. I've still got some pull with reporters, you know," she said, smiling. "So what exactly is the deal you cut with the DA?"

"Alexander steps down, and I plead guilty to the misdemeanor charges of petition fraud. They had me nailed on gathering those petitions anyway."

"That makes sense," she said. "The DA gets rid of both of you without a big mess. He probably knew he couldn't get Alexander. Conspiracy is almost impossible to prove. But I'd say Brett Alexander owes you big time."

"No. Nobody owes me anything. I'm just glad it's all over."

"Good. And that reminds me, Rick wants you to come work for his law firm. You'll be his assistant. Hollywood, babe. It's a great opportunity."

"Tell him I appreciate it, but no thanks. I'm tired of chasing things. Actually,

I'm tired of chasing myself, Samantha. I want my life to mean something, to me. That's all that matters. For the past two years I've been chasing my own tail like a haunted dog, but all along I should have been running along the beach and jumping for Frisbees and rolling in the grass and falling in love with the pretty girl down the street. I've missed all the best gifts nature's been trying to give me."

"I got into reporting with those same kinda dreams. God, that was so long ago . . ."

"I know you did."

"Well, we're throwing you a big party in the spring, babe. That's only eight months away. And I've got this girl I really want you to meet. She works—"

"Samantha."

I kissed her long and sweet on the mouth. We would always have each other and the things we did. She wrapped her arms around my waist and rubbed her cheek against my chest. "Be happy, Boo-Boo."

"That's all I want." I kissed Samantha on the forehead, then I watched her and my brother drive away. The sun was bright and warm and it made me squint as I walked the short distance to prison.

one year later . . .

EPILOGUE

It could have been anything. For me it was politics. I don't blame the system or other people—I made my choices. My first week locked up was the hardest. I laid in my cell staring at the springs and mattress above me. My bunk was a place of terrifying solitude; I was afraid to leave it, almost as if the mattress itself was suspended thousands of feet above jagged cliffs. I never moved, never spoke. Not even for meals; trays were brought to my cell. I was deeply depressed, full of shame and resentment. Iron bars and thick concrete stood between my body and the freedom I was born with. Honestly, it hurt.

But resentment is an emotion I have since learned to live without. A man only has time to live his life. Once I fully understood this, prison become a place of learning for me. Besides being the perfect environment for rebuilding my body, prison transformed into a sort of spiritual haven for me. Winter and my brother kept a steady supply of books coming in. I read them all, over and over again. Literature was my sanctuary. I spent nearly all my time thinking about the kind of man I would be when I got out. The loneliness went away after I got a cell mate, T-Rex, a 315-pound former dealer. The dark was the worst time in prison, especially the hour just after lights-out—always the longest. But T-Rex and I stayed up for hours talking about our lives and planning for the future. I could tell it was difficult for him, but one day T asked if I would teach him to read. We started with *The Old Man and the Sea*, then moved on to *Cannery Row* and later *The Stranger*. "Motherfucker talkin' 'bout the same shit I be goin' through," he said of the latter. For me it was like reading those books for the first time again. T-Rex looked after me.

Edward Winston has dropped out of public view. He's back working on Wall Street, which is probably best for everyone. Meanwhile Mariella has become the Republican Party's brightest luminary—a rising star on television. I always knew she would. The other day I got a card from Cynthia Winston. Her parents hadn't told her why I was away, and she said she missed me "a million tons." That card made my week. I have not seen or heard from Bill Crutchman since the night he pulled me out of Blackie's bar. He got back every penny of the bail money he posted for me. No further words are necessary between us; when he dropped me in front of my parents' house that night, I know he saw the gratitude in my eyes.

Rachel West is working at the Veterans Department in Washington, DC, with Frank Buckman. I have learned to take pity on both of them. John Griggs left his think-tank job to write speeches for the governor, but he's hoping to get out of politics soon. John just finished a screenplay about a former Supreme Court justice. I've read the first draft, and it's quite good. Renee Tumler now works for Dale Spencer's gubernatorial campaign; we keep in touch. Samantha Gellhorne is married to Rick and still working as a reporter. If you watch television in Los Angeles, you'll see her. Brett Alexander is now vice president . . . of his family's car dealership in Orange. Brett occasionally sends me political articles over E-mail, and sometimes I get excited over some new development, but it always passes. The world holds so much more for me.

As for me, right now I'm kicking my bare feet up on a wicker table on Bud's dock, enjoying the warm Caribbean sun and tossing garlic-fried shrimp to my friend Papa, the dolphin. The German lady is playing reggae music at the restaurant, and it makes me want to stand up and dance. Bud is in Washington closing down his office. After Stan Williams lost the presidential race, Bud quit politics forever, or until someone pays him "a shitload of dough" to come out of retirement. Maria and I look after the place when Bud is back in the states. I think I'm falling in love with her. It will be my first time. I've been down here in paradise for three months, and I figure I'll stay for at least another year. Bud hired me to help write his memoirs, which should be a spicy affair. I'm warming up by writing short stories on my laptop. I wrote one for Maria the other day, and she said: "I love it and it is very beautiful, *Jeem.*"

My parents and Jake visited last month. They stayed at the new resort down the beach. Bud took my pop and Jake out marlin fishing on his forty-two-foot boat, *At Water*. I don't think my dad knew quite what to make of Bud—who the hell does?—but we all had a great time. I miss my family every day I am not with them. But Winter is coming down to visit next week. I can't wait to see her. She's living in New York, working as an on-air personality at MSNBC. But like many of my friends, Winter says she wants more out of life. "Party politics is dead," she wrote to me in a recent E-mail. She couldn't be more right. Republicans and Democrats have abandoned the Constitution and left its authors out in the cold to die; now the parties are locked in a despicable, futile struggle, picking at the skeleton of freedom. The system is at a dead end. Until the Libertarian Party gets its act together and rises up to what it will someday be—the driving force behind the first true political revolution in seventy years—until that time, politics is dead to me.

Some say I got off easy. I say it's all about learning, and I've done a world of that. As I gaze out across the blue and green horizon, it occurs to me that our lives are like the ocean—every stream runs into them, but like the sea, our souls are never full; and what could possibly be more elegant and inspiring than that?

Maria likes to sit with me on the dock when I write. She is with me now; her soft tan legs are draped over my lap. Maria's favorite writer is Gabriel García Márquez. I hope to fill that slot someday. She's smiling at me now and I think we'll go for a swim with Papa.

ACKNOWLEDGMENTS

I would like to thank five special people:

My parents, Allan and Olanda—the best dad a guy could ever hope for, and the most caring, wonderful mom imaginable. Their support made a writing career possible, and their love made everything else possible. My brother, Dave, who helped convince me to write a novel over a blazing campfire and a twelve-pack of Keystone Light high up in the Sierra mountains that one fateful night. Flat broke, with nothing going for us, we've stuck together and done what we said we'd do—our first step into a much larger, wide-open world. My literary agent, Mike Hamilburg, a man of the rarest qualities—honor, integrity, and truthfulness. Despite our slight age difference, Mike is one of the youngest people I know at heart; he has a contagious, almost childlike enthusiasm for everything he does, and I consider myself damn lucky to call him my agent, and my friend. And finally, my editor, Dan Slater, at Pocket Books. Dan was the first person in publishing to recognize *Spin*, and I can honestly say that without his enormous work and personal dedication to this book, it might not have happened. We have shared a vision for this book from the very beginning, and Dan has fought time and again down in the trenches to preserve that vision. He's also become a hell of a good friend. Take my word, Dan—you're a dope editor.

I would also like to thank Will Swain, Jean Pasco, Harold Johnson, and Gary Ginsburg at *George* for their early editorial help; my uncle, Dave, for use of his glorious lakeside cabin; Riccardo for the free coffee, chair, and table; my film agent, Bill Contardi, at William Morris, for his trememdous work; my entire family; John Roberts, Jennifer Grossman, Chris Jester, and John Herr for their friendship; and Maria Hanley for her unfailing love.